# The Orphanage

Laura Laberge

# THE ORPHANAGE

Layout and Publishing: BoD – Books on Demand GmbH, In de
Tarpen 42, 22848 Norderstedt
Printing and Production: Libri Plureos GmbH, Friedensallee 273,
22763 Hamburg

ISBN: 978-3-7597-4149-3

# CONTENTS

After five years of work, the story is finally written.

It is a rather complex mix of adventure and crime with many different characters. For easy reference I therefore name most of them in the beginning.

I would like to take this opportunity to thank all the people who have supported me in my work in one way or another, and who have often helped me with constructive criticism.

Thank you to my husband Barth for his ongoing motivation, support and graphics.

Thank you too to my friends and acquaintances. I have often been able to gather valuable material from our various discussions, without you perhaps realising it!

I want especially to thank Georgette, Isabelle, Linda, Henrietta and Maria for 'proofreading', and all those who have patiently listened to me and supported me with suggestions during the years.

I would also like to thank my editor at projekt-lektorat.de. The task required a great deal of empathy from an external perspective, and you've done a truly outstanding job.

A special thank you to my friend Alan, who, in real life heading to the Dominican Republic, forgot his mobile phone on the back seat of our car on the way to the airport. That incident was the start and motivation for this story.

Any resemblance to living or deceased persons is purely coincidental and in no way intended by the author.

Luxembourg author Chantal Welter writes under the pseudonym of Laura Laberge.

Previous publications (in German language):
- Nur wegen dir
- Eine Spur von Leben
- Geheimakte Frank Mayer

llaberge@pt.lu

# CHARACTERS

| | |
|---|---|
| Alan Moore | friend of Thomas, David, Alfonse |
| Thomas Walter | graphic designer |
| David White | friend of Alan |
| Alfonse Weis | retired ex special police |
| Matthew McKenna | magician and medical doctor |
| Jeff McKenna | medical doctor and Matthew's brother |
| John McKenna | director of the McKenna clinic in Luxembourg, father of Matthew and Jeff |
| Claire McKenna | wife of John McKenna |
| Lis Chandler | Spanish teacher |
| Eric Chandler | the son of Lis Chandler |
| Caro Klein | girlfriend of Eric Chandler |
| James Hammer | private investigator |
| Bernard Bouvier | bank director |
| Franz Kramer | childhood friend of Matthew McKenna |
| Diane Van Helden | daughter of Gerard Van Helden |
| Gerard Van Helden | father of Diane and Laetitia Van Helden |
| Emily Fox | wife of Gerard Van Helden and mother of Diane and Laetitia Van Helden |

| Laetitia Van Helden | sister of Diane Van Helden and wife of Klaus Schmitt |
| Klaus Schmitt | husband of Laetitia Van Helden |

# DIANE

## *FRIDAY, JULY 5*

Friday night, 10:30 p.m. Alan Moore was finishing his beer. "Time to catch the last bus, lads," he said to his poker buddies, Alfonse Weis and Thomas Walter, glancing at David as he stood up. The four long-time friends had met for an after-work beer, followed by a round of poker and a nice dinner, as always discussing the week's events. Tonight, they were gathered at Alfonse's house in Fentange, a small village nestled in a quiet area not far from the capital.

Alan Moore, 53, a British citizen and banker, had lived and worked in Luxembourg for over twenty-five years, and resided in a beautiful apartment in the city centre.

Thomas Walter, 55 years old, a Dutch citizen and graphic designer by profession, had been divorced for over twenty years and now lived in Bivange, a small town near the capital. He loved his work and dedicated himself wholeheartedly to every project.

Alfonse Weis, a 60-year-old Luxembourger, was a retired intelligence officer but had only left the service a few months ago. He was of medium build, slim and fit, with grey hair, a determined gaze, and a good sense of humour. During his tenure in the police force, Weis had brought down numerous criminals, and once he took on a case, nothing and no one could deter him until the culprit was apprehended. Since retiring, he had more time for his family, which brought much joy to his wife Madeleine. However, he somehow missed the daily challenges, although he didn't discuss this with his wife or friends; it was simply a sentiment that anyone who knew Alfonse could sense.

David White, 50, a long-time friend of Alan Moore, hailed from Scotland and was visiting Alan for a few weeks. David, a former soldier, had served in multiple military operations abroad, though he rarely spoke of them. In Scotland, he had worked as a police officer until falling ill and taking early retirement.

"Right," David stood up as well.

"Time for another pint in the Irish pub on the way home," he said to Alan as they bid farewell to Alfonse, whose wife Madeleine had gone out for the evening to ensure the men's poker night went undisturbed.

Thomas dropped Alan and David off at the next bus stop on his way home.

"See you soon and have fun."

"I'll catch you later, Thomas. Thanks for the lift," Alan replied as they exited the car.

A few minutes later, the bus arrived and both men took their seats. There were only a few people on the road at this hour. When the bus reached their stop for the pub and came to a halt, Alan suddenly changed his mind.

"David, I'm too tired for the pub tonight. I'm heading straight home. You've got the key; I'll see you in the morning. That last beer really hit me."

"Sure thing. Catch you later or tomorrow," David said as he disembarked. A thunderstorm rolled in and soon, heavy rain began to fall.

Alan settled in, gazing out of the window. He was exhausted after a stressful day at work covering for vacationing colleagues. It was a struggle to stay awake in the warm bus. As it stopped at the next station, he noticed a tall, slender woman boarding. She appeared somewhat anxious, glancing around nervously. Clad in a black raincoat and with a vibrant scarf protecting her hair from the rain, the woman seemed caught off guard by the sudden downpour. Her blonde hair hung wet over her shoulders. Hastily, she selected a seat one row ahead of Alan, positioning herself halfway so as not to be visible from outside.

As the bus prepared to depart, a man in a black hoodie boarded at the last moment, taking a seat in the front row behind the driver. He was equally drenched from the rain.

Upon spotting the man, the blonde woman stood up abruptly, crossing over to sit beside Alan. Strands of her damp, blonde hair framed her face as she looked at him.

"Excuse me, sir, may I ask you a favour?" she whispered, her voice trembling slightly. From her flawless, beautiful, albeit slightly gaunt face, two large, fearful blue eyes gazed at him.

"That depends," he replied with a friendly smile.

"I have to get off in the city centre and I'm afraid the man in front of me will follow me," she whispered to him in a low voice. "I would be very grateful if you could get off the bus with me and accompany me to my apartment door. It's not far from the city park, Avenue Monterey. Please. I'm serious."

Alan saw pure fear in her eyes. Despite wearing jeans and a black coat, the woman exuded elegance. She attempted to shield part of her face with the scarf.

"What makes you think Mr. X will follow you?" he asked in a whisper.

"Instinct! When I was waiting at the bus stop, I noticed him immediately; he was staring at me. When I looked at him, he tried to look away, but you can tell when you're being watched, you know. And then he got on the bus after me."

"And why would he want to follow you?"

"I can't tell you that. Firstly, I don't know you, and secondly... Oh, I have to get off at the next stop."

As Alan watched, the mysterious man also stood up as if to disembark. So far, the woman appeared truthful.

"Okay, I'll come with you," he decided spontaneously and rose from his seat.

Upon hearing these words, the relief on her face was evident. "Thank you!" She briefly touched his arm.

She has a dazzling smile, Alan thought as he followed her off the bus. Perhaps it's a twist of fate?

Mr. X also disembarked, but through the rear exit.

"It's not far," she said, pulling her scarf further over her head, now obscuring part of her face as they hurried through the city park.

As they walked, they periodically glanced back to see if the mysterious man was indeed following them.

"Look, he's coming towards us!"

She tugged briefly on Alan's sleeve when he turned to look again.

The man strode purposefully while speaking into his cell phone. He briefly glanced up and slowed his pace upon realising he was approaching too swiftly.

"How about I just give you a hug now and we wait until it's over?"

Before the woman could respond, Alan enveloped her in his arms. "Don't worry," he whispered, "I'll release you in a moment."

She peeked over his shoulder and saw the man had stopped, talking loudly on his phone while gesturing with one hand. His tone suggested annoyance.

"Hmm…" Alan slowly released his arms from her and looked over his shoulder. "He's stopping. We'd better keep walking; he really looks like he wants to follow you." By now, Alan had also become suspicious. There was something strange about this person's behaviour.

At last, the rain had almost stopped. Alan Moore and the beautiful stranger continued on their way. About five minutes later, she stopped at the first block of flats on the corner of the main street and hastily pulled a key out of her pocket.

"I'm so grateful that you came with me. I… would you mind coming in with me, I mean, just to see if everything is okay? Please!" The 53-year-old Englishman simply couldn't resist the look in those blue eyes.

"No problem, now that I'm here!" said Alan kindly. "Perhaps in return, it would be fair to give me a brief explanation of all these events when we're at your apartment?"

"Yeah, sure, as soon as we get upstairs," the woman said as she hastily opened the front door; they both entered and took the elevator to the sixth floor.

The stranger's penthouse was on the right-hand side; she opened the door, and they both entered. Once inside, she immediately locked the door and closed the security chain.

"Thank you," she said again. "Now I'm reassured. Please have a seat. Can I offer you something? A coffee, or…?"

"A coffee would be nice, thank you."

A few minutes later, she came back from the kitchen with two cups of coffee, put them on the table, and sat down opposite Alan. She leaned back on the couch and brushed a few loose strands of hair out of her face. What a beautiful woman, he thought. It was the right decision not to go ahead with David tonight.

"My name is Diane. Diane Van Helden."

"Pleased to meet you, Diane… although the circumstances seem a little confused. I'm Alan Moore. Who is following you and why? I assume this isn't the first time someone has followed you, is it? In that case, you should report it to the police."

Alan stood up and looked out of the large window. "You have a fantastic penthouse here and a great view!" Then he sat down again.

"Yes, it's very nice here. I like it." She paused. "Okay, then I'd better start from the beginning. I don't know why I should involve you in this, but I have a feeling that I can trust you."

"That's entirely up to you. But it would be a bit late not to trust me now," Alan remarked somewhat mischievously.

By now, it was almost midnight. Alan called David briefly and told him that he wouldn't be home until much later.

"The story I'm about to tell you sounds pretty crazy, but it's the truth. I swear it." Diane looked at him with wide eyes.

"I'm listening carefully, go on." Alan felt wide awake again, especially at the sight of the woman's elegant beauty.

"About six months ago, I met a man, handsome, charming, in his mid-fifties, with blond but greying hair. Over the weeks, we got closer and started a relationship."

"That sounds normal so far," Alan commented.

"That's right. He had a good sense of humour, was educated, and told me that he worked for the Ministry of Family Affairs and was regularly away on business trips. He also told me quite early on that he was still married but in the middle of a rather unpleasant divorce. He later took this as an opportunity not to invite me to his home because his wife was refusing to move out until everything was financially settled and the divorce was finalised.

"Mark, as he was called, often stayed here overnight and when he had to work late, he sometimes arrived here in the middle of the night and then went to work from here the next day. He told me that he was sometimes on the road at weekends too.

"He also told me that he spent a lot of his free time in the Dominican Republic because he was working in an orphanage in the capital, and supporting it financially. The orphanage is called 'Pequeños Angeles', which means 'little angels.' Whenever he had some free time, he would travel there to help, send materials, whatever was needed. I thought that was a pretty noble activity."

"We got on very well and about two months later we went on vacation together for a week to the island," Diane continued her story. "Mark was often away on business during the day, but we always met up for dinner in the evening. So, I was often alone during the day. I'd go sightseeing in the city and we'd meet up at the hotel in the evening. Once he took me to his orphanage. Everything was exactly as he had told me. As I speak some Spanish, I was able to talk to some of the staff there. I also saw the young girls and toddlers who lived there. They all seemed to be between two and ten years old. What struck me was that all the girls there looked rather European, and none of the children were indigenous. When I asked Mark about it, he just said it was different. I didn't really understand, but I was under the impression that I shouldn't interfere or ask any more questions.

"When I returned to the orphanage the next day, I met this little girl called Kim. She was so sweet, indescribably shy and timid. She had just turned six, had big brown eyes and kept looking at me. She spoke German.

"Her parents had died when she was a baby and she had been living in this orphanage ever since. She captured my heart immediately, I don't know why, but I couldn't help it.

"I then spent the remaining three days with her during the day. When we returned to Luxembourg, I kept thinking about the little girl and after a few days of careful consideration, I made the decision to adopt little Kim.

"The next day I was full of enthusiasm and told Mark about my decision, but to my great surprise he didn't seem at all enthusiastic about it. On the contrary, he advised me not to rush into such an important decision and to wait until our next visit. I insisted that he should at least inform the orphanage immediately to make sure that Kim was no longer available for adoption. He simply ignored my request and said we would sort it out on our next visit.

"At my insistence, we returned to the island one month later and during the trip I sensed that something was wrong with Mark. He was suddenly acting so differently. When we arrived at the orphanage and I asked about Kim, I was told that the girl was no longer there. Mark told me that he had just found out that Kim had already been adopted. It was all so strange. I was of course very disappointed and angry at the same time. And so, the two of us got into quite a heated argument. He then didn't want to talk about it anymore and invited me to an expensive restaurant that same evening. There he told me that he wanted us to move in together but I wasn't impressed, which of course he noticed. Since that incident, there has been some tension between us.

"I had a very strange feeling about him," Diane continued. "He spent more than a whole day with business people, didn't tell me exactly what he was doing or when he would be back. He basically ignored me.

"On my very first visit to this orphanage, I had the strange feeling that something was wrong there. I can't explain it. Later, I asked him how it was possible that Kim could be adopted so quickly, but he avoided the subject. On the last day before we left, I was alone in the hotel again. Without telling Mark, I returned to the orphanage. As the staff there already knew me, they let me in without any problems and then I met a young woman who worked there. When I asked her about Kim, she said she recognised me from my last visit.

"Suddenly, she discreetly pulled me aside and said that little

Kim had not been adopted, but had been taken to the hospital for a few days at the request of Dr Mark Lamborelle. He suspected an illness. I explained to her that I was and am still willing to adopt her. The young woman just said I had better stay away from this case and do nothing more. She begged me not to mention what she had confided in me under any circumstances, otherwise she would be dismissed.

"At that moment, I realised that Mark had appeared and was standing behind me, so I couldn't ask anything else. The next day we flew home.

"Later, I asked him why he didn't want to help me adopt this girl, to which he replied rather gruffly that if we were to continue our relationship, he certainly didn't want a child to be part of that.

"In the days that followed, I made the decision to break up with Mark. He was not the man I had originally thought he was, and certainly not the man I wanted to continue being with. That was a week ago.

"Since then, he has called me a few times and asked me to re-consider my decision. He has told me that he loves me and that maybe we could find another daughter for me, he wouldn't be completely averse to having a child. But I have been very short with him. I've told him our relationship is over. And I also said that I had the feeling that there was something wrong with the orphanage and that I would go to the police, with or without his blessing. And that was the last time I spoke to him."

"Quite a temperament!" said Alan. "When was the last time you spoke to him?"

"Five days ago," Diane said. "Since then, he has tried to speak to me again and again, but I haven't returned his calls. And ever since then I've had the feeling that I'm constantly being watched and followed, I don't know, maybe I'm paranoid about this story. But I have the feeling that someone is after me. The night before last, I saw a van with darkened windows parked across from here all night, and I was suddenly very scared. But nothing happened. And the same scenario happened last night. The same van, but again nothing happened."

"What a story, Diane," Alan said. "But are you sure this surveillance is coming from this man and not just... well, could it be someone else?"

"I suppose so, yes. Because before that, I mean before I wanted to break up with him, I've often had the feeling that someone was following me or watching me."

"But why would he still be after you? Do you have connections to people who could be useful to him?"

"No, I don't think so. My father lives in Holland, my mother died in a car accident, and I can't imagine why my departure has made him so angry. He might assume that I'm going to the police and having the orphanage investigated. But first of all, it's not in this country, and besides, I would never do that. And if he's so reluctant, then there's probably something really wrong, otherwise why didn't he tell me that little Kim was in hospital for an examination?"

"One reason could be that he didn't want to have a child in your partnership," Alan said.

"My gut feeling tells me that there's more to it than that, but I don't care now. I'll get in touch with the orphanage myself soon, go there and meet the lady who spoke to me. Then I'll look for little Kim and, if I'm lucky, I'll adopt her or at least make an application. And I will make sure that Mark Lamborelle is not there at the same time."

"Well, that won't make him very happy when he finds out."

"I couldn't care less! I'm a free person and someone like him can't intimidate me."

Outside, it was storming and raining cats and dogs. Alan looked out of the window onto the street.

"I still think you should go to the police," he said. "This story needs to be reported at the very least; you never know what good it could do. I don't necessarily mean the orphanage story, but I would definitely report your suspicion that you're being followed. Maybe his face is not unknown to them."

Diane thought about it.

"Yes, you're right. You know what, why don't you stay here tonight and then accompany me to the police station first thing in the morning?"

"I ... here ... okay! I'll do anything for a beautiful woman," Alan said and smiled. He had nothing to lose, except that he was falling in love with this woman. *I never dreamed it would be this easy to meet the woman of my dreams,* he thought.

He quickly called David and told him not to expect him until tomorrow morning. David had the key to his apartment, and it wasn't the first time he had been there.

"Well, Alan, I wish you something," David said with a grin.

Alan spent the night on a soft and comfortable couch and thought for the best part of the night about the strange story that this breath-taking beauty had revealed to him.

## *SATURDAY, JULY 6*

Saturday morning, 8 a.m. Diane had already prepared coffee by the time Alan woke up. Within seconds, the story of the previous night came back to him.

"Are you from Luxembourg?" he asked after a long shower. He sat down with Diane at the kitchen counter.

"Yes and no. My mother is, well, she was Luxembourgish, Emilie Fox, and my father is Dutch but has lived in Luxembourg since he was a child. His name is Gerard Van Helden. My mother died in a car accident when we were both very young, my sister and I."

"That must have been terrible for you."

"Yes, it was. We lived with my grandmother in Amsterdam for many years; my father was unable to look after us for a long time after the accident. He survived but it took him over a year to fully recover.

"And when I finally returned to Luxembourg, my sister stayed with our grandmother. I immediately found a job here that I love. I work with people who have hearing disabilities; it gives me a lot when I can teach them something."

"I'm sure that's no easy task?"

"Not at first, but as soon as you can communicate with them, you want to do everything you can to teach them and help them."

"So, you can read lips?"

"Yes, I can do that," she smiled.

"The name—Van Helden—maybe your friend was after money? Your name sounds a bit royal. Do you come from a noble family?"

"No, no, we're just a normal family." She smiled and stood up.

"All right, let's go to the police station and see what they can do for us. Would you accompany me, please?" Diane asked hesitantly.

"By all means, "Alan said. "I won't leave you there alone."

"You know, when we get this over with, I'd love to take you out for a really fancy dinner," Diane said.

"Agreed. With the greatest pleasure." *Today is my day*, he thought.

Together they got into the elevator, went down and left the building. Diane looked up and down the street.

"Everything seems to be fine," she said, "nothing unusual."

"It looks clear to me too," Alan said.

A few meters further on, they stopped at traffic lights which were still red for pedestrians. It was fairly quiet on the road that morning, very little traffic. The school vacations had just begun.

When the pedestrian traffic light turned green, Alan and Diane stepped off the sidewalk onto the street at the same time. Without warning, a car came around the corner at incredible speed, partially drove onto the sidewalk and hit both of them, throwing them onto the street.

When he came to, the only thing Alan could remember was the screeching of brakes and the sight of a couple of pedestrians running towards him from the other side of the road. A few meters away, he could see Diane lying on the road with a great deal of blood around her head. He heard screams, words like "call an ambulance" and "accident", and then he was unconscious again.


"Mr. Moore, can you hear me?" a man's voice called Alan back to life. He slowly opened his eyes and saw a blurry person in a white coat leaning over the bed and pointing a lamp at his eyes.

"I'm Dr. Malone. You're in hospital, you've had an accident, you were hit by a car, can you remember that? Please follow this light with your eyes. Yes, very good, up, down, left, right. Perfect!"

Alan rubbed his eyes. "My head hurts like hell."

"Is there someone we can call?"

Alan gave him David White's name and number, and within an hour David was at his bedside.

"Boy, what are you doing? I thought you were sleeping with a woman?" David's joke fell flat.

"David, that's a very, very long story."

Alan looked around the hospital room, trying to remember

exactly what had happened before he lost consciousness. He tried to get up, but his head hurt too much.

"How long have I been here, what time is it?" When he looked at his watch, he realised that it no longer worked. The glass was broken.

"It's 1 p.m. now. Please don't worry," said the doctor, approaching Alan's bed. "You only have a slight concussion and a few bruises, you'll be fine. I'll leave you now but I'll be back." Then the doctor left the room.

Now Alan managed to sit upright.

"Where is she, where is Diane?" he looked anxiously at David. "Where is the woman who was brought here with me?"

"Hey, lie down, wait, I'll call the doctor," David said.

David went out into the hallway and asked for someone who could give them information about this woman. After a few minutes, Dr. Malone came back in. "Mr. Moore, you should stay in bed and rest for at least a day," he said in a firm voice when he saw that Alan was already half-dressed. "That's not a very good idea," he warned.

"Where is Diane? Is she next door?"

"You mean the lady who was with you? Well, my colleague just told me that she left the hospital this morning, she's fine and after some tests there was no reason to keep her here any longer."

"But there was a lot of blood around her. There was blood all around her head. How could she be all right?"

"It was probably a laceration on your arm or blood from your head, Mr. Moore. I wasn't the doctor who examined Mrs. Van Helden. But in a state of shock, the brain can imagine things that aren't necessarily there. I assure you that Mrs. Van Helden has been examined and is fine."

"Okay. Thank goodness. Thank you, doctor, but I have to go too."

"Not without my permission, Mr. Moore. Not until tomorrow at the earliest."

"I'm signing out now, at my own risk, Dr. Malone. Thanks for everything, but I don't have any more time."

Climbing out of bed, Alan called to his friend, "Come on, David, let's go."

Without waiting for David's reply, Alan put on his shoes and about ten minutes later he and David left the hospital. They took a cab and during the ride, Alan told David what had happened since he had met Diane on the bus.

"Oh dear, that smells like trouble," David said. "I suppose we're on our way to the lady's apartment."

"You bet!"

The cab dropped the two men off on Avenue Monterey, right in front of Diane Van Helden's house. Alan rang the bell several times, but there was no answer.

"Maybe she's not here yet, or she's just gone shopping, or she's looking for you, or ..."

"And we hadn't even exchanged phone numbers yet! Who could have known ..."

The two men then decided to go home and come back later that afternoon.

In the meantime, Alan had filled his friend David in on all the details of Diane's strange story. He also had a long phone conversation with his friend Alfonse Weis, who had hosted the poker evening the night before. The former intelligence officer confirmed that the woman's disappearance was indeed strange, but since Alan didn't really know her, it was difficult to start any kind of search. Alfonse suggested waiting a few days, but that wasn't what Alan Moore had in mind.

In the early evening, he and David tried to ring her doorbell again, but there was no answer.

There was not the slightest trace of Diane Van Helden. No one answered the door, and after the two friends asked again at the hospital that evening, they only received confirmation that Diane Van Helden had been discharged from hospital that morning.

"David, something's wrong. That's what my instinct tells me."

They looked at each other. "And now what?" asked David, seeing in his friend's face what he had already been thinking about.

"I'm going to look for her, no matter what. Someone has kidnapped her, or she has gone into hiding for a while because someone is after her again. I can only sincerely hope that she's still alive."

"But where will you look for her?"

"I don't know, but I'll think of something. Maybe I'll fly to the Dominican Republic and visit the orphanage, 'Pequeños Angeles.'"

David looked at his long-time friend with some concern. He knew that Alan would not be put off from pursuing this project.

# CLAIRE



## *SUNDAY, JULY 7*

In the Parisian theatre, rue Blanche, the illusionist and magician was bowing to the audience, enjoying the overwhelming applause. The audience was fascinated, whistling and shouting, rising finally together to give the actor a standing ovation. Matthew McKenna was enjoying the atmosphere to the full. He extended kissing hands to the audience; his beaming smile visible to everyone in the audience. He felt carried away by the atmosphere, as if he were in a trance. His mischievous smile and the look in his eyes left no room for doubt: He was simply happy. Tears of joy welled up in his eyes.

This show was Matthew's third and last in Paris for this season. The dark-haired, handsome forty-two-year-old Luxembourger took his last bow. His black suit, white silk shirt and black bow tie suited him very well. His warm brown eyes lit up as he kissed his assistant's hand: "Mesdames et Messieurs, mon assistante Nathalie." Another overwhelming round of applause filled the hall.

"Merci, infiniment, merci et à très bientôt. Je vous aime!" He gave his assistant a beautiful and grateful smile, and disappeared behind the red curtain within seconds.

*How I love this magical atmosphere that evokes the same feelings every time*, Matthew thought. He was a medium-sized and rather muscular man, popular with women who liked his charming and boyish manner.

That feeling of being carried away by the audience's applause still filled Matthew with as much joy as his very first performance. He enjoyed being on stage and he adored the world of magic. He loved to cast a spell over his audience for a few hours, to amaze them, to enchant them with his tricks. After every performance, he felt deep inside that he was born for this and nothing else.

However, the magician also had a second profession. Matthew McKenna earned his living as a general practitioner in Luxembourg, where he had his practice in Howald, a suburb of the capital. This career choice had not actually been his own decision, but that of his father, the owner and director of the most prestigious private clinic in Luxembourg. The world of magic had fascinated Matthew since childhood and he knew even then that he would one day be on stage. Over the years, he had managed to combine these two activities, and few people could really understand how a professional doctor could spend weeks a year traveling the world and performing his shows as a magician and illusionist.

When Matthew finally disappeared behind the curtain, his cell phone rang. It was his younger brother, Jeff on the phone.

"Matthew, Mum's not feeling well. I think you should come home as soon as possible."

Matthew and Jeff's mother, Claire McKenna, had just turned sixty-five last year when she was diagnosed with bowel cancer. After an operation and several months of treatment, the cancer seemed to have been beaten. However, a few weeks ago, shortly before Matthew was due to leave for Paris, Claire's condition had deteriorated rapidly. Matthew had the impression that she was getting weaker by the day. The chemotherapy had simply weakened her body too much.

"I'll be back in the morning, Jeff."

Silence.

"Hey, Jeff, I said I'd be home tomorrow ... all right?"

"No, I don't think so. Professor Weydert has asked us all to come to the hospital tonight, and ... "

"You're calling from the hospital. Let me speak to Mum!"

"She is not conscious. She is under morphine because of the severe pain."

"Okay, I'm leaving now. I'll be there as soon as I can!" Matthew interrupted the conversation without waiting for Jeff's answer.

As if in a trance, he informed his team that he would not be able to attend their usual closing dinner.

"Thank you so much for your tireless efforts. You have all been fabulous and without you, I wouldn't be able to do what I do."

He hugged every member of his team and shortly after 8 p.m. his white Golf Variant with the large inscription "My world is MAGIC" and a photo of a black hat with a white rabbit and a magic wand sped down the highway towards Luxembourg.

"Oh Mum, please wait for me, please ... I'm on my way ... please ... if there's a God out there somewhere, a creator, please, just give me five minutes with her ... please! I have to say goodbye to you, Claire."

Tears rolled down Matthew's cheeks. He sped up his drive. Images from his childhood flashed through his mind. He saw himself as a ten-year-old boy coming home from shopping with his mother. She had just bought him his first magic box, a plastic toy for children, but for him it was the most precious object he had ever owned. He was filled with immense joy and pride. Matthew had wished for nothing more than the little magic box.

His father, on the other hand, would have preferred to see him with a plastic stethoscope, a complete children's pharmacy, but that didn't interest the sensitive little boy at the time. His brother

Jeff, two years younger, quickly adapted to his father's wishes and thus automatically received his greater affection. John McKenna's private clinic was the best-known and largest clinic in Luxembourg, and he was a respected and renowned surgeon. Yes, this was his world, the only one that ever meant anything to him. And anyone who did not share his interests did not fit.

Jeff was and remained the preferred and perfect son for Prof. Dr. John McKenna. It took Jeff three more years to complete his medical degree, but he finally did it. He then married and gave his parents two sweet grandchildren, the perfect family life.

Matthew had never fitted into this pattern. He had graduated from medical school with honours and then had worked as a doctor to earn a living. However, the world of illusions, so full of wonders and surprises, had continued to fascinate him. He had kept his first magic box as a very precious, irreplaceable memento, the most important memory of his childhood.

A few years later, after an internship at his father's clinic, Matthew, then thirty, broke free. He took a break from the world of medicine and spent four years in the United States, studying the magical world in depth.

Matthew found it sad that his father was visibly ashamed of his son, a fact that he expressed in every possible situation. He never missed an opportunity to make fun of Matthew and looked down on him.

A renowned doctor and head of a hospital with a son who was a magician, a son who conjured white rabbits out of a hat; for John McKenna this was a disgrace. Although Matthew had passed his final exams with ease, Jeff always remained the favourite son.

Sometimes Matthew wondered what Jeff would have really liked to do with his life if he hadn't had to live under this constant pressure to perform in order to realise his father's dream.

However, Jeff would never talk about it, especially not to his brother.

Their mother Claire, however, always treated the two sons the same. She made no distinction and did her best to comfort Matthew in every possible way when it became increasingly clear that their father favoured Jeff and was visibly distancing himself from his youngest son. The final break came when Matthew officially made "illusionist" his second profession and then announced this publicly. His father only briefly commented that this was not a profession, but nonsense, and that his son would eventually realise that he could not make a living from it.

Speeding towards Luxembourg, Matthew was distracted by the pleasant summer evening, warm, with very little traffic. Finally reaching the clinic, Matthew parked in front of the door and ran up the stairs.

As he reached his mother's room, his father was just coming out. Matthew stopped and looked at his father as he waved his head in denial and looked at his son with tears in his eyes. Claire McKenna's life had ended just moments before.

## TUESDAY, JULY 9

It was just after 12 p.m. when Lis Chandler drove to the supermarket. "How nice to be back in my home country," she thought as she turned into the parking lot. The forty-year-old, slim woman with long, dark brown hair had returned to Luxembourg for good a few weeks ago. She had lived on the Spanish island of Mallorca for the last twenty-five years, working as a foreign language teacher.

This spring, however, she had decided to return to Luxembourg.

She had applied to the local university as a Spanish teacher and was promptly accepted. With a job starting in September, Lis had a good two months to settle back into life in her home country. For the time being, Lis had rented an apartment on Rue Lavandier, near the city centre. Later, she wanted to buy a small house somewhere, but it was still too early to decide where that would be.

Lis Chandler was a somewhat strange character. The attractive woman with the green eyes had a black belt in karate and was also familiar with several other martial arts. And not without reason. Almost no one in Luxembourg knew where she had first come from, and after so many years, hardly anyone remembered. As a child and teenager, some of her friends had called her the girl with the sad eyes. She did indeed have a rather melancholy expression on her face.

Lis' father, Bernard was a respected and internationally known bank director and a member of the board of a large local bank, as well as its main shareholder. Matthew's father and he met regularly on the golf course.

She had just got out of the car when her mother rang her on her cell phone.

"Hello Lis, do you have a moment, I have some sad news."

"Hey Mum. Sure, what happened?"

"Claire McKenna died the day before yesterday. The news is in today's paper."

"Claire … Matthew's mother! How sad for him."

The news touched Lis deeply and within moments, the thought of Matthew had transported her twenty-five years back in time.

Lis had just turned fifteen, he was eighteen. They both wore the same style of jeans, attended the same college, and were in love with each other. Matthew was Lis' first great love.

The more she thought about the past, the more tears came to her eyes.

She leaned back in the car as the many memories spontaneously took over. Matthew and she had spent a lot of time together back then. Both her parents were close friends and belonged to the upper class of wealthy families in Luxembourg.

Matthew had been an adventurous boy but at the same time, very sensitive. He was always ready to perform a magic trick out of the blue. Countless times, he and Lis had walked around the neighbouring forest, talking about everything and nothing. They had had a close relationship for more than six months, and nothing and no one could keep them apart.

Despite meeting as children, they had only become a couple much later during a local summer festival. Back then, Matthew had shoulder-length hair and looked more like a hippie, a fact that had always caused tension between him and his father. That night at the festival, he had plucked up his courage to ask Lis to dance. They danced all night, until the early morning, when their first evening together had ended with a kiss. It was a beautiful memory. They had been a couple since that night, and their friends and classmates and the whole neighbourhood quickly knew it. Claire McKenna always brought fresh pastries on Sunday afternoons when Lis was at Matthew's house. It was a nice, simple time, free of worries and obligations.

And then came the abrupt separation, triggered by an incident that Lis never wanted to be reminded of again. She had tried to erase it from her memory and from her life.

Later, she had moved to Mallorca and the capital Palma, where her parents' vacation home was located, became her new home.

Matthew went to London to study medicine, but the practical side of his lessons caused him problems. It took him a long time to become immune to the physical nature of medicine.

After graduating, he returned to Luxembourg and completed his internship at his father's clinic.

When Matthew had his doctorate in his pocket, he decided to make a fundamental change in his life, saying to his father one evening: "Dad, I'm thirty now and I've spent too many years of my life doing exactly what you expected of me. Now I'm going to go in a different direction, I want to find out who I really am, at least I'm going to try. I need a break from medicine and want to explore the world of magic, my world."

This news hit both John and Claire McKenna very hard, although it didn't come as too much of a surprise to his mother. All that mattered to her was that her son led a happy life and did what he thought was right.

Matthew had made a fair suggestion to his father to work two days a week at the clinic and use the other three days for his magic, but his father said he couldn't have a doctor who would conjure white rabbits out of a black hat. He was worried it would have a negative effect on the McKenna Clinic's reputation.

This was the final break in the father-son relationship. It was very painful for Matthew's mother, who had always tried to avoid this situation and keep things between them peaceful.


Matthew moved to the USA and lived in Las Vegas. When he returned to Luxembourg after almost five years at the age of thirty-five, he opened a small medical practice, and thanks to the excellent reputation of the McKenna Clinic's name and his father, Matthew quickly gained many patients. John McKenna, however, was furious. He thought it was a disgrace that a McKenna was traveling the world as a magician instead of becoming a senior doctor. It was an even greater disgrace to his father that Matthew had put up posters of himself as a magician in the waiting room of his surgery.

Lis returned to reality when she heard her mother's voice again.

"Lis, are you still there? Why are you so quiet? Will you come to Claire's funeral?"

"Yeah, yeah, sure. I'll pick you up, Mum."

Lis got out of the car and hurried into the supermarket. She quickly bought the few items she needed and went to the express checkout. While she waited in the queue, she looked around until she suddenly spotted a familiar face in the queue right next to her.

Their eyes met almost simultaneously. The tall, dark-haired man looked a little surprised at first, then he smiled. "Hey, Lis! I would have expected anyone else right now, but not you."

"Thomas! Well, if that's not a coincidence!"

The man paid and waited for her at the other end of the checkout.

"I'm so glad to see you after so many years." He spontaneously hugged her.

"Are you on vacation?"

"No, I recently moved back to Luxembourg."

Thomas Walter was visibly happy to see her again.

They had met a few years ago on Mallorca when Thomas was on vacation there. This developed into a rather loose relationship. He spent his vacations with her, usually renting an apartment on the island or traveling around. They rarely spent the days at her house. They had spent many hours together, until the day Lis broke off the relationship abruptly and without warning. She told Thomas that she wasn't cut out for a long-term relationship or to live with someone. She needed a lot of freedom. Thomas had no choice but to accept this brief explanation.

Thomas had lost none of his charm; on the contrary, he looked better than ever, Lis thought. A few grey hairs had blended into his black hair and his green eyes still held the same charm that she had succumbed to many years ago. After the break-up, however, she had made sure there was no more contact, apart from annual birthday and Christmas cards.

"Are you free for dinner tonight? I'll invite you!" he asked spontaneously.

"Yes, with pleasure."

"There is a new Spanish restaurant in Alzingen."

"It's a deal! 8 p.m.?

"Perfect, I'll see you there," Thomas said.


At 8 p.m. sharp, the two met in front of the restaurant. Thomas hugged Lis warmly.

"How nice to see you, Lis. Your hair is longer than ever," he greeted her. He let a strand of it slip through his fingers. "And still that melancholy look in your eyes."

"They say that the eyes are the mirror of the soul," she said and smiled.

They entered. A friendly waiter greeted them and escorted them to a table by the window, where they took their seats.

"Tell me, what brings you back to Luxembourg now, homesickness? Have you had enough of all the Spaniards?"

"Both, actually! I just wanted to live here again, I missed this small country, my language and my mother."

"And your father?"

"Oh, my father ... Not so much, actually. Bernard is still as married to his bank as ever. I often wonder how my mother deals with it, he's hardly ever home. He's not only president of his empire but also a board member of a number of other companies and associations. She just loves him very much. It's her decision."

"You never spoke much about your father back then, why?"

Lis raised her shoulders. "You know, Thomas, we've grown very far apart over the years. When my brother Georges died in that bike accident at the age of fourteen, my father's world fell apart. He had big plans for his son."

"He was your twin brother, right?"

"Yes, that was him. We were so close. Georges was such a lively personality, funny, crazy, clever. According to my father's plan, Georges should have taken over the entire private bank. His empire should have been called & Son, not & Daughter."

"You wouldn't have wanted that anyway, would you?"

"No, but that was never an option either, until after Georges' death. After that, my father told me to study economics, with the idea that he would then introduce me to his banking world. And from the moment I told him that his whole financial world didn't interest me at all, I was no longer the beloved daughter. I knew that when I was fifteen and I knew that would never change. Later, when I was living in Mallorca, he didn't visit me very often. Every now and then he would come with my mother for a short vacation, but we were quite far apart."

"That's sad. But it's never too late to improve the relationship a little."

"Well, it would take a lot more than just 'a bit of patching up'. But that doesn't bother me anymore."

Thomas and Lis took a break from their chatting to order food.

"And you, Thomas, what's new in Luxembourg? Are you still single?"

"Yes, I've been waiting for you," he replied half-jokingly, half-seriously, with a smile on his face. He was as charming as ever.

Then Lis' cell phone rang.

"Please excuse me." She took the call.

"Hello ... Eric, what's going on here? I'm ... what? Oh no." She shook her head. "Sure, I'm at the Spanish restaurant in Alzingen. I'll see you in a few minutes."

She put the phone back in her pocket and looked at Thomas.

"Someone is standing outside my front door and can't find the house key," Lis explained briefly. "And now this 'someone' wants to pick up the key from me."

"Aha!" Thomas was curious to know who this 'someone' could be.

About fifteen minutes later, a tall, slim, rather good-looking young man in his mid-twenties entered the restaurant. He had well-cut, light brown hair and was wearing jeans and a white shirt. He looked around and spotted Lis.

"I think your lodger has just arrived," Thomas said with an ironic undertone to Lis, who was sitting with her back to the door.

She turned around and signalled to Eric with her hand.

The young man approached the table, put his hand on her shoulder and kissed her on the cheek. She introduced the two men to each other.

"Thomas, this is Eric! Eric, this is Thomas, an old friend."

"Hello," said Thomas. "I'm delighted to meet you! Although 'old' refers to the years of our friendship, not my age," he said jokingly.

"I'm pleased to meet you." Eric gave him a firm handshake with an open look.

"I'm sorry, Lis, I just can't find that damn key. I'm so sure I put it in my pocket, but ... "

"No problem. Voilà!"

She took her key out of her pocket and handed it to him. "But please remember to be home later, otherwise I won't be able to get in."

"Okay, I'm not going out tonight."

"I'm so glad you're back!" she said.

"Me too," Eric whispered, kissed Lis on the cheek once more

and said goodbye to Thomas with a handshake. "It was a pleasure to meet you. Enjoy your meal."

Thomas looked at Lis a little suspiciously.

"What?" she asked with a somewhat ironic look.

"Didn't you always say that younger men weren't your thing?"

"Yes, I did!" She had to smile as she looked at Thomas, who was obviously quite surprised and curious.

"Don't tell me this young man is your age ... Not that it's any of my business, don't take this the wrong way, but ..."

"But you want an answer, don't you? You're funny, Thomas!" She looked at him mockingly.

"Of course, you don't owe me an explanation."

Lis smiled mischievously. "Maybe I can answer two questions at once."

Thomas looked at her curiously. Of course, he really wanted to know.

"Eric is my son."

Thomas, who was about to bring the fork to his mouth, almost dropped it and slowly put it back on his plate.

His facial expression spoke volumes, changing from complete surprise to thoughtfulness, confusion, incomprehension, and then he quickly counted backwards in his mind. Mallorca, a good ten years ago. He quickly came to the conclusion that Eric had already existed back then. Lis had never mentioned him.

"I can see a lot of questions on your face," Lis said. "I never mentioned Eric because you said quite early on in our relationship that you would rather have your freedom and that children were not an option for you."

He interrupted her abruptly. "Hey, that was a bit different. I didn't want a baby; I didn't want a fresh start with a child ... But you ... I ... Of course ... I would have tolerated your son ... I mean accepted, embraced. You should have talked to me about it. But where was Eric when we met at your house, when we were on vacation together?"

"He often spent his vacations with my parents in Luxembourg. And he also spent some time at a boarding school."

"But ... this boy, I mean this young man, how old is he, he looks quite grown up?"

Lis looked at Thomas for a while before she replied: "He's twenty-four!"

"He's ... I see ... So, you were about sixteen when you became a mother. What happened, a one-night stand?"

"You could call it that ..."

"His father?"

"That wasn't the right thing to do. I don't want to dwell on this topic. Eric is a great boy, now a man, and that's all that matters to me. And I love him more than anything."

Thomas thought it was a good idea to change the subject. He didn't want to burden his first meeting with Lis with any more questions.

"Hey, I'm so happy to see you again," she confirmed.

"Me too." When Thomas looked at her, he still felt the same butterflies in his stomach as back then. She had the gift of looking at someone with that melancholy gaze, with her clear green eyes, and the man opposite her literally melted away. Her long hair framed her oval face with its flawless skin, the perfectly shaped lips, the thick black eyelashes, no make-up; she was simply a natural beauty.

When she appeared in a tight dress, it was easy to mistake her for a movie star. But most of the time she wore jeans and a blouse or T-shirt.

The two of them talked at length about the past years, exchanging stories about many things that had happened. They left the restaurant quite late.

"We'll keep in touch, yeah?" Thomas held her hand. It was obvious that he wanted to see Lis again.

"By all means! I'll call."

He accompanied Lis to the car and when she got in, he gently held her arm for a moment.

"I have another question: back in Mallorca, you had that weird knife tied around your ankle the whole time. Is it still there?"

Lis, who was already seated, looked at him and then pulled up the leg of her right pants. A leather shaft with a knife in it was tied around her ankle.

"Some things never change, even over the years." She looked at him, half smiling, half serious, and winked.

"And I still don't like surprises." She gave him a wonderful, open smile and then closed the car door.

As Thomas was on his way home, he thought back to his romance with her. Lis. He hadn't expected to see her again, but he had to admit to himself that he was still in love with this mysterious woman. He had realised that again tonight.

When they had spent their first night together in Mallorca, he had seen the knife when she had taken it from her ankle. For a moment, he thought she was going to attack him. He had never met a woman who took off her knife before going to bed with him. The explanation she gave at the time was simple: I don't like surprises.

Thomas thought this was a bit exaggerated and asked her if she could handle the knife. She said that she had been in a precarious situation before and that it would never happen to her again.

He also recalled that they were once walking through the streets of Palma late at night when they were suddenly followed by two rather drunk youths. When they caught up with them, one of them pulled out a knife and threatened them to hand over their money and cell phones.

Within moments, Lis managed to lay one of them flat on the ground with a few lightning-fast movements. She put her foot on his arm, took the knife from him and told him to go to hell. The other one had already run away, and the second one did the same as soon as she took her foot off his arm.

Thomas was perplexed and later asked Lis about the incident. She simply explained that she had attended some self-defence courses in earlier years. She looked a little too professional for that, he thought at the time, but preferred to leave the subject alone.


When Lis came home, Eric was in the kitchen making himself a cup of coffee.

"Hey, it's good to see you home again."

"Yes, I'm glad too. We've spent so little time together. But Mum, I want to introduce you to someone soon. I've found the love of my life!"

"Hey, I almost thought so. You've been walking around in a particularly good mood for a few days now, humming songs ... but I didn't want to ask."

"I can't hide anything from you," he laughed.

"What's her name?"

"Caro. Caroline, to be precise. She looks so good and she's so sweet!"

"Do you have a photo?"

Eric picked up his cell phone and held it out to Lis.

On it was an image of a young, attractive woman, with blonde, shoulder-length hair and wearing a leather jacket and pink leggings.

"Very beautiful at first sight! When will I meet her?"

"I'll ask her when I get the chance if she wants to meet her future mother-in-law yet or if it's still a bit early."

"Oh, you're so bad! No, seriously, Eric, I'm happy for you. What does she do for a living?"

"She works at the McKenna Private Hospital in the admissions department. I'm going to meet her there tomorrow at lunch. She suggested it this morning."

"Fine!" She pressed a kiss to her son's forehead and then retired to bed.

# WEDNESDAY, JULY 10

Eric had already arrived at the hospital half an hour before his date with Caro, he didn't want to be late. When he arrived, he thought about passing the reception counter to wave to his new girlfriend but as there were several people in the queue, he continued on to the cafeteria where he sat down at one of the tables and watched the people passing by. There were patients as well as doctors and nurses taking a break in the cafeteria.

While Eric was people watching, a rather tall, fully bearded man with sunglasses and a leather jacket came over and sat down at the table next to him. The man moved a coffee from his tray, placed it on the table, and immediately unfolded his daily newspaper, behind which he then disappeared. He didn't seem to take off his sunglasses.

Finally, Eric saw Caro coming towards him from a distance and immediately forgot everything else.


He stood up and they greeted each other warmly with a hug and an intense kiss. "Hello, nice to see you," he said.

"I'm so glad you came." Caro said as she sat down. Eric quickly bought two sandwiches and a salad, as well as drinks from the counter.

"You look so good. I could fall in love with you right now," he whispered when he returned. "A lot of work?"

"Yes, it's been crazy the last few days and ..." She broke off in mid-sentence. "There, look at the man at the far right. That's the head of the clinic. Prof. Dr. John McKenna himself. And next to him, his son Jeff. He's the head of radiology, I think."

"I see, should I know them?"

"No, you don't, but it's important for me to know who my bosses are."

Just as they had started eating, a man in a white doctor's coat approached them. Eric spotted him first and then Caro saw him too.

"Dr. Lamborelle, good afternoon." Caro greeted the new arrival.

When the bearded man heard this name, he looked over his newspaper and briefly glanced at Caro, Eric and the doctor. Then he disappeared behind the newspaper again.

"Hello Caro and bon appétit!" Dr. Lamborelle said, looking at Eric. Then he turned to Caro again. "Maybe I'll see you later. I'm busy for another two hours, then I'll come by the counter."

"Yes, sure ... See you later, Dr. Lamborelle."

The doctor continued walking past their table in the direction of the two Dr. McKennas, who were still engrossed in conversation.

"He's a doctor who comes by here from time to time and often attends meetings with Jeff McKenna," Caro said. "He's very friendly and waves to me every time I see him."

"Is he a specialist?" asked Eric.

"I don't know. He's never said what exactly he does, and I don't want to ask. I think he looks good though, blond hair, blue eyes, tall."

Eric looked at Caro seriously, but with a twinkle in his eye. "Well ... I hope you don't like him too much!"

"No, there's someone here I like much better who has even more magical eyes," she laughed.

"That's very good, beautiful lady. Will I see you at the weekend?"

"I think it will be possible," Caro said at first with a serious face, then she laughed.

"I really hope so." Eric kissed her goodbye very deeply.

Lost in thought and daydreams, he then made his way home again.

## THURSDAY, JULY 11

Thursday dawned with a rainy morning. Both Lis and her mother were due to attend Claire McKenna's funeral. As they entered the funeral hall, all the McKenna family members were standing together. Lis saw Matthew long before he saw her. She looked at him. He stood motionless, wearing sunglasses and looking exhausted. His hair was no longer shoulder-length as it had been when they were young, but about an inch long, and he was unshaven. The look suited him. His father John was standing right next to him, followed by his brother, Jeff. Next to them were a few more people Lis didn't know.

She placed her condolence card in the box provided. When she came to Matthew to offer her condolences, the words stuck in her throat and tears blurred her vision. Matthew was visibly surprised to see Lis standing before him. He held her hand for a long moment and Lis had the impression that their eyes met, even though she couldn't tell through his sunglasses. Then she continued on her way to the row of chairs where her mother sat.

Finally, the ceremony was over and Lis returned home. Her thoughts had been with Matthew all evening and all night. He had become so thin.

It was the first time that she had seen him with such short hair. *Claire's death must have hurt him a lot*, Lis thought. He and his mother had been very close all his life. She had always given him the love his father never could. Matthew was a very sensitive person, even as a child, Lis remembered.

Lis had felt a strong desire to comfort him, to take him in her arms, to talk to him or just sit quietly and listen. When they were both teenage lovers, they discovered they had so much in common. They were both highly sensitive people, which brought them even closer together.

Then Lis' life had changed abruptly and with it, her trust in Matthew. This incident was also the reason why Lis ended their relationship. Back then, Lis had told him in confidence that she had seen her dead brother Georges, that he had spoken to her when she was in a really bad way, that he had come to help her and to reassure her that she would not die.

What had brought their relationship crashing down was the fact that Matthew didn't believe her. He told her that she should see a psychiatrist. Lis had never spoken to anyone about this encounter and when he didn't believe her, Lis stopped answering his calls.

Later, Lis came to understand better the reactions to expect when talking about a deceased person. After this incident, she never spoke to anyone about it again.

And what had happened then was long time ago ... Forgotten and forgiven, and perhaps no longer so important.


## *FRIDAY, JULY 12*

Friday morning. The phone rang shortly after 8 a.m. It was Lis' mother.

"Good morning, my darling. I'm late, I'm on my way to the dentist. But I just had a call from Matthew. He thanked me for attending the funeral and gave me his cell phone number. He asked me to give it to you. He would like to talk to you and if you feel the same way, he would be very happy to hear from you. He doesn't dare to ring you, after all that happened so long ago. He'd rather leave it to you."

"Thanks, Mum." Lis wrote down the number and found she was glad that Matthew had rung.

As she was preparing a hearty breakfast, Eric came into the kitchen.

"Morning, Lis." He kissed her on the cheek, took a cup of coffee and sat down with her.

"You know what, I've been thinking about moving back to Luxembourg for a few days now. I don't think London is my future."

"Because of Caro?"

"I've been thinking about it for a while now. But Caro makes the decision easier for me. What do you think?"

"Of course, I'll be very happy when my son is within reach again. But what are you going to do with your studies? Are you going to study here or are you going to look for a job?"

Eric looked at Lis. "Do you want me to knock on Grandpa's door?"

"You know he'll welcome you with open arms. But if I were you, I would do it on a trial basis first. The gentleman who is your grandfather is a tough one. I know him, believe me!" Lis looked at her son seriously.

"Why don't you ask him if he would take you on for six months? You'll find out if that's your world and, more importantly, you can take the chance to get to know him. Because if not, then his bank is not for you."

"I'm okay with that. And nobody has to know that I'm his

grandson. I have a different name anyway. And there's no one to make the connection. He just has to be okay with it."

"I think that's good. Talk to him, Eric. But if it doesn't feel right, please don't do it just because of Caro. We can always find you another financial company here in the country."

"Grandpa wouldn't survive if I went to the competition."

"Oh, he's had to put up with other disappointments. And he got through them well, trust me," Lis added a little sarcastically.

"Okay, I'll do that."

After Eric had left, Lis immediately dialled Matthew's number. She could hardly wait to hear his voice again after all these years. Somehow, she was already a little excited.

"McKenna."

"Hi Matt. It's me, Lis."

She could hear a sliver of brightness in his voice as he replied, "Lis! How nice of you to call right back."

"Once again, my heartfelt condolences," Lis said on the verge of tears.

"Thank you so much." There was a pause and Lis could sense Matthew's overwhelming sadness return.

"Are you free tonight?" he asked spontaneously.

*Strange,* she thought, *it's as if we had only parted yesterday. Talking to each other, so easy, so familiar, after all these years.*

"Absolutely!" They arranged to meet at a local Japanese restaurant at around 8 p.m..

Matthew was already waiting outside the entrance when Lis arrived that evening. He was wearing a white T-shirt and jeans. She took one last look in the mirror, then got out and walked towards him. They stood still for a few moments, just looking at each other.

Twenty-five years had passed, but Lis felt as if she had last seen him yesterday.

"Hey!" he said finally.

"Hello Matt. It's good to see you! I'm so sorry about Claire." Lis began to cry.

Without saying a word, he took a step towards her and they embraced for a long time.

"It hurts so badly," he whispered.

"I know," she said, "I know." Brushing his tears away with the back of his hand, Matthew took Lis' elbow and steered her towards the restaurant.

The waiter led them to their table and they took their seats.

Lis checked her make-up in a small compact she took from her purse.

"It's so nice to see you after all these years," he said. "It's been so long and you've hardly changed, you're just as I remember you. Only then you were a teenager and now you're a beautiful woman."

"Well, the twenty-five years have made me a little older. Your haircut has changed. Normally shoulder-length, now just a few centimetres," she replied, a little embarrassed. "But it looks good on you. You still have that boyish, mischievous look. But tell me how you've been. How does it feel to be a doctor, you're the one who decided to go in this direction."

"Partly. I'm a part-time doctor *and* a part-time magician. Crazy, isn't it?"

"No, I think it's great. So, you resisted all the pressure. Well done!"

"I did find it hard to stand up to my father, as you can imagine," Matthew said. "And without his financial support, I would never have been able to realise the other side of my career. But when I revealed to him after graduation that I was going to the States for a while to become a professional magician, that was the end of our father-son relationship. Well, if there ever was one.

"When I didn't want to join his clinic, but wanted to run my own practice so I could work the way I wanted to, I ruined things with him forever. And my super brother Jeff, of course, did everything our father expected him to do. But what about you, Lis? What have you been doing all these years? I want to know everything."

Matthew looked at the beautiful woman sitting opposite him. Her hair was even longer than he remembered. Her clear green eyes still had a hint of melancholy. She seemed very calm.

"When did you get back to Luxembourg?" he asked as he continued to look at her. His extremely short haircut suited him, but his eyes looked tired.

"I've only been back in the country for a few weeks. I've had enough of Mallorca and all the tourists. It's been long enough and I'm glad to be back."

"And how ... are you ... I mean ... how does it feel to be back in this environment? Are the memories no longer too present?" Matthew dared to ask.

"It's actually better than I thought at first. I've been wanting to come back to my home country. The distance was necessary to continue living. I worked a lot on myself and it took many long months before I was able to walk around normally again.

"I no longer suffer from paranoia, I can move around freely, I no longer stare at people as if I see an enemy in everyone. The only thing that has remained is the claustrophobia. I can't bear to be locked up somewhere if I can't see a direct escape route. I also have a big problem with getting on an airplane, but I can control it, at least for short distances. The regular flight to and from Mallorca was good training for me."

"I'm glad you're doing so well, Lis. I've asked myself so often how you're doing, what you're doing. You banished me from your life and quite rightly so. I was a fool in many ways."

Before Lis could answer, Matthew continued.

"I know I acted like an idiot back then, but I didn't realise it until later. And I'm very sorry about that. I've thought about it a lot, and if I could have undone anything, it would have been what I said to you. It was so damn unfair and reckless of me."

"No, it wasn't that. Back then, you couldn't really understand what I was saying to you. But now I understand a lot more, believe me. I've learned that this kind of conversation is only possible with people who have already had similar experiences, because they know it's reality, but otherwise ... well, let's leave the subject, okay?"

"Yes, of course. I'm just very happy to see you again," Matthew said, briefly touching her hands.

Lis looked at him. Yes, when she looked at him, she still had that familiar feeling of butterflies in her stomach. But she wanted to keep that to herself at the moment.

The food was served. As Matthew had hardly eaten anything in the last two days, he was finished in no time at all.

"It's so unbelievable that Mum is no longer there, that I can never speak to her again, that it's all over. Death is so damn final."

"Yes, unfortunately it is. And on top of that, you realise that things will never be the same again."

"When your twin brother Georges died, you must have felt the same?" Matthew asked.

"Yes," Lis said. "It was like someone had taken half of me away, we were so close ..." She ran her fingers through her hair.

"Did you never get married?" Lis asked, impulsively changing the subject.

"No, I never have," Matthew replied. "I have a relationship with a married woman. She's uncomplicated and we have agreed to keep it that way. I don't want to move in together or get married at any point, and she has accepted that ...Well, we agreed that four years ago. Brigitte is a very nice and clever woman. We get on well together."

"And it wouldn't be enough for more?"

"It's never been important to me, until now. I want to be free and to be able to travel whenever I want. I want to be unattached and not have all these complications of relationship stress. It's just not for me. And you?"

"I never got married either. But this week I met an old friend again in the supermarket. We met on Mallorca and fell in love. But the relationship was ... let's say, complicated. Thomas is a very nice man. I'm glad to have met him again after more than ten years. I'm gradually settling in very well here and hope to see some old acquaintances and friends from back then.

"And I have a son, Eric, who is now twenty-four."

"A son?" Matthew asked. "And his father?"

"I raised Eric on my own."

"If Eric is twenty-four, then you were..?" Matthew calculated back in a flash.

"Sixteen."

"Did you fall in love with the first Spaniard you saw when you were there?" Matthew joked.

"Not quite so ... maybe we'll save that topic for another day," Lis replied.

"Why did you just run away and leave the country back then?"

Lis leaned back a little and played with her hair.

"It wasn't easy to get back on my feet after the whole incident and I wanted to get away from everything and everyone. You remember we had this huge summer house in Mallorca and that was the ideal solution for me. I was able to finish my studies there. We had a housekeeper, my mother was often there, and so the years went by. Over the years, I familiarised myself with some martial arts, got my black belt in karate and ..."

She made a head movement and pointed to her leg under the table while discreetly pulling up her right trouser leg. Tonight, too, she had her knife tied to her ankle.

Matthew looked, wide-eyed, and then looked back at Lis.

"That's not part of karate training, is it?"

"No, it isn't. But I feel safer with it and can defend myself if the situation requires it."

"Do you really think you can hurt someone if you're attacked?" Matthew was surprised after all.

"Not only that," she looked at him seriously. "I could kill someone if they challenged me."

Silence. Matthew took a sip of wine.

"If anyone ever attacks me again or tries to, Matt, they will only have one chance. The first attempt has to be so precise that I can't make my move. Otherwise, I'm fast enough to kill anyone. But enough of this topic. We're here to have a nice evening." Matthew was shocked and surprised by this statement.

"You know, my dear father wasn't particularly interested in Eric when he was young. But that has changed for the better in recent years, ever since Eric decided to study economics and banking. Bernard has been much more sociable with his grandson since then. He fawns over him here and there, takes him to the bank now and then. I can see him working there."

"Is that what Eric wants?"

"I don't know. I have the feeling that he doesn't really know himself yet. But if that's what Eric wants, that's fine with me. As long as he doesn't feel forced to do it. He's been studying in London for the last five years and has now been back home for a few days. I need to discuss this seriously with him. He's now considering staying in Luxembourg, not least because of his new girlfriend."

"To pick up on the theme about us in earlier years," Matthew was a little nervous. "There was the fact that I advised you to see a psychiatrist immediately, just because you had told me that you had seen your deceased brother."

"To be honest, it didn't make my situation any worse, that's how bad I was at the time. Actually, the total change of country and environment did me a lot of good. The first few years on the island were very hard. It took me a long time to get back on my feet, at least mentally. My mother often came to visit, my father, well ... from time to time. He never really had time. After a few years, I would come to Luxembourg to go on vacation when we had both gained some distance from what had happened."

"Neither of us are blessed with our fathers, are we?" said Matthew.

"No, we're not! But we've always had enough money, as if that could replace love, understanding and time together."

"Have you ever really been able to talk to your father about this, Lis?"

"No, not really. Now, of course, he's proud of his grandson, but we don't see each other too often. Bernard hopes that Eric can one day take over his empire, step into the position that I never wanted and that his son Georges never could. But the wall that has been built up between him and me over the years is very high, almost impenetrable."

"Oh yes, I know that wall too. I thought that if I didn't have any real fatherly love, at least I didn't lack money, so I accepted his regular transfers without a guilty conscience. Whether it was right or not, I don't know and now I don't care."

Matthew looked at her lovingly and hesitantly placed his hand on hers. She let it happen.

"I've often thought about you, Lis. You were so fragile when we met at your house before you left the country. It broke my heart and I wish I could have been with you to at least help you through the worst of it. I tried to talk to your mother a few times to see if I could visit you, but she said you needed distance and rest. Eventually I gave up and went to London to start a new life and study medicine. But you and I, we were so close, didn't you miss me a little?"

Lis stroked a strand of hair from her face.

"I was so devastated at the time that I didn't even know whether it was worth going on living or not. Eric finally gave me a reason not to put an abrupt end to it all. At the time, I thought I would never be able to banish all the images, faces, smells, and voices from my mind. But I did it, even if it took many years.

"Are you happy with your life?" she asked Matthew impulsively.

"Actually, yes. When I'm on stage, I forget everything around me. I float in the applause of the people and that gives me life energy. But it also gives me great satisfaction when I can heal a patient. Yes, I'm happy with my life as it is."

They talked for a long time that evening and when the restaurant owner was about to close and politely asked them if he could serve them anything else, they decided to leave.

It was almost midnight. Time had flown by.

They stayed outside for a few more moments.

"It was very nice tonight. We've just been looking back over the last twenty-five years," he said quietly, standing there like a shy boy.

"Yes, it's crazy how life goes. When did you get that short haircut? You look good!"

"As a doctor with long hair, I was viewed somewhat sceptically by patients, I noticed that. Besides, this is much more practical," he said. "Will I see you again?"

"Absolutely. If you can trust a woman with a knife tied to her ankle." She smiled.

"I think I'll take that chance." He kissed her gently and she got into the car. "Take care." He waved and waited outside his car until she was out of sight.

# SATURDAY, JULY 13

At Saturday lunchtime, Eric and Caro met up with Lis in a large shopping centre near the city. Eric wanted their first meeting to be relaxed and away from home. A casual lunch would be a good start. Both were already sitting at the table when Lis arrived after shopping. They greeted each other and it seemed as if the two women hit it off straight away, immediately finding common topics of conversation.

"Eric has such a young mother," Caro exclaimed at one point. "That's nice and you both have so much time together in one life."

"Very true. It's also difficult to be a mother at a very young age, but I grew into the role quite quickly."

"I'm actually an orphan," Caro admitted, much to Eric's surprise.

"I see," was his spontaneous reply.

"Yes, I was adopted as a one-year-old child by Mr. and Mrs. Klein here in Luxembourg. I couldn't have wished for better parents."

"And what happened to your biological parents?" asked Lis.

"They were killed in a car accident. I was in the car too, in the back seat, but I was the only one who survived."

"I'm very sorry to hear that," said Lis.

Eric put his hand on Caro's arm without saying anything.

"I was so young back then that I can't really remember my biological parents. But maybe that's a good thing. I'm very grateful that I have such wonderful adoptive parents."

"So, were you in a home here in the country?"

"Yes, in Clervaux. There's an orphanage there, quite small, quite unknown, it seems."

"I don't think I know it, but I have been abroad for many years," Lis explained.

Time passed quickly and the conversation moved to easier matters. In the early afternoon, Lis said goodbye and went home.

## SUNDAY, JULY 14

Eric spent the night with Caro and returned home on Sunday morning.

"Caro is working the early shift at the hospital," he explained briefly as he made himself a coffee in the kitchen.

"She's a very nice person, Eric. I say that because I can feel it. She has a good heart."

"Yes, she's wonderful. But the adoption thing surprised me a bit. It must be weird not knowing your real parents, I don't know my dad, but at least I know my mum." He walked over to Lis and gave her a kiss on the cheek.

"And she's doing super well." He winked at her.

"Oh, I'm glad," she said, looking at her son with a loving smile.

"Where did you meet Caro? You haven't been back in the country that long?"

"Actually, at the reception desk of the hospital where she works. When I went to my doctor's appointment the other day."

"Did you then invite her out straight away?"

"You're so curious," he said. "She had to re-enter my details into the system and then her computer froze, so she had to wait a while. I took the opportunity to ask her if she did that on purpose to get to know me better."

"You're crazy."

"Maybe, but it got me to the point where I could invite her for a coffee. No more, no less."

"I'll ask my mother when I get the chance if she knows about this orphanage in Clervaux," Lis said spontaneously. "I've never heard of it. I didn't know we had anything like that here. We already have an organisation for orphans, but I've never heard that you can adopt directly here in Luxembourg."

On this same Sunday afternoon, the poker friends were heading towards the local airport. Thomas Walter was speeding along the highway in his dark green Saab Cabrio 9.3 in the direction of Luxembourg's Findel Airport.

In the passenger seat was Alfonse Weis, the ex-secret service agent and the back seat was occupied by Alan Moore.

"Alan, I don't want to interfere with your plans, but I have to say it again. You've got a lot on your plate. How on earth are you going to find this woman? The orphanage will hardly give you any clues," said Weis. "Trust me."

"We'll see about that, boys," Alan said sadly as he checked one last time that he hadn't forgotten anything. His hand luggage was next to him, and he had put a large suitcase in the trunk. Cell phone, passport, boarding pass, credit cards and laptop.

"I have no other leads or clues. The hospital is pretending not to know anything. Diane is not at home in her apartment, and she had specifically told me that she would soon visit this orphanage herself and look for the little girl. So that's where I'm going to start. She's worth the effort, I'm sure of it.

"David is already there. He thought a little adventure would do him good. Besides, he has experience in dealing with criminals, should it be necessary. He's a trained soldier, after all."

"That's true," agreed Alfonse, "The Dominican Republic cannot be compared with Luxembourg in terms of crime."

"It's more like South Africa," said Thomas, who had lived there for fifteen years.

"We're way too early," he added, glancing in the rear-view mirror. "There's still enough time for one last local beer." The suggestion was unanimously accepted.

"I also think your plan is pretty risky," said Thomas. "I have to agree with Alfonse. You have zero clues, you have nothing at all except the name of this orphanage, Pequeños Angeles. And the name of your missing beauty, Diane Van Helden. Where will you look, what will you do? You only speak a few words of Spanish. Allow me to say that you have no chance of finding anything there."

"Besides, you don't even know if Diane is there. She could just as well still be in Luxembourg. Or anywhere else in the world?" Alfonse added.

"That's exactly it. Or somewhere else," Alan agreed. "I can't just sit and wait, hoping she'll turn up one day. You know me. When I've decided to do something, I do it. Besides, who else is going to find her? She's just disappeared and that's not normal. I checked with the local police. They made a note, that's all. I don't even know where exactly she works, otherwise I would have already contacted this organisation. And her story sounded so believable. I'm flying to Santo Domingo and then I'll see. There are two of us and we will plan the next steps when we get there. I'll keep you posted."

While Alan checked in, Thomas parked and waited with Alfonse in the cafeteria with a cold beer.

"Cheers, boys! In a few weeks you'll at least be speaking fluent Spanish," said Alfonse, raising his glass.

"Oh yes, and with a little female help it goes even faster," joked Thomas.

"I hope so," Alan said with a smile. "I've also sent you the address of our hotel. Hotel Discovery, sounds exciting, doesn't it? I'll let you know when I arrive. It's about thirty kilometres from the airport to the city centre."

The men finished their beers and said goodbye. Alan went through passport control.

"I don't have a good feeling about what he's doing," said Alfonse on the way back from the airport.

"You know he's an adventurer and always will be, he likes that, and he must be terribly in love with this blonde beauty. Diane Van Helden. Sounds noble."

"Yes, yes," Alfonse agreed. "I'm curious to see where this leads him. I have to admit, though, that it's strange that she just disappeared like that. It almost arouses my professional interest to look into it. But let's first hear what he thinks of the situation when he gets there. Then we'll see.

"You know, I'm still in close contact with my best former partner, Bob Wagner. He helped me a lot back then—even off-duty— when we had to solve the murder of the banker Frank Mayer. Boy, oh boy, that was a great job."

"And you were still on duty then, weren't you?" asked Thomas.

"Yes, but I was taken off the case by some officials. We didn't know why at the time, but in retrospect it turned out that a high-ranking government official was involved. Well, I needed Bob to do the research and we both worked hard at weekends and late into the night. Bob took a big risk, but the man is one hundred percent reliable. So, if I need anything, I can always knock on his door. Plus, he especially loves research like this because it's a change from the usual paperwork he has to deal with."

"Maybe Diane had to go away spontaneously, family, boyfriend or something ... And she'd only just met Alan. They don't owe each other anything," Thomas concluded.

"That's true. But it's still a strange thing."

"It's a shame you're no longer on duty, Alfonse." Thomas looked at his friend in the passenger seat.

"I'm no longer officially on duty," muttered Alfonse, "but that doesn't mean we can't do a little investigating ourselves if the situation calls for it."

"Sounds good. I like that approach!"

"But let's wait and see what they find out there first and then we'll see," said Alfonse calmly.

## *MONDAY, JULY 15*

On Monday, Thomas invited Lis to lunch. The tall, black-haired man loved his freedom, his independence and his spontaneous decisions and actions. Perhaps that was the reason why he had never settled down with a wife and family, but had always slipped from one casual relationship to the next. As long as the woman didn't want to move in with him, everything was fine.

"Hello," Lis kissed him on the cheek as she got in to the car. As they reached their destination, a small pizzeria not far away, a cell phone began to ring as Thomas was just about to park the car.

Thomas looked at Lis after a few more rings. "Aren't you going to answer it?"

"It's not mine, it's yours that's ringing," she replied.

"No, mine has a different ringtone." Lis looked at him a little suspiciously.

"Hey, that noise is coming from the back seat," Lis said, turning to look behind her.

"There's your cell phone!" she said triumphantly to Thomas. She pushed the button to answer the call.

"Hello? ... Who, David? No, this is ... Hang on, I'll give you Thomas Walter."

He picked up the phone. "Hello? What do you mean, me? Yes, but ... aha? Now I understand. This is Alan's cell phone. It must have slipped out of his pocket on the way to the airport.

"So, David! What's going on in the Dominican Republic? Good climate, beautiful women?"

Then Thomas' face became serious.

"Hm ... Not arrived yet? But can't you ask at the airport? Ah, the plane landed on time ... Yes, I know you don't speak a word of Spanish, but can't anyone at the hotel help you in English?"

Thomas paused. David seemed very excited; Lis could faintly hear his voice.

"Absolutely yes, I think you should call the police ... How? ... Okay ... Let's see what you can achieve. Call me back later, but please use my number. Bye, see you then."

Somehow Thomas was a little worried. "Well, the phone belongs to a friend of mine, Alan Moore. I drove him to the airport yesterday and apparently the phone fell out of his pocket because it was lying in the back seat."

"And the man who was on the phone then asked about ..." Lis asked.

"Yes, he's looking for Alan. David White, his friend, wanted to know where Alan is. He was supposed to meet him four hours ago at the Discovery Hotel in the Dominican Republic, but Alan hasn't arrived yet. It was barely twenty kilometres from the airport David was at. The plane had landed on time. Hm ..."

"And now what?" Lis asked.

"I don't know. The bus must have got stuck somewhere. Nothing to worry about."

"Let's have something to eat first, and then I'll ring our poker friend, Alfonse Weis. He used to work for the police. But maybe Alan will have turned up by then. Or maybe he caught the wrong bus and couldn't call to let David know because we have his cell phone."

"Yes, that sounds plausible," said Lis.

"Alan's trip to Santo Domingo has an interesting backstory," Thomas explained as they sat down on the terrace of a nearby café.

He explained the disappearance of Diane Van Helden after she and Alan were on their way to the police station and were hit by a car.

"That sounds like a detective story," Lis commented. "And he hasn't been able to find the woman since he was hospitalised?"

"No, he never actually saw her in the hospital. He was alone in a room when he woke up and only found out in the morning that she had already been discharged, even though he saw her lying there after the accident, apparently with a lot of blood loss. Very, very strange."

"Which hospital?"

"The private McKenna clinic."

"Ah," was all Lis said when she thought of Matthew. "I know Matthew, the eldest son of John McKenna, the director."

"Does he work there?"

"No, they don't get on that well, he and his father. He only goes there from time to time when one of his patients has been admitted. Otherwise hardly ever. But Eric's new girlfriend works there. I'll ask her when I have time."

"That would be great, Lis! Then we could help a bit from her too. Alan is sure to turn up soon and the mystery will be solved," Thomas added.

"Pretty brave of him to just fly there alone with his friend and go to that orphanage. I assume he thinks this woman is there?"

"Yes, and that's his only clue. He's tried everything to find her here in Luxembourg but he doesn't have her phone number. She wasn't in her apartment either. He knocked on her door several times but she didn't answer."

"And your friend Alfonse was with the police, didn't you say?"

"Yes, but he can't get private cell phone numbers either."

"I'll see what Caro can find out, I'm sure she'll be very discreet."

"Thank you, Lis, I really appreciate that!"

# MATTHEW

## *TUESDAY, JULY 16*

By Tuesday morning, there was still no indication of what had happened to Alan Moore. David had contacted Thomas several times. He was very worried.

"Listen Thomas, something is wrong. I'm seriously worried. First of all, I speak next to no Spanish and no one here is cooperative. Fortunately, the receptionist at the hotel helped me a little and accompanied me to the airport. The bus left there on time but no one can say if Alan was on it. But he had landed with the plane, at least that much we could confirm. I don't understand it."

Thomas paced back and forth during the conversation. He had also become nervous in the meantime.

"Have you been to the police yet?"

"Yes, I've filed a missing person's report, but everything here seems very relaxed and laid-back. No panic, no excitement, no stress. Basically, a bunch of lazy civil servants."

"I'll talk to Alfonse. He usually has a sensible suggestion. As a former police officer, I'm sure he can tell us what to do."

"Do it soon, preferably today. I have a bad gut feeling." David was worried.

Thursday, almost midnight. The ringing of her cell phone woke Lis up. She had fallen asleep on the couch. Matthew's photo appeared on the display.

"Hi Lis, I'm sorry I'm calling so late ... But do you think we could meet? I have something to tell you ... It's very important ... Really, really important."

"What's happened? Are you in trouble?"

"No, no, but I can't explain it on the phone. I'm totally confused, and I don't know who I could talk to ... Except you."

Still half asleep, Lis rubbed her eyes and looked at her watch.

"Okay, then why don't you come over. I'm alone anyway, Eric's spending the night at Caro's. I just need a few minutes to wake up."

"Thank you, I appreciate it! I'll be there in twenty minutes."


Lis was a little worried now. So suddenly and in the middle of the night? *What's going on*, she wondered to herself.

Shortly afterwards, the doorbell rang.

"Hey, thanks a lot and sorry for the late hour," Matt whispered as he kissed Lis on the cheek when she opened the door.

"Come in, have a seat. What happened, Matt? I have to admit, you've got me curious."

They entered the living room.

Matthew looked a little funny. "I had a whole bottle of red wine after I went out with a friend. But I need to tell you the whole story. Can I ask you for a coffee?"

Matthew looked deep into Lis' green eyes, which still fascinated him. Or was it the red wine?

He ran his fingers over his hair, or rather what was left of it since his new haircut. There was no mistaking the deep sadness in his eyes. He bit his lower lip.

Lis came back with two coffees and sat down next to him.

"What's got you so excited?"

He spontaneously took her hand. "May I?"

"You may ..." she said, a little confused.

"You know, there are so many things I need to tell you. Since I saw you again at the funeral, since our dinner the other night, the years that have passed have come back to life in my mind. I'm going back twenty-five years now. I was so confused that night, that evening." He took a sip of coffee.

"I remember clearly that you tried to talk to me several times and tell me that you had seen or met your brother Georges after he died, but I didn't want to know. I thought you were going crazy because of the grief."

"Hey, Matt, we agreed that we'd never bring this up again! And that's fine with me. Forgotten and forgiven. Really, it's fine with me."

"No, that's not it, Lis. I was so damn unfair. I know I even referred you to a psychiatrist back then because I was sure you were hallucinating. And now ..."

Matthew looked so helpless in those moments. "And that's exactly the reason ... Well, part of the reason I'm here now. Please ... Please listen to me."

He took her hand again.

Lis looked him firmly in the eye. "I'm listening, shoot!"

"I have to tell you what happened to me earlier. I can't talk about it with anyone but you."

Matthew was excited and confused. He leaned back, stretched out his legs and first looked into space, then closed his eyes. Like on a psychiatrist's couch, yes, that's how he felt now. But it did him good to know that someone was there and listening.

"Tonight, I met up with a friend on the Place d'Armes, we had pizza. There were a lot of people there. The streets and terraces were full.

"We talked about this and that, and from time to time my eyes wandered to the people at the neighbouring tables, as you do. Suddenly, at the end of the square, near the Cercle Municipal building, I saw a small, elderly woman leaning back against the wall.

"She reminded me a little of my mother and also the colour of her dress with the wide black belt. This woman had her eyes on me, and even though she was quite far away, I could really feel that she was practically staring at me.

"I told my friend that I had to leave for a moment because I had just seen someone I knew. By now it was almost dark outside. I walked towards the woman and the closer I got, the more I recognised her face, the face of my ... My mother, Claire."

Lis raised her eyebrows. "Oh!"

"When I was almost to her, she walked away, turned around and gave me a hand signal to follow her."

Matthew paused. "You can't imagine what moved me at that moment, what I felt, but I had to follow the woman. I had almost caught up with her and then suddenly she was gone, disappeared as if she had never been there. It was Claire, my mother, I know it for sure. I'm one hundred percent sure."

Now Matt opened his eyes, which were filling with tears, sat up straight and looked at Lis.

Lis frowned without saying a word and looked at Matthew.

"Say something, don't tell me I just imagined it, tell me what's wrong with me, Lis. What happened there? I didn't imagine it. When you told me about your brother, when you saw him, was it like that?"

Lis nodded in agreement.

"Am I leaving you speechless now?" asked Matthew.

Lis' eyes filled with tears.

"Hey," he said and grabbed her hand again.

"It's crazy. Now you're having exactly the same experience I had with Georges back then. No wonder, you have exactly the same abilities, you're just as sensitive," she whispered.

"You believe me, as simple as that?"

"Yes, of course I believe you. I am the best proof for myself that such things simply exist."

"What should I do now?" Matt asked, his head in his hands. "Lis, I need your help, your guidance. I want to see her again, talk to her, ask her so many things, I still have so much to tell her. I feel so confused and overwhelmed.

"Do you see Georges regularly? What do you talk about? How do you talk to each other? My head is spinning. Normally I could discuss everything with my friend Franz. Do you remember him? He used to come to our house a lot."

"Yes, I remember him well. Is he no longer in Luxembourg?"

Matthew shook his head and his expression darkened. "He died in April of this year. It wasn't that long ago. He was helping his friend who was suspected of murder, then there was a shootout and Franz was hit. He died a day later, shot through the lung."

Matthew cupped his hands in front of his face. Tears rolled down his cheeks.

"Him and now Claire. The two big pillars in my life, just gone, disappeared. Almost at the same time. Franz was a kind of father substitute for me. And a brother substitute. He was there when my father didn't have time, he often took me fishing, on his boat, he took an interest in my little magic tricks. We had so many wonderful moments together. Real buddies, especially when I was little. Although he was much older. I think almost twenty years older, but I didn't care.

"Later, when I came back to Luxembourg after my studies, it was as if I had never been away. I had grown up and a different kind of friendship had developed. We talked about so many things. He told me a lot about his childhood, how he had to work hard to survive. I think there were five or six children and only little money. He was a great guy. And now I can't tell him anything. He would have understood me too."

"You can already tell him, Matt! Just tell him. He'll hear you, believe me."

Matthew looked at Lis a little strangely. "That's exactly what I have a problem with. And that's why it totally blew my mind when I saw Claire earlier."

"You don't have to believe in it right away. But at least allow for the possibility that this world exists. And then you will see it."

"You mean they're going to contact me?"

"If they think it's necessary, they'll do it. And you seem to be open to it. From what you've told me, your mother seems to want to give you a message, maybe talk to you?"

"Yes, but that doesn't mean I should die too, does it?"

"No, no, definitely not. There must be a good reason why she went to so much trouble to make contact with you. After all, the spirit world needs quite a lot of energy to make itself visible to us."

Matthew listened to Lis. By now he no longer knew whether he was in reality or whether it was all just a dream.

"Are you telling me that the deceased live among us and can take form at any time if we wish it as much as they do?"

"I don't think so. It takes a certain amount of concentration and willingness to make contact on both sides. And there needs to be a reason why contact should be made."

"Then why did your brother contact you?"

"Back then, when I was in this terrible situation, Georges

came to me regularly to reassure me that I would hold on, that I wouldn't die, and that everything would work out. He told me to trust him. I thought every day that I would rather take my own life than be hurt by these creatures.

"On several consecutive days he appeared again, and suddenly I got the hang of it, and all I had to do was think about him, and then I saw him. It was wonderful. We talked about a lot of things during those nights. When I say 'talked', it was more through telepathy. Because they don't have a physical body anymore, they don't have a physical voice, right? You can see that in your mind's eye. The very first time Georges revealed himself, I saw him in his real body. It was at night. I was lying awake, thinking about when I was going to be killed, and suddenly I saw this faint light, a body form reaching for me, slowly coming closer."

Matthew was speechless.

"Then I heard a voice whispering my name, then the voice said, 'it's me, don't be afraid, I'm Georges' ... Now, and then we could connect mentally, at night, when everything was very quiet. Matthew, that was the only thing that kept me alive, he gave me hope. Do you understand that?"

"I think I understand, at least a little," was all Matthew could say. "So, this other world really exists, this other world that we hope for really exists. And you're sure you didn't imagine it? I'm sorry to have to ask you that."

"Did you imagine seeing your mother? No. So, here we are! Of course, there is this 'other' world, but not everyone is interested in connecting with it, as I said before. But remember, Matthew, it's almost impossible to tell anyone about it, forget about convincing anyone. Besides, the people around us at this moment can't see the person you saw, the person I saw."

"Why not?"

"Because they don't make a direct connection to that person at that moment. But if we were to focus on your mother together, we would probably both be able to see her."

"I'll go crazy if I don't keep reporting on Claire. It's so over-whelming. There really is a world that exists alongside ours. And everyone should realise that."

"You can forget that at the moment. Do it for yourself and only for yourself. And let the others find out for themselves if they really want to and are looking for it."

"Hm … Ok," Matthew propped his chin on his hands and looked directly at Lis.

"Sometimes they also manifest based on a melody, a song or a smell, something that connects the two of you. That's usually easier for the person on Earth to associate the connection and the person."

He looked at Lis questioningly.

"What now?" she asked with a smile. "Keep asking questions if you want. I'll give you answers as far as I know them myself."

"It's not that, at the moment I have something else to think about, and that makes me very ashamed."

"I think I know what you're going to say."

He nodded in the negative and wiped the tears from his eyes. "And I sent you to the psychiatrist back then, and I didn't even listen to you. You must have felt terrible when even I didn't believe you. I'm so incredibly sorry!"

"That was so long ago now, Matt. It's forgotten and forgiven. And besides, I can't even blame you for not believing me. How would I have reacted if the opposite had happened?"

"But that's why we broke up, isn't it?" Matthew said quietly.

"Yes, we did, but even without that incident, I don't think I would have been able to have a normal relationship at that time. I had to get away, I had to find myself again."

"I don't know what to say anymore." Matthew rubbed his face in his hands, visibly exhausted by the intense conversation.

"You need some time to digest our conversation now, okay? Go ahead and do that, and we'll continue our talk in a few days."

"Oh, one more thing: I visited Claire in hospital before I left for Paris and that was the last time, I spoke to her. She held my hand. I wanted to cancel my shows, but she insisted I go. She knew how much this world meant to me and she understood me. Maybe she didn't know that she only had a few days left to live. I keep seeing this scene in my mind's eye, I see her in the hospital bed and I'm sitting next to her, and we talked about so many things, and she told me how much joy I brought her as a child, I always had my magic suitcase with me." Matthew could no longer speak; he was crying too hard.

Lis sat down with him again and held his hand. By now it was half past one and she was very tired.

After a few minutes of silence, he wiped away the last of his tears. "I'm totally exhausted, I'm sorry, Lis, for just steaming in here and overwhelming you with all this in the middle of the night."

"That's okay, honestly! But I'm really exhausted now. I can give you a blanket and you can fall asleep here on the couch if you want." She looked at him.

"I'm happy to accept that suggestion," he said. As he took off his shoes, Lis handed him a blanket.

"Thanks for everything," Matt said, closing his eyes. "And sleep well."

Lis watched him for a moment before leaving the room.

Matthew had a very restless sleep that night. He tossed and turned a million times and dreamed a lot of chaotic and confusing things.

Matthew woke up in the morning drenched in sweat. It was already light outside. Lis was already sitting in the kitchen with a cup of coffee.

"Well, did you sleep well?" she asked as he slowly got up.

He rubbed his eyes. "No, I feel like I've got a massive hangover. And we only had coffee."

He got up and sat down at the kitchen counter with Lis. "Morning!"

"Don't you have any patients today?" Lis asked.

"No, I'm closed on Mondays and Fridays; that fits in well with my gigs, which usually take place at the weekend. But I work all day on Tuesdays, Wednesdays and Thursdays. And I've kept the whole of August free. Sometimes I need a longer break."

"Do you perform abroad then?"

"No, not in August. I just want to rest, buy new material, whatever comes up."

He took a sip of coffee. "I'm telling you, I've been dreaming strange things. That's why I'm so down, I think."

"Yes, we've done too much at once. I'm still tired too. It's going to be a very slow start today."

"I had a dream about Claire. She was sitting at a table and showed me a picture of Franz," Matthew suddenly said. "Why would she show me a picture of him?"

"Maybe you should focus on him a little more?" Lis suggested.

"Do you really believe that dreams have a meaning?"

"There are dreams and then there are dreams. Some are just the result of our daily routine, while others are also clues and messages. If you look into it more deeply, you will realise that some dreams are more real than others. When you wake up in the morning, you know that you have really been in contact with someone."

Matthew looked at Lis. "Oh yeah?"

"Absolutely! And I get the impression that Claire is really trying to tell you something. It's a shame you weren't with her when she died."

"I know, but hey, wait a minute. Now I remember something. When I got to the clinic that night, Jeff told me that Claire had been asking about me so much, that she really needed to talk to me."

"Ah, now we're getting a bit closer. You see, it makes sense. There's something she wants to tell you."

Matthew looked a little confused. "Yes, that makes sense, you're right. When will she get back to me?"

"When she feels that the situation is appropriate. You have to be patient and think about her often. You can ask her in your mind what message she wants to convey."

"Lis, I have to process all this and deal with it first. It's too much for me."

"That doesn't surprise me."

To change the subject, Lis roughly informed him about Thomas Walter and his friend Alan Moore, who had not shown up in Santo Domingo.

"It's strange that this Alan was on the plane but never arrived at the hotel."

"Yes, that's strange. I'm sure there's an explanation for that," said Matthew.

" Hopefully he'll turn up again and have a logical explanation. But that doesn't happen every day."

"You're right about that. I hope he's turned up by now," Matt said, "I have to go now, Lis. Will I see you again soon?"

"We'll call, okay?"

"All right."

Matthew turned around in the doorway. "Thank you for your time, for your explanations. It meant a lot to me last night."

"You're welcome, Matt." They hugged each other warmly.

Lis didn't want to mention to Matthew that she was planning to ask Caro for help with Diane Van Helden and to ask to look at her hospital file. He certainly wouldn't support that, especially as it concerned his father's clinic. Maybe he could have helped, but right now she wanted to keep him at a safe distance.

# FRIDAY, JULY 19

David White had made no progress. The local police were not being helpful; a missing person's report had been registered and that was it. He'd been brushed off with the words that people disappear every day and that the police didn't have enough time or staff to investigate every single case. He was told to contact the relevant embassy or set off on his own in search of the missing person.

# SATURDAY, JULY 20

This Saturday, Lis met up with Eric and Caro for lunch at a nearby pizzeria. She was pleased to see her son so entranced with his new girlfriend.

During their conversation, Lis briefly told them about Alan's disappearance and the accident that had preceded it.

"And then he woke up in the hospital and all he was told was that Diane Van Helden had already been released that morning, which makes little sense when, according to Alan's testimony, she was lying in the street covered in blood as far as he could remember."

"And the woman's ex-boyfriend should be able to be tracked down, right?"

"Alan Moore hadn't mentioned his name, at least no one knows what this man's name is."

"Then it will be difficult. But it's strange," Caro said. "It's quite unlikely that the hospital would discharge a patient so quickly without doing further tests to make sure there are no internal injuries. Unless she insisted and discharged herself. Where was she?"

"Well, in the same clinic where you work."

"I see," Caro said. "When did this happen?"

"Sometime at the beginning of the month. I don't know the exact date."

"You know what, I'm on the night shift at reception tonight. We don't have an ER tonight, so it'll be pretty quiet. I'll check our database and see what I can find. Diane Van Helden, right? And Alan's last name?"

"Moore, Alan Moore."

"Okay, I'll see if I can find any information under those names."

"Just make sure, Caro, that no one notices that you're looking at personal data."

"No, no problem at all. I'll just look at the computer. There's no one checking what I'm doing."

"It would be great if you could do that," said Lis.

"Sure, I'll let you know as soon as I find something or not."

In the evening, Eric and Lis stayed at home waiting impatiently for a call from Caro, who was due to start her night shift at 9 p.m..

"What about you and Thomas?" asked Eric, who was standing by the window. "You were lovers years ago, right?"

"Yes, but he's a friend now, I'd say. A very good friend."

"And Matthew?"

Lis smiled. "Hard to say at the moment. I was so in love with him when I was fifteen and he was crazy about me, too."

Eric turned around. "I can see it in your eyes. No more questions."

"What do you see? Besides, he's busy!"

"That can change, Mum!" Eric grinned. "It still sounds unusual when I call you mother, you know. Ever since I was a kid, you've been more my friend than my mother."

"It wasn't the easiest childhood a son could imagine, was it?"

"No, it wasn't! But we managed and I can't imagine a better mother, Lis! And despite everything, I was brought up very well!" Eric joked. He hugged her warmly.

"I have to compliment you, Eric. You're always so well dressed. You hardly ever walk around in T-shirts and those baggy pants with your butt hanging down to your knees."

Shortly after 10 p.m., Caro finally called.

"Hey, Caro. We're dying to get some information. What did you find out? I'll put you on speakerphone."

"Hello Eric, hello Lis. So, Diane Van Helden is in the patient database, admitted on Saturday, July 6. But strangely, she has not been discharged, at least there is no entry in her file that she has left the hospital. When I look at the records of her condition at the time, she was diagnosed with a severe concussion, then complications arose and a week later she was placed in an induced coma. She still seems to be in intensive care. In any case, there is certainly no record of a discharge anywhere."

"Well, that's strange! Who's treating her?"

"Dr. Peter Lamborelle."

"Do you know him?" asked Lis.

"Yes, but not personally. That's the man who greeted us in the cafeteria the other day."

"Ah yes, the blonde playboy." Eric couldn't help himself.

Caro laughed. "I don't know if he looks like a playboy, but he's very good-looking, I find, and he's been always super nice to me, right from the start."

"He likes you! No wonder! I just hope he doesn't like you too much."

"Well, it's still too early for jealousy, my dear!" Caro added jokingly. "No, but seriously now. I think I'll go upstairs and see if I can get in there."

"Do you have access?"

"I don't know, I'll try."

"Do you want me to come with you? I hate to leave you alone with something like this."

Caro thought for a moment.

"Why don't you both come, then Lis can wait outside in the car. You never know what good it will do. There seems to be something strange about this patient file if it doesn't contain the whole truth."

"I think so too. I'll text you when we get there," Eric said.

"Park near the main entrance, but somewhere on a side street so as not to attract attention. It's very quiet tonight, but it's better to be safe than sorry."

Within five minutes, Eric and Lis were seated in Lis' white VW Golf, driving to the hospital ten kilometres away.

"You don't like this Dr. Lamborelle?" she asked.

"At first glance, he seemed to like Caro too much. But it could also be that I'm wrong. I don't know, but my gut instinct was throwing a spanner in the works."

"It's strange," Lis agreed. "Why tell Alan she's been discharged when she's in a coma and still there? And she has no family here in the country. Surely they've checked with her place of work for contacts there at least."

"Yes, a lot of things don't seem to match up," Eric said. "Unless they accidentally made the wrong entry in her file."

"I can hardly imagine that," Lis said.

Drawing up to the hospital, Lis took a left at the main entrance and parked in a side street as Caro had suggested.

"I'll wait here, Eric, don't do anything illegal, okay? And text me if there's anything wrong."

"Don't worry, I'll call you. We're just going to have a look around. We won't get a better opportunity than this."

"Be careful. Nobody likes having their clinic spied on. Here!"

Lis pulled up the leg of her trousers and gave him the knife she always carried with her, along with the leather case and strap.

"Now, tie this around you. You never know." Eric looked at her strangely.

"Please!" Lis repeated resolutely. "Just do it, okay!"

Eric knew about Lis' paranoia, but had come to terms with it. He eventually took the knife, but really more to see his mother reassured than for his own protection.

"Satisfied?" Eric got out then turned back to Lis. "You know what? This is very exciting," he said. Then he closed the door and walked towards the main entrance.


When he was almost at the door, Caro opened it and he went in.

"Come with me to my counter, just around the corner. I'll lock the front door again."

She showed Eric Diane Van Helden's patient file on the screen.

"And at the bottom, you see, it doesn't say anything about

discharge or anything like that. The woman has been in a coma here since … Well, that's a fortnight now."

"Room 1112," Caro read aloud. "Shall we have a look at the room?"

"You bet! That's why I'm here," Eric said. "Are there a lot of staff here at night?"

"I don't think so. I never see everyone down here who's on the night shift. I know, why don't you put on a doctor's coat and a face mask? That makes it a bit more credible in case we're seen and you won't be immediately recognised. Wait, there should be something like that here in the radiology doctors' back room."

Caro went into the back room to have a quick look. A short time later, she returned with a white coat and a mask.

"There you go, you're already a junior doctor. Try it out."

Eric put on the doctor's coat and found it fitted well, if a little on the large size.

Then they walked along the corridor and up the stairs to the second floor. There they turned right and walked along the corridor. Suddenly, a door opened further ahead and a person entered the corridor.

"Hey, stop, come in here," Caro whispered spontaneously as she grabbed Eric's arm and pulled him into a small room. It appeared to be a room where a stock of medical equipment and products was kept.

She peered through a narrow gap in the door into the hallway to see who was there and where they were going.

She could only see the person's back; the man was also wearing a white doctor's coat. He walked briskly forward and then entered a room at the top left of the corridor, closing the door behind him.

"A doctor," said Caro, turning to Eric. "He must have been called to a patient. Normally, the intensive care patients are only monitored by the nursing staff at night. We'll have to wait."

Ten or fifteen minutes passed, time in which Eric and Caro became a little impatient.

At last! The doctor stepped out of the room again and came down the corridor. Caro's head was back in the room in a flash, but she left the door ajar to watch him pass. She pointed her finger at Eric's mouth to give him a signal that he had to be absolutely quiet.

As the doctor walked past the room where they were hiding, Caro recognised him.

"That was Dr. Lamborelle," she said with a surprised look on her face.

"So what? What's so special about it?"

"He never works the night shift."

"Then it's probably an emergency and he was called in." Eric tried to find a simple explanation.

"Come on, let's find Room 1112," said Caro. As they walked down the corridor, Caro realised the room they were searching for was that which Dr. Lamborelle had just exited.

"This isn't a normal intensive care room. Normally, they're all connected and there are always a couple of nurses monitoring the whole time," Caro said.

"Let's go inside. If anyone sees us now, we'll just have to pretend we're on a tour. You're a new doctor and I'm showing you the ICU. It's your first night shift, okay?"

"Okay. But Diane should be in a coma, right?"

"Actually, yes, she should." Caro slowly opened the door and blinked cautiously. They both entered quietly.

In the bed lay a blonde woman, intubated and connected to a

number of machines. The couple looked at each other, both thinking the same thought. If Diane van Helden is here, then why was Alan Moore told that she had left the hospital on the same day?

Eric pulled out his cell phone and took several photographs of the sleeping woman.

"She's beautiful," Eric said.

"Now get out, come on," whispered Caro.

They both left the room, walking carefully but quickly back down the corridor, down the stairs, to reception and Caro's desk, where she immediately took her seat again. Eric was in the back room about to take off his doctor's coat when he heard a man's voice.

"Good evening, Caro. You're on the night shift again?"

"Good evening, Dr. Lamborelle. Yes, but it's very quiet. What brings you here tonight? An emergency?"

"I wanted to check on a patient. I'd been told that her heartbeat was irregular, so I thought I'd pop in myself. I was in the area anyway."

"Ah, yes, I see," Caro was deliberately speaking louder so that Eric could hear.

"Well then, I wish you a good night, Dr. Lamborelle, and a nice weekend."

"I wish you the same. It was nice to see you, Caro. Maybe there's a chance of a coffee together in the next few days?"

Without waiting for her answer, he walked to the elevator that led to the parking lot.

Caro was visibly relieved.

"You can come out, Eric! Phew, now I felt really queasy," she confessed. "Imagine if he had caught us in her room."

"I don't understand, Caro. Why are they hiding the fact that the woman is still here?"

"Maybe they didn't want to tell Alan Moore because he's a stranger to them here?"

"But they were brought in together, weren't they? Surely everyone knows they belong together? He was asking for her explicitly and he also knew her address."

"It's all quite mysterious," Caro said. "Why don't you give your photos of the woman to Lis so she can pass everything on to Alan's friend, Thomas."

"Good idea. Maybe he can make something from it. The story doesn't seem entirely smooth to me."

"No, not for me either. Well, I'm going back to the switchboard. Sleep well, Eric, and I'll see you tomorrow!" Caro hugged him tightly, they kissed, and then Eric went back to Lis' car.

On the drive home, he told Lis what had happened and immediately sent her the photos on her cell phone. However, he didn't say that they had almost been caught, he didn't want to upset his mother unnecessarily. After all, everything had gone well.

"That sounds very strange," was Lis' reply. "The woman is still in hospital but they told Alan that she had left the same morning. Why is that?"

"I don't know. But please be careful if you want to get involved in this," remarked Eric, who knew his mother only too well. She always had a strong desire to get to the bottom of an injustice and, if someone was in trouble, to help them as much as possible. He handed the knife back to her.

"I'll speak to Matthew when I get the chance, but not about this incident, because he won't be very pleased that we did this on our own initiative and trespassed in his father's clinic."

# SUNDAY, JULY 21

Throughout the week, Alfonse had tried several times to contact the local police in Santo Domingo, but had failed to make contact. When he met up with Thomas this Sunday evening for a bottle of red wine to further discuss Alan's situation, they both decided to travel to Santo Domingo as quickly as possible. They could not and would not simply abandon their long-time friend to his fate. In the meantime, David was also panicking. He didn't know what else to do there and urgently needed help and support.

"Communication will be difficult, Thomas. Be aware of that. None of the three of us speak fluent Spanish. How are we going to deal with that on the ground?"

Thomas grinned. "Hey, here's an idea! I know someone who would be the perfect interpreter for us." Alfonse just looked at him, confused.

"Okay, then you go ahead. Because without an interpreter, we can forget the whole mission, if you ask me."

# MONDAY, JULY 22

Thomas didn't want to lose another day. On Monday night, he invited Lis to dinner. He picked her up and parked outside a sushi restaurant in Howald.

As they reached the restaurant, he held the door open for her.

"So, you really want to go there?" she asked, somewhat surprised, when Thomas told her about his plans once they were seated.

"We have no other choice. David is desperate and doesn't know what to do. At least Alfonse and I could help him and coordinate with the local police. Alfonse is a retired policeman after all, with a lot of experience. But Lis, we need someone who speaks Spanish. And more than just a few words here and there." Thomas looked at her urgently.

"Oh no, you mean … You don't mean ME, do you?" She looked at him and frowned.

"Mhm!" Thomas nodded silently, looking at her expectantly and waiting for her reaction.

"Whew," Lis took a deep breath. "You're asking a lot of me. I don't know if I can do it. You know my fear of flying."

"Yes, I know, and I'm also aware of what I'm asking of you. But I don't know anyone else who would qualify."

"A real interpreter?"

"No, we can't afford the costs and no information must be leaked, Alfonse made that very clear. After all, he was in the secret service and knows what he's talking about. And besides, what am I supposed to explain to a hired interpreter? That my friend is missing somewhere in the Dominican Republic and I want to look for him? That it could take a week or even a month, if we find Alan at all? I know it's a bit of a strange situation, but I need your help, Lis. Please think about it, sleep on it."

"Who else is going?"

"Just the three of us. Well, I mean, the two of us and hopefully you."

"I really need to think about it, Thomas."

"We don't have much time; I'm asking you to help us. Besides, you are very good at defending yourself when you are challenged."

"I don't know if my black belt will help me if someone threatens me with a gun."

"Sure, but it won't come to that. At least I hope not."

"When would we leave?"

"As quickly as possible. Every day is vital."

"I'd like to meet this Alfonse first, if you want me to travel with you. Is that okay?"

"He's all right, believe me. A very fine guy, honest, calm and very attentive."

"I would like to see him before I set off with him on a journey into the unknown."

"But of course. What about tomorrow? Are you free?"

"Yes. There's not much going on here. Shall we meet on a terrace somewhere?"

"Okay. Deal."

# ALFONSE

## *TUESDAY, JULY 23*

Thomas and Alfonse met Lis on a rooftop restaurant terrace on Tuesday evening. At last, the tropical heat that had prevailed over the last few days had eased somewhat. It was still a summery twenty-four degrees, but much more pleasant than before.

"Do you want to join us?" said Alfonse after they had greeted each other and taken a seat on the terrace.

"Yes, if there's no other option and that doesn't seem to be the case. I can come for a week or two."

Alfonse was looking at Lis very intensely, a fact which Thomas noticed immediately. *Why would he do that*, he asked himself. *That's not like Alfonse at all.* He was normally rather reserved, but here it seemed to be the opposite.

"Thomas told me that you just got back from Mallorca."

"Yes. That's why I'm not working yet, not until school starts in the fall. I have a job at the university."

"Forgive me for asking, but don't we know each other from somewhere? Your face looks familiar somehow."

"That's hardly possible. I have lived abroad for over twenty years and have only been back in the country for a few weeks."

"It could have something to do with my profession; Thomas has probably told you that I worked for the secret service."

"Yes, he did. I might have some information that could be

relevant to your case," Lis said. "My son Eric's girlfriend, Caro, works at the McKenna Clinic. I told her about Alan and Diane Van Helden. Caro looked through the patient lists for us and found an entry that shows Diane is still entered in the database as if she were still there and in a coma. On Saturday night, I went to the clinic with Eric, and he and Caro went into the room unseen and found her there."

"That is strange," said Thomas. "You've already done a bit of detective work before we started."

Lis then showed them the photos.

"If that's Mrs. Van Helden, then there really is something wrong," Alfonse concluded in his calm and relaxed voice. "Hm ... this could even turn into a real criminal case," he muttered, more to himself than to those present.

Lis wondered what had to happen to upset this man.

"Then there must be a good reason why this information was kept secret from Alan," Alfonse said.

"Exactly!" said Lis.

They looked at each other thoughtfully.

They talked for quite a long time that evening. Lis liked Alfonse's good sense of humour, but she realised quickly that this man was not one to be dealt with lightly as an investigator.

"That means," Lis summarised, "that you'll be wanting to leave for Santo Domingo as quickly as possible."

"Exactly," agreed Thomas and Alfonse.

As the meal drew to a close and good-byes were being said, Thomas hugged Lis and couldn't help but whisper to her, "So?"

She winked at him with a smile. "I'll consider the trip, seriously!"

Thomas and Alfonse drove home together. As they pulled up to Thomas' house, Alfonse paused.

"Lis' face looks strangely familiar," he said. "I have a very good memory for faces."

"Oh yes, and then where from?"

"I don't know, not yet. Somewhere … But I'll find out. I never forget a face."

With these words, the two friends said goodbye.


# WEDNESDAY, JULY 24

Lis called Matthew during his lunch break.

"Hey, you don't sound too good," she said after they had both exchanged a few words.

"Brigitte is annoyed because her husband is going on another long trip and won't tell her where or what."

"If he's traveling, that works in both of your favour, doesn't it?"

"Yes and no. She would like to move in with me for these weeks, but I don't want that. And besides, I have other things to do. But you called for a reason, what's on your mind?" he asked.

Lis explained the situation with the flight to Santo Domingo. "I have decided to accompany these people. I can't let them go there alone where nobody speaks a word of Spanish. They would get pretty lost."

"I see," Matthew agreed, "but it won't be a vacation, as far as I can tell from what you've told me."

"No, I know. But they seem so helpless otherwise. And their friend Alan must be in quite a mess, otherwise he would have contacted them somehow. But hey, Matt, don't you fancy coming along? A change of scenery, get away from it all for a while. And I'd be so happy if you flew with me?"

Silence at the other end.

"Dominican Republic … Actually, not a bad idea. When do you want to go? And what about the visa?"

"We don't need that. We all have Luxembourg passports."

"Okay. Tell me when you're going. You're booking my flight too?" Matthew had decided spontaneously and instinctively. Then he didn't have to explain to Brigitte why she couldn't move in with him while her husband was away.

"Are you really coming?" she asked to make sure.

"Yes, I'll go with you. It could be quite cosy and nice, we're sure to have a beach and beautiful areas there."

"Sure, I'll take care of the booking. Thanks Matt. Really, I appreciate it very much."

Lis was delighted with his spontaneous acceptance. She felt safe with him, even after all these years of no contact.

"Goodbye!"

This Wednesday was a night with a full moon. Matthew had a confused dream. First, he saw himself traveling to Santo Domingo with Lis. Then he saw his mother again. She was standing far away from him in a forest. Matthew ran after her. Suddenly she was standing right in front of him. *You have to talk to Ingrid,* she whispered. Then she was gone and Matthew woke up in a cold sweat.

He got up, went into the kitchen, and fetched some water. He stood at the window, looking out at the beautiful, clear full moon. He couldn't get the dream out of his head. *You have to talk to Ingrid,* Claire had said to him. Ingrid was a good friend of his mother's, she had come to visit regularly, and since Claire had been battling her cancer, Ingrid had been particularly present. She would pick Claire up for shopping, coffee afternoons, or walks. Ingrid was an extremely friendly woman.

*What should I say to Ingrid when I call her?* Matthew thought about how he could best explain himself to her without making a fool of himself.

That afternoon, Alfonse turned up at Thomas' apartment spontaneously and without prior arrangement.

"Hey Alfonse, what's up?" Thomas let him in and served them both a cold beer.

"I thought a lot about how I might know Lis, or who she reminded me of. I just couldn't get her out of my head."

"Well, so what? Have you solved the puzzle?"

"Are you sure your Lis is really called Lis Chandler?" Alfonse asked, as relaxed and comfortable as he always used to be.

Thomas knew that Alfonse sometimes spoke in riddles but he didn't understand this question at all.

"Can you express yourself a little more clearly so that a normal person like me can understand?"

Alfonse frowned and looked at his friend a little mischievously.

"What do you know about her past? Maybe there's a lot she's hiding from you?"

"Hmm ... What do I know? She teaches Spanish here, she lived in Mallorca for many years as a young adult, she, yes ... She has a twenty-four-year-old son."

"Mhm." Alfonse rubbed his chin thoughtfully. "Is that all?"

Thomas leaned back on the couch. Suddenly he smiled and looked at Alfonse.

"There are two more things. She has a rather strange habit: She always, and I do mean always, carries a knife on her ankle, the knife is in a leather case. She says it's just for her safety. And she has a remarkably long scar on her lower back."

"On the lower back!" Alfonse repeated. "So, you've already moved on to deeper investigations!"

"Yes, yes." Thomas laughed. "We've known each other for quite a while."

"Did she ever tell you where the scar came from?"

"No, she just said it was an injury from a long time ago."

"That's a strange thing about the knife. But it would fit my theory. I don't think Lis Chandler is her real name."

"Excuse me? What makes you think that, Alfonse?"

"I told you the day before yesterday that Lis' face looked somehow familiar. But then I pushed the thought aside again until suddenly I remembered something. So, I got up in the middle of the night and went through my archives. And there it was: the Bouvier case. You can see it here."

"The Bouvier case?" Now Thomas could definitely no longer follow his friend.

Alfonse took out his briefcase and pulled out a file. He opened it and took out an excerpt from an old newspaper article, which he presented to Thomas.

"Take a look at this and read the full article."

Elisabeth Charlotte Bouvier, the daughter of a wealthy bank director, had been finally released after three months in captivity.

*After a three-month search, 15-year-old Elisabeth Charlotte Bouvier, daughter of the wealthy president and main shareholder of the private bank Bouvier & Co, Bernhard Bouvier, was found and freed by a special unit today. The teenager is safe and well and back with her parents. The family insisted that no further details be given to the press.*

Next to it was a black and white photo of a young girl with long, dark hair.

"Now take a good look at the photo." Alfonse held it closer to Thomas.

"That was twenty-five years ago," explained Alfonse. "The then 15-year-old daughter of the very rich private banker Bernard Bouvier was kidnapped and was in the hands of the kidnappers for three months. First, they demanded a small sum. The father paid. Then came a second demand for payment, which was also paid, but the girl was not released. Then a special police unit was deployed and, in cooperation with foreign units, she was finally found. Two young men were arrested and brought to court.

"The official version," said Alfonse, "is that the two, who were in their early twenties at the time, wanted to play a joke, at least that's what they claimed. A few weeks later, after the liberation, Elisabeth Bouvier suddenly left the country. She was never seen again, not a word about it in the press. Many months later, it leaked out that she had gone abroad for therapy. And after that, nothing was ever reported about her again. The whole event just disappeared and the girl never showed up here in the country again."

"Why are you associating Lis with this girl?"

"Her face looks too much like her, it's just my detective instinct, that's all. Besides, it was me, among others, who was on the case at the time."

Thomas looked at the photo again. "Hmm, I don't know … Well, she does look a bit like Lis, but maybe I'm just imagining things. I'll could just ask her, I guess?"

"By the way," Alfonse continued, "contrary to the newspaper report, she was not found by the special police unit, but was released by the kidnappers after her father had paid the third sum. And when I say sum, I mean two million euros. Only Bernard Bouvier wanted the press article to be worded differently. Under no circumstances did he want to tell the public that the police had completely failed and had been unable to locate the girl. It was only later, with the help of the girl and her descriptions of the place where she was staying, that the two young men were located. They were Luxembourgers and came from wealthy families.

"I remember the girl so well when we were questioning her. She was so fragile, so emaciated, so scared. She was sitting in the chair in my office, her parents were there too, and she was exhausted. Unfortunately, we couldn't spare her from having to make a statement. I sat in the next room and watched. As I was responsible for the secret investigations, I wanted to remain unseen and stayed in the back room. She didn't see me. She was a real beauty, green, clear eyes, long black-brown hair. What struck me at the time was that she didn't cry once. That was the thing that amazed me the most. It was like she was in a trance. It must have taken a lot out of her. Three months in a container, not knowing if she would ever get out of there alive."

"How can it be that you couldn't find any traces?"

"There were no clues, nothing at all, I'm telling you. One day she didn't come home after school and that was it. No one had seen or heard anything. Her classmates said they left school together and then she went on her way, just like any other day. We asked everyone: neighbours, people who live on the way to school, teachers, friends, family. Nobody had seen anything. There was no direct motive, except that Bouvier himself was and is so rich. Sure, that was a reason, but then where do you look for a perpetrator?"

"It's terrible that the police were so useless," Thomas said angrily.

"I had her house and the bank under surveillance for 24 hours without the slightest result, not the slightest clue."

"And what's with the scar on her back?"

"During the three months she was locked up, she tried to escape once. One of the two men threatened her with a knife, as she reported afterwards. She attacked him, bit him and then he pulled out a knife. During the melee, he stabbed her in the back. The scar was badly infected when she was rescued and needed urgent treatment. So much for the scar on her lower back."

"What a mess," Thomas whispered more to himself. "Well, after hearing all that, Alfonse, it might fit her profile. I'll ask her, first thing in the morning. We'll sort it out quickly if she's the Bouvier girl. I'll let you know then.

"But if she is that girl—which I'm not convinced of yet—then it doesn't make any difference to our trip, does it?"

"Not at all, no. I just thought I knew that face and that was the only reason I mentioned it to you."

# SATURDAY, JULY 27

Thomas was very surprised by what Alfonse had told him last night, and he wanted to resolve the matter as simply and quickly as possible, so he arranged to meet Lis at a nearby restaurant.

"Thomas, I know you too well. What's on your mind?" Lis asked as they took their seats and she looked at his face.

"Why do you think I have something on my mind?"

"I know you a bit," she said, winking one eye.

"Yes, you do. Alfonse said to me the other day that your face looked somehow familiar to him when he met you. And it took him a while to figure that out. He told me something that I can't really relate to and I want to ask you about it directly."

"Aha, so I remind him of someone?" said Lis.

*Her eyes are beautiful*, thought Thomas. *I love her eyes.*

"He thinks you might be the 'Bouvier girl.'"

Thomas put his face in his hands and looked at Lis questioningly.

Lis returned his look with piercing eyes. She remained silent.

"So it was him who was discreetly entrusted with the case back then," she said quietly and leaned back.

"Yes, he's ex-secret service. Is it you then? You're the Bouvier girl?" Thomas stared at her.

She nodded in agreement. "Yes."

Silence from both sides.

"I don't know what to … What to say … I'm sorry that … That something like this happened to you … I can't find the words," Thomas stuttered.

Alfonse's words ran through Thomas' mind. *The girl must have been a mental wreck after being locked up for three months, all alone.*

"Did he tell you the whole story?" she asked.

"As far as he knows himself, yes."

"That was many, many years ago. And yet …" she whispered.

"But now I'm really surprised," said Thomas. "Speechless. All these years, you've never mentioned anything to me."

"I couldn't do that then because I wasn't ready for it. I couldn't talk about it, and besides, what difference would it have made?"

"But the perpetrators were arrested and punished, weren't they?"

"Yes and no. Two of them, yes, they were arrested. But there was a third man. Nobody believed me when I told them about this third man. And then, for my own peace of mind, I didn't say anything more about it in the end. There was no trace of a third person anywhere. This person always wore a black mask and gloves. Only his mouth and eyes were visible. The police never found fingerprints from a third person and the other two testified under oath that it was just the two of them. They went to prison for ten years, but were released after five years because they had rich parents and had behaved very well."

Silence from Thomas. Then he had to ask, "What happened to this third man?"

"He raped me two days before I was rescued. And more than once."

And if someone had pulled Thomas' chair away at that moment, he probably wouldn't have noticed; her words really hit him hard.

"You were … You were …" Thomas thought back to their time together in Spain in a flash.

"Eric?"

She looked at him seriously and nodded affirmatively. "Yes. Eric."

"I … Aah …" Thomas couldn't think straight.

Lis noticed the state he was in at the moment. "It was a long time ago and I've learned to deal with what I experienced back then. I've dealt with it well with professional help."

"No one can imagine what you must have gone through."

"No, that's true. But no one should have to imagine it either. Now you're asking me if I'm damn sure about that third person, since everyone was wearing a mask, right?"

She smiled at him, which lifted the unease in the atmosphere a little.

Thomas just nodded. Suddenly tears came to his eyes. He had to clear his throat and took a deep breath. "I'm so sorry," he whispered and wiped his tears away.

"To be able to close the whole case, to just file it away, finally, I said that I was wrong and it really was just two men. I was so fed up with being asked the same questions so many times. The police had nothing more to do, the case was closed, I had my peace, and so did the police. Because that was what they wanted. To close the case as quickly as possible. But this third man had a special feature. He had a black spot in his left eye, right next to the pupil of his clear blue eyes. I had enough time to memorise it for the rest of my life."

"That's all you've ever seen of him?"

"Yes. He was never found or identified. I still think from time to time, what if I were to come face to face with him one day and look him straight in the eye? Of course, there are other people who have a spot like that in their eyes, but it's relatively rare, you know."

"And everything was kept secret here in Luxembourg?"

"At the time, there were no further examinations because my father was too worried about his reputation. My father asked me to have an abortion. He offered to arrange everything here in Luxembourg. He knew an excellent gynaecologist, everything would be handled with the utmost discretion, and I could start a new life, without any burden, as he called it. As if you could start a new life straight away after something like that. I would never have been able to just move on after a rape and an abortion. In my father's eyes, everything can be settled and solved with money. His condition was to have an abortion or leave the country. And I decided to have the child and leave the country. Maybe it was a bit of a defiant reaction against my father, to show him that money alone can't solve all the world's problems. My mother suffered a lot but she often came to Mallorca to our house. Here in the country, the investigation was dropped and the story was shelved. My parents have a large residence in Mallorca, Eric was born there, and then I gradually worked through what had happened to me with a psychiatrist and other really nice people. I got used to the island."

"And then you met me," Thomas added.

"And then I met you," said Lis.

"And Eric?"

"Eric thinks his father was a one-night stand and that's why I wanted to stay in Spain."

"That means he doesn't know about your kidnapping?"

"About the kidnapping, yes, but he doesn't know that one of the kidnappers is his father. He thinks I met this lover as soon as I arrived in Spain. And I want it to stay that way, please! I then changed my surname to Chandler because I was constantly afraid that people would find me with my real name. I still don't know who I was dealing with. Would he try to find me and kill me, so I couldn't testify at some point? I felt safer after the name change. I'm also glad that Eric doesn't have the name Bouvier."

"Man, oh man, what a story!" Thomas was astonished. "But why was no gynaecological report drawn up and your rape confirmed?"

"Because I didn't tell anyone about the rape, I only told them that a third person was involved and I said I didn't want anyone to touch me to examine me, I wanted to go to my room at home and not see anyone. I told them they hadn't hurt me, and hoped and prayed that I wouldn't be pregnant. My father was happy that everything was kept under wraps, because he wanted to keep the press and rumours out of his world. It was only when I realised I was pregnant that I spoke to my mother and then, of course, to my father, who then suggested an abortion. Anyway, there were no fingerprints of Mr. Unknown. Whoever this person was, he was well protected and must have come from a wealthy and well-known family like the other two. That was my conclusion. And believe me, I have had enough time to go through the entire three months I spent there in detail."

Thomas didn't know what to say, he was in shock.

"I, on the other hand, took a long time to distance myself from the idea that Eric's father was such a bastard of a man. But by the time Eric was born, all that was forgotten, and you know, never having seen the man's whole face, I don't see a spitting image of him in Eric, which is certainly an advantage. I could never tell Eric what really happened. I think he wouldn't be able to cope and would turn the whole world upside down to find this man. It's better for everyone. He probably thinks quite often that there's a man living somewhere who is his father, but he's not looking for him, thankfully. That would be pretty difficult too."

Thomas was visibly taken aback.

"I don't know what to say, Lis," he said hoarsely. "I feel more than sorry for you. This whole kidnapping must have changed you a lot inside."

Lis nodded in agreement. "It took away all my illusions about life. If I hadn't had Eric, I think I would have taken my own life. I had a horrible period of paranoia, panic, fear of enclosed spaces and so on. My child gave me the strength to regain my balance to a certain extent."

"Today seems to be my day of surprises," said Thomas.

"Looks like it!" She took his hand. "I'm really fine, Thomas, believe me. That was all a long time ago."

"That explains why you're always walking around with a knife!"

"Yes, I wanted to make sure that I could defend myself in an emergency. And I've also learned to shoot, I have a black belt in karate. If anyone ever tries that again, they'll have to be very good and fast. Otherwise, he's dead. And that's where we change the subject. Now you know, and that's a good thing."

Thomas swallowed.

"And the father-daughter relationship between you and Bernard Bouvier?"

"We've both been working on it ever since. And over the years he's seen Eric more regularly, and now that Eric has studied banking and knows his way around the financial world, Bernard has actually become very sociable. He probably always secretly wished that my son would one day take over the entire Bouvier bank. He sees Eric as the future of his empire. Let's see what comes of it. I've explained to Eric in many conversations that he should never feel obligated to do so, but if he needs his grandfather in any way, he shouldn't hesitate. But Eric's interest in finance seems to be in his genes. He certainly didn't get it from me."

Lis paused for a moment.

"And now the good news, Thomas," Lis said, changing the subject. "I will come with you to Santo Domingo. But I'm coming with Matthew, my old friend. He needs a change of scenery and can help us."

"Aha! Matthew."

"It's a long story, but he's a doctor and it can't hurt. We won't be there until Wednesday, though. Is that all right with you?"

"That's wonderful, thank you, Lis. I really appreciate it. You're sweet!"

He kissed her amicably and then said goodbye.

That night, Thomas dreamed strange things and woke up a few times in a cold sweat. He couldn't get Lis' story out of his head.

## SUNDAY, JULY 28

On this Sunday, Thomas had a very detailed conversation with Alfonse.

"I was sure of it. It could only be her," Alfonse said. "I'm not at all surprised that she's good at defending herself. If I had been in her place, I would have done the same. And I was almost certain at the time that she only changed her story to say that it was two men, so that she could finally have her peace. She had insisted for a long time that there was a third man, but then at some point she just said she was wrong. She had everyone against her. Sad, isn't it?"

"You can say that! Damn unfair!"

"So, what's the plan?" asked Alfonse.

"We'll meet tomorrow morning. And she'll arrive with this Matthew on Wednesday."

"Wonderful, then we have reinforcements and another man to help us, and a doctor to boot, which can't hurt. See you then, Thomas." said Alfonse.

## MONDAY, JULY 29

On Monday morning, Thomas felt worse after his bad night, worse than after a night of poker and a lot of beer. With a lot of effort, he managed to get to the airport on time and took the 7 a.m. flight with Alfonse to Frankfurt and from there to Santo Domingo, where they arrived late in the evening. At least they were able to get some sleep in Business Class.

## TUESDAY, JULY 30

Late evening in Luxembourg is already 6 am local time in Santo Domingo. David was waiting for Thomas and Alfonse at the airport, and together they drove back to the Hotel Discovery.

"I don't know about you, Thomas, but I need a few hours' sleep, otherwise I'm useless," said Alfonse, yawning. "I'm dead tired. I just can't sleep well enough on a plane."

"I agree with you, Alfonse. David, I'll meet you for lunch later." The two men went to their rooms, where Alfonse sent his wife Madeleine a text message to say that they had arrived safely at the hotel.

Shortly after 2 p.m., Alfonse appeared on the hotel terrace, followed shortly afterwards by Thomas. After a light lunch, they drove with David to the local police station to put everything on record again, this time with Alfonse's help. He knew exactly what to ask but as almost nobody understood English, it was a rather short conversation with no real result.

They had to wait another two days for Lis and Matthew, but David was relieved that he was no longer alone in dealing with the disappearance of their friend.

"Do you have any idea who owns the orphanage here?" Alfonse asked David.

"I don't know, I looked around a bit on the net, but there's only the address and a contact number."

"Then I'll call Bob. I think he can track down some information for us."

Bob Wagner was Alfonse's former colleague and faithfully helped him wherever he could.

"Hello Bob, this is Alfonse."

"Mr. Weis, this is a pleasant surprise. How are you?"

"I'm in Santo Domingo. We, that is, some friends and I, are looking for a poker friend of ours who has disappeared here. I'll give you all the details later, but maybe you can help me and do some research on an orphanage called 'Pequeños Angeles' here in the city. Who owns it, how it's registered and anything else that might be of interest. It also seems to have a connection to Luxembourg. That's all I know at the moment."

"That sounds pretty exciting, Santo Domingo", Bob said enthusiastically. "I'll do it as soon as I can!"

"As soon as we know who owns the orphanage, we will plan the next steps," explained Alfonse.

## WEDNESDAY, JULY 31

It was half past six in the morning when Eric and Caro drove Lis and Matthew to the airport. They still had time for a coffee together, during which Lis introduced them to Matthew as a childhood friend.

"This is going to be an exciting journey. I hope you find this man again," said Caro. "In the meantime, I will inquire about Mrs. Van Helden's condition. Discreetly, that goes without saying."

"Just be careful, you two," said Eric.

"Mrs. Van Helden? Who's that?" asked Matthew. "Is she also part of this mysterious story?"

Caro and Eric looked at Lis at the same time and realised that there was still a lot to explain. Lis bit her lower lip.

"Yes. There's something else. Alan and this unknown woman were hit by a car and injured the morning after they met. When Alan woke up later in the hospital, he was told that his friend had already left the hospital. When I found out that Caro worked at the same clinic, I asked her to check the patient file. She discovered that the woman was still in the clinic and in a coma. And then Caro and Eric, when Caro was on night shift, went into the room to check ... well ..."

Matthew looked at the three of them in amazement. "I see, and ...?"

"Diane Van Helden is still at the McKenna Private Clinic." Lis was prepared for Matthew to be angry because she had kept this from him but she felt she had to explain it to him now.

"Oh really! And I find out now, an hour before departure?" Matthew was not amused by the late information.

"It all happened so quickly, I would have explained everything to you on the plane because we didn't have time beforehand. At least now we know that the woman is still in hospital."

"I might have been able to help you there, yes? Wasn't that an option?"

"I know I should have told you sooner, but it's too late now anyway."

"You're right about that though!" Matthew said, "I'm not thrilled about this, but we have to go now, or we'll miss the plane."

"Thank you, Dr. McKenna," Caro said kindly. "And have a good trip, take good care of yourselves, both of you."

Lis hugged her warmly. Then she and Matthew went through to passport control.

Check-in went smoothly. The flight seemed to be fully booked. Everyone had already taken their seats and were waiting when a man was let on at the last minute.

He was tall and muscular with dark, short hair and a three-day beard. As he walked down the centre aisle, it was impossible not to notice that he was watching all the passengers. He took a seat in the very last row. The doors closed and the plane was ready to take off.

"Are you okay?" Matthew looked at Lis as they reached cruising altitude. She finally seemed a little more relaxed.

"Yeah, I'm fine." She smiled.

After changing to a Boeing 737 in Frankfurt, Lis and Matthew then had a direct flight to Santo Domingo. They sat roughly in the middle of the plane; Lis had an aisle seat. The tall man with the beard from the first plane was seated two rows behind them.

"We'll be landing in less than ten hours. Make yourself comfortable," said Matthew.

"Yes, I will get through this too, with you by my side. I'm so grateful to you for taking all this on for me. I appreciate it so much, Matt!" She put her hand on his knee for a moment.

"A change of scenery is exactly what I need right now," he said. "I want to avoid any relationship stress with Brigitte, but sometimes it's unavoidable when her husband and I are away at the same time. Then she feels let down by everyone."

Lis looked at him. "In a way, I can understand her, but, well, you'll have to find out for yourself."

"Mhm ..." he said and Lis understood that it was time to end this topic.

"Maybe we're in a real crime story here and we just don't know it yet. What do you think?" she asked.

"It sounds very strange when a doctor at the hospital confirms to Alan that his friend has left the hospital, and then we discover that this is not the case. Somehow, I doubt that this is just a mistake. Surely the doctor has access to this patient's file. When we get back, I'll take a closer look at this incident."

"I really should have told you this earlier, I'm sorry."

"No problem, we'll sort it out later. You know, I dreamt about Claire again last night."

Matthew mentioned the second dream about his mother and this woman called Ingrid.

"Hmm ... You really should get in touch with this woman. Maybe there's something else she wants to tell you that Claire might have said?"

"I hardly know her. She looked after Claire when she was ill and visited regularly, but what should I give as a reason for visiting her? And what should I talk to her about? Besides, she could have contacted me, I can be found on the internet. And I'm sure she knows my name too."

Matthew made himself comfortable and closed his eyes. "We'll see when we get back. And if I'm in the mood for it."

After the food had been served and cleared away again, it became quiet. Most of the passengers went to sleep.

Lis and Matthew did the same. She fell asleep quickly and survived the first five hours well.

When she woke up, she found that Matthew had already been served coffee.

He looked at her.

"I was just thinking that you really are a tough person! Why are you going on this crazy trip? And for someone you know only slightly or not at all?"

She smiled. "That's right, I don't actually know this Alan at all. But after hearing his story, the disappearance and then reappearance of his friend, and now his disappearance on the island ... I might be projecting here, but if he's been kidnapped because he was doing research and is locked in a basement with no windows, not knowing if he'll get out alive ... "

She looked at Matthew. "I can't just sit back!"

He looked at Lis. "This is bringing back memories?"

"Yes, it brings back memories. A lot of memories. And if there's anything I can do to help him, I certainly will."

"I understand. But tell me, the fact that this Diane is still in my father's clinic makes me curious. Why would the attending doctor lie to Alan Moore and say that she left the clinic that very morning, when all the time she's in a coma in intensive care? It all seems very strange to me; a lot of things don't add up."

"Certainly not! And then Alan disappears when he gets to the island, if he got there at all. Sounds more like a detective story, doesn't it?"

"Yes ..." Matthew admitted. "Do you have the doctor's name?"

"No, but I'm sure Caro can figure it out."

"Look here." Lis took out her cell phone and showed Matthew the photo Caro had taken of the woman in the hospital.

He took the phone and looked at it closely. Then he looked at Lis and frowned.

"And you're certain that that's the same woman, Diane Van Helden?"

"I've never seen her myself, but that's the woman in the room whose name Caro tracked down that night. As for her appearance, only one person can give us confirmation and that's Alan himself. But we have to find him first."

Matthew nodded. "Send me the photo on my phone too. Then at least we'll both have it."

"You're not going to send it to Jeff or anyone at the clinic, though?"

"Of course not! Don't worry about it. I don't want Caro to be dismissed without notice."

Lis closed her tray. "I need to stretch my legs a bit." She stood up and then walked down the aisle. The flight was very quiet. Most of the passengers were sleeping.

Just as she was standing in front of the door of the occupied toilet, a man came out. He seemed a little hectic and bumped straight into Lis.

"Oh, I'm so sorry, it was my fault," mumbled the tall blond man, who had stepped on Lis' toes. "It's just too crowded in here."

"Yes, that's true," she replied kindly, looking the man straight in the eye.

She immediately felt a shiver through her whole body and her blood ran ice-cold. There was a black spot in the man's left eye. Cold sweat ran down Lis' back and her blood pressure dropped within seconds. She lowered her gaze, quickly went inside the cubicle, and immediately locked the door with trembling hands.

She leaned back against the door as her breathing quickened.

For a moment, she thought she was going to suffocate. She quickly cooled her face with cold water and thought about what she had just seen.

The man's eyes were familiar to her. Lis had not experienced such a terrible feeling of fear since she was fifteen years old. She stayed on the toilet for more than twenty minutes until she regained her composure. She tried to take a deep breath to better process the incredible shock she had just experienced. Then she put on her sunglasses, took a quick look in the mirror and stepped outside.

When Matthew saw her walking back, he immediately realised that something was wrong. She was as white as a sheet of paper and drenched in sweat.

She sat down. Her hands were shaking.

The man with the full beard looked up briefly; he had also

noticed that Lis was agitated as she walked back to her seat. Then he returned to his book. No one noticed that he discreetly took his cell phone and snapped a few photos of Lis and Matthew. He continued to observe the situation as he pretended to read his book. A few moments later, he sent the photos on via MMS: "Hey Mike, please identify them both. Thanx!"

"What's wrong, Lis? Did you get sick in there?" Matthew asked, looking at Lis, who had closed her eyes and was still shaking.

She nodded in the negative and said. "Wait, please, just let me rest for a few minutes." She breathed irregularly.

Matthew looked at her with serious concern. He felt her pulse, which was racing. "Come on, tell me, what happened? Are you feeling ill?"

"Yes, but not like that ... Did you see the man who came out of the bathroom just before I went in?"

"No, not at all. I didn't look up."

Lis turned to Matthew, looked him in the eye and whispered in a shaky voice. "Matthew, I've just looked into the eyes of the man who raped me that night, the third man ... who never officially existed. It was the same eyes; he had the same black spot in his left eye."

"What, are you sure about that, Lis?" Matthew was visibly moved. "How can you be sure that it was that man? Don't you think that's jumping to conclusions?"

"No, those eyes are unforgettable. I had enough time to memorise them for the rest of my life, believe me."

"First, breathe in and out calmly and deeply. We'll take care of the rest later. You have to get out of this state first."

"I have to get out of here, Matthew. Now, or I'll suffocate!"

Her breathing quickened again, drops of sweat beaded on her forehead. Her mouth went dry.

"Hey, hey, Lis, look at me," Matthew said. She did.

"You're not going to pass out here and now. Everything is fine. It's just your thoughts that are putting you in this state. Everything has been fine for the last six hours. You're about to put yourself in a very unhealthy, uncontrollable state. Stop doing that. Come back here." Matthew spoke in a firm, serious tone.

Lis' breathing was too short and too fast. "I'm so scared of him, Matt!" She then squeezed his hand tighter and tighter.

"You're safe here. Nothing can happen to you. I'm with you!"

"You have no idea what he's capable of, Matthew."

"Listen, this man is back in his place. He doesn't know who you are, and he can't do anything to you in here."

"I know that, but I'm overcome by the feeling that he'll recognise me next time. And then …"

"Lis, drink some water." She took the glass with a trembling hand and drank it down in one go.

He wiped the sweat from her forehead.

"I thought I had everything behind me," Lis said in a panic. She was still shaking.

It took a long time for her to calm down a little. Matthew held her hand and they were both silent for a while.

"This man, are you really sure it's him from back then?"

She nodded in agreement.

"When those eyes looked at me, I was in a state that I wouldn't wish on anyone, a state that is impossible to describe. Because I could only see his eyes, I stored them away for all eternity. I thought about how I would kill him, what I would do to him. But I have long forgotten that." And again, she breathed faster. "I don't even have my knife with me, it's in the suitcase."

"And if you did, I don't think you can use it here!"

Then Matthew did something he hadn't planned at all.

He turned to Lis, put his left hand on the back of her head, held her gently and kissed her. First he placed his lips on hers, and when Lis let him, he stayed like that for long seconds. Then he let go of her.

At first she didn't react at all, then she looked at him hesitantly, and a smile briefly appeared on her lips.

"Hey! You're using this opportunity in your favour."

"Absolutely!" He looked deep into her eyes. "It was a way of calming you down and taking your mind in a different direction," he whispered.

"Indeed, it was."

"Listen to me, Lis: I will never let anyone hurt you, okay? As long as I'm around you, no one will hurt you. And locally, as you explained to me, we have an ex-elite soldier and an ex-intelligence officer. If that's not enough protection ..."

Lis was surprised, confused, and happy. A wall of emotions came crashing down on her.

"I'm going to go to the toilet now too and you stay here, okay? Where is the man? What's he wearing?"

"He must be sitting somewhere in the front rows near the toilets. He's wearing a white polo shirt and jeans, I think."

"All right, I'll have a look."

"Okay, I'm a little quieter. Maybe it's your kiss that's working, I'm not sure."

Matt smiled. "I'll be right back, don't worry. And don't run off, will you?"

Then Matthew walked slowly down the corridor.

About ten minutes later, he returned to his seat.

He sat down without a word. He was deep in thought. Then he looked at Lis in amazement with raised eyebrows.

"Well, tell me, have you seen him?" Lis waited impatiently for his answer.

"I hate coincidences like that," he whispered more to himself.

"What now? Did you see him or not?"

Matthew turned to her. "Lis, I know who that man is."

"You … You know him?" she said loudly.

"The man in the white polo shirt," Matthew whispered, "is Biggy's husband. His name is Peter Lamborelle."

"Whose husband?"

"Brigitte, my … Well … The woman I told you about, my girlfriend. I call her Biggy."

"Her husband … That man there?! Wow!"

"Exactly!"

Lis was completely speechless.

"But how do you know him, have you met him before?"

"Yes and no, once at a cocktail party after a medical conference. I hadn't started the affair with her yet. But there's no doubt about it. It's him. And in fact, this man is violent. Biggy has told me enough about him."

"So, what now? Do you think he'll recognise you, Matt?"

"Could be, I don't know. We'll just act normal. And once we're out of here, we probably won't see him again."

"But what's he doing in Santo Domingo?" Lis wondered.

"He's on a business trip, like Biggy said the other day. He's supposed to be away for a month."

"Where does he work?"

"He has quite a high position in the Ministry of Family Affairs. Biggy often talks about how irascible he can be, suddenly starting to shout out of nowhere, becoming aggressive and sometimes even violent."

"And then he beats her up?"

Matthew nodded in agreement. "Exactly, rarely, but it does happen."

"Do they have children?"

"No. She can't have children. It's probably better that way."

"Why doesn't she leave him and report him to the police?"

"Ask me something simpler! I've told her so many times. But she thinks she has so much freedom, so much money, she can do what she wants, and if she leaves him, he'll destroy her."

"Only she gets beaten half to death from time to time without saying what else she has to put up with?"

"Exactly! But there's nothing I can do for her. We agreed from the beginning of our relationship that we would never live together or have a committed relationship. And that was fine with her."

"Couldn't you live with her?"

"No, I can't do that!" Matthew said quite firmly. "We should try to get some more sleep now."

He had abruptly broken off the conversation. As he leaned back in his seat, he closed his eyes. "I hope you can get some sleep too and forget about the incident."

Lis couldn't sleep for a long time. The man's face kept coming back to her.

*So, this is what my son's father looks like*, she thought. *It's amazing. If I told anyone, I saw the face of the man who is my son's father for the first time today, they wouldn't believe me. And not even an uninteresting looking man. Blond hair, broad smile, charming.*

Lis was no longer sure whether this trip was a good idea. She should have just told Thomas to get an interpreter from somewhere else.

It would be nice to hear from Georges again, she thought. He had helped her once before when she was almost at the end. But no one had believed her. Of course she had seen him, spoken to him. Now she was in a difficult situation again, wasn't she? *I think so,* she said to herself.

Peter Lamborelle. It was a name that Lis was completely

unfamiliar with. Had this man also recognised her now, from back then? She decided to wear her sunglasses from now on and use the toilet at the other end of the plane.

A very unpleasant feeling crept over her, which she couldn't shake off. Matthew, meanwhile, was fast asleep.

Her thoughts turned to Biggy. How often would she have had to put up with his aggression, among other things?

Lis forced herself to slow down and reorganise her thoughts. She was well on the way to sinking back into a panicked state. And that was hell.

Fortunately, the stewardess came and offered refreshments. Matthew woke up.

"Well ..." he said, still half asleep.

"You're sleeping the sleep of the just," smiled Lis, who was glad that she could talk to him again. "I don't have a good feeling about this man."

"Don't go crazy with it now. There's nothing we can do at the moment, we're safe, you're safe, and we can only hope we don't run into him on the island. We'll probably never see him again."

Lis wasn't so sure, however. In fact, her inner feeling told her something completely different.

"You know Matt, I need to tell you something, better now than sometime later. I just want to ask you to keep it away from Eric, okay?"

Matthew looked at Lis rather curiously. "Today seems to be the day of surprises, doesn't it? Okay, no problem, shoot!" He leaned his head back and closed his eyes as if he was listening to a confession.

She almost whispered: "Peter Lamborelle is Eric's father."

Matthew thought he hadn't heard properly. He opened his eyes and looked at her in surprise. "He's ... Who?"

"Yes, you heard right. He's Eric's father."

"I thought you had conquered a Spaniard after you arrived in Mallorca."

"No, no, it wasn't like that."

Matthew couldn't take his eyes off her.

"I'm going to kill him, Lis. I'll kill him for this!"

"Matt, please, calm down," she whispered, "calm down! Now I'm back in control and I want us to ignore what I said for now, okay?"

"How can I just ignore this? There's the man who did this to you and he's free and ..." He called the stewardess and ordered a coffee for both of them.

Then he closed his eyes for a few minutes, stretched out his legs, and took a deep breath.

"Okay. We'll put this whole mess on ice for now. But we won't forget about it. When we get back home, we'll talk about it. We're not going to leave it untouched, no way."

"Yes, well, we'll see what we can do," she agreed.

Matthew had regained his composure. "And when we get back home, we'll find out what's going on with that woman in the hospital. After all, I have access to the hospital and the files. I also have a small consulting room there but only for emergencies when a patient is admitted."

"You mean we're going there unannounced."

Matthew looked at Lis again. "I think that's best for a start. Because if something isn't right, we have the advantage of the element of surprise."

"Good idea!"

"It would be good if your two children, I mean Eric and Caro, didn't continue searching on their own. If they're discovered doing something illegal, Caro will lose her job, and both of them will have a lawsuit on their hands. My father is as tough as nails."

"I'll talk to Eric again when we land. I'll make it clear to him then."

"Yes, you should do that. It's better to be on the safe side, and yet I find it extremely strange that one of the doctors at our clinic told Alan that she had gone home, and in fact she's still there. I can't understand that. But at the moment there are so many things we don't understand. It's suddenly all mixed up!"

Matthew closed his eyes again and leaned back.

"I wonder what kind of surprise is coming next?" He smiled and fell asleep shortly afterwards.

# SANTO DOMINGO

## *THURSDAY, AUGUST 1*

They had finally arrived. The landing went smoothly and all the passengers were taken to the airport terminal by bus. Lis kept an eye on Peter Lamborelle, who was sitting at the front of the bus. She and Matthew boarded through the middle door.

Once they arrived at the airport building, they queued at the conveyor belt to collect their luggage.

Peter Lamborelle didn't seem to have a suitcase with him. He was only carrying a small piece of hand luggage and walked quickly to passport control.

The attractive man with the beard was not far from him and also joined the queue. He also only had hand luggage. He turned around again briefly and took a quick, unobserved look at Lis and Matthew. He waited patiently in the queue, looking around from time to time and observing the people in front of him.

"Once we've got our bags and have passed through passport control," Lis said, "I'll give you something before we leave the building."

While they were waiting for their luggage, Lis turned her cell phone back on. She sent Eric a text message to confirm her safe arrival.

"What have you got for me?" asked Matthew. "Can't it wait until we get to the hotel?"

"No, it can't."

Their suitcases quickly appeared on the conveyor belt as Peter Lamborelle passed through passport control.

"Good, then we've got rid of him for now. Lamborelle has just left."

"Ah, you kept an eye on him anyway."

"You bet I have."

The bearded man seemed to follow Lamborelle unobtrusively but quickly as he read the answer on his cell phone.

*- Woman: Born Elisabeth Charlotte Bouvier, she changed her name to Lis Chandler at the age of 16.*

*- The reason?*

*- Not specified.*

*- Bouvier ... the banking guru?*

*- Yes, her father, Bernard Bouvier! The man: Matthew McKenna, father Prof. John McKenna, private clinic in Lux.*

*- Aha! She was panicking when she hit my target.*

*- So, she knows him!*

*- Yes, I think so. Stay in touch. Thanx Mike.*

The man put his cell phone away again, walked on and kept an eye on Peter Lamborelle from then on.

"So, what have you got for me?" Matthew was curious after all.

Lis drew Matthew to the side of the luggage collection area and opened her case with a code. She took out two knives, each with a leather case.

"You can't be serious, Lis. Am I supposed to tie this around my ankle now?"

"Yes, you must. We're in uncharted territory here and a little survival knife like this can come in handy sometimes. You know I can be a bit paranoid.

"I'll go to the bathroom first, you stay with the bags," she said and before Matthew could say anything else, she was on her way.

*What have I got myself into*, he thought, watching the other travellers who were all heading for the exit. He took his cell phone out of his pocket and sent Brigitte a short message.

*Just landed, everything is fine. We'll see each other again soon.* He didn't mention that her husband Peter was on the same plane. That would only lead to discussions and Matthew wasn't in the mood.

A short time later, Lis had returned. She stood directly in front of Matthew and looked him in the eye.

"You took me quite by surprise on the plane with your spontaneous kiss!"

Then she put her arms around his neck. He could feel her breathing.

"I ..." Then she kissed him, very superficially at first, and when he returned her kiss and hugged her tightly, it turned into a long, intense kiss that took them both twenty-five years back in time. He gently stroked a strand of hair from her face.

"Hey!" Matthew looked at her lovingly and wrapped his arms tightly around her.

"I actually wanted to say ..." Lis mumbled to herself, not knowing exactly what she wanted to say. "I don't want things to get difficult between us ...you have Brigitte, I'm ...oh forget it ...!"

She kissed Matthew again. She had thousands of butterflies in her stomach when he smiled at her.

"I'm also in favour of it not being difficult," he said as he reluctantly let go of her again.

He nudged her nose with his finger. "The girl with the sad eyes," he added, looking at her urgently. "Back when you were out of my life, I kept thinking about our last day together before you were taken. We came out of the movies, goofed around all evening, walked through the city park in the dark, it was a hot summer evening."

"Exactly! We were so crazy," she continued. "We kissed, hid behind a very old, big tree, and then we came home after three in the morning. I remember everything, I haven't forgotten a single moment!" She stared at him.

"And then you were suddenly gone, just like that. I went crazy. I didn't know what to do," he confessed. "Knowing that someone could have done something to you was the worst thing."

"But I'm here now!"

They kissed again, for a small eternity. They both had to smile at the same time.

"Come on, tie the knife quickly around your ankle and let's get out of here." She kissed him on the nose. "You know what my mum said the other day when she saw you at church with that short haircut? He looks like Matthew Fox from my favourite show 'Lost.'"

He looked at her a little thoughtfully. "Well, I can only hope that our trip here doesn't end up with the same plot."

"I hope so, too. After all, our flight was much more pleasant without the crash landing! I have one more request: please give me that smile again."

Lis had her cell phone in his hand and spontaneously snapped a photo of Matthew before he noticed.

"As a souvenir of this trip!"

"Okay, ma'am, I'll go downstairs quickly. I'll be right back."

Another quick kiss and then Matthew hurried down the stairs with his rucksack.


Lis watched him go. She had a gentle smile on her lips. She looked happy.

About two minutes later, she received a text message from him. *Lis, I've missed you so much all these years!* She read this line at least six times and a dreamy expression appeared on her face.

Ten minutes passed and Matthew hadn't come back. She looked at her watch and told herself that he was probably freshening up a bit, that the bathroom was probably filled with other travellers.

Another ten minutes passed. Lis picked up her cell phone and called Matthew's number.

It went straight to voice mail.

As she looked around, Lis saw Thomas and Alfonse on the other side of the arrivals area. She took the two suitcases and went through passport control, straight to Thomas and Alfonse.

"Hello and welcome!" said Thomas and gave her a warm hug.

"Matthew went to the toilet a good twenty minutes ago and he hasn't come back yet. That's not normal! I'm very worried! Please help me look for him!" she said.

"Hm, let's go in and find out," said Alfonse. "Thomas, you stay with the suitcases. We'll be right back. There's probably a lot going on down there," muttered the retired secret service agent.

Lis explained to the man at passport control in Spanish what was going on and he called an officer over to take a look.

They went downstairs and into the men's room.

"There's no one here," Lis said in a complete panic. "Alfonse, something's wrong here. Matthew, where are you?" she suddenly shouted, pushing open all the doors that weren't locked. "Oh no, Matthew ... What has happened? MATTHEW!!!" But there was no answer.

"Maybe he used a different exit?" said Alfonse to reassure her. He knew that what he had just said was complete nonsense. There was no other exit from the bathroom.

"He's gone, just disappeared." Lis ran frantically from one door to another, looking in every cubicle again. "Look, here's his scarf, Alfonse."

Lis picked it up. "Something's happened to him. My God! They've taken him too ..." Then she burst into tears.

Alfonse hugged her tightly. "Come on, let's go up to Thomas and report it to the police immediately."

Within minutes, the security staff had been called and Lis, Alfonse and Thomas were trying to explain the situation.

Yes, she did have a photograph of him. Thank God, she had taken one on her cell phone! She tearfully showed it to the officers and told them all the details she could think of.

Matthew had disappeared. They searched the airport building while Alfonse waited with Lis and Thomas, recording anything that might be helpful in any way. The policeman had promised to get in touch with them as soon as they had some clues. Lis couldn't be calmed and was crying incessantly.

In the meantime, an entire police patrol with search dogs was on the scene, but after more than two hours of pointless searching, there was still no trace.

"I shouldn't have come here in the first place; I should never have asked Matt to come with me. What if he's dead?"

"Lis, listen to me." Alfonse held her tightly. "Why would he be dead? You'll find out what happened, I'm sure of it. There's nothing we can do from here now. Let's wait a little longer and then go to the hotel."

Finally, Alfonse and Thomas convinced Lis to leave the airport and they drove to the Discovery Hotel where David was waiting impatiently for them.

Everyone was visibly exhausted and had taken a seat on the hotel terrace in the backyard.

"We have no choice, we're going to have to trust the local police here," said Alfonse. "We won't find either Matthew or Alan on our own. But I suggest we take a look at this orphanage first thing in the morning and decide from there what to do. I don't see any other option. It is our only point of reference."

Thomas agreed. "We have to find Alan and Matthew; I'm not leaving without them."

"Me neither," Lis confirmed.

The waiter came and everyone ordered. Then Alfonse's phone rang. It was Bob Wagner. Alfonse moved away from the table and walked to the side. He returned a few minutes later.

"Well, here's something very interesting!" Alfonse sat down again. "Our orphanage here in the city has its entire administration in - where do you think? - Luxembourg. Well, now you're surprised and so am I!"

Silence. They looked at each other in confusion.

"In Luxembourg?" David repeated. "That means it has to be registered there and also have a legal company. But it doesn't seem to be publicly listed anywhere on the net."

"Who is the manager?" asked Lis.

"Well, no details seem to be known." Alfonse scratched his chin.

"Normally, all companies, regardless of their status, can be found in the business register, with the names of the business owners. We'll have to take a closer look when we get back to the country. In any case, this is not normal!"

Lis took off her shoes and leaned against the back of the chair. She was exhausted.

"So, Alfonse, you were on my case many years ago," Lis said, much to Thomas' surprise. He had deliberately not broached the subject.

"Yes and no. I was one of the three officers who investigated the case. I know that the special unit hadn't tracked you down back then and that the kidnappers only released you after your father had paid the ransom. The press was told a different version to stop copy-cat offenders."

"Yes, I'm aware of that, Alfonse. I was suddenly released and left blindfolded somewhere for the police to find me."

"And then at some point you completely changed your statement and said that there was no third man. But there was? Had you mentioned him often enough?"

"Nobody believed me, and all the back and forth to convince the officials in charge wore me down so much that I couldn't take it anymore. In the end, it didn't matter whether there were two or three. Nobody cared. They wouldn't have caught the third one anyway, there were no fingerprints, no picture, no nothing. And I had the impression that everyone was so relieved when I confessed that there were only two. Because that closed the case and my beloved father could continue his business as usual."

"At the time, I worked very hard on your case and spent a long time trying to find a motive for your kidnapping. But I never found one, apart from the money. Did you find anything else?" asked Alfonse.

"I always assumed it was about getting as much money as possible from my father Bernard Bouvier, right?"

Alfonse looked thoughtful. "I'm not so sure about that. The two young men came from quite wealthy families, they didn't really need the money in that sense."

"Okay, while we're being open with each other, I need to tell you what happened on the plane when Matthew and I flew here."

Thomas looked at Lis with great interest.

"As I was on my way to the toilet, I bumped into another passenger who had just come out. We looked into each other's eyes for a moment. And I panicked. When I looked into this man's eyes, I knew that this was the third man from back then. He had a special dark spot in his left eye. It's very rare, I've never seen it on anyone else. But I'm damn sure it was him."

There was total silence at the table.

"Wow," Alfonse broke the silence after a few moments. "That's a strong statement, Lis! That means this man is here on the island with us now?"

"It seems so, yes, but there's something more."

Lis took a sip of red wine.

"When I returned to my seat, Matthew immediately realised that something had happened to me, and it took quite a while for me to calm down and relax. I then asked Matthew to have a look at this man too, which he did. He also made his way to the restroom, and when he returned a few minutes later, I immediately noticed a very strange, confused look on his face. He said that he knew who this man was. His name is Peter Lamborelle."

"How does he know him?" asked Thomas.

"This Peter is the husband of Matthew's girlfriend. He met him at a cocktail party."

"Aha!" Alfonse was now very interested. "Assuming you're absolutely sure, we'll have the kidnapper's name straight away, won't we, Lis? Isn't that great?"

"Yes, I'm as sure as I can be, and no, that's not good. Because I definitely don't want this case to be reopened and for me to have to start all over again. Besides, how am I supposed to prove it now? No, I certainly don't want that, Alfonse. I can't go through that again. It would kill me."

"Okay, okay, I understand. First of all, stay calm. I could do some private research myself to see if this name is connected to Bouvier Bank, you never know. That could be a motive as to why you, of all people, were kidnapped."

Lis thought about it for a moment. She wasn't particularly enthusiastic about the suggestion.

"Okay, you're welcome to do that, but please, Alfonse, do it very discreetly and make sure that my name doesn't appear anywhere, neither Lis Chandler nor Elisabeth Bouvier. And I say that on purpose, because this man is dangerous! Don't underestimate him. Besides, I just want us to find Matt and Alan; this man is no longer important to me."

"Boy, oh boy," David said, ordering another bottle of red wine, "this is going to be a couple of weeks. So much confusion and mysterious happenings ... and I thought I was only going on a two-week vacation in Luxembourg."

"Well, that's what you thought?" Thomas joked and then his face became serious. "If we had Alan and Matthew here, that would at least be something."

"We'll take care of that tomorrow, there's nothing we can do today," David said. "Cheers! Here's to a good night's sleep."

Lis spent a very restless and almost sleepless night. Every time she closed her eyes, she kept seeing Matthew's face in front of her. Then Peter Lamborelle came to mind, the person she least wanted to meet in her thoughts and dreams. The look in those eyes had frightened her beyond belief. At one point, she actually expected Georges to turn up. But he was the only person who didn't invade her dreams.

During the night, Lis got up several times and looked at her cell phone, hoping for a sign of life from Matthew. *Oh Matt, please come back. Let me know you're alive, I beg you!* she thought.

## *FRIDAY, AUGUST 2*

6 a.m., Friday morning. Matthew's head was pounding as he slowly regained consciousness. His eyes were still closed but he could feel that he was on solid ground. Where was he? He did not have the slightest idea. He tried to remember. What had happened? Gradually, his thoughts returned to the airport building. Yes, he had kissed Lis. He smiled at the thought and saw her face in his mind's eye. He remembered walking down some stairs and

entering the men's room. He tied the knife around his leg, then he texted Lis— he remembered exactly what he wrote—then he opened the door and started washing his hands and then ... yes, then suddenly someone was standing behind him and he had received a brutal blow to the head.

And then everything went black.

Matthew slowly opened his eyes. He felt a big bump on his head, which hurt like hell when he touched it. But at least it wasn't bleeding.

As he tried to sit up quickly, he lost his balance and fell down again. He looked around. It was still quite dark in the room. At the top, just below the ceiling, there was a small, hatch-like window. The wall seemed to be at least four meters high. His rucksack was lying right next to him. He put his hand on it.

Then he lay down again and waited until it got lighter. He must have fallen asleep, because when he opened his eyes again, it was much brighter around him. Full light was coming in through the hatch, allowing him to see the inside of the room clearly.

Matthew sat up and looked around again. He still felt quite dizzy. As he took his bearings, he got a huge fright. A man was lying on a mattress in the other corner of the room. *Was he asleep or no longer alive*, he asked himself as he quickly picked up his rucksack and opened it.

His first thought was to look for his cell phone. Hastily, he pushed his hand down to the bottom of the rucksack and felt the device still where he had stowed it after texting Lis. Strange. Maybe the kidnapper hadn't found it? He tried to switch it on, but there seemed to be no power. The battery was almost flat. No wonder.

Then he took a pair of handcuffs out of his rucksack, which he had put in there as a precaution as he was packing. Whatever this was, it couldn't be a professional kidnapping, otherwise the cell phone would be gone, Matthew concluded to himself.

He stood up quietly. Suddenly he remembered the knife. Yes, it was still there, tied to his ankle. *Oh, Lis, how can I thank you for that? At least I have this to defend myself.* He immediately pulled the knife out of its leather sheath and took it in his hand, ready to attack. He walked slowly towards the man.

At least he was still breathing, Matthew realised as he stood next to him, but he seemed to be fast asleep. He was lying on his stomach.

Matthew very slowly placed the handcuffs around one of the man's wrists while holding the knife to his throat as a precaution. He quickly closed the cuffs with his other hand.

The man seemed to have noticed this and started moving.

Matthew, who was still holding the knife to his throat, put his foot on the man's leg and said: "Hey, wake up! Very slowly and don't panic. And above all, don't move."

It was quite a while before the man in jeans and a dirty T-shirt gave any sign of life at all; he tried to turn his head a little and looked, still half asleep, at Matthew.

He seemed to slowly realise that his hands were tied.

"And now what?" he asked in a weak voice, blinking at Matthew.

"Who are you?" asked Matthew. "And what are you doing here, where are we?"

Then the man spotted the knife. "Hey, always nice and slow. One at a time. Can I get up?"

"Sure, but slowly. And I'm not removing the handcuffs. Don't fall over, don't try to attack me and no uncontrolled movements!" Matthew took his foot off his leg and stood in front of him with his knife. Until now, he had never threatened anyone with a knife in his life.

The man stood up slowly and looked rather dazed. "My head is heavy. Last night's sleeping pill must have been stronger than usual. My name is Alan, Alan Moore," he then said to Matthew's great surprise and relief at the same time.

"Alan Moore? You ... You're here? Well, that changes the whole situation immediately."

He quickly released the handcuffs.

"Have we met before?" Alan asked, looking at him again in confusion and surprise. Alan's short, greyish hair was sticking out in all directions, as if he hadn't washed it for days.

"I've heard all about you. You're the reason I'm here. I've come with some other people who are looking for you: David White, Alfonse Weis, Thomas Walter and a woman called Lis, who speaks Spanish."

Alan rubbed his eyes. "And how did you get here, where are the others?"

"That was more of a coincidence, I'd say. They locked me up with you. Where are we here? I'm Matthew McKenna, a friend of Lis, who is a friend of Thomas Walter. It's a long story."

Alan looked at Matthew a little suspiciously. "Sounds like it."

"Alan, where are we, who locked us up? What's happened?"

"I haven't got the slightest idea. Well, I'm sure you know that I came here to find a woman. When I arrived at the airport building and was waiting for my suitcase, I was kindly asked to accompany two men who were holding a gun to my back. When we were outside the building, I felt a strong blow to my head and then found myself here in this room when I regained consciousness."

"Yes, I know about this woman and I also know that David was waiting for you at the Hotel Discovery."

Matthew then told Alan what had happened when he and Lis had landed and what the situation looked like, as far as he knew it by now.

"What a crazy situation," Matthew continued. "After we picked up our luggage at the airport terminal, Lis insisted on taking her knife out of her luggage. She always carries a knife on her leg for safety. And she insisted that I do the same, she had brought one especially for me. I only did it to do her a favour, but now, I'm grateful to her for that. That can be helpful in our situation."

"Oh, by the way," Matthew picked up his cell phone again, searched for something and then handed it to Alan.

"Is this your Diane?" He showed Alan the photo of the woman in the hospital room that Caro had taken and he received from Lis.

Alan's expression changed abruptly. "My goodness, yes, that's her. Where did that come from?

What's wrong with her?"

Matthew explained that Diane Van Helden had never left the McKenna clinic in Luxembourg.

"What, she's still in the same clinic? And I was told exactly the opposite. Those bastards! Whoever they are, Matthew, we've got to get out of here somehow and fast."

"Yes, I agree with you. We need to get out of here. Do they bring you food regularly?"

"Yes, they push it in through the opening in the door. I haven't seen a soul since I've been here. I hear voices, the two men who picked me up at the airport seemed to be locals, they only speak Spanish to each other."

"That means they haven't spoken to you and might explain why you're here."

"No, not at all. I screamed, I shouted, but there was no reaction."

"Strange," said Matthew.

"At least they left me my rucksack with a few things in it, and there's an old shower around the corner, behind the door, and a toilet if you need it," Alan continued. "I still don't understand why they picked me up right at the airport," he added.

"And then me. Also strange. We must have been followed. But who could have guessed that I would end up here today?" Matthew asked. "We must have fallen into the hands of a gang of scammers who ambush passengers and then kidnap them as soon as they set foot on the island. They take their money, but then, why do they lock you up here? That makes no sense, if you ask me."

"Give me a few minutes," Alan said, went into the other room and came back a moment later.

He had washed his face with cold water.

"Hey, you're limping?" Matthew saw that immediately. "Sprained foot?"

"No, something hurts under my foot when I step on it hard. I already had it before I left Luxembourg but I didn't think anything more of it. I assumed it was from the accident and would go away in a few days. But in the last few days it has been quite sore. It's only a small spot, but it hurts a lot."

"Can I have a look at it?" asked Matthew.

"Sure. Do you know anything about it?"

"Yes, I'm a doctor."

"Oh, that's a good thing." Alan stretched out his foot as Matthew sat down on the floor in front of him." And the fact that you have handcuffs in your luggage, is that part of a doctor's basic equipment?" he asked.

Matthew picked up his cell phone with the small flashlight and illuminated the spot. "No, that's part of a magician's basic equipment," he said with a smile.

Alan looked at him in confusion. "A magician?"

Matthew glanced at him: "That's a longer story. My battery is almost dead, but the lamp still works, well enough."

He looked at the sole of Alan's foot and pressed lightly on various spots.

"At first glance, I can't see anything. Except for a small bulge here." He pressed lightly.

"Hey, right there," Alan said. "Right there it hurts, yeah there."

Matthew took a small bag out of his rucksack.

"Did you bring your whole medical kit?"

"No, but a small emergency bag, just in case. Yes, I'm a part-time doctor and part-time magician, it sounds funny, but it's true. Here, put your foot on the backpack so it's a bit higher and I can see it better."


Matthew continued to examine the painful spot.

Suddenly, a soft beep sounded from Matthew's backpack.

"Did you bring an alarm clock?" joked Alan, "Maybe some basic equipment too?"

Matthew looked confused for a moment. Then he opened his bag.

Then he looked at Alan enigmatically.

"What?" the latter asked. "An alarm clock after all?"

Matthew shook his head in the negative.

Then he pulled a small device out of his pocket, which triggered the signal again.

"Of course! I'd forgotten all about that!" was all he said. "But it's weird!" He held the device further away from Alan and the beeping stopped. He brought it closer again and it started up again.

"What is that? What are you measuring on me? Am I radio-active?"

Matthew played with the distance a few times, sometimes closer, sometimes further away, and the sound adjusted accordingly.

"Come on, what's going on here?"

Matthew looked at him again.

"This here, Alan, is a chip reader from a vet friend of mine who lent it to me the other day for my neighbour. She wanted me to find out if her stray cat was chipped or not. In fact, I forgot to give it back to her later and so it's still here in my bag. Now I must have accidentally pressed the button and switched the device on but ..."

"And that means it reacts to me?" asked Alan, who no longer understood anything.

"Only if there is a microchip in the immediate vicinity."

"A microchip?"

"Exactly." Matthew took the device in his hand and held it along the sole of Alan's foot, whereupon it beeped incessantly.

"Have you ever had an operation where metal was inserted into your ankle or foot?"

"No. After the accident the other day, when I was run over with Diane, I had a slight sprain in my foot, that's what they told me in hospital when I woke up."

"Hmm, I think the chip reader is reacting to something in the sole of your foot."

"No, that can't be. I'm not chipped, come on." Alan was now very suspicious of Matthew.

"Come on, hold it to another part of your body. This device is giving false signals. Maybe it's reacting a bit confused, broken from the impact earlier?" Alan tried to explain.

Matthew ran it all over his body but the device only registered a tone at the sole of Alan's foot.

"But there's no code to read. Animals have a number on them. The registration number that can be used to trace the owner. You're chipped, Alan. I'm sorry, but you have a chip on the bottom of your foot. That's this little bulge here. And that's why you're in pain."

Alan looked at Matthew a little suspiciously.

"I know it sounds strange but I don't have a better explanation. You've got something metallic there and it can only be a chip that the device is reacting to."

"Check the soles of your own feet," said Alan, who now seemed slightly annoyed.

"It won't change anything, but if you insist, I'll do you the favour, Alan."

Matthew slowly brought the device up to the sole of his foot, first to the right, then to the left and to his great surprise, a tone sounded.

Matthew was startled. He looked at Alan speechlessly and tried again. From left to right. He repeated this a few times. Yes, no doubt about it, there was something there.

The two men looked at each other without saying a word.

"So you're chipped too, are you?" Alan was curious about this answer.

"That's impossible. I would know that for sure! Who would have chipped me?"

"I have the same question: who would have chipped me and for what purpose?" Alan said.

Matthew felt the sole of his foot carefully. "Nothing unusual, nothing painful. But here, hey, not directly under the sole of the foot, but a little above it. A very small bulge. Almost impossible to feel."

"If I'm being hunted for trying to help Diane, then I don't understand why you're walking around with a chip too," Alan concluded.

"Let me think for a moment," Matthew said, holding the device to his foot again and again.

"Where could you have been chipped?" Alan asked. "That could only have happened at the clinic, or in a doctor's office, but you would have noticed such a procedure. Diane and I were admitted to the McKenna Private Clinic. But you know all about that, that's where Diane's photo was taken."

"Today really is my day of surprises," Matthew said. "You've never had foot surgery before this last one?"

"No, I haven't! Why do you ask?"

"No, because this clinic belongs to my father and is run by him."

Alan now looked at Matthew in genuine surprise. "Ah!!! And what have you got to do with all this?"

"Me? With what?"

"I don't know. But ... If I was chipped at the clinic and now you arrive here with a chip?"

"I have nothing to do with any of this. But it certainly wasn't done at the McKenna Clinic. No way," Matthew said with conviction. "Not there. My father is an extremely honourable doctor. He and I don't exactly have a fantastic father-son relationship, but he is, after all, a top doctor and surgeon, integrity and honour are essential to him. I'm confused, Alan."

"Well, and your chip, Mr. Wizard?" asked Alan. "When was it used and where? We seem to have the same source, don't we? It suddenly makes sense now!"

Matthew looked at Alan even more confused and felt his bump on his head again. "I've only been to our clinic once, for two days. I hurt my knee so badly on stage that I had to have meniscus surgery, that was about four months ago. But ... No, I'm already starting to get paranoid. I don't believe it. Why would someone do something like that? It doesn't make any sense at all."

"There we go ..." Alan just commented, "We agree on that. It doesn't make any sense."

"I can't believe I have a microchip in my foot. It must be this machine, it's sending the wrong information ..." Matthew said and put it aside.

"I wish you were right, but I think we both been chipped, unfortunately," Alan concluded, looking at Matthew with concern.

"Listen to me, Matthew, I'm serious now. If we're both chipped, then we can be tracked down. That would explain why they were expecting me when I arrived here at the airport. And if we keep thinking logically, why were you followed and beaten up as soon as you arrived? It kind of fits together, doesn't it? Can you give me a better version of the story?"

"But I have nothing to do with you. No one could know that I'm here because of you. No one, I mean, no outsider."

Matthew pondered. "I presume that Lis doesn't have a chip. That's why they were able to track me down and then kidnapped me, but not her."

"If your theory is right, then we need to get rid of this thing as quickly as possible. Can you cut it out for us?" Alan suggested.

"Let's take a look. Now I'm really grateful to Lis for this knife. She has some strange habits, but this could save our lives."

"Who is this Lis? Your girlfriend?"

"Hm ... More like a good old friend, my first love from teenage years. It's a long story. Put your foot here and keep it still." Alan held out his foot again and Matthew felt the sole.

"What else have you been able to find out since then?" asked Matthew, while he was busy removing the chip.

"Nothing. All I know is that Diane got into this mess through her ex-boyfriend, at least that's what she says, he seems to be connected to this orphanage here. She had told me about him. Obviously a strange guy. And that's why I came here, because I didn't know where else to start. When I called the orphanage from Luxembourg and asked about this man, they knew immediately who he was. Somehow he must have some elite connections if you know what I mean."

"What's her ex's name?" Matthew asked cluelessly.

"Mark Lamborelle."

Matthew raised his head instantly and looked at Alan, frowning. "Say that again!"

"Mark Lamborelle. Don't tell me you know him!"

"No. I know a Peter Lamborelle, but ..."

"But what?"

"He's the husband of my friend, well, actually my lover. And this man, I mean this Peter Lamborelle, he was on our flight here. He's also here on the island. Blond hair, tall, slim, doesn't look particularly friendly, but pretty good-looking, I'd say."

"Hmm, that description could fit the face of Diane's ex-boyfriend," Alan said thoughtfully. "She showed me some photos the night before the accident. I'm still wondering if we're talking about the same man here, though. This seems like a pretty criminal guy who wants to get Diane out of the way. The reason is still unclear."

"Funny!" Matthew was trying to figure out a way to fit it into this. "And the chipping is even weirder. So, now I want to see how I can remove the chip from your foot, Alan. Because if our theory is right, then we really have to get rid of these things, otherwise we won't get very far, assuming we get out of here at all."

"Well, I hope so. Two of us can do it, and you have the knife. So far, only one person has ever brought the food. I've never heard two people talking outside when they bring food. We'll think of something."

Matthew was infinitely glad that he had his emergency bag in his rucksack and that it hadn't been taken away from him.

Within half an hour, he was able to remove the chip from Alan's foot with a tiny incision. It was easy to feel the exact spot under the skin, so it was easier than expected.

Now Matthew had to try the same thing on himself. Alan held

a small mirror in front of him, which he had fetched from the bathroom next door.

He held the mirror up to Matthew so that he could see where he needed to make the incision.

In his case, the chip was on the side of the foot, and he came to the conclusion that in Alan's case, it had probably slipped and ended up under the sole of the foot. Matthew had now also removed the chip from his foot. A larger incision had been necessary. Drops of sweat stood on his forehead as he stuck a plaster over the cut.

"If this keeps up," he said as he packed everything back into his rucksack, "we will have to be prepared for anything. This story is taking strange turns."

"You're telling me," Alan confirmed. "Very strange twists!"

By now it was well after 8 a.m.

Matthew tried to use his phone again, but there was no network. He prepared a text message to be sent as soon as a connection was available.

*August 2: Lis, I'm alive, don't worry, I've found Alan. We're locked up somewhere and trying to escape. I don't have a network here, so you won't get this text until we're somewhere else. I'll call you as soon as possible.*

"What did you tell your lover about where you were going?"

"I simply told Brigitte that I was going to the Dominican Republic for two weeks with friends. She told me that she wasn't very enthusiastic because her husband, probably 'our' Peter Lamborelle, would be away on business. She wondered why she needed a lover who would also be away most of the time."

"Hmm ... sounds like you need to take her out for a really nice dinner when you get back home."

"I don't care, we made an agreement at the beginning of our ...

well, togetherness. We made an agreement: no living together, no orders and certainly no restrictions on freedom."

"Sounds good," Alan agreed, "exactly my philosophy. And it seems that this Peter is indeed our man, same timing."

"I think so too. Alan, we need to make a plan to get out of here. We can't wait for someone to cut our throats, if that's what they're planning. Anyway, they're not that professional or they would have taken my rucksack. My passport and credit cards are here too, down in the rucksack. But they've taken my wallet. I had it in my trouser pocket. It only contained a copy of my passport and some cash though. For security reasons, I always like to spread my valuables out in two different places. This time, the precaution was worth it."

"You're right about that. They don't seem very professional. But the blow to the head wasn't bad," Alan said. "I think my luggage got lost somewhere. I had a small piece of hand luggage, but they left it with me. Of course, I had already noticed at that point that I didn't have my cell phone with me."

"Yes, you lost it in Thomas' car, it must have fallen out of your pocket. But your suitcase arrived at the hotel with David, I heard."

"Well, at least that's something. I wish we were there already!"

"Your luggage is the least of our problems at the moment," Matthew said. "Shouldn't we try to break down the door somehow? We've got the survival knife here. I'm sure we can get out with it. It's not as if they expect us to have any tools with us."

"We can definitely try, come on."

"Do you have any idea where we are?"

"No," Alan said. "I can only assume we're near the orphanage in case there really are illegal things going on there, which Diane was convinced there were. I sincerely hope she's still alive when we get back to the country."

"We should at least assume that. Even if she's in a coma, that doesn't necessarily mean she's almost dead. So let's get to work."

Matthew took his knife and all the other small tools he had in his backpack and both men knelt down in front of the door. They examined the lock and Matthew used various tools to try to unscrew or pull the lock off. Of course, they wanted to do this as quietly as possible, as they didn't know how many men were outside.

After half an hour, the two men gave up without success.

"We won't be able to do that," said Alan, after they had really tried everything. The lock seemed to be secured from the outside and therefore couldn't be broken from the inside.

"We'll wait until tonight. You say the food will be delivered?"

"Yes, around 7 p.m."

"It might be easier to escape then."

"But how do we get out of here?" asked Alan.

Matthew stood up as well. "Here's what we're going to do." He moved closer to Alan and whispered in his ear for a few minutes. There was no way he wanted anyone to overhear. There didn't seem to be a camera connected, as far as Alan could tell. At least not in this room.

The latter nodded silently. "Good plan!"

Then Matthew took the handcuffs he had used earlier, and gave them to Alan who put them in his pocket.

# *SATURDAY, AUGUST 3*

On Saturday morning just after 9 a.m., Lis was the first to arrive for breakfast on the terrace. She felt exhausted and was very worried about Matthew. How much she missed him. She felt constantly on the verge of tears. She ordered a strong coffee and helped herself to the breakfast buffet. It looked quite good, unlike her room. A single bed in the corner, furniture that was at least

30 years old, and a bathroom, if you could call it that, with an old shower and a toilet with a washbasin next to it.

She had asked at reception if there was a room available for Matthew. Alan's suitcase from the airport was already in his room.

A few minutes later, Lis received the text message that Matthew had sent yesterday.

*August 2nd. Lis, I'm alive, don't worry, I've found Alan. We're locked up somewhere and trying to escape. I don't have cell service here, so you won't get this text until we're somewhere else. I'll call you as soon as I can.*

She read the message at least three times. What a relief! He was alive. Matthew was alive. Tears rolled down her cheeks. She could hardly wait to feel him again.

Thomas and Alfonse appeared shortly afterwards and a few minutes later, David showed up too. They seemed to have quite a hangover from the night before. They had probably drunk a few bottles of wine.

Lis immediately showed them the text message from Matthew.

The three men sat down at a table together and, after a strong coffee, a conversation gradually got going. The atmosphere was oppressive.

"That's something! Wonderful!" said Alfonse. "Then they'll turn up here at some point. It's better if we don't call when they're somewhere tricky, so let's leave it for now. They'll find their way to the hotel somehow."

"If they're still well," David commented.

"They're big boys," said Thomas. "Of course they're fine, they'll both be fine. There's nothing we can do anyway; we haven't the faintest idea where they could be."

"What's our plan, where do we start?" asked Lis, looking at each of them.

"You can forget about the police here," David spoke up. "What I've achieved with the police in the last few days has been zero."

"And what we've achieved in the last two days hasn't been much better. They only speak Spanish and broken English, but I don't think we'll get anywhere with them," said Thomas. "We went to the orphanage yesterday morning to see exactly where it is, but we didn't go in. We thought we'd wait for you in case they only communicate in Spanish," added Alfonse.

"Well, then I suggest we go there," said Lis. "Maybe we'll find some clues there. Anyway, that's the only clue Alan has."

"Right," David agreed, "we need to get in there, maybe under the pretext that we need information about a possible adoption?"

"Sounds good," Alfonse agreed. "I came up with a plan last night, but only if you agree to it, of course."

"What plan?" asked David.

"Thomas and you, Lis, are a couple considering adoption. You got this address from a good friend, Diane Van Helden, and now you're here on vacation and wanted to come by to check things out. David and I will be staying somewhere out of the way, otherwise it will look pretty weird. Alan had mentioned that Diane's ex-boyfriend's name is Mark Lamborelle. Perhaps you could mention that name as a reference during the interview?"

"So, this can only be a brother of this Peter, or his son?"

"As long as it's not Peter Lamborelle, we can do it," Lis agreed.

"I still suspect that guy from the plane was just a coincidence," Alfonse said, looking at Thomas.

"Okay, let's try the plan. Do you think Alan and Matthew could be there too?" asked David.

"I don't know, but there's only one way to find out. We'll go along, and while you two keep the contact busy and distract her with questions, we'll check out the building as far as we can get in."

"I hope Matthew and Alan are okay. I'm still so worried," said Lis. She was on the verge of tears again and Thomas put his arm around her to comfort her.

"They'll get through, believe me. They'll make it!"

Alfonse made a note of the address of the orphanage and together they caught a cab shortly after 1 p.m., even though their destination was not far from their hotel.

The cab took them to a side street near the orphanage. Thomas and Lis walked hand in hand to the front door, while Alfonse and David kept their distance.

If Thomas and Lis weren't back within two hours, they would ring the doorbell and see what was going on.

Lis and Thomas were standing in front of the entrance door of 'Pequeños Angeles'. They were both a little nervous. They were aware that they might not be able to get in without an appointment but it was definitely worth a try.

Meanwhile, Alfonse and David walked around the building and inspected the back of it.

Thomas cleared his throat. "This is going to be something," he muttered to himself. "I'm taking you to an adoption interview."

"It has to look real now, otherwise we won't get anywhere anyway," Lis added and gave him a beautiful smile.

"Yes, ma'am!" He looked at her urgently as he rang the bell. "Let's do it."

Just as Thomas was about to ring the doorbell again, the door was opened. A tall, slender lady in her mid-fifties, elegantly dressed in a dark blue dress and with grey hair, appeared and greeted them in Spanish.

"Hello, what can I do for you?"

Lis took over the conversation. "Good afternoon, señorita. We have come from Luxembourg on the advice of a friend. She said we could come by spontaneously for a preliminary talk and get information about a possible adoption."

The lady looked at her very closely. "Who recommended this house to you?" she asked in a rather stern voice.

"Mrs. Van Helden, Diane Van Helden," Lis said, hoping that this was not a mistake.

"Ah, Mrs. Van Helden! Of course, please come in!"

*Well, at least we're in*, thought Thomas. *That was easier than I had expected.*

"My name is Antonia Sanchez; I am the assistant to the director of this facility. Please follow me."

Lis briefly introduced herself: "My name is Martina Kaufmann and this is my husband, Alexander."

Lis and Thomas were led into a well-furnished large room right next to the front door. It was filled with stylish furniture—a desk with two chairs opposite, while further back in the room, a seating area consisted of two single armchairs and a couch made of dark brown, expensive leather.

Antonia Sanchez took a seat at the desk and Lis and Thomas sat opposite her.

"Mrs. Van Helden hasn't been here for a while. She seems to have a lot of work in Luxembourg at the moment. But it's very nice that she recommended our orphanage."

"Yes, she had nothing but positive things to say about it, and we're so glad we finally decided to adopt, aren't we, darling?" Lis took Thomas' hand and looked at him.

"It wasn't an easy decision, but yes, I'm very glad we've decided to do it." Thomas could hardly believe what he was about to say.

"We would first like to find out about the general conditions and guidelines for adoption," he continued.

"Yes, first of all we have to check your identity, your family situation and your financial situation, I'm sure you understand that. Then you will be introduced to our director, who will give you more details about the possibilities of adopting a baby. Surely Mrs. Van Helden has already explained all this to you?"

"Yes, yes, of course!" Lis lied convincingly. "Do you only place European children?"

"Ninety percent, yes! Then you probably also know our subsidiary in Luxembourg. Everything is managed from there to facilitate the entire process."

"Mrs. Van Helden mentioned it briefly, but didn't elaborate. Where exactly is the orphanage in Luxembourg?"

"In Clervaux. It's a very modest house, we're not very wealthy, you know, but it's important that we have a presence there too. You will adopt your child through Luxembourg, which simplifies the adoption process and all the necessary legal documents enormously."

"Clervaux?" Lis remarked involuntarily, spontaneously thinking of Caro. She had mentioned that she came from an orphanage in Clervaux.

"Yes, Clervaux. A small town in the north of your country. Do you not know it?" Mrs. Sanchez said a little sharply.

"Sure, I just thought your orphanage would be more in the city centre."

Thomas looked at Lis, somewhat confused.

"And the children themselves, what kind of backgrounds do these parentless boys and girls come from?" Lis thought it was time to divert the topic.

"It's very different, Mrs. Kaufmann. There are children whose parents have died in an accident, car accidents are not uncommon, or young, single mothers who give their baby up for adoption directly because they are still children themselves and can't or don't want to take on the responsibility. As you can see, there are many situations that make a child available for adoption. And that is very sad. That's why we are always very grateful when adoptive parents are found who can give a child a nice home and look after it with love and care."

"That's all very understandable." Lis looked at her watch. "But we don't want to take up any more of your time now, Mrs. Sanchez. We are very grateful to you for answering our questions immediately. We will get back to you as soon as we have all the documents ready for review."

"Yes, please do." Ms. Sanchez handed Lis her business card.

"I have one more question," Thomas said. "Is Dr. Lamborelle here in the house today too? It would be nice to meet him now that we're here."

Lis thought she hadn't heard correctly. She stepped on Thomas' foot.

"Mr. Kaufmann, you're really lucky. Mr. Lamborelle is currently in the country and is also in the house now. If you can kindly wait a moment, I'll see if he's available for a brief meeting. I'll be right back."

Mrs. Sanchez stood up and walked out of the office.

Lis looked at Thomas with angry eyes. "I'm not sure that was a good idea. We didn't talk about this, Thomas!" There were footsteps outside.

"Don't worry, it'll be fine," he tried to reassure Lis. "We'll never get a better opportunity."

The door opened and a tall, well-dressed man in a black shirt and white linen trousers entered.

"Hello, Mrs. and Mr. Kaufmann!"

Lis and Thomas turned around at the same time when they heard the voice.

"It is a great pleasure for me to welcome you to our clinic. My name is Dr. Peter Lamborelle. A warm welcome to you!"

They stood up and he greeted them with a firm handshake.

"Good afternoon, Dr. Lamborelle," said Thomas enthusiastically. "We are very grateful that you have the time to meet with us. Thank you very much!"

Lis thought she couldn't see properly. She was looking into the face of the same man she had bumped into on the plane. Their eyes met immediately as they took their seats.

She felt her pulse increasing by the second. *Oh my God, the black spot in his left eye. If he recognises me now, I don't know what will happen*, she thought, panicking.

Thomas, on the other hand, seemed to have the situation perfectly under control and took over the conversation. However, he seemed to underestimate the state of anxiety Lis was in and didn't notice. She behaved very discreetly and was able to control her thoughts with great effort, so that she at least managed to stay in the room.

"Of course, we can't tell you the exact date yet, but an adoption should actually be possible within six to eight months. There are so many homeless children and infants who are longing for a family life, for loving parents. It is very nice that you have decided to adopt."

"Yes, we're very glad we made this decision too, aren't we, darling!" Thomas took Lis' hand and looked at her lovingly.

"Yes, we've thought about it very carefully," she added, almost in a whisper.

Dr. Lamborelle once again explained the exact process of the administrative matters.

"We will request all the necessary certificates of our identity, fill out the forms and send everything to you personally," confirmed Thomas.

"As I mainly work in Luxembourg myself, we can meet there at a later date, and if you have any questions in the meantime, I'm always available," said Dr. Lamborelle, handing Lis and Thomas his business card.

"Do you have any other questions that I might be able to answer now?" he asked, staring at Lis. The blond, tanned man really didn't look like a criminal, Lis thought. Her thoughts spontaneously wandered to Eric.

"Martina, do you have another question?" Thomas brought her out of her thoughts.

"No. No, not at the moment. Or no, just one. Will we also find out the story of the adopted child at some point?"

"That's actually against our regulations, Mrs. Kaufmann, mainly because we don't want the adoptive parents to develop any prejudices. Often these children come from very poor backgrounds or even from very unsocial family circumstances, which could later be a burden for both parents and the child. But I can assure you that we examine all the details very carefully in this regard before we approve the adoption procedure."

"That's reassuring," Lis said. She realised that the longer she was in this man's presence, the worse she felt. Her blood pressure was dropping as she struggled to focus on something else. She was beginning to feel very unwell. Her mouth had become very dry. Then small black dots became visible in front of her eyes, accompanied by a slight ringing in her ears that turned into almost complete deafness within seconds.

As Thomas and Dr. Lamborelle stood up, Lis got up too. Just as she stood, she collapsed and fell unconscious on the floor.

"Oh no! Hey, Martina!" said Thomas and they both knelt down next to her.

"Help me, Mr. Kaufmann, we need to put her legs up. I'll get some refreshment and a cold compress in a minute. Don't worry, it's probably this oppressive heat and it's particularly humid today. I'm sure it's getting to your wife." Then he hurried out.

"That must be it," Thomas replied. "Martina, hey, look at me. Are you all right?"

He patted her cheeks lightly. After a while, Lis slowly opened her eyes.

A short time later, Dr. Lamborelle returned, followed by Mrs. Sanchez. He brought a wet towel, which he placed on Lis' forehead. Then he knelt down next to her and took the glass of water that Mrs. Sanchez handed him.

"So Mrs. Kaufmann, have a few sips!" He caringly held the glass to her mouth.

"Thank you," she whispered, taking the glass and bringing it to her mouth.

"Are you feeling a little better?" Dr. Lamborelle asked, checking her blood pressure. "Yes, it's very low. I thought so, she was white as a sheet when she got up from the chair earlier," he confirmed to Thomas. "It's better if she stays seated for a few more minutes."

Thomas excused himself to find a toilet and went out.

Lis was still lying on the floor. Peter Lamborelle towered above her with the glass of water. It's those eyes, Lis thought. She was freezing cold and hot at the same time.

"Mrs. Kaufmann, are you all right?" he asked in a low voice, looking at Lis.

*And he's even worried*, she thought. Suddenly tears came to her eyes, the way he was looking at her ... how strange. She found herself in a jumble of emotions.

"Please, let me help you up." He held out his hand to her and Lis sat back down on the chair. She quickly wiped away her tears.

"Yes, I'm fine. Thank you very much. I just can't stand this heat. I'm very embarrassed about this incident."

"Please don't be, it's not a problem at all. It's quite normal, not everyone can find their feet straight away in this climate." He smiled kindly. "But Mrs. Kaufmann, didn't we see each other on the plane the other day?"

At that moment, Thomas came back. Lis stood up immediately. "I'm fine again, we can go."


Without answering his question, Lis shook hands with Dr. Lamborelle and Mrs. Sanchez, who escorted them to the door.

As Thomas and Lis were exiting, a tall man was walking up the front steps towards them.

"Good afternoon," he greeted Mrs. Sanchez. "My name is Winther, I have an appointment with Dr. Lamborelle."

When Lis looked at the man, she recognised his face. It was the fully bearded man from the plane. Their eyes met for a moment.

Then Lis went on with Thomas and the man came in with Mrs. Sanchez.

Lis turned back around, and strangely enough, the man was doing the same. Their eyes met again.

"Do you know him?" Thomas asked, a little surprised.

"No, but I think he was on our flight over here."

"Ah yes, that happens," said Thomas. "Come on, let's go."

Lis and Thomas walked slowly down the street. "Are you really all right again?" asked Thomas, still looking worriedly at Lis. She was leaning against a wall. "I don't know. No, somehow nothing's all right. But yes, we got out all right and I have to digest who was standing in front of me first."

"Phew, that was a tough one. I was a bit nervous too," commented Thomas.

"How do you think I felt?" Thomas could see that Lis wasn't feeling well at all. "That was Peter Lamborelle, Thomas! Personally!"

Tears rolled down her cheeks again.

"Come here, Lis!" Thomas hugged her and held her for a while.

"I'm sorry I asked to see Dr. Lamborelle. It was on the spur of the moment. I had no way of knowing, but I shouldn't have."

Alfonse and David caught up to them. They had been waiting further down the road.

They were briefly told what had happened during their meeting.

Lis stood directly in front of Thomas and put her hands on his shoulders. "Listen Thomas, Caro, Eric's girlfriend, comes from this house in Clervaux. She was adopted as a toddler or baby and comes from there. She mentioned that the other day when she came to visit me."

Thomas became very attentive. "I see. Well, maybe she'll have more to say about this house. Or about her parents?"

"That's quite possible. But it's probably more of a coincidence," Lis added.

They walked back to the hotel together. In the afternoon, they all met up again in the hotel bar.

"I went to the police again," explained Alfonse. "They have no leads but they are continuing the search based on the photo. My Spanish is zero and these police officers hardly speak any English."

"Do you think we could do something ourselves?" Lis asked anxiously and nervously. "I'm really worried about Matthew."

"No, at the moment we can only wait and see," said Alfonse.

"Two people have already disappeared. We can't just sit and wait, can we?" Lis was annoyed.

"But at least we know they're together somewhere. I tried all these avenues before you came and still got nowhere. Wait and see, at least until tomorrow. It's too late now anyway. Tomorrow we'll see how to proceed." David tried to reassure her.

"And besides, we all need sleep," Thomas added. "Do you fancy joining us for dinner later?"

"No thanks, Thomas. I'm going to stretch my legs a bit and have a look around. My day is definitely over."

Lis' thoughts revolved around Matthew. She was really worried about him. Then she thought about Mr. Winther, the bearded man who had come to the door of the orphanage as they were leaving. She should have talked to him, maybe he knew more? Or at least, she should have warned him if he was considering adoption.

Lis grabbed her sunglasses and sun hat and went outside. She wanted to go for a walk to take her mind off things. It was 6 p.m. and she wanted to be alone for a while. She knew that Thomas would have liked to have dinner with her but even that was too much for her now.

She strolled through the streets, stopping here and there to look at some shop windows and market stalls with fresh fruit.

Just as she crossed the road to get to a café terrace, she half-stepped on the sidewalk with her foot, tipped to one side and fell to the ground.

"Oh, blimey!" she said. Her foot hurt and she remained sitting on the ground for a moment.

While she was trying to get up again, she heard a man's voice: "Have you hurt yourself? Wait, I'll help you up," and she saw a hand reaching for her.

When Lis looked up, it was the face of Mr. Winther that was in front of her. The man from the plane, the same man who had entered the orphanage earlier when she came out with Thomas. He was wearing jeans and a white shirt and was at least 1.85 m tall, Lis estimated quickly.

"Have you hurt yourself?" he asked again. Lis was so astonished that she didn't know what to say.

"Are you all right?" he repeated his question.

She felt her foot. "Thank you! Yes, it hurts a bit, but I think it's all right." She moved her foot back and forth.

"Why don't you sit for a while?"

Mr. Winther accompanied Lis to the terrace of the café nearby and she sat down on a chair.

She stretched out her leg, pulled up her trouser leg a little, loosened the leather shaft with the knife and placed it on the table.

Mr. Winther was a little surprised. "You're prepared for the worst, I see! May I offer you something to drink?" Lis continued to look at him and his bright blue eyes were more than mesmerising. That look struck her like a lightning bolt. Somehow those eyes were strange, mysterious, maybe they scared her a little, she wasn't sure. Or was it because he looked so serious?

"Coffee?" he asked.

"Yes, I'd love one, thank you."

The man ordered in Spanish.

Lis moved her ankle, it didn't seem broken, probably just slightly sprained.

"We've already met once today," she said, looking at him again. "Today at lunchtime in front of the orphanage."

"That's right. I'm Michael Winther. Pleased to meet you." He looked at her intently.

Now Lis didn't know which name to mention to him. Since he had to be connected to the orphanage somehow, she quickly decided that she was Martina Kaufmann for the time being. If he had nothing to do with them, she could always tell him her real name later. "Kaufmann. Martina Kaufmann," she introduced herself.

"Kaufmann?" the man repeated, knowing full well that this was a lie.

"Yes, Kaufmann!" Lis said resolutely. Then she picked up her knife and strapped it back on. "Well, you never know what it might be useful for in a foreign city," she explained briefly.

"You're right about that. You're also from Luxembourg, we were on the same flights over here," Winther remarked.

"Yes, that was us. You were the last passenger to board in Luxembourg," said Lis.

"I was quite late, but I couldn't help it. Are you on vacation?" he asked. Lis had calmed down in the meantime and was somehow enjoying the man's presence. But what was he doing at the orphanage? She reminded herself that she had to be very careful with her answers.

"Yes ... Yes, we're here on vacation." She knew for a fact that Matthew was with her on the plane and Thomas was with her at the orphanage. She wondered if he had noticed the two different men.

"And you?" Lis then asked to keep the conversation going.

"I'm here on business." The conversation somehow didn't seem to get off the ground. It sounded more like a game of cat and mouse.

"Well, Mr. Winther, I'm going back to the hotel. Thank you for your quick offer of help and the coffee."

He stood up. "The pleasure is all mine. I hope you enjoy yourself."

"And you too!" replied Lis.

Then she strolled on. When she arrived at the hotel, she went straight to her room and had a snack brought to her.

For the time being, she didn't want to tell anyone about her encounter with this man. After all, it was probably irrelevant. However, she wouldn't mind seeing him again, she had to admit to herself. An interesting man at first glance, she estimated him to be in his late thirties or early forties.

8 p.m. Matthew and Alan were sitting on their mattresses when they heard a noise outside.

"Here comes dinner," Alan said quietly, winking at Matthew.

Within seconds, Alan fell to the floor and Matthew rushed to him, screaming and grabbing him violently by the collar. He screamed for help as loud as he could, and they repeated the whole scenario for several minutes until someone opened up from outside and immediately approached the two men with a gun.

"Stop right there!" shouted a man in jeans and a T-shirt, pointing the gun at Matthew. With a precise movement, Alan kicked his leg towards the man, knocking the gun out of the man's hand and on to the floor. At the same time, Matthew turned around and grabbed the man's hands. Alan stood up, quickly pulled the handcuffs out of his pocket and put them around the man's wrists while Matthew pressed the knife to his throat.

Matthew then hit him hard on the head. Fortunately, despite the noise, no one else came in.

"Now let's get out of here," Matthew said, reaching for his rucksack and checking his knife on his ankle. He also picked up the man's gun.

"Wow!" Alan grabbed his jacket, and then both men quickly left the room.

They found themselves in some kind of backyard. The room they had just left was appeared to be a large, modified container. All around them were hundreds of other containers, stacked one on top of each other.

"We have to get out of here, and fast. I don't know where we are, but we'll find out."

Matthew looked at his cell phone, he now had a network connection, but shortly afterwards his battery was completely dead.

"Damn!"

Alan could walk but his foot still hurt a lot. Matthew helped him to walk on; they had no other chance to escape.

"I'll sort out our chip story when we get back home," Matthew said, "you bet your life I will. What a mess. Someone from the McKenna clinic is going to jail for this."

"Well, I hope so, of course. But first we have to find out who put us in here and why. There's so much I don't understand at all. It all makes no sense, Diane must have found something that makes her a danger to someone, to this man?"

They continued on their way.

They walked for hours on a country road where there was not a soul to be seen, neither by car nor on foot. It wasn't until late in the evening that they reached a small snack bar where a few cars were parked. It looked pretty uncomfortable, but that didn't matter. They went inside together in the hope that someone would be able to help them.

Lis woke up. She had fallen asleep after all. It was just after midnight. Half asleep, she got up and got herself something to drink. Then she looked out of the window.

*What will we do if we don't find Matthew or Alan? Are they even still alive? I should never have brought Matt here*, she thought.

An inner restlessness overcame her. She picked up her phone and sent a text message to Eric.

*Is everything OK at home?*

It was already 8 a.m. in Luxembourg and Lis assumed that Eric was still asleep. But he answered immediately.

*Everything is fine, Lis—but there's one thing that is strange.*

Lis was immediately wide awake. She called him within seconds.

"Hey Eric, what's happened?"

"Hello, Mum! Don't worry, we're fine. But you know, this lady's patient file ..."

"No names on the phone please, better safe than sorry," Lis interrupted him abruptly.

Eric was a little surprised at first, but continued. "Okay. So, in this patient file, it says that the woman left the hospital around noon on Saturday, July 6, after being examined by her doctor. Caro only saw this last night, but, and here's the thing, she's still in the same room, only now there's no name on the sign by the bed. What do you say now?"

"What, are you really sure there isn't another woman lying there now?"

"Caro says it's the same woman, for sure. I wasn't there the second time. But she took a new photo, and if we compare it with the other one, it's the same woman, without a doubt."

"Listen Eric, listen to me carefully: You two are not to do anything more. Please. There's so much that doesn't fit together, there's a lot going on, but we'll talk tomorrow, okay?"

"Yeah, sure. Don't worry, we won't do anything else. Do you know when you're coming back?"

"No, not yet. We'll talk tomorrow. Have a good day. Give Caro a hug for me and thank her for everything she's done!"

"I will, take care of yourself!"

Then they hung up.

Lis lay back down on her bed. *Diane is still in the hospital, and her patient file has been changed? Someone wants this woman gone, or at least not able to talk.*

She had barely finished her thought when there was a knock at the door.

With one jump, she was out of bed again. She picked up her knife and walked slowly to the door, which was locked.

There was another knock. "Lis ..." She heard a voice.

"Thomas, is that you?" The door had no peephole.

"It's me, Matt."

"Matt?!" Lis could hardly believe it. Matthew!

She quickly unlocked the door and fell into his arms before he could even enter.

"I'm so happy to see you," she said.

He hugged her tightly and kissed her as he brushed a strand of hair from her face. As he did so, he looked at her.

"It's all right now," he whispered and closed the door behind him.

"You look completely exhausted. What happened?"

Matthew first sat down, had a drink and then briefly recounted what had happened since he had gone down the stairs in the airport building to go to the toilet.

"Oh my God! You were very lucky, we certainly wouldn't have found you. And neither would the police, I think by now."

"That's for sure." He took her face between his hands. "It's good to see you."

Then he kissed her again.

"Alan's in his room now too, but I really need to check on his foot and bandage it properly."

"Your suitcase is in your room, right next door," Lis explained.

"Wonderful! I haven't even been there yet, I had to see you first." He pulled Lis to him and kissed her again.

"I was afraid I'd never see you again," she whispered. "I'm really sorry I dragged you into this mess."

"It's too late for that now. We're in the middle of it and we have to see how we get out of it. At least we have Alan back with us. He's not in great shape, but he'll be fine. I'll just go and see him quickly," explained Matthew.

"You'll be back, won't you?"

He looked at her and took her face in his hands again: "You bet!"

Lis held on to him for a moment longer. "I spoke to Eric earlier. Caro says that Diane's patient file has since been changed and it now confirms that she left the hospital on July 6 after being examined by her doctor. But according to Caro, she's still in a coma in the ICU and now there's no name on the bedside. I think things are happening that your dear dad hopefully has no idea about!"

Matthew looked at her thoughtfully.

"I'll take care of it when we get back. I can't do it over the phone, and besides, I have to make sure who's on our side at the clinic first. Because this …" He felt the lump at the back of his head from where he had been hit. " …I don't want a second time. Some people at the clinic are playing games, it seems. So, see you in a minute." He hurried outside.

Alan was almost asleep when Matthew knocked and then entered.

While Matthew thoroughly disinfected Alan's foot wound, he told him what Lis had just said.

"What's going on here?" Alan asked, rubbing his eyes. "I don't understand the connections. You and I, we have nothing to do with each other, but we get locked up together. Diane is on the run because her ex-boyfriend is going crazy and spying on her, scaring her and then getting to both of us, at least that was her theory. My question is: Why? She said he did some weird stuff in connection with the orphanage. Maybe because she's distanced herself from him, he thinks she could be dangerous to him."

Alan sat up. "Does that sound logical? What do you think? Thanks for looking after me so well, by the way." He patted Matthew on the shoulder.

"You know what Alan, I can't think today. Let's get this on the table tomorrow. I'm just too tired right now."

"I totally agree," Alan said, dropping back onto the bed. "And don't wake me up tomorrow, please! I just need to get some sleep in a proper bed so I can feel alive again."

Matthew smiled. "I understand. See you tomorrow, then. Good night!"

When Matthew returned to Lis, she was lying on the bed. He went to her. "Alan's fine, but he's tired, like all of us."

She sensed his hesitation. "What now?"

"By the way, Diane Van Helden's ex-boyfriend is called Mark Lamborelle," she said. "Maybe a coincidence, maybe not."

"I don't know. Lis, I'm so tired." He leaned his forehead against her shoulder.

"Me too! There's a very comfortable double bed here!" she replied.

"Unanimously agreed." He smiled. "I don't snore."

"Good." Lis had a smile on her lips as she lay back down. "Me neither!"

Matthew lay down on the bed, Lis next to him. With his eyes closed, he reached for her hand.

"We don't know who is after us and, above all, we don't know why someone is after me. They can't be all that professional, otherwise they would have taken my rucksack and my cell phone. My passport and money were still in there too. I don't understand this. I assume I got in their way at short notice. And with the microchip, they were able to track me down immediately."

"But who planted that in you, Matt?"

"As I said to Alan, the only place I can think of where something like this could have happened is at the McKenna Clinic, because that's the only place I've been under anaesthesia. And that's where I'm going to confront someone on the spot, believe me. I've had this chip for months, imagine that. I'm going to find whoever did this, and they're going to have a very bad moment. You can bet on that."

"It's quite incomprehensible. I also don't understand where it's all leading." Lis said. "By the way, as we were leaving the orphanage, a man who was on our plane and got in at the last moment entered the place."

"Yes, I remember. He went in there?"

"Yes, strange, isn't it?" said Lis. "Maybe he wants to adopt a child?"

Matthew no longer answered, he had fallen asleep.

Before falling asleep, Lis turned the events of the day over in her head again and again. She couldn't get Mr. Winther out of her mind for a long time, she didn't know why. Maybe it was his striking blue eyes?

## SUNDAY, AUGUST 4

It was already daylight when Matthew woke up. He dared not move so as to not wake Lis, who still seemed to be fast asleep.

He looked at her and his feelings took over. *What am I going to do with you? What am I going to do with Biggy? At that moment, I wish I was standing on a stage somewhere, forgetting everything around me and just doing my show like I always do. Then I'd see my patients and everything else would be the same as always. But that will hardly be possible. Oh Lis, I thought I'd put my feelings for you behind me, been done with them. There have been so many years in between. And somehow it seems like yesterday ...*

Matthew got up quietly and took a shower. When he came back into the room, Lis had just woken up and was looking at him. He pulled the bath towel into place and fastened it.

"Good morning. Did you sleep well?" he asked.

He went to her bed and bent down. Her long, half-wavy hair was slightly dishevelled. "Right now, I feel like I've been transported back to the day we first kissed but so many years have passed between us."

"Then I'll close my eyes like I did back then and wait for you to kiss me." Lis closed her eyes and smiled.

He leaned down towards her and their lips met in an intimate kiss.

"I'm still in love with you, you know that! I thought, believed, hoped that you and I could be good friends, but it's going to be hard," he whispered.

"I see it as difficult too," she whispered and pulled him to her again and kissed him. "We'll see what happens when we get back home," she added.

"That's a good suggestion. You mean without obligation, here and now?"

"That's exactly what I mean. I shouldn't have cut you out of my life so easily back then, but it was all so damn hard, I had to fight for my survival. My whole perfect world was turned upside down."

"Sure, you did the right thing," he said. "For you and for your son. There was no room for someone like me, who certainly wouldn't have understood what it was like for you at the time." Then he lay down next to her.

"And now we're here as if nothing had ever happened in between. Life is a strange thing."

"You know," Lis said thoughtfully, "ever since I looked Eric's father in the eye, I've wondered a dozen times what would happen if he found out one day that he had a son. And what Eric would do then. I hope it will be a while yet, because the thought scares me."

"Maybe he'll never know? I hope you never meet this man again and despite everything, he's not the man you think he is and that he's just doing some job here."

"Do you want me to tell you something?" Lis looked at him seriously. "I've already met him."

"What?"

"Yesterday, Thomas and I went to the orphanage posing as a couple thinking about adoption, hoping to get some clues. And we were introduced to Dr. Peter Lamborelle, with whom we had a conversation afterwards." Lis explained to Matthew how she had collapsed.

"...And then I got up again. Dr Lamborelle helped me, took my blood pressure and then Thomas and I left very quickly. But before that, he asked me if we hadn't already met on the plane. At that moment, Thomas came back in and we said goodbye."

"So it's him, despite everything. You took a damn big risk! It could very easily have gone wrong!"

"Yes, that's him. It was an almost unbearable situation for me."

"We still have a tiny hope that he's not the one you suspect, don't we?"

"The chance is zero, Matt! I'm damn sure of it. But is it possible that he's after you because you're friends with his wife?"

"And you think that's why he put a chip in me? I hardly think so, because how would he be able to influence anyone, in the clinic, I mean?"

"Maybe he's got someone to play along? Come on, let's go and have breakfast and then see what we're going to do today. Actually, now that Alan's back, we can go home, what do you think?" asked Lis.


"I still think we should talk to the local police and take another good look at the orphanage, but preferably in the evening or at night. Can't do any harm," suggested Matthew.

"Do you want to play detective now too?" asked Lis.

"Now that we're here? I'm sure Alfonse will approve."

An hour later, everyone met for breakfast.

"Alfonse, David, this is Matthew McKenna," Lis introduced him.

"Hey," Alfonse stood up and shook his hand with a firm grip. "So you're the doc!"

"Nice to meet you, Alfonse. Yeah, you can say that again." Matthew grinned. "The one who spent the night in the container with Alan."

David greeted him too.

"Then, finally, we are now complete," said Alfonse.

"Alfonse," Lis said, "I know we all came here to find Alan, but we'd also like to take a look inside this orphanage now that we're here."

"By all means! I'm going to see the orphanage with David tonight. We discussed it in detail last night," confirmed Alfonse, pouring himself another cup of coffee. "When we looked at the building yesterday, including from the back, I analysed the alarm system. We can get in without any problems and the office seems to be on the second floor. We'll have a look around there. If we can get to the files, we might find some additional information. Thomas and Alan, I could use you out there to warn us if something happens there or someone shows up unexpectedly."

"Okay, let's go!" said Thomas.

"You're actually going to break in there?" Matthew asked, a little surprised.

"I don't think they'll show us the files voluntarily, Doc," said Alfonse, grinning.

"Well, I'm game. We could hole up somewhere outside, and keep an eye on the road, or whatever it takes?" Lis said.

"Yes, a good suggestion," Matthew agreed. "Let's work out the exact plan this afternoon."

Then Lis turned to Alan.

"I didn't want to bother you with any more news last night, but I spoke to my son during the night. He and Caro have discovered something."

"Shoot, anything that will help us," said Alfonse.

Lis told him about Diane Van Helden's patient files at McKenna Hospital.

"So, Diane is still in this hospital in Luxembourg?" Alfonse asked, very surprised.

"Yes, she is in a coma and in intensive care. Over the last few days, however, the name attached to her bed has been removed, and her patient file now states that she left the hospital on Saturday, July 6, after examination. Strange, isn't it?"

"What? My God, what have they done to her? I knew straight away that she was seriously injured. I have to get back as quickly as possible." Alan was visibly anxious and worried.

"That's right, we do," said Alfonse. "But one thing at a time. Now that we're here, let's make the most of today, tonight and tomorrow morning, and if nothing unforeseen comes up, we'll go back to Luxembourg. Are you all in agreement?"

"Then we'll book our return journey for tomorrow. In that case, we should stop by the orphanage tonight," Alan added.

Lis then briefly mentioned that Caro grew up in the orphanage in Clervaux.

"I'll do my best to find out more information about this Peter Lamborelle," Alfonse explained. "You can find me in my room during the day. By the way, Alan, see if you can find a photo of Mark and or Peter Lamborelle somewhere on the net."

"Good idea, will do."

Turning to Lis, Alfonse then said: "I know, Lis, you are convinced that this man was also involved in your kidnapping. Do you know the name Lamborelle from somewhere, perhaps from your father's side? I've been looking for a motive for your kidnapping, ever since it happened. It was never clear why you, of all people, were kidnapped for ransom."

"Yes, but you know that the large sum demanded has its appeal for young adults, especially if they can use it to prove their power over others, in this case over my father and his empire," Lis said.

"Sure, but don't forget that the two young men came from very wealthy families and didn't necessarily need the money."

"You're right, Alfonse. Of course, I thought long and hard

about an explanation, but I couldn't come to any other conclusion."

"Why didn't you insist on keeping up the search for this 'invisible third party' back then?" asked Alan.

"I'd had enough, it was so humiliating having to face all these questions. They didn't believe me, they thought I was crazy and imagining things. And my father was more interested in his bank's reputation than my well-being."

"Yes, that was a shame," Alfonse agreed.


"Yes, that's it," Lis said. "Listen, I'm going to go on a little sightseeing tour at lunchtime today while we're here. Anyone fancy coming along?"

Thomas and Matthew accompanied Lis, while Alan, David and Alfonse did their research and stayed at the hotel.

She noticed that Matthew often received text messages from Brigitte, which he answered quickly and briefly. She had the impression that this annoyed him somehow.

"Does Brigitte know we're going home?" asked Lis when they both arrived back at the hotel in the late afternoon and Thomas was enjoying another beer on the hotel terrace.

"Not yet, but she's already announced that she's coming to pick me up. Listen Lis, I know our situation isn't easy, you must know how much you still mean to me, but I want to maintain my current relationship with Brigitte at the moment. I think it's the only way we can get more information about her husband. If I cut off that source of information now, then we won't know what this guy is up to, assuming he has anything to do with any of this, and if he's related to this Mark Lamborelle or whatever.

"By the way, I haven't even thanked you for literally forcing your knife on me when we landed here. If I hadn't had that, I don't know how Alan and I could have escaped so quickly."

Lis didn't reply to his explanation about Brigitte. She didn't want to think about that now either.

"No problem, I'm glad it served a purpose," she said.

Following the sightseeing tour, the group all met at the hotel for dinner and discussed their plan in detail once again.

Alfonse took his cell phone, looked something up and then held it out to Alan. "Here, this is Peter Lamborelle. Does he look anything like Mark Lamborelle? Take a closer look. This is the only photo I could find of him anywhere. Just this one, and only this one. It's strange. On the government website of the Ministry of Family Affairs there is only this photo. But it seems to be a few years old."

Alan took the cell phone and looked at the display. "That doesn't just look a lot like Mark. That is Mark Lamborelle. I saw some pictures of him that Diane showed me the night I brought her home."

"Hm, but that's Peter," Alfonse corrected him.

"Let's see," Lis said, and Alan handed her the cell phone.

She only had to look at it for a moment. "Oh yes, that's Peter Lamborelle, no doubt about it. The man who was on our plane and who is here with us, or at least was."

Matthew then looked at the photo too.

"That's Peter Lamborelle, no doubt about it!"

"Twins?" asked David.

"Maybe! Matthew, do you know anything about this?"

"No, Brigitte never spoke of her husband's brother. But I might be able to find out," said Matthew.

"The more I think about what's going on here," Alfonse said calmly and matter-of-factly as always, "I'd just say, guys, we need to look for a connection. I do believe in coincidences, here and there, but I hardly think that the disappearance of Diane Van Helden and the kidnapping of Alan and Matthew is just coincidence. Nor that this Peter Lamborelle was on the flight to Santo Domingo by chance."

"You mean that my kidnapping from back then is also connected to this?" asked Lis.

"No, not necessarily that, but everything else, hmm ... When we get home, I'll do some intensive research and look at all the people involved. I'm still in good contact with one of my former colleagues, Bob Wagner, who is still active. He will help me discreetly, I'm sure of that. We worked very closely together."

For a few minutes, everyone looked at each other thoughtfully.

"Okay, we're leaving at 11 p.m.," said Alfonse. "Please dress in dark clothes. The plan is made. I'll take the window from the back yard with David and get in. Thomas and Alan, you take the front and find a dark corner from where you can watch the building unseen. Matthew and Lis, you secure the back. Please remember to put your cell phones on silent. If someone is watching you for a while, change position. We will only text, no talking if possible. No phone calls. Alan, you bought a new cell phone today, we all have your number. If for some reason we have to split up and leave, we'll meet at the hotel. Before you go out on the street, make sure no one is following you or watching you. Otherwise, do a few laps and return. We don't know who we're dealing with here, so be careful, guys!"

Once the clock reached 11 p.m., they set off two at a time.

Matthew and Lis walked briskly, talking intimately together. "You know what worries me, Matt?"

"Tell me!"

"If this Peter Lamborelle turns up somewhere and meets up with Eric, or if Eric somehow finds out who he is, it will mean a major life crisis for my son. I will do everything I can to ensure that he never meets him and never finds out that this man is his father. Please promise me that we will never talk about this when Eric is around."

"Sure, you don't have to worry about that. But you're right. It would be a very painful situation for Eric if it's confirmed that this man is his father."

"It's him, I can't have been that wrong, those eyes, that look. I'd better not think about it now."


Once they reached the orphanage, Thomas and Alan took the front. They positioned themselves between two houses facing each other, where the street lighting did not expose them.

Matthew and Lis went into the backyard of the building. It was quite large and some trees provided shade from the streetlights and they stopped behind a fairly dense tree.

Unbeknown to any of the team, Mr. Winther was standing further away in an unlit corner. He was astonished when he saw someone trying to break into the orphanage. He stayed in the background and watched from a distance. *What on earth are they doing*, he wondered. Of course, he hadn't missed seeing Lis, alias Martina Kaufmann.

Alfonse seemed to have quite a few tools with him. He first cut a cable under the window and within a few seconds he had opened the back window without the slightest noise. He and David crept in.

"I hope it goes well," Lis whispered and looked at Matthew. They were standing close together.

"It'll be fine," he said softly. How he would have loved to kiss her right here and now, just like that. Maybe she had just been waiting for this? Or maybe not? Since he had said that he didn't want to give Brigitte up, she had somehow distanced herself a little, even if it wasn't immediately visible. But he could feel it. *Was she somehow right, or not? Oh, I don't know. But I still love her! It's not easy to just switch off feelings like that.*

He was torn from his thoughts when a pale light became visible in the second-floor office.

"They're in the office now," Lis whispered, glancing at her cell phone from time to time so as not to miss a possible text message from one of the others.

"It's quite an unusual feeling to be doing something illegal," said Matthew.

She spontaneously took his hand. "I am so grateful to you for accompanying me on this journey."

He squeezed her hand and held it tightly.

"Lis," he put his mouth very close to her ear. She waited for a word. "No ... Nothing." Then he kissed her on the cheek and looked down.

"We have to guard the building," he said resolutely, letting go of her hand and taking a step forward.

On the other side of the street, where Thomas and Alan stood, everything was quiet.

"What are you going to do when we get back? Go to the hospital and look for Diane?"

"You bet I do! I'll storm in there, and if I have to turn everything upside down, I'll find her."

"If only it were clear what this is all about," said Thomas. "I don't understand what's going on here. Mrs. Sanchez was super nice and accommodating yesterday when Lis and I were here, and we're supposed to get in touch with her as soon as we've got all the paperwork for our phony adoption together. That's all quite normal, isn't it?"

"Yes, it looks that way. But something must be wrong, otherwise Diane wouldn't have gotten into so much trouble when she broke up with that guy and then told him that things weren't right here. She thought the orphans were European kids and that in itself is quite strange."

At that moment, a light was switched on in another room on the third floor.

"Oh dear, there's someone exactly a floor above who has either woken up or ..."

Thomas hurriedly wrote Alfonse a text message.

The light in the second-floor office was quickly shut off.

*That's typical Alfonse,* thought Thomas.

A few minutes later, Alfonse and David climbed out of the window, much to the relief of Matthew and Lis.

"Whew, finally," Lis said.

As they all made their way back to the hotel, Alfonse filled his friends in on what they had found.

"I have photographed some interesting documents that are kept in a filing cabinet. I'll show them to you once we stop," Alfonse remarked briefly.

It was already half past one when they arrived back at the hotel. They went straight to the hotel bar and ordered a round of beers.

Then they sat down on the terrace, which was empty at the time.

"We had to break open a hanging locker, but look here."

Alfonse took his cell phone and showed them a document signed with the name of Dr. Peter Lamborelle.

"This wasn't the only document with his name on it; all the documents in this folder were signed by him. I didn't have time to read through everything, but his name kept coming up. He seems to be responsible for communicating with the adoptive families. Anyway, this is a document where a couple makes the application, and he approves it."

"Well, Brigitte's husband is definitely not a doctor," said Matthew, "I can guarantee that. He may work for the Ministry of Family Affairs, but he doesn't know anything about medicine.

Brigitte has said that often enough. He's a bureaucrat who only does paperwork."

"Well," said Alfonse, "then he seems to have skills that his wife has no idea about. I'm going to bed now," he said, getting up. "Good night everyone, tomorrow we'll book our return flights."

As he walked towards the stairs, he turned. "And I recommend that none of you start another mission on your own tonight," he remarked with a grin.

"No way," Alan confirmed. "I'm finished. If Diane's in Luxembourg, it's really time we got her out of there. There are so many things to sort out, I think! See you tomorrow and sleep well!"

David and Alan went up the stairs, leaving Lis with Matthew and Thomas.

"I'm done for the day too. See you tomorrow and have a good night."

Then Thomas also went up the stairs.


"What a mess!" said Matthew. "There really is a lot to sort out!"

Then Lis and Matthew went up the stairs too.

"What now? What are we going to do with the night that's already begun?" asked Matthew as he opened his door and turned back to Lis.

"We should definitely discuss it," Lis said, walking up to him and kissing him as she shut the door behind her locking it from the inside.

Later, they lay close together in Matthew's room.

"I've thought about you so often in the last few years," Lis whispered. "And I wanted to call you, then I didn't, then I convinced myself you had your own life and surely never wanted to see me again after I broke off contact so brutally."

"Actually, Claire brought us back together. Because otherwise we would have never seen each other, except by chance in a supermarket one day," he said.

"Perhaps I would have chosen you as my doctor?" said Lis.

"What do you think, can you handle the situation if Peter Lamborelle really is Eric's father?"

"I don't know. Honestly, I've been so confused since I met this man. I can't describe this feeling to anyone. When he handed me the glass of water and was so concerned, I would never have suspected him to have such a depraved character. It's hard to understand."

"I think that's it. I know Brigitte still loves him despite everything he's done to her. I can hardly understand it. He beats her, he leaves her alone most of the time, but then, when he needs her to accompany him at parties with the country's elite, she is only too happy to present herself as his happy wife at his side."

"I could never do that," Lis said. "Do you love Brigitte?"

"I like her very much. We know each other well. Let's not talk about her now, it won't get us anywhere."

Matthew kissed Lis deeply. "We'll see where life takes us. There are so many unknowns to take care of right now. And after that, we'll see where we both stand."

"Yes, we'll see."

"I think it's funny that Alfonse calls you 'Doc.'"

"Yes, from the very first moment. He seems to enjoy it!"

Lis looked at him tenderly. Then they fell asleep in each other's arms.

## *MONDAY, AUGUST 5*

Alfonse was an early riser and had already planned for the departure. After breakfast together, the return flight was scheduled for the same evening. There was no reason to stay on the island any longer and there was more than enough to do in Luxembourg.

# INGRID

## *TUESDAY, AUGUST 6*

The plane landed in Frankfurt at 6 a.m. and a connecting flight had them back in Luxembourg by 10 a.m.

"You know Brigitte's picking me up," Matthew kissed Lis as they waited for their luggage.

"It's okay, I'll survive." She didn't look particularly happy however.

When they had all passed through passport control, Brigitte came up to Matthew and hugged him.

She was a tall, slim and elegant woman with short blonde hair, wearing a rather tight calf-length linen dress and black leather shoes.

Matthew looked over her shoulder at Lis, before briefly introducing Brigitte and saying goodbye.

"See you soon, get home safely," Lis murmured.

As they turned to leave, Alan approached. "Matthew, I don't know how I would have got out of this alive without you. I'm deeply in your debt and would love to invite you out one evening. We'll keep in touch."

"You're welcome, Alan!" Matthew gave him a friendly hug. "We'll keep in touch, and I'm looking forward to our dinner. Thank you very much." Matthew didn't want to reveal any more in Brigitte's presence.

Thomas was still watching the two of them. *Brigitte seems a very smart woman,* he thought. She left a lasting impression on him.

Alfonse, Thomas, Alan and David said goodbye to Lis. As she took the elevator down to the U1 parking lot, she saw the tall man with the three-day beard, who had also been on their return flight. He was leaning against the wall and talking on his cell phone. She looked at him briefly; he was wearing a long black leather jacket and jeans. He had already seen her, and his eyes followed her until she got into her car and drove away.

When Lis came home, Eric had just got up and was sitting in the kitchen eating breakfast.

"Hello, my dear son. Was it a long night?"

"Hey, Lis! No, it wasn't. Caro stayed here and then went to work. She had an early shift today and had to start at six. But by then, I had already fallen asleep again."

Lis made herself a coffee and sat down with him. There were so many things she wanted to talk about. She couldn't tell him everything, especially not that she had met his father. *What would this situation look like*, she wondered. She knew that one day, she would have to tell him the truth, and she wasn't looking forward to it.

Brigitte drove Matthew home. In the kitchen, he made coffee for them both.

"Matthew, I'm so incredibly glad you're back, I've missed you so much."

She hugged him tightly and made as if to lead him straight to the bedroom.

He freed himself from her arms and stopped in the corridor. "Biggy, I've been flying for over ten hours, I'm jetlagged, I'm tired and I just want to hang out today. Okay?"

She then let go of him with a somewhat sour expression on her face. "Do you want me to make us breakfast?" she asked.

"That's very kind of you, but I'd like to take my time now and just be alone for a bit. We'll see each other again in the next few days, I promise. But I'm done for today." He kissed her on the forehead. "When is Peter coming back, or is he already back?"

"No, he called yesterday. He'll be back the day after tomorrow. But I don't care if he comes back the day after tomorrow or in a week or not at all, and you know that too."

She picked up her handbag and jacket and headed for the door. "Before I upset you, I'd better leave you alone." She kissed him again. Then she disappeared. Secretly, she still hoped he would hold her back, but he didn't.


After Matthew had listened to the messages on his answering machine and checked the mail, he took off his shoes and flopped down on the couch, leaning his head back and stretching his feet across the table. He closed his eyes.

*So,* he thought, *I don't want to worry about other people's problems today. But I will call Ingrid, my mother's friend. I can't imagine what I should talk to her about, but we'll see.*

He searched for her name. Ingrid Meyer. She still lived here in the community, in Alzingen. *Wonderful. Let's get this over with now. It will probably sound pretty stupid when she asks me why I'm calling, and I say I don't know.*

"Meyer," a woman answered after the second ring.

"Hello, Ingrid. This is Matthew McKenna."

"Matthew? Matthew! Oh, how glad I am to hear from you. How are you? How are you all?"

"Yeah, I'm fine, we're fine, I miss Claire as much as you can imagine. It's hard, especially because I didn't get to see her before she died."

"That must have been very difficult for you. But Matthew, I think we should meet for a coffee as soon as you have some time. Would that be okay with you?"

Matthew became attentive. *How strange …*

"I'd love to, Ingrid. Tomorrow afternoon? You're making me curious."

"Good, that would make me very happy, Matthew. My husband will be off bowling and I'll be on my own."

"Okay, let's do this. I'm excited too!"

*Well, if I can comfort her, why not. Then we can both talk about Claire and old times and probably cry together.*


The day flew by. Matthew had slept through the afternoon and now at 10 p.m., he was wide awake.

After grabbing something to eat, he stood at the window and looked out at the quiet and empty street. Spontaneously he decided to pay the clinic a visit and look into Diane's room and his own office.

Matthew put on a sweater and made his way to the hospital. He parked in the basement. Then he got into the elevator and went straight to reception. On the way, he put on his white doctor's coat and hung his stethoscope around his neck. He looked as if he had just been called to an emergency.

The nurse from the night shift at reception greeted him in a friendly manner. Then he went up the stairs and stopped in front of Room 1112. By now it was 10.45 p.m. and the corridor was empty. Nevertheless, he prepared himself for the possibility of meeting someone unexpectedly and had a credible answer ready in case questions arose.

Matthew waited a few moments and when no voices could be heard from inside, he pressed the handle, quietly entered and quickly closed the door behind him.

He carefully approached the bed. There lay Diane Van Helden, connected to a ventilator and equipped with all the necessary monitoring systems. She was alive. There was no patient information in the room. *If she's been lying here since July 6, a month ago,* Matthew wondered, *what could be wrong with her?* Matthew came to the conclusion that all looked most confusing and unclear.

Then he walked to his own office, sat down at his desk and logged into his McKenna Clinic profile. He tried to see if he could retrieve Diane Van Helden's data.

Yes, he had access. Wonderful.

With a few clicks, he had her patient files on the screen ... Room 1112, attending doctor ... *aha,* Matthew thought ... Dr. Peter Lamborelle!

*Well, that's strange. Is there anywhere that name doesn't appear? Now I don't understand it either. This man is not a doctor, he never studied medicine, I'm sure of it, because Brigitte had already mentioned that several times.*

He continued reading.

*... Severe concussion as a result of an accident ... The patient has not regained consciousness since ... But where are the CT scans and test results? Why is nothing stored and entered here?*

Matthew didn't want to inspect Lamborelle's office right now. It was too late and since Lamborelle since would only return on Thursday, Matthew intended to check out his office tomorrow night. He made his way out and took the elevator back down to the parking lot.

Half an hour later, he was back home, exactly at midnight and stayed awake for a long time wondering what this was all about.

When Matthew woke up, it was already midday. After a shower and two cups of coffee, he called Lis. He told her about his visit to the hospital yesterday.

"Yes, she's lying there peacefully, but when I looked at the patient's file, I found nothing. No CT scan, no tests, nothing. I don't understand it. Or it was coded by Dr. Lamborelle. But that's not normal. I'll look into it later. This afternoon I'm meeting with Ingrid, I called her and she immediately suggested we meet."

"You see, it was no coincidence that Claire pointed her out to you in your dream, I'm sure of it!"

"Looks like Claire might have a secret treasure chest hidden somewhere for me," Matthew joked. "I'll keep you posted. Is everything else okay with you?"

"So far, yes. Eric was here yesterday. Everything is fine. I'm still exhausted. And Alfonse will be exploring in all directions these days. I can't wait to see what he finds out."

After this conversation, Matthew also rang Alan and told him that Diane was still in hospital but that there were no reports.

"I really need to see her, Matthew. Is there any way you can make that happen?"

"Then it must be tonight. Our suspected doctor, Lamborelle, will be back in Luxembourg tomorrow and I don't want to cross his path or arouse his suspicions for the time being. Until we all have clarity about the background, we should be careful not to underestimate him."

"Yes, I understand. Can't we get her out of there?"

"We can't do that at the moment. We don't know what injuries she has. And remember, she's been there for a month, we don't know if she has been in a coma from the start. We can't just move her."

Matthew thought for a moment. He knew only too well that Alan wanted to see her.

"Okay, why don't you come and see me tonight, after 9 p.m.? We'll drive to the hospital together and then you can see her briefly in the room. I'll give you a doctor's coat to wear."

"That's a plan, will do! Thank you, Matthew. I really appreciate it."

"With pleasure! I'll see you later."

Matthew then drove to Ingrid's house and found a car park out front. She was already at the window, waiting for him.

"How nice to see you, Matthew. Come on, let me give you a hug."

They hugged warmly and he presented her with a small bouquet of flowers.

Ingrid was a petite, slender person with short grey hair; she and Claire had been schoolmates in primary school.

"Hello Ingrid. You look good!"

"Oh, you're a charmer. Why don't you come in with me? Just like when you and your mother used to come here for coffee and cake from time to time."

"Yes, I remember that very well. And you talked and chatted for hours, and I played soccer outside with the boys."

"Yes, yes, the nostalgia. It often catches up with me too," she added.

They sat down in the garden. Ingrid had always had a penchant for roses of all types and colours, and her garden looked beautiful.

"I've thought about you a lot in the last few weeks. After Claire's funeral, I wanted to call you straight away, but then I thought you might need some rest, some distance."

"Yes, that really hit me hard. You know how close she and I were, we had such an intimate relationship. She gave me all the love that my father never gave me. And the fact that I never really got close to my father made my bond with Claire even stronger."

"I know, Matthew. I was at her bedside the day before she died. She told me you were in Paris. Oh, she was always so proud when she told me about your performances. And she really wanted to talk to you, she knew she was going to die soon. She wanted to wait for you, but she didn't make it."

"No, that night it was me who couldn't make it home fast enough. That was cruel. But Jeff and Dad could have let me know sooner. I think I was five minutes late, five lousy minutes."

Matthew fought back tears.

"I've replayed these moments in my head countless times. I wanted to say goodbye to her so much."

Ingrid made coffee and put a homemade marble cake on the table.

"It was Claire's favourite and yours too, if I remember correctly," she said as she took her seat again.

She looked at Matthew.

"I spoke to Claire for a very long time that day. We talked about a lot. After all, we had been through so much together. We were best friends for most of our lives."

"I believe that. Girlfriends know more about each other than their own husbands or children?"

"That may be true. But there's something in Claire's life that really only me and one other person know about. She asked me to tell you something in case she didn't manage to see you again. I promised to do that."

"I'm listening." Matthew leaned back and stretched out his legs.

Ingrid's expression became serious.

"Claire and I got married in the same year. And we were both the happiest young women imaginable. I had found the love of my life with Jean and Claire was also very happy with John. But your father, as you know, was married to his job on the one hand and very busy on the other."

"You can say that again. I think if he was home one night a week, that was a lot."

"I know! At some point, Claire met a young man who was very much in love with her. And they met more often than they originally wanted to."

Matthew looked at Ingrid, somewhat confused. *Why would she want to tell me such a story from the past? Maybe she just wants to relive her youth with Claire and share it with me,* he concluded.

"This young man knew very well that Claire was married, very married, but they got on so well and he had time, lots of time. And then the day came when Claire told me she was expecting a baby." Ingrid now waited for Matthew's reaction, but he just looked at her questioningly.

"And that was me," he said with a grin.

"And that was you, Matthew."

"What are you saying?" Now he was puzzled.

"I'm trying to tell you that you're ... I'm trying to tell you that you're not the biological son of John McKenna. Claire really wanted you to know that. And that's what I'm doing now."

Matthew looked at her, stared at her.

"Who is it?"

"What I'm about to tell you is going to hurt you a lot, Matthew. I'm so sorry. It was Franz Kramer."


Those words hit him very hard. Matthew got up at once and walked a little further into the garden. Ingrid followed him and compassionately put her hand on his arm.

Within seconds, Matthew saw countless images in his head. How, as a child, he often went fishing with Franz Kramer, the supposed family friend, how he played soccer with him, how he had time for him when his father, or rather John McKenna, wasn't there. And when he was there, Jeff was always the favourite son. At least that was understandable now. That's why there was always this distance, these unspoken differences of opinion. And when Matthew chose magic over medicine, the father-son relationship was finally in tatters.

Matthew turned and looked at Ingrid. Tears rolled down his cheeks. He took a deep breath.

"Whew! I'm ... not sure how I feel. Franz Kramer, he died in April, didn't he? That was only four months ago. So I had my real father so close to me the whole time, so close, and ... Did he know? He must have known, right?"

Ingrid was also overwhelmed by her own feelings and had tears in her eyes. "Yes, he knew all along. But Claire didn't want to leave John, she loved him despite everything, he gave her security, financial security. He really isn't a bad person and never was. What's more, Franz Kramer was an adventurer. Claire knew that and Franz knew that. And they all three agreed that you would never find out."

"That's why John was often such a stranger to me. Jeff is my half-brother, he's the doctor, he did what his father expected him to do. Does he know about it?"

"No, Jeff has no idea. Nobody knows about it except me, you and John."

"Wow, today is not my day!" Matthew wiped away his tears.

"I think, Matthew, for Claire it would be good if you could accept this one day - I'm not saying immediately, of course - I mean one day. Without doing too much damage with words. But that's easier said than done. Claire certainly wouldn't have been happy if you turned your back on John now."

Matthew looked at Ingrid as if he had just received a beating. He nodded in confirmation.

"Mhm … Yes, probably. I need to digest it all first."

"Yes, do that, it takes time, a lot of time."

"Oh yes, you can say that!" Matthew stepped closer to the petite woman, placed his hands on her shoulders, and hugged her tightly for a long time.

"Thank you, dearest Ingrid, for telling me that. I have to go now, okay?"

"Of course, Matthew! But take some advice. Before you argue with John or accuse him of anything, wait a few days and let it all sink in. Please!"

"You're right. Nothing will change anyway. And besides, I have a few other things to sort out."

He hugged her once more and then said goodbye.

*Franz is my father and he knew that all the time. That must have hurt him a lot. All those years we were together, when he took time for me, took me on an outing. I think I'm suffocating.*

Matthew drove straight to the cemetery and went to Franz Kramer's grave. He sat down on the gravestone and looked up at the sky.

In his mind, he saw himself in the garden with him again. Claire was making coffee, Jeff was five years old at the time and had just started kindergarten. Matthew was two years older. Franz helped him with his schoolwork from time to time. *That's why he was with us so often, and I just thought he was a friend of the family. Well, that wasn't really the case. But how could John take it all so matter-of-factly and casually?*

Matthew had the feeling that something was strangling him. He began to cry because of all the time he had lost and also because of the fact that he would probably have liked to have called him father, which Franz would have liked.

Matthew was glad to be alone in the cemetery. He could cry out all his feelings.

After an hour, he got back into his car and drove off. On the spur of the moment, he decided to stop by Lis' on the way.

Matthew rang Lis from the car and was outside her house within a few minutes. By now it was 7 p.m.

Lis was at the door waiting for him.

"Hey," he said when she had opened the door.

"What's wrong Matt? Come in. You look like you've been slapped."

"Somehow I think I have been! I just found out that John is not my biological father, but Franz Kramer, our family friend!"

Matthew settled down on the sofa.

"What?"

Then the words just poured out of him. As he spoke, he was swept up in his feelings; he smiled, cried, laughed, and was angry, all at the same time. Matthew no longer knew what was happening to him. The emotions of his whole life had caught up with him and were overwhelming.

He ended up crying. "And I spent so much time with this man, he was always there for me, and Claire and John knew it for a fact, and neither of them said a word. I never understood why I got so much more affection from a family friend than I did from my own father. But why did I never doubt that John was my father?"

"How could you? You have trust in your parents, that's what you grow up with. As a child or even as a teenager, you don't simply distrust your parents, unless it comes to very serious situations."

"Hmm ... Maybe, yeah ... I feel somehow cheated. Franz was always happy about my little magic tricks that I was allowed to show him as a child. How this person must have suffered inside.

How often he must have wished he could tell me that he was my father."

"Maybe not just him, but all of them. Even your mother and father."

"Am I supposed to feel sorry for them now?" he asked gruffly.

"No, not that. I don't know! But I have to admit, that was the last thing I would have expected. Now it's clear why Claire made herself visible to you after she died."

"Yes ... There's that too. I'll talk to her when I've cleared my head a bit."

"Do that, she'll be very happy."

"I'm so confused. But by the way, I called Alan and promised him he could come to the clinic with me so he could see Diane for a bit. He'll be with me at 9 p.m."

"Are you sure about that?" asked Lis.

"We have no choice, it has to be tonight. Peter Lamborelle is coming back tomorrow, Biggy told me."

Lis could no longer hear that name. Yes, she was jealous, and rightly so. But she couldn't bring it up now, it was definitely the wrong time. There were already enough unresolved problems.

"Are you hungry?" she asked.

"A little."

"Is pizza okay?"

"Of course, thank you. Lis, why has no one ever spoken to me about this?" Matthew asked.

"Because everyone acts as if they have a perfect family life. Just like they did with me back then. Nothing to the public, everything swept under the carpet, sending their own daughter out of the country instead of owning up to what had really happened and protecting me and my child."

"Our families have a lot in common," concluded Matthew.

"Oh yes, and our fathers too, I mean the official fathers. Are you going to talk to John?"

"I suppose I will have to. But I'm not sure when that will be yet. I need to digest it all first and calm down. At the moment, it would end in a terrible argument and an explosion of emotions. And I don't need that these days.

"Besides, I can't really be mad at him, it's not his fault, at least not directly. Sure, Claire was alone most of the time, he has to take the blame for that, but ... In my case, it's too late anyway.

"Franz is dead, and I was always so happy to be with him. It's too bad I didn't know earlier. I would much rather have said 'father' to him than to John. It's just too much right now.

"But we need to find out what's going on with Diane very soon, because if she's there much longer, I'm afraid she won't survive. Alan would like to take her with him, but that's not so easy when she's in an induced coma. We can't just carry her out. I have no idea where to start."


Matthew was exhausted, but he had to take Alan to the clinic as promised.

"Give Alfonse a few days, he'll do his research and I imagine he'll find something," Lis said.

"At least I hope so," Matthew said. "Otherwise, I'll have to turn to Lamborelle for information about Diane. But it would be better if he continues not to know that we know. I need to find out where his office is."

"Caro can help, she'll know for sure."

"No, let's leave her out of it. I don't want her to know, at least not yet, that there's something wrong with this 'doctor'. Tonight, I'll take a closer look and try to find his office. Alan can help me with that. Actually, he could come straight here, if that's all right with you. Then I won't have to go home."

"Yeah, sure, call him, no problem. He can eat with us too, if he wants."

"I'd love to sit in a quiet corner and pull a big blanket over my head so no one could find me or talk to me. And then one day I'd wake up and everything would be back to normal, all the unresolved difficulties would be gone and forgotten, and everything could go on as it was before this whole mess."

"Wonderful, but you know it doesn't work like that. I have days too when everything is too much for me and I want to hide from the world. Come on, we can do this, Matt, we'll manage somehow."

An hour later, Alan arrived, and the discussion was continued over a glass of red wine and pizza.

"No, as long as we don't know what Diane's injuries are and what her general condition is, we can't just take her off the machines. I'll find out what her exact injuries are first, but to do that we need to find Lamborelle's office," Matthew said.

As the two men were leaving, Matthew turned to Lis. "Caro's not on the night shift tonight, is she?"

"No, Eric is traveling with her."

"Right, I'll get back to you." Spontaneously, he came back to the front door. He took Lis' face between his hands and kissed her. "Don't worry, we're big boys!"

"That's exactly the reason I'm worried! Here, please take my knife."

Without objecting, Matthew tied it around his ankle and they drove off. In the car, Alan put on the white doctor's coat that Matthew had given him earlier.

They reached the hospital shortly after 10.30 p.m. and after parking the car in the parking lot, they both got into the elevator.

As they walked past the reception desk, a quick glance at the reception desk reassured them that the nurse on duty wasn't Caro. The night shift had started at 10 p.m. and no staff changes were expected until 6 a.m. the following morning. Matthew greeted the receptionist briefly before they disappeared into the elevator.

"That doctor's coat looks good on you," Matthew joked.

"Well, if you say so. I hope Diane pulls through, I really do."

"We're doing what we can, Alan."

The second floor was empty.

"The room is up here, on the right. But let's go in here first, come on," Matthew said.

He held the door to a storeroom open and pushed Alan in front of him, then closed it from the inside.

"I want to go in alone first. If there's someone in the room, I'll find an excuse. It'll be a bit harder with two people. You can peek through the opening here and when I give you a sign, you can come out. Not before, okay?"

"Got it!"

Then Matthew walked out, leaving the door ajar, and headed towards Room 1112.

Just as he was about to press the door handle, he heard a voice and footsteps coming around the corner. Matthew turned and hurried back to Alan.

With his finger over his lips, he looked sternly at Alan and signalled him not to say a word. Matthew squinted out through the gap. He quickly closed the door completely.

"What's going on?" whispered Alan, who was standing close behind Matthew.

"It's my brother Jeff! That's all I need right now. We'll have to wait."

"Did he go into her room?"

Matthew nodded in agreement. Then he opened the door a

little and peeked out. A few minutes later, Jeff left the room, followed by a nurse with whom he was having a lively conversation. They stood outside the room for a few more minutes, and while Jeff talked, the nurse made a few notes. Then they both continued down the corridor and turned the corner.

"They've gone." Matthew turned back to Alan. "A few more minutes, then I'll go and give you a sign. We have to take the risk, otherwise it won't work."

"Okay, you decide."

"I have no idea either, but we'll have to try. If someone shows up, we'll have to improvise." He stepped out again, walked down the hall, opened the door, and went inside. There was no one inside the room except for Diane, who was lying in the bed.

He quickly signalled to Alan, who rushed in and closed the door.

He hurriedly approached the bed. "Oh no, Diane." He leaned over her slightly and looked into her face. "What have they done to you! Matthew, can you diagnose anything here? She looks so pale."

"Hey, Alan, listen. Look at me." Alan turned and looked at him.

Matthew put his hands on his shoulders. "There's nothing we can do now. She's pale because she's been lying here for a month. You're sure it's Diane, that's very good. I'll find out what's going on tomorrow or in the next few days but we can't do this alone, and we certainly can't just switch everything off. The people next door will get an alarm signal and we definitely don't want that. Besides, if her condition is serious due to the accident and we switch the machines off, she's dead! Is that clear? Now let's go again, come on."

Alan took one last look at her and put his hand on her forehead. "Diane, I'll come back, I promise you that. I'll get you out of here," he whispered, tears in his eyes.

The two men went again into the storeroom.

"My brother knows about this woman, so perhaps he also knows about Peter Lamborelle. Interesting!"

"Are you going to talk to him about it?"

"Not for the time being. As long as they feel safe, I don't think they'll do anything brutal. So, we'll leave it at that until we find out more. After all, I still have to have a conversation with my adoptive father. What a mess! Okay, let's go find Lamborelle's office."

"And then?"

"Then we'll go inside. Maybe this will give us some information." He showed Alan a small tool used for picking locks that he had pulled out of his pocket. "This will get us in, trust me."

"Aha, yes, if you say so. You're always good for a surprise!"

"My magic tricks are sometimes quite useful, especially when it comes to getting away from a place. Let's go."

The two 'doctors' walked down the corridor and then made a round of this floor, checking the name tags in front of the various offices.

Then, on the second floor, they found what they were looking for. Peter Lamborelle had a corner office.

With no one around, Matthew was able to open the door in seconds without being seen or making any noise. He and Alan disappeared into the office.

"We can't turn on any lights, but we can use the lights on our cell phones. That shouldn't be visible from the outside."

"What are we looking for?"

"I don't know, let's see what we can find. Files, documents, anything. I can't get to his computer. We'll have to take care of the papers and files. I'll take this side of the shelf, you take the files opposite. We'll go from there. There must be papers somewhere that give clues to the orphanages or adoption files."

"That may be, but don't you think he'd rather keep it at home?"

"No, his wife would have found it already, believe me."

"Really?"

"Yes, she doesn't trust him, she's home alone most of the time, so she can have a good look around his office. I would say there's definitely nothing at home."

"What if everything is stored in the Cloud?"

"Then we're out of luck. There must be original documents somewhere. And they can only be here or in Clervaux, at least that's my guess, Alan."

"Okay, let's get started." The two men went through one file after the other. It was very quiet outside in the corridor. Matthew had also locked the door from the inside with his tool. He went through all the files on his side but found nothing of interest. Then he sat down at the desk and searched through the drawers.

"Hey, come here." Alan held a black file in his hand and opened it in the middle. On the first page was a document addressed to a person from the orphanage in Clervaux.

In this correspondence, Peter Lamborelle seemed to be both a doctor and a director of the orphanage. He had signed with both titles.

"The man has no scruples," Matthew said as he examined more documents.

"These look like adoption applications, and in this letter, he is confirming an application. It would be good if we could take out one or two family files and then have a closer look."

"This is where we really commit a crime?" asked Alan.

"What about him? I'm sure he can be prosecuted for everything he's ever done here."

"Shouldn't we take the whole file?" asked Alan.

"We could do that, but what if he notices?"

"Maybe he'll think he's put it somewhere else."

"Okay," Matthew agreed, "we'll take it with us. At least it will give us some information about the house in Clervaux."

The two men left the office quietly and inconspicuously, Alan with the file in his arms as if it were the most normal thing in the world.

"We should avoid reception, at least you with the file. You know what, I'll go up to the nurse for a minute and engage her in conversation, while you go to the elevator as usual and head to the parking lot."

"Okay, good plan."

Matthew walked down the stairs and straight towards the reception.

"Good evening. Another exhausting day! But now I'm off home." He gave the young woman a warm smile.

"Have a good evening, Doctor, and see you tomorrow!"

"I'll see you tomorrow, and don't worry too much about the night shift. It should stay quiet."

Matthew then also took the elevator to the basement carpark, where Alan was already waiting.

"It was worth it, our visit tonight," Matthew said on the way home.

"I think so too," Alan said intently, looking through the files. "Do you want to take them with you and when we meet with Alfonse at the weekend, you can bring the file with you?" he said to Matthew.

"Yes, we could do that. I'll go through it at home."

Matthew dropped Alan off at his apartment and then drove to his own place.

It was almost midnight again. Matthew sat down on the couch with a cold beer. Brigitte had already sent him four messages asking where he was and why he wasn't answering.

While Matthew didn't feel like answering, he was also aware

that he couldn't destroy his connection with her now, as dishonest as it may be. He wrote back, inviting her to lunch tomorrow.

# *THURSDAY, AUGUST 8*

2.00 a.m. Matthew had been reading through the file without a break and had discovered several interesting facts. The file seemed to contain contracts that Dr. Peter Lamborelle had signed with Luxembourg families. These families all wanted to adopt European babies or toddlers.

Despite the late hour, he texted Lis. "Hey Lis, what are Caro's parents' names and how old is she, do you know?"

Lis must have had her cell phone right next to her bed, because he received an answer within five minutes. "Caro KLEIN is 23 years old and lives in Bridel. Parents, no idea. Why?"

"I'll tell you tomorrow. Thank you and sleep well."

In the file was a contract from a couple named Annette and Pierre Klein, living in Bridel. Twenty-three years ago, they had applied to adopt a European child. *Hmm ... it looks like this file contains all the adoption contracts from many years ago, but whether it really has a connection to Caroline is unknown. But there is a possibility*, Matthew thought.

After a few hours' sleep, he called Lis again and told her about his and Alan's visit to the clinic and what they had found there. "Peter Lamborelle is also returning to Luxembourg today."

"It could be that it's one and the same family, but it doesn't have to be. I haven't found any details online, but maybe I can ask Eric if he can investigate discreetly, but without stressing Caro. I'm sure she would wonder why we want to research her adoptive parents."

"And now I'm going to have lunch with Brigitte. I'll be in touch again."

"Ah yes, well then, bon appétit."

"You too, see you later."

Lis wasn't particularly thrilled about this, but what did she expect?

After Matthew had left, Lis spontaneously called Thomas and arranged to meet him for lunch in an Italian restaurant in the city. The well-known restaurant was very busy and had a lovely terrace with a view of Luxembourg's old town.

Thomas picked up Lis and they had to wait outside for a while until the customers in the queue in front of them had taken their seats.

Suddenly, someone tapped Lis on the shoulder.

When she turned around, she saw Matthew, accompanied by Brigitte. Thomas also turned around. They greeted each other.

*An embarrassing situation*, Lis thought. *This is not at all the person I would like to meet right now.*

"Hello," Thomas said with an enthusiasm that made Lis angry. "Why don't we sit at a table together if there's one free?"

*This can't be true*, Lis thought, looking at Thomas as if she wished she had never called him.

The waiter had a table for four and took them there.

Lis sat down opposite Matthew, while Brigitte took a seat opposite Thomas.

Thomas and Brigitte had plenty to talk about, as it soon became clear. Lis, on the other hand, was desperately looking for a suitable excuse to leave the restaurant.

However, when the food was served, she relaxed slightly. As always, it was exquisite.

"You seem restless," Matthew remarked, looking at her fondly as they all ordered coffee to finish their meals.

How she would have loved to be here alone with him. But there was Brigitte, sitting right next to him. Lis wasn't in a particularly good mood.

"Yes, I didn't sleep well and I have a headache." She looked at her watch.

"I think I have to go now, I still have a few things to do today."

She stood up and said goodbye first to Thomas and Brigitte, and then to Matthew.

"Don't you want me to take you home?" said Thomas, tearing himself away from his conversation with Brigitte.

"No, it's all right, I'll walk. It'll do me good."

Matthew stood next to Lis. "Nice to see you," he whispered knowingly.

"See you then, have a nice afternoon."

She paid as quickly as she could and went out.

*What a relief,* she thought outside. *I can't help it, but this woman at Matthew's side is not my cup of tea.* She hurried off to catch the bus at the next stop.


An hour later, she was back home. She let herself fall onto the sofa and closed her eyes. *Why didn't she just let it all go, Matthew seemed to have everything he wanted with this woman. Or not?*

*Maybe I should see less of him when our mission is over. I need some distance from him. That will be beneficial for everyone involved,* Lis was thinking as her cell phone started to ring.

It was Matthew.

"Hey, Lis!"

"Hello."

"It wasn't the ideal situation at lunch, but it was unavoidable."

"It certainly wasn't ideal, to say the least. But Thomas and Brigitte seemed to have a great time," she added.

"Yes, I thought so too." Lis didn't feel like talking about the lunch anymore.

"Come on, I want you to understand me, Lis. Brigitte is in a very tense situation. She knows that her husband is involved in very dangerous things, and she is afraid of him, afraid for her existence, for everything in fact. If everything comes out, her life will be ruined."

Lis thought she hadn't heard correctly.

"Oh yeah?! She's afraid for her existence? Does she actually know what her wonderful husband is involved in, what he has been doing all these years? Of course, her existence will also suffer. But if we talk about it, how many children have lost their parents because of him?"

Matthew realised that he had gone a little too far with his remarks.

"And what about me? Do I also have the right to say that I don't agree with all this crap? But let's not discuss this today, Matt. Come on, we both need peace and quiet!"

"I think so too," he whispered.

"Are you still with her?"

"She's upstairs on the phone," he replied.

"Good, then sleep well, we'll talk later! Good night!"

Lis didn't wait for his answer, but simply hung up.

He's with her, or rather, she's with him, and he feels sorry for her ... Damn!

With these thoughts in mind, Lis went to bed early.

## FRIDAY, AUGUST 9

Lis woke up. She stayed in bed for a while, her thoughts returning to the previous night. She reviewed the intense hours she had spent with the man she had met as a teenager and about whom she actually knew very little. The sensitive boy from back then was now a sensitive man with whom she was still just as in love as she had been then. But at the moment, it was difficult to judge how things would go on. There were still too many hurdles ahead of them both. Somehow that scared her.

The ringing of her phone snapped her out of her daydreams. It was Alfonse Weis.

"Hello Lis, am I too early?" Lis looked at her watch, which just showed half past seven.

"Hey Alfonse. It's okay, but I'm still in bed. How's your research going? Anything new?"

"Yes, quite a lot. That's why I'm calling. Are you free tonight?"

"Absolutely. Have you found anything interesting?"

"More than that. There are some extremely interesting and strange connections. Can we all meet at your place tonight? It's easier if we all get together. I mean, will you bring the whole crew, Thomas, David and Alan?"

"Sure, you make it sound really exciting."

"Yes and no. Will Eric be there too?"

"No, Eric is out with Caro."

"Good, because it's better if he's not there for now. I'll see you around seven?"

"Perfect, Alfonse. I'll see you then. I want Matthew to be there too, okay?"

"Of course, he is also part of it, just like all of us."

*He can really keep the tension high*, Lis thought afterwards and hopped out of bed. *Typical Alfonse.*


That evening, Thomas, Alan, David, Alfonse and Matthew gathered at Lis' place.

They ordered Italian food at a local restaurant.

"Well then Alfonse, let's hear the news, you made it sound so exciting on the phone," said Lis.

"It was easiest to all meet together, and for now it's better if we keep all the information strictly between us before we decide what the next step will be."

Alfonse looked at each of them very seriously.

"So, Lis, I've been doing some research with a former work colleague who is still on the force. If you're asking me if it's completely legal, no, it's not, but we all want to find out what's happening and why. Well, that was the only way to hopefully get it discreetly. And now listen. There is a very interesting connection that will more than surprise you.

"Peter Lamborelle's father is Auguste Lamborelle and is seventy years old. Diane Van Helden's father is Gerard Van Helden and is also seventy years old. And your father, Lis Chandler alias Elisabeth Charlotte Bouvier, is Bernard Bouvier and is also seventy years old."

Everyone listened very attentively.

Lis looked wide-eyed at Alfonse, who glanced at his notebook from time to time.

"At this point, they are just three people of the same age. But when you factor in that Bernard Bouvier, Gerard Van Helden and Auguste Lamborelle were also classmates at primary school in Luxembourg City, there is a strong indication that they know each other.

"Auguste Lamborelle later joined the Ministry of Family Affairs and became a civil servant, just like Gerard Van Helden, who later also took up a position there.

"At some point, Auguste Lamborelle came under suspicion of embezzling money, and it was none other than his former schoolmate Gerard Van Helden who provided the evidence supplied the rope that hung him, so to speak. The case went to trial and Auguste Lamborelle was sentenced to ten years in prison, which he had to serve in full.

"When this happened, Peter Lamborelle was just twenty years old, which in turn means that Peter was thirty when his father was released from prison. Lis, you were kidnapped while Auguste Lamborelle was in prison. Your two other kidnappers, the teenagers whose names were known, testified that they acted alone, and so the case was quickly shelved after you also confirmed this."

The doorbell rang, startling the group. Dinner had been delivered.

Lis had been in a trance ever since her father's name had come up. Silence reigned as those gathered ate their meals.

"There must be some point to it, some connection," Matthew said at last.

"Quite a mess, if you ask me." Alan added.

"Lis, you understand what I'm getting at, don't you?" asked Alfonse. "I see you look pretty confused."

"Yes, I am," Lis replied. "And you think my father has something to do with it?"

"Maybe, but I don't know, not yet. By the way, Mark is Peter's middle name, a simple explanation to this name confusion. What's strange, though, is that Peter Lamborelle has been following this woman Diane Van Helden ever since she broke up with him. And the fact that she is still being held at the clinic, even though Alan has been told she is no longer there, is another mystery. Then I'd like to know why Peter Lamborelle kidnapped you and demanded money from your father. Where is the connection?"

"Maybe there isn't one? Bernard, I mean my father, would have said so, he would have testified, wouldn't he? Do you think he knows more about my kidnapping than he pretended to know at the time?"

"It is possible," Alfonse said. "There's only one person who can ask him about it off the record and ..."

" ... And that's me," Lis said calmly. "It's all very confusing. There are quite a few pieces of the puzzle still missing."

"I think so too," confirmed Alfonse. "But my gut feeling is that we're on the right track. What do you think?"

"Hmm ... Sounds like it. There can hardly be that many coincidences," said David.

"I don't think so either," Alfonse agreed. "But there's something else." He poured himself another glass of red wine.

"Gerard Van Helden's wife, born Emilie Fox, Diane's mother, died in a car accident here in Luxembourg over 20 years ago. They not only had a daughter, Diane, but also another daughter, Laetitia Van Helden, who is married to Klaus Schmitt. She is two years older than Diane.

"This couple had a daughter who was kidnapped during a summer vacation in the south of France and disappeared without a trace, according to the files. When this happened, the girl was barely a year old and never reappeared."

"Are these two people still alive?" Matthew asked, and then told him about the file he had found in Lamborelle's office at the clinic, which mentioned Annette and Pierre Klein, who had adopted a little girl called Caroline.

"Very interesting, Matthew! I don't know if they're still alive, I haven't researched it yet. We haven't got that far yet."

"But that's where Diane could help us, if she survives."

"Absolutely!" Alfonse confirmed. "And it's very interesting what you are saying, Matthew, because here it comes. Laetitia van Helden's daughter was called Caroline Schmitt."

"Yes, but ...?"

"Nothing per se. But you once mentioned that Eric's girlfriend Caro comes from an orphanage here in Luxembourg. Caro, Caroline?"

"Oh, my God!" said Lis. A cold shiver ran through her body.

"You mean ... No, why would there be a connection, Alfonse. The name is the same, but ..."

"But?"

"Yes, indeed ... Oh dear ..." Now Lis became very thoughtful.

"Peter Lamborelle has been busy for years placing orphans with rich families here in Luxembourg, hasn't he? Somehow, he transports them here to Luxembourg from the Dominican Republic. But where do these European children who are placed in the orphanage in Santo Domingo come from? That's question number one. Question number two: are they really all orphans living without parents, or are they 'made' into parentless children?"

Lis put down his knife and fork. "It could well be that it's all hidden behind his smooth façade."

"Absolutely," Alan agreed.

"We'll find out," said Alfonse firmly. "Lis, my sincere wish is that you don't let Eric know about this for the time being. He loves Caro and would tell her everything, but that's no good, because at the moment we only have assumptions, nothing more. I'd like to know more about her adoptive parents, I'd like to visit that home in Clervaux one day, but then I'd also like to know what Bernard Bouvier has to say when you ask him about his two classmates? That is the question!"

"I certainly will! My dear father won't be very amused about it, but I will go and see him tomorrow, Alfonse. It would be really hard to bear if he knew much more than he has been admitting all this time. But then he would have to know that the name Lamborelle is somehow connected with my kidnapping, wouldn't he?"

"I don't know, but it's possible! Are you going to find out?"

"You bet!"

"I know you don't have the best relationship with him, but it could help us a lot."

"I will definitely do it, Alfonse. And I thank you for all your time and effort, and also your anonymous former work colleague. Please pass on my thanks to him."

"I will."

Matthew stood up, took a document from the folder he had brought with him and placed it on the table.

"But then everything fits together. This contract here from Annette and Pierre Klein, imagine if it was actually from Caro's adoptive parents?" Thomas said.

"Oh my God, you mean she was taken from the Van Heldens and then the Kleins adopted her?!"

"This could be how Lamborelle's system works," said Alfonse, "we need to find out more details about it."

"Well, if Bernard Bouvier is in any way connected with this Auguste Lamborelle, then there is certainly an explanation for your kidnapping."

"It looks like this Peter Lamborelle wanted to take revenge on the entire Van Helden family because Auguste Van Helden put his father in prison! As crazy as that may sound," Thomas postulated.

"Very likely! That makes sense!" Alan agreed. "That's why he's been trying to get to Diane, but what's he planning to do with her?"

"If Caro is the biological child of Laetitia Van Helden and Klaus Schmitt, then this couple doesn't even know their daughter is alive," Lis said.

"No, they don't," Alfonse agreed, "and Caro's adoptive parents adopted her in good faith because they believed Caro's biological parents were probably dead."

"Oh dear, that won't be a pleasant revelation if it's true," said Thomas.

"It certainly won't. But we're not there yet," said Alfonse. "Before we go to the police with anything, we have to be absolutely sure and uncover everything ourselves. Otherwise, we'll get shot at from both sides, you can bet on that."

"That's for sure. We have to hurry, or Diane will be dead. Don't forget that," Alan reminded them all.

"She could give us more insight," said Alfonse.

"Yes, but if we make noise in the hospital now without proof, they'll sue us. Besides," said Matthew, "we still have to find out why and how Alan and I were implanted with chips. It could only have happened in our clinic. I'll sort that out with my … non-biological father when we're ready."

"Non-biological father, Doc?" Alfonse asked, looking rather surprised at Matthew.

"Yes, that's another surprise. It's a long story and I only recently learned the truth. John McKenna doesn't know that I know yet, so let's keep a lid on this one for now too! First things first."

"And then we also need proof that Peter Lamborelle wants to clean up the Van Helden family," said Alfonse. "Somehow that sounds plausible. But would that mean that the mother of Diane and Laetitia Van Helden, Emilie Fox, didn't die in a simple car accident either?"

"I don't think so, if this man is that reckless and crazy!"

"And that man is Eric's father!" Lis was on the verge of tears. "I don't know how to deal with this situation. And I certainly don't know how to tell my son."

"Are you really sure about that, Lis?" asked Alfonse.

"I'm so sure. And when I talk to him, I'll make sure, Alfonse. I have to get through this confrontation anyway. Otherwise, it's not over for me yet."

Everyone looked at Lis.

"Wait a minute, Lis," Matthew looked at her sympathetically and put his arm around her shoulder, "we're not there yet. Maybe things will turn out differently after all."

With all the information on the table, the group decided to part ways for the night. After the others left, Matthew stayed behind to talk to Lis.

"I'm sorry about yesterday," she said, "I wasn't in the mood."

"Me neither." He took her in his arms. "It's been a difficult day too."

"Actually, it all makes sense," whispered Lis. "Peter Lamborelle is suffering from the fact that his father was in prison for ten years and has been seeking revenge on the Van Heldens. That would indeed be a very logical motive. He kidnaps the baby from Laetitia Van Helden and her husband, destroying that side of the family. Then he spies on Diane Van Helden, and when the opportunity arises, he makes a pass at her. But he already knows who this woman is. He knows everything about the family. Oh my God, can this be true?"

"I think we're at least very close to the truth, Lis. As unpleasant as it is. But where do you fit in?" Matthew asked.

"It could be that I only got into this story by chance because my dear father has a lot of money and the boys needed money at the time," Lis concluded.

"I don't think so, they came from rich families, they didn't need any money."

"So it was just a brutal teenage game, a competition between friends?"

"Well," Matthew said, "I imagine a teenage game to be rather harmless and not a kidnapping followed by ...."

"Say it for what it is: A rape with kidnapping and blackmail for money."

"Yes," was all he said.

"Okay, I'll talk to my father tomorrow," Lis said. Her eyes looked very tired. "If my father knew all along, or at least suspected, who had kidnapped me, he should have just said so. Even if it was just his guess."

"Come here," Matthew pulled her to him and hugged her, then kissed her.

"Is anyone else waiting for you tonight?" asked Lis.

"Actually, yes ... I should already be at Brigitte's, but I'll call her now to say I'll see her tomorrow." He sent a text message to Brigitte, then turned off his phone.

"Sleep well, Lis," Matthew hugged her to him again, "and good luck with your father tomorrow. I know you're not looking forward to that conversation."

"You can say that. Thank you for everything, for being there, for being with me, for understanding that ..."

"Hey, hey, lots of compliments!"

Despite his attempt to be cheerful, Matthew could see that Lis had tears in her eyes.

"What's happened?"

"Nothing ..." She leaned her head against his shoulder. "I'm afraid of the moment when I face Peter Lamborelle and then when I have to explain everything to Eric. I don't think I'll be able to cope with the situation."

"You'll rise to the occasion, Lis. I'm sure you will!"

"I'm also very afraid that I'll completely overwhelm Eric and he might have a crazy reaction. I wouldn't want to lose him for the world."

"You won't. He's a young, open-minded man. In my opinion he'll probably need some time, but then he'll be fine."

"I hope you're right, Matt. I really do."

Then they said goodbye and Matthew drove home.

Lis couldn't get a good night's sleep that night. She dreamed

strange dreams, with her thoughts revolving around the conversation she knew she had to have with her father.

# JAMES

## *SATURDAY, AUGUST 10*

Lis had guessed right. Her father was often in his bank's office on Saturday mornings so that he could work in peace for a few hours without any employees around him. When Lis called him, she did so under the pretext that she was in the city centre and would like to stop by for a coffee.

"Hello, Lis. Since I don't believe you're a coincidence, I assume you have something on your mind." Bernard Bouvier, a tall, handsome and elegant man, stood in the doorway. He wasn't wearing a suit or tie today, but jeans and a white shirt. His full grey hair was cut very short, and he was wearing modern glasses.

"You know me well, Dad. Hi, thanks for your time."

"Come next door, we have to make our own coffee. I can ask my assistant to do it during the week, but not on Saturdays."

Father and daughter sat down.

"How are you?" he asked when he saw that Lis was tired and somewhat agitated.

"Well, well. I need your help. And no, it's not about money and it's not about Eric."

"Okay, then let's hear it. It's rare that you ask me for help. Or rather, not anymore ..." he added quietly with a somewhat sad undertone.

"You had two classmates at primary school called Auguste Lamborelle and Gerard Van Helden."

He looked piercingly at his daughter over his glasses. "You weren't born then. How do you know these names?"

"It's a long story that I don't want to tell in full, at least not yet. But I would like to know whether you and Auguste Lamborelle have had or still have something that connects you in some way. Was there anything between you back then, many years ago?"

"How can you make assumptions like that? You don't even know these people, do you?"

"So, there is something after all?"

Bernard Bouvier looked at his daughter, somewhat confused and thoughtful at the same time.

"There's an old story that no one really knows, and it also falls under the secrecy of a bank director, Lis."

"Is it also covered by banking secrecy if this old story could have something to do with your daughter's kidnapping?"

Bernard Bouvier looked at Lis in amazement. "What are you getting at?"

"I'm not sure yet, but what was that story or connection? Please, Dad, I need your help with this! If you want to restore our relationship in any way, it's now or never!"

Lis looked resolutely at her father. "What was it between you and Auguste Lamborelle?"

She did not take her eyes off him.

"Okay! But I insist that you explain to me exactly what's going on here."

"All right, but first I need to hear your story."

"Okay, it's a deal! Many years ago, Auguste Lamborelle came to me and asked for a loan, a very large loan. He said he needed the money to hire a star lawyer. He had been accused of embezzling money, which had been uncovered by the third person in the group, whose name you already know, Gerard Van Helden.

Both men worked at the Ministry of Family Affairs, which you probably also know."

Lis nodded in agreement.

"And you didn't give him the loan, right?"

"Exactly!"

"Why not?"

"Because he had no guarantees, because he would never have been able to pay it back and because he was guilty anyway and would have gone to prison, with or without a star lawyer."

"I understand," Lis said both thoughtfully and sadly. "I understand a lot of things now. What else can you add?" she asked, knowing that he wouldn't say anything.

"What else can I say?"

"Perhaps now, for once, you have the opportunity to side with me and do what you never wanted to do, for the sake of your empire's reputation, for the sake of your personal reputation as a banker, for the sake of ... I don't know what else ..."

"I haven't the slightest idea what you're alluding to here, Lis?"

*Does he really have no idea that Lamborelle was responsible for my kidnapping? I can't imagine that*, Lis thought.

Lis stood up. "Then let's leave it at that, at least for now. I'll get back to you. Thanks for the coffee."

"Hey, but Lis, now explain to me what your unusual questions are all about. How do you know these names?"

"Everything in its own time and at the moment it's just not ready yet. There are still a few things to sort out and then I'll tell you everything. I promise!"


With these words, Lis left the office, leaving behind a man who was suddenly asking himself a lot more questions about the past.

Throughout the day, Lis thought about what she had learned

from her father. Suddenly many connections became clear to her. Many things began to make sense.

Lis did her shopping and then made herself comfortable at home while she tried to organise her confused thoughts about all the past events and information she had received from her father.

Somehow, she still couldn't shake off the conversation with him.

Matthew called her briefly and she explained to him what her father had said. In the evening, she called Alfonse, told him briefly and they arranged to meet the next evening.

The orphanage in Clervaux also played in her mind. Finding no peace at home, she spontaneously decided to go there, just to have a look around. She put on black clothes to remain inconspicuous—a jacket with a hood, black jeans, hiking boots—and took her gun with her as a precaution. No one knew that Lis had a firearms license and was trained to use it.

After about an hour, she reached the village and parked the car in a small side street a few hundred meters from the property. It had become dark in the meantime.

Clervaux was a small and touristy village. The orphanage itself was located at the end of the settlement, directly on a forest slope and barely visible from the main road.

Lis decided to walk the rest of the way. She didn't yet know what she could hope to gain from her visit, but her curiosity grew with every step. She just wanted to have a quick look around, nothing more. This time Lis wanted to do it alone.

She took her gun from the car and put it in her jacket pocket as a precaution.

When she had almost reached the main gate, it opened automatically. She just managed to hide behind a bush as a dark green Jaguar drove past her and entered. Then she walked on briskly until she stopped behind a tree right by the gate and watched the car. She realised that Peter Lamborelle was the driver, which didn't surprise her.

The gate slowly began to close behind his car. *It's now or never*, Lis thought. Quick-witted, she slipped inside just before the gate slammed shut. At that moment, she hadn't thought about how she would get out again later. The wall surrounding this property was extremely high, at least two meters. No one could get in or out so easily, especially not without being seen.

The long walk to the orphanage lay ahead of her. A large park surrounded the house. Lis walked carefully through the grass so as not to be caught on camera.

Finally, she reached the building. It was stately and of beautiful architecture. *No wonder no one noticed it straight away*, she thought. She saw the Jaguar in the parking lot right next to the main entrance.

Slowly and very attentively, she continued on her way, circling the building. There was still light behind many of the windows, but some were dark. By now it was almost 11.00 p.m..

Lis had just finished walking around the building and was standing behind a tree when she noticed a lighted window on the second floor. Shadows could be seen behind the curtain.

Just as she was about to take a step forward to take a closer look, she was startled to feel a presence right behind her.

In a split second, her heart started pounding in her throat. Just as she was about to catapult this person to the ground with a deft grip, she felt a gun touching her back. At same time, a hand gripped her right arm tightly, preventing her from drawing her weapon.

"Don't move and stay calm, please!" she heard a strong male voice. "Then turn around very slowly, without making a wrong move. Be careful, I don't want to have to hurt you, okay?" Lis nodded in the affirmative. She was scared. Within a second, the man had taken the gun out of her pocket in one swift movement and seized it.

"And now your cell phone, please!"

She felt uneasy and trembled slightly. Then she slowly turned around.

Lis was astonished and surprised to find herself looking directly into the face of Michael Winther. He was also looking at her with a surprised look.

He held his open hand in front of her and she put the cell phone in it. He switched it off immediately and put it in his pocket.

"Mrs. Kaufmann! What on earth are you doing here? You're certainly not in the right place!" he whispered, still pointing his gun at her. "If you had walked another three meters or so, the alarm would have gone off. There are countless infrared cameras here that will trigger all the surveillance spots, and that's not in your interest or mine, is it?"

"Mr. Winther?" asked Lis, completely confused. "You scared the life out of me. Were you following me?"

"No! I only noticed your shadow."

"Are you guarding the house for those inside?" she asked.

"Not really, otherwise I wouldn't have warned you, would I? Listen, we have to get out of here as quickly as possible! Otherwise, it won't stay this quiet for much longer and then we'll have visitors we don't want. Come on!"

Without waiting for her answer, he spontaneously took Lis by the hand, and they walked towards the forest, which was a good hundred meters away.

"I'm putting my gun away now," he said, "please don't try to attack me with your knife or whatever. Because it won't end in your favour, I promise you that!"

She was still reeling from the shock. "Of course not!" She

brushed her hair out of her face and looked at the man again, she was still shaking. *Winther. The man with the mesmerising eyes. Whoever he really is, those eyes have a magical attraction,* Lis thought. *Actually, a completely inappropriate thought given the situation.* She was a little less anxious now.

"Are you from the police?" she asked as they walked on briskly.

"That was me!" He looked sad for a moment. "We need to talk; we seem to have common interests."

"How do we get out of here and how do I know I can trust you?" Lis asked suspiciously.

"Then I suggest we start by me finding a way out of here."

"How do you know the way?"

"I've been here before. Are you a good climber?" he asked in the same breath.

Lis looked at him questioningly. "That depends on how high!"

"Let's go!"

"Where are we going?" she asked, albeit a little anxiously.

"Just come with me, it's not far."

They walked towards the forest and after about three hundred metres they reached the high wall that surrounded the property.

"I can climb, but I can hardly get up there," Lis realised.

"You don't need that!" In a few simple steps, Mr. Winther had fetched a ladder from the bushes. It was right against the wall and couldn't be seen under the leaves. He looked at Lis, who only said 'Aha' while he stabilised the ladder on the wall.

"Please, after you!" He held the ladder tightly and made an almost inviting motion with his hand. She had no other choice if she wanted to get out of here unseen and safely.

Once at the top, he pulled the ladder up and put it down again on the other side.

He climbed first and jumped the last bit.

Then he looked up at her.

"Jump, I'll catch you."

Lis climbed down and when she had almost reached the ground, she jumped the last bit straight into his arms.

They were very close for a few moments.

"Thank you," she said, brushing her long hair out of her face. Then he let go of her.

He immediately grabbed the ladder and hid it right against the wall under the bushes and leaves.

"I don't understand anything," said Lis. "Do you come here often?"

The man didn't answer her question. "My car is parked quite far away from here. Come with me and then I'll drive you back to yours? And just in case you don't trust me yet, remember one thing: I could have let you walk straight into the hands of the other side, but I didn't, right?"

"But then you would have been discovered too!"

"No, not necessarily."

They quickly walked on together until they reached his black Mercedes SUV about ten minutes later. Lis got in with mixed feelings.

However, he didn't start the engine. She looked at him suspiciously and took off her cap.

"Better?" He looked at her briefly, because he must have noticed that she felt uncomfortable.

"I don't know yet. You really scared me earlier."

There was actually nothing frightening about his behaviour, but somehow his striking eyes scared her a little.

"I had no other choice," he interrupted the short pause. "I didn't want either of us to get caught here, under any circumstances."

"Yes, I understand. That was good too. Thank you."

"Mrs. Kaufmann, what are you doing here at this time of night, alone in the dark and with a gun? I also saw you at the orphanage at night in Santo Domingo." He looked at Lis somewhat mischievously. "Shouldn't we play with all our cards on the table?" he asked.

"I ..."

Without waiting for her answer, he said: "My real name is James, James Hammer!"

"Oh, so Winther is a fake name?"

"I had to come to the orphanage incognito, but I can explain that later. Now back to my question: what are you doing here alone with a gun in front of this place? It's none of my business, but don't you know how dangerous it is to spy here? Are you looking for a child who is in this orphanage? Or are you also on to something and know of a connection between the two orphanages here and on the island?"

Lis was a little exhausted now. "Yes, I know about a connection. No! I'm not looking for a child, but I ... I'm involved in a complicated story that actually started innocently enough. And I believe that part of the solution lies in this orphanage."

She looked out of the window. "My name isn't Martina Kaufmann and the man who was with me isn't my husband. My name is Lis Chandler."

James had to smile secretly. After all, he had known that since their flight together, when Mike had told him her real name by text message. *At least she seems to be honest. A good start,* he thought.

"Another person using a fake name?" he smiled.

"I didn't have a choice either," Lis explained and as she spoke, tears came to her eyes, and she leaned her head back.

"I'm sorry ..." She wiped her eyes with her hand.

He handed her a tissue.

"Thank you!" She looked at him again. "But you were at the orphanage in Santo Domingo, and the woman who opened the door knew you by name. What do you have to do with all this?"

James Hammer looked sympathetically at her.

Without answering her question, he said: "I remember the scene on the plane. You were on your way to the toilet and then almost collided with a man who had just come out of the toilet."

"You were watching me?" asked Lis, who was surprised by his statement.

"No, I wasn't watching you, but rather the other person, the grey-blond man, whose encounter apparently frightened you so much that you completely panicked."

"Do you know him?" asked Lis.

"Yes and no. Yes, because he is the director of the orphanage on Santo Domingo. No, because there are other criminal activities involved and I haven't found out exactly what's going on. I've been following this man and watching him, so I couldn't help but notice the look on your face. He really scared you. Why?"

"He's a … He … I don't know if I want to tell you that."

"And," James added, "the man who was on the plane with you was different from the man who came to the orphanage with you. There are some things that don't add up there either, do they?"

Lis looked at James again. He seemed somehow amused that he had noticed all this.

"Yes, maybe some things aren't so coherent," Lis said more to herself.

"All right, brave, pretty lady. First I'll tell you why I'm after this man, then you can do the same or not, as you wish. But I'm warning you. You must keep this information away from the others in your group, at least for now. I want to continue working undisturbed and most importantly alone, okay? We all seem to have the same interests. But if you don't keep this to yourself, we could all get into serious trouble and put ourselves in danger!"

Lis nodded in agreement. "Sure, no problem. No one knows I'm here at the moment anyway."

"Good," he said. "But before I explain, are you hungry?"

Now Lis looked at him in astonishment. "Hungry? Now?" It was just after midnight.

"Yes, because I haven't eaten anything tonight and I have a small picnic basket in the back seat for situations like this. I've already spent many hours here, and I was planning to stay here all night, that is, on the premises, to keep an eye on everything that's going on, who's coming in and out."

James Hammer reached into the back seat and pulled out a basket, placed it on his lap and took out a sandwich.

"I've just picked up some cheese and ham with tomato; would you like one?" He handed it to her, wrapped in a small bag.

"You're serious," she said.

"Of course I am," he replied as he unpacked his own.

Lis had to smile now. "I don't know … What to say." Their eyes met again. "Are we having a picnic here now?"

He smiled. "Call it what you like. Go ahead and have some if you're hungry, I brought three of them."

She took the sandwich, removed the bag and took a big bite. James did the same.

"It tastes really good," said Lis.

"I think so too, home cooking!" he confirmed.

"I've only brought water. Please help yourself." He handed her a bottle of water and a cup.

"This is a totally crazy situation," Lis commented, holding the cup. He filled it halfway with water.

"True, but the world is crazy. And we're both here to find out something. So let me start by explaining why I'm here."

"Peter Lamborelle is involved in a very dirty business. He, or rather his organisation, kidnaps children from tourists in the Dominican Republic, maybe elsewhere too, I don't know yet. Then he keeps them in the orphanage on the island for a long, long time until the situation has calmed down, the real parents have stopped looking for them, and the police have more or less finished their job. Then he sells them as orphans for a lot of money to wealthy families, especially here in Luxembourg. Because he works for the Ministry of Family Affairs, he has all the necessary connections for such actions. He has to be well-connected because he has to get the children into the country legally somehow, under a different name and with a fake passport and so on. But there must be more people involved, because how else could they create all the legal entries, papers and whatever else is necessary so easily?"

"How do you know all that?" Lis asked.

"Three years ago, my wife and I were on vacation in the Dominican Republic with our then three-year-old daughter Sarah. At the time, we were living in Germany, just over the Luxembourg border, and were already planning to move to Luxembourg. But we weren't registered here yet, we still had an address in Germany.

"Then one night our daughter Sarah was kidnapped from our rented vacation home, right from the room next to ours. She was never found again. We did everything we could, both locally and here. I was still a police officer at the time and despite all my connections, I came up against so much resistance. Nobody wanted to help us because the kidnapping hadn't happened here in the country.

"When I investigated further, I was told to leave it alone and concentrate on local crimes and my work.

"Then, a year and a half ago, the terrible certainty came to the surface purely by chance. We saw the announcement of our daughter's death in a local Luxembourg newspaper. We both recognised the face immediately, it was our daughter Sarah, although she had been given a different name. We tried to get in touch with her parents, but after a few phone calls we were banned from the house by the police and charged with trespassing. Although we had a lawyer, we had to give up because everyone was against us. Sarah's parents were very dismissive. My wife then committed suicide. She couldn't bear the thought that our daughter had been so close to us all the time and we had known nothing about it."

"And you were sure that it was really your daughter and not a girl who looked like her?"

"Yes, we were absolutely sure. After my wife's death, when I was finally back on my feet, I was suspended because it was discovered that I was using the police data too much for my own research. Then I really started researching. I found out that Sarah had been adopted a year after she was taken away from us, after she had gone missing on the island. And she was from the orphanage in Clervaux, which means she was only with her adoptive family for about six months before she died. But I have no idea from what she died. It wasn't in the obituary."

"Do you know which hospital she died in?"

"Yes, at the McKenna Private Clinic. That's because the announcement in the paper included a special thanks to the paediatric department and staff at that clinic."

Lis almost choked when she heard that name. "Oh dear, it all fits together!"

James looked at her. "Do you know this clinic?"

"More than that. I'll explain it to you in a moment."

"I assume that Sarah was held in Santo Domingo after the kidnapping until the dust had settled," James Hammer continued.

"Back then, after the kidnapping in Santo Domingo, we really did everything we could, including in Germany, but there was no trace, no information, no help. Nothing, absolutely nothing. Yet we were so close to her the whole time. The adoptive parents live in Moutfort. I want this Lamborelle arrested, I want to find out who is behind this, and I want to speak to him personally!"

James paused to catch his breath. He was on the verge of tears.

"I'm so sorry for you," Lis said, briefly placing her hand on his. "Then you also know that he's somehow connected to the clinic?"

"I'm not sure exactly what's going on, but I was able to track him twice as he drove into the parking garage of the McKenna clinic. So, I strongly suspect he has a connection there."

"Something like that," Lis whispered.

"Since I left my job, I've been following this man privately," James continued. "During the first year after Sarah disappeared, I found out quite a lot but I didn't have the access rights I used to have. A friend helped me a little. I found out that Sarah had been placed with her adoptive parents through the orphanage here in Luxembourg. And then I found the connection to the Dominican Republic, to the orphanage there. I spent a month in Santo Domingo and followed the trail to this orphanage and the connection back to the orphanage here in Luxembourg. During my surveillance and research, I saw this man come and go many times. When I started my investigation here, I saw the same man again and I followed him. That's why I was on the same flight as you."

"But how did you know about his travel plans?"

James Hammer looked at Lis. "Business secret! But at least I have the man now, although I don't know yet who's protecting him in the government or anywhere else, and I don't want to kill him until I find out."

"You can't kill him that easily," Lis said firmly.

"Why not? I have nothing left to lose. And if I don't do it, who will? You? No, I don't think so! I won't give up until I find him and his connections. He, or rather they, whoever that may be, have taken everything that was important in my life, everything

I lived for. There is nothing left, I have nothing to lose! You may say revenge isn't the way to go, maybe you're right, but you know what; I don't care. He will pay for what he did, not just to me, but many parents, I'm afraid. He will pay. I'll get him, I swear it."

"I understand that. But how did you get into the orphanage when we met? Did you say you wanted to adopt?"

"Yes. I asked about the adoption conditions and had many other questions. But I was only introduced to a lady, not the man himself."

James looked at her continuously with his hypnotic eyes.

"And what did he do to you? Did he kidnap your child?"

Lis nodded in the negative. "No, rather the opposite," she turned her face towards him and leaned against the headrest. She wiped her tears away again.

"Sorry, but I don't quite understand," James said quietly.

"It's different ... I ... " Lis didn't know how to begin but she wanted to explain to this man why she was here. She had a strong feeling that James was telling the truth.

He looked at her. "You don't have to explain anything to me, if you don't feel like it. You can get out of the car, no problem. Just stay away from the orphanage, unless you want to get killed there!"

However, Lis didn't feel the slightest urge to get out of the car. Somehow, she felt at ease in his company, now that she had calmed down somewhat.

She leaned her head back and looked at him.

"I was kidnapped as a teenager and my father was blackmailed for a lot of money. I spent three months in a room with no windows and he, this man, was one of the three kidnappers. They were young adults at the time, and he raped me the night before I was released. When I was freed, no one believed me that there was a third perpetrator. He was wearing a black hood and a mask;

I only saw his eyes when … well … when it happened. And then we collided on the plane, as you noted, and I saw his eyes. He had a black spot in his right eye, very rare, but just the same as the man who raped me. I hadn't seen him again until then."

James was visibly shocked. "Oh, and I thought I'd been through a lot."

"So you have, we've both been through hell," said Lis.

"That's why you lost total control when you met him again! That's more than understandable, to say the least."

"Exactly!" Then Lis told him what had happened when she was kidnapped. "And I have a son of whom he … is the father, but he doesn't know anything about it!"

"Your son or Peter Lamborelle?"

"Both of them. Neither knows anything about the other."

"It sounds complicated, but it all fits together," James said, looking at her sympathetically. "What a story, Mrs. Chandler."

"Call me Lis." She was surprised that she wanted to be so open with this stranger.

"How did you cope with it all?"

"It took a long time. Things have gone quite well over the last few years, until the moment when this man came back into my life. Then, the past came back to life in a matter of seconds. And I thought I had put it all behind me. But when I saw those eyes, I was sure it was him because I'll never forget them."

"You didn't know who you were dealing with until then?"

"No, not at all, we were just on our way to Santa Domingo to look for a friend who had disappeared. I was asked if I could join the group because I speak Spanish."

Then Lis also talked about the reason for her trip to the Dominican Republic, about Matthew and Alan.

"And the man you saw me with on the plane is Matthew McKenna, the son of the clinic director." Of course, James Hammer already knew that, but Lis couldn't have known.

"I don't know what to say. Then Lamborelle also has allies at the McKenna Clinic, how else would these two men have been chipped? And the fact that my Sarah died there is no coincidence, is it?"

"At least it wasn't a coincidence that she was taken there. It's all so surreal and sad at the same time."

"And what are you going to do now?" he asked.

"Tomorrow I'm meeting up with the friends who were on the trip with me, and then we'll decide what we do next," Lis explained. "Among them is a former intelligence officer. Maybe this man can help you?"

"No, that's not an option! Please, don't mention me in any way to outsiders. I work alone and only alone, okay? And I trust very few people."

"Ah, sure that's all right. Is there somewhere I can reach you if ...?"

"I would prefer to be able to get in touch with you. I use different cell phones for security reasons," explained James Hammer. "And if they've tracked me, I definitely don't want them to know about you."

"I understand. Thank you for stopping me earlier," said Lis.

"It could have gone very wrong ... For both of us."

Lis gave him her cell phone number. Then James drove her to her car and stopped.

"Strange coincidence," he said.

"Yes ... So many strange coincidences ..." As Lis opened the door, James continued to look at her as she got out.

"Good night," she said before closing the door.

"Don't underestimate them," he warned. "They'll kill anyone who gets in their way, don't forget that!"

Their eyes met again for a few seconds. "Thank you," Lis said.

Then she got into her car and drove off. James waited until she had gone.

It was after 3am by the time Lis made it home.

# SUNDAY, AUGUST 11

Lis had hardly slept in the remaining hours of the night. She had not yet spoken to Alfonse or Matthew about yesterday. She didn't want to mention this mysterious James at all.

*An interesting man,* Lis thought secretly, *strange eyes. So this Lamborelle had had something to do with the kidnapping of James Hammer's daughter. And then later, when the girl got sick, or whatever had happened when she was with the adoptive parents, he took her to the McKenna clinic. The girl was already three years old when she disappeared, and then a year in that orphanage .... and then, six months later, she dies. Hmm ... too bad I don't know the adopted name; Caro could discreetly check that out.*

Lis called Alfonse around noon and told him what she had learned from her father about the connection between the three men in question, Gerard Van Helden, Bernard Bouvier and Auguste Lamborelle.

"Wow. Give us a day so I can think about how to proceed. We don't want to cause panic anywhere, especially as the police have to be kept away for the time being," was Alfonse's instruction.

# MONDAY, AUGUST 12

Monday morning dawned raining. When Eric got up, it was half past eight. Lis was in the kitchen when he entered.

"Hello Lis, you look tired!"

Lis was standing by the window with a cup of coffee, looking thoughtful.

"Hm, I had a restless night. And you?"

"Everything's fine," he said. "I had a long talk with Caro

yesterday and decided to stay in Luxembourg and look for a job. I'll talk to my grandfather soon."

"You get on very well with Caro; that makes me happy for you, Eric!"

"You like her too, I can see that."

"Yes, I like her very much. She's an open and intelligent young woman. You're a good match, as far as I can tell."

Then Eric's cell phone rang.

"Hey Caro, I've already had breakfast, I ... Yes, I hear ... What?! What do you mean, disappeared?"

Lis pricked up her ears.

"But ... Hmmm .... No, don't do anything on your own! It's too dangerous. Yeah okay, see you later, I'll pick you up at two.

"Just imagine, Lis," he said, turning to his mother, "The woman from Room 1112 is gone, just disappeared. The room is empty and the file says she left the hospital on July 6."

"Damn," said Lis. "We have to tell Alfonse. What have they done to her?"

Lis called Alfonse and explained to him what had happened.

"Yes, the room is empty, just as Caro reported. Are you worried, Alfonse?"

"Listen, Lis, we're all going to sit down tonight and discuss what we're going to do."


After Lis had also spoken to Matthew, Thomas, Alan and David were also notified. They all agreed to meet at Lis' home that evening.

After lunch together, Eric left.

"I'm going to meet Caro after work at 2 p.m.. I'll pick her up and spend the night with her."

"Okay. I'll see what Alfonse suggests. Our problem is that we have no evidence. And I'll also talk to Matthew, he's coming here too. Say hello to Caro for me and have a nice day. And Eric, please don't play detective on your own. I don't want my son to put himself in danger, okay!"

"Roger, Mum!" He kissed Lis on the cheek. "I love you!"

"I love you very much, Eric!"

Then he went out.


2.30 p.m.. Lis felt drained, tired and impatient to get back into a calmer routine. She had just laid down on the sofa and was almost asleep when her cell phone rang. It was Eric. He sounded very excited.

"What's going on? Change of plans?"

"No, but Caro is missing. I can't find her."

"What do you mean? Where did you want to meet her?" Lis sat up and immediately heard how stressed Eric sounded.

"I waited as usual, on the street right next to the clinic, I never go into the parking garage if it's only for a few minutes. But she didn't show up. Then I tried to call her but her cell phone was turned off. I went to reception and they told me she had just left. Then I went back outside but she was nowhere to be seen. She couldn't have left in her car; she took the bus this morning because I was supposed to pick her up. I'm so worried. I don't understand this. What am I supposed to do?"

"Go back inside. Maybe she ran into someone or she's waiting in the cafeteria, maybe she misunderstood you?"

"No, but fine, I'll go back in. Maybe I'm overreacting because of everything that's happened recently." He had already hung up.

Lis sent him a quick text message: *"Please let me know if you find her."*

*"I will, thank you Lis!"*

Lis spent most of the afternoon asleep on the sofa. She was exhausted from the excitement of the last few days and weeks.

When she woke up, she saw that Eric had sent her a text shortly before: *Everything's fine, see you!*

*Great*, Lis thought. *Well, I can understand why he was worried. We're all pretty tense these days.*

Shortly after 8 p.m., everyone had arrived at Lis' house: Matthew, Alan, David, Alfonse and Thomas.

Alfonse explained to them in detail the connection that Lis' father, Bernard Bouvier, had with Auguste Lamborelle, Peter's father.

"Well, at least we now have an explanation as to why Peter Lamborelle kidnapped you. It was to punish your father for his own father being in prison for ten years. He blamed everything on Bernard Bouvier," said Alfonse.

"Yes, exactly that. But Bernard, I mean my father," Lis explained, "would have had to have known or at least had a very strong suspicion about who might have kidnapped me, wouldn't he?"

"I think so too, but maybe he really didn't believe that Auguste Lamborelle's son could be so crazy? I don't know. You know your father best."

"Well ..."

"And now?" asked Alan. "When should we get the police involved?"

"It's still too early," Alfonse insisted. "We have no evidence and we really need to find out who is involved in the clinic. I'll try to find out about Caro's parents' past and their lives. Whether they still exist and where they live."

Lis thought of what James had told her.

"Alfonse, if you find something, we should be very careful that Caro doesn't find out, at least until we're sure."

"We should definitely not overwhelm her with such

information, but her biological parents would also have to be informed at some point."

"The simplest solution would be to get Peter Lamborelle to confess!" suggested Alfonse, looking at Lis.

"Are you kidding?" said Matthew.

"Okay, I'll do it, Alfonse!"

"You're going to do what?" Matthew asked, very surprised by Lis' statement. "Have I missed something here?"

"I have asked Lis if she would be prepared to get Peter Lamborelle to confess," Alfonse admitted. "To do that, she would have to meet him, pretend to be Mrs. Kaufmann again, and then gradually lay her cards on the table.

"We can't get in there without an official reason. It's a huge property with a very high and solid wall around it, an alarm system, cameras and so on. I've already been there to check it out," Alfonse added.

"I'll wear a microphone and then get him to give the necessary answers. I ..." Lis knew she had to be very careful not to reveal that she had been there herself and had spied around the building during the night.

"You're crazy, you're both crazy, have you lost your minds? That's not an option. What if he shoots you!" Matthew was upset. "Alfonse, this is madness," he added. "We'd better call the police."

"No, we won't," said Lis firmly.

"As long as Lamborelle thinks he's on safe ground, he won't be that dangerous. Besides, we don't have a shred of evidence. And your brother Jeff feels safe too, everyone feels safe, and that's our chance," said Alfonse.

"I'm not afraid of this man!" Lis emphasised, "Tomorrow I'll call and see if I can get an appointment."

"We will go there as Mr. and Mrs. Kaufmann," said Thomas resolutely.

"No, I will go without Mr. Kaufmann."

"I want to come with you, Lis, it's safer for you," said Thomas.

"That's sweet of you, Thomas, but I'll do it alone. I'm going to have to face this man anyway, sooner or later. I'm going to get it over with."

"I don't know," said David, "I don't like this plan. If even the slightest thing goes wrong, it will blow up in our faces!"

"Well," said Alfonse, "it might work. Besides, if anything goes wrong, we'll be outside, and I'm a professional after all, don't forget that. To be on the safe side, I'll put Bob in the picture, because he's already helped me discreetly with the data investigations. You never know. And if there are any problems, he can call in reinforcements. Better safe than sorry!"

"Why don't we involve the police right from the start?" asked Thomas.

"We have no evidence, we don't even know who else is involved, and we don't want to carry out a police operation with a hundred men because if Commissioner Kraus marches in, it will be with special forces and all the trimmings. We need evidence for that, which we don't have, not yet. It will be an endless conversation that will get us nowhere. And then we might be charged over it, depending on how it's judged. I'm in favour of handling this discreetly and in my own way.

"Besides, we don't want to cause mass panic in the hospital," Alfonse continued. "A task force storming the McKenna Clinic, I can already see it on the news. No, no, absolutely not. Bob can act in an emergency and call for backup. Then there's still time to call in Kraus if things get really dicey."

Alfonse insisted on this approach.

"Well, as far as our hospital is concerned," Matthew said, "I'm sure Jeff, my half-brother, is at least involved in Diane's disappearance, because I saw him coming out of Room 1112 that night when I checked. I can't imagine he's innocent. Besides, someone from the clinic must be fully in the picture because who else could have implanted the microchips in us?"

"Of course, there must be at least two or three involved," said Alfonse. "But if Peter Lamborelle suspects that we're on to him, he'll certainly consult with Jeff."

"Listen, we're in dangerous territory here. Who can guarantee that these people won't turn violent when they realise that everything could blow up and we're on their trail?" Alan didn't think this planned action was ideal either.

"Well, they already know what's going on, otherwise they wouldn't have wanted you and Matthew out of the way, would they?" said Lis. "But it can only be in connection with Diane. No one knows yet that we know what happened then and no one knows that we know about the adoption thing, do they?"

"I wouldn't be so sure about that," said Matthew. "I just don't think it's a good idea for you to go there alone."

"Yes," said Lis, "I'll call first thing in the morning and make an appointment. And I'm sticking to it! I've made up my mind!"

"And where should we start then?" asked Alan.

"Well, we have another problem in the meantime," Lis confessed. "Caro called this morning. She noticed that Diane Van Helden is no longer in Room 1112, and her file now says that Diane left the clinic on July 6."

"Oh no, Diane!" said Alan in a panic. "Well, you do your thing, I'll go to the clinic tomorrow and then I'll keep looking there. She must still be there. What do you think, Matthew?"

"I assume so, because she was in a coma a few days ago and it takes time for someone to get back on their feet. Except ..."

"Except what?" Alan looked at him seriously.

"We don't want to assume that but ... unless something has happened to her."

"No, I can't and won't believe that. And in that case, why would they have let her live so long?"

"Well, I'll go to the clinic with Alan and have a look around. We'll do it discreetly. We can't all go to Lamborelle's office anyway," David suggested.

"Good, then I'll take Thomas with me," said Alfonse. "Lis and Matthew, you're going in a car together. Let me know as soon as you have an appointment. Now is the time to hurry," said Alfonse.

"Who actually owns the orphanage here in the country? Who is it registered to?" asked Alan. "To Lamborelle?"

"No," corrected Alfonse, "I looked it up and it's only registered as Little Angels Asbl, non-profit company, but the business owners are not listed in the company register. I find that a bit strange, because that's where you normally find every company and its owners and shareholders."

"That is indeed strange," commented Thomas. "And the orphanage on the island?"

"Even less information. Pequeños Angeles and the address, and nothing else. But I'm less surprised there, but here in this country?"

"Can you ask your colleague to do some research on Clervaux as well?"

"Bob is still on it, but there doesn't seem to be an owner listed. He'll keep looking."


It was a long evening with many lively discussions but the original plan remained in place. Lis was to make an appointment in Clervaux and try to seek out Lamborelle with a hidden microphone. Thomas and Alfonse would support her from outside.

David and Alan would go to the clinic and try to discreetly find out something about Diane; how, they didn't know exactly yet.

Matthew stayed on after everyone had said goodbye. He was standing opposite Lis in the corridor.

"You have nothing to worry about, believe me." She saw that he looked worried. "I'll manage."

"I have my doubts about that, Lis, to be honest. I'm seriously worried that if you're alone in a room with this ... this criminal, the situation could escalate quickly, are you aware of that?"

Lis took a step towards Matthew and put her arms around his neck.

"I can do it. And besides, and this information is just for you, not for Alfonse or for the boys. I'll have a gun in my pocket."

"You ... What? No, Lis, that's really enough. There's no way you're doing that!"

"I know how to handle a gun, Matt, I learned how to shoot. Trust me. And please don't say a word to Alfonse."

"I don't like it and I don't understand why you have to do it. You don't have to prove anything to yourself or anyone else!"

She kissed him on the nose. "It's not about proving anything to anyone. I want to clear everything up, once and for all. You'll keep this to yourself, you have to promise me that. And I'll do what I've planned. Don't worry, I'm not planning to shoot the man. That would be far too easy for him. I want to hear him tell me the truth and Alfonse needs to nail him. That's all. The gun is only for my defence if, and only if, it will be necessary, okay?"

"No, not okay, not okay at all. But okay, I won't say anything. Come on, you're asking a lot of me!"

"I know. We have to put a stop to this, Matt. Think of all the children who weren't orphans, think of the parents!"

Matthew hugged her tightly. "What about Jeff and my adoptive father and Brigitte, who must have realised something's wrong by now? Do you know how I feel? I want to sit in a corner and pull a big blanket over me and forget about this whole world for a while."

"That wouldn't be so bad. Once all the problems are solved, I'll come to you straight away."

They stood together for a long time, without many words.

"How's Eric?" Matthew finally asked.

"He's with Caro. He called briefly to say he couldn't find her, she was on duty until 2 p.m. and was supposed to meet him. They probably passed each other by, but he texted shortly afterwards to say that everything was fine."

"Good to know," said Matthew and went home too.


Lis had just showered and was about to lie down on the sofa in her bathrobe when her cell phone rang.

"Hello Lis, this is James."

"James! Has something happened? You sound restless."

"No, do you have a moment, I have something to tell you?" Lis looked at her watch, it was already 10.30 p.m.

"Yes, sure. Right now?"

"Actually, I'm right outside your front door. Can I come in or would you like to get in the car with me? It's really important."

"You're ... at my door ... Yes, then come in. Give me two minutes and I'll open it."

She quickly slipped into a purple tracksuit, tugged a little at her wet hair in front of the mirror in the hallway, and then opened the front door.

James Hammer was standing there in jeans, a black shirt and a leather jacket.

"I'm really sorry to disturb you at this late hour, but something seems to be brewing."

"Come in first and have a seat. Coffee?"

"Thank you, yes!"

Lis let him into the living room, made two coffees in the kitchen, and then sat down opposite him.

"Now I see you in the light. When we first met, everything was pretty dark," Lis said with a smile.

James looked at her closely, her long, wet hair hanging loose in her face.

"Well, that's true. It was a great night," he confirmed. "Please give me your phone, you'll get it back when I leave your apartment."

"My what? Is that necessary?" Lis thought it was excessive, but she did it without protest and put her cell phone on the table. James Hammer took it, switched it off and immediately put it in a case, which he pulled out of his pocket and then placed on the table.

"Thank you! At least now we're sure that no one can listen in," he explained briefly.

"I see ..." She looked at him suspiciously. "So, what's happened?" she asked impatiently.

"The thing is: Over the last three evenings, our man has driven around your block of flats several times without stopping. But he has only ever looked past this building and then driven on. So I would ask you to be particularly careful! I assume he's up to something."

"You're watching my apartment?"

"Yes and no, I wasn't actually planning to do that. But since I was following his car, I quickly found out that he was driving around here. When it happened once, I didn't think anything more of it. But after two more nights, I started to find it disturbing."

"And you knew exactly where I lived?"

"I didn't know until then. But when I drove around here the second night, I found out. He must have been looking for something interesting, otherwise he wouldn't have done it three nights in a row. He didn't get out, but stopped for a few minutes, then drove on and watched this building. Your address is nowhere to be found, but since I had your name, it wasn't difficult."

"Ex-secret service, I see."

"Yes, that's the way it is. I'll be honest, I didn't have to tell you all this. I could have just waited without warning you and then seen what he was up to."

"That's right. Somehow we're in the same boat." Lis said thoughtfully as he continued to let his eyes rest on her. *He looks a little sad*, Lis thought, discreetly loving to look at him.

James Hammer was very taken with this woman. This surprised and frightened him at the same time, as this had not been an issue since the death of his wife.

"Then he's probably looking for me. Maybe he recognised me on the plane?"

"Quite possibly. If you had recognised him straight away, he might have done the same," James guessed. He leaned back on the sofa.

"The lady in the clinic, I mentioned her, she is no longer in her room either," said Lis.

"How do you know that?"

"My son's girlfriend works there and noticed it."

"Then maybe she's in danger too."

"I don't think so, nobody suspects her as an employee. Besides, nobody knows about this connection."

"That's what you think! But I wouldn't be so sure."

"Yes, but ... Now you're scaring me."

"That's not my intention, I just want you to be careful and not underestimate these people for a second."

James looked at his watch.

"What should I do now?" asked Lis, a little worried.

"Nothing at the moment, we have no clues as to what he's up to. Besides, it's already pretty late."

"Was he here again tonight?"

James nodded in the affirmative. "When I called you, he'd just left. I waited a few minutes after that, but he didn't do the usual round the block, he didn't come back."

"You said 'these' people. Who are they?"

"I don't know yet who exactly the people are who are working with him, but I'll find out," James said quietly but firmly. Lis could see the resolve in his eyes.

"And then?"

"I'm not that far yet. I'll find out when we reach that point."

"You're really determined to bring these people down. Then you'd better watch your own life while you're at it."

"I'll do my best." He smiled. "I'll keep you in the loop as much as you want, and you'll keep me in the loop?"

"Good plan. After all, we're both involved in this, each in our own way, but we've both suffered a lot because of this man."

"We sure have," James became thoughtful for a few moments.

Somehow Lis sensed that James Hammer was in no hurry to leave.

"The day we realised that our daughter had just disappeared, it was like ... I still can't explain it. You know, I told her a bedtime story every night, even on that last night. And this story, this very last story that I told her, I haven't been able to get it out of my head since. I think about it every night, even now. I don't know how many times I've remembered those last moments when I was close to her. She looked so happy, we laughed, we chatted."

Suddenly James realised he was reminiscing and cleared his throat. "I'm sorry, I didn't mean to bother you with this, we have other problems to solve ... I ... better get back on the road."

"I can well imagine those moments," Lis said sympathetically. "I don't know if it will ever be possible to get over it."

"I don't know either." He had tears in his eyes. "I don't know," he whispered.

Lis' eyes met James's again and without words they looked at each other intensely.

"Would you like another coffee?" Lis asked, a little unsure whether she should.

*Oh dear*, she thought, *this is getting more and more complicated.*

"No, thanks." James stood up. He was also a little lost for words. Lis stood up too.

He took the case with her cell phone and gave it back to her.

"It's time for me to go home. I'll be in touch again. And please be careful not to tell your friends about our encounter!"

"Sure!" said Lis, although she was a little confused. She walked with him to the front door. "Thank you for warning me!"

He turned around once more. Her heart beat faster.

"You're welcome. Please be careful and don't underestimate our man. He really is dangerous."

*I have the impression that the man in front of me is the more dangerous one at the moment*, Lis thought.

James was just about to turn back to the door when he felt Lis' hand on his arm.

Then he looked at her and took a step closer.

He gently touched her face and let his fingers glide over her cheek.

"I'm not sure if this is the right time," he whispered as he gently pulled her towards him.

"Me neither," Lis managed to say before their lips met. A simple kiss that quickly became more intense and intimate.

James wrapped his arms around Lis and she held him tightly.

He looked at her, brushed a strand of hair out of her face and touched her cheek again.

"There's something magical about your eyes," Lis whispered and gave him a beautiful smile.

"When I saw you outside the orphanage and a little later on the street when I fell over, I knew I really wanted to see you again. But the situation was too delicate," she confessed.

"Yes, that was and unfortunately still is the case," he agreed.

"We'll get through this together," said Lis. "We'll have to."

"Right. Now, brave and pretty woman, take good care of yourself, lock the door when I'm out, and be vigilant. I'll be in touch as soon as I know anything, okay?"

"I promise." She put her arms around his neck, and they kissed again.

"I'm also very good at defending myself if I need to. I'm trained in self-defence."

"That's very good, for a start. But if someone points their weapon at you, you can't necessarily use yours. You still have to be careful and vigilant!"

"I promise, James." She looked at him intensely and felt butterflies in her stomach. She had fallen in love.

He hugged her one last time.

"Sleep well! See you tomorrow!" He tapped her nose with his finger and looked happy at that moment. He smiled slightly.

Lis was completely overwhelmed by his hypnotic gaze. Then he left and she locked the door as agreed. She leaned against the door and thought for a few more moments about what had just happened.

She had deliberately not told James Hammer that she wanted to pay an official visit to the orphanage tomorrow with her friends. *It never hurts to be careful*, she thought, *despite his hypnotising eyes.*

## TUESDAY, AUGUST 13

The night was filled with chaotic dreams and thoughts. After breakfast, Lis called the orphanage in Clervaux and, as Mrs. Kaufmann, was able to make an appointment with Peter Lamborelle for 3 p.m. the same day.

David and Alan had decided to look for Diane on their own and made their way to the clinic around midday. They didn't yet know how or what exactly they were going to do there. They started with a coffee in the cafeteria and discreetly observed the visitors and staff. At home, they had memorised the faces of Jeff and John McKenna, whose photos could be found on the clinic's website.

Matthew had arranged to pick Lis up at around 1.30 p.m.. Alfonse would drive with Thomas and they would all meet later in Clervaux.

James Hammer was following Lamborelle's car again. He was all the more surprised to see Lamborelle driving in the direction of Lis' apartment.

It was just after 12 p.m. when Lis heard the doorbell ring. As she was expecting Matthew a little earlier, she immediately pressed the button and opened the front door to the building.

She opened the front door straight away and heard footsteps shortly afterwards. "I'm in the kitchen, come in Matt!"

The footsteps came closer, and just as she was about to turn around, she felt the barrel of a gun in her back.

"Calm down and don't do anything rash, Elisabeth Bouvier!"

Lis felt like she had been struck by lightning as she turned around.

Peter Lamborelle stood in front of her with a gun.

"You?" She was in shock and almost paralysed with fear. She hadn't even put her gun in her handbag yet.

"We don't have much time! Here, tie yourself up! I'm not here to argue, so do it or your son won't survive today, do you understand that?"

"Eric? Where is Eric, what have you done with him?"

Lis did as he ordered and handcuffed herself. She was trembling.

"He and his super-curious girlfriend à la Miss Marple have been in a safe and, above all, escape-proof place since yesterday. Why do they have to stick their noses in everything that's none of their business? Leave it to the professionals!"

"Tell me where they are, right now. Where is my son?" Lis shouted.

"Later, get out of here first, let's go! It's all very simple. The gun is under my jacket and pointed at you. My car is parked a little further up the road. You sit in the back seat. And Elisabeth Bouvier, I'm only going to say this once, if you try an unexpected stunt, your son and his girlfriend will be dead. Have I made myself clear?"

"I'll kill you, Peter Lamborelle, I've wanted to do that for a long time!"

Then they went downstairs. There was no one in the foyer nor in the stairwell.

James Hammer was sitting unseen in his car further up the street. He watched the two come out of the house.

*Damn,* he thought. He quickly got out and followed unobtrusively at a safe distance. He couldn't possibly take his car now; that would attract too much attention.

When Lamborelle and Lis reached the Jaguar in the side street, he opened the rear door.

"Inside!"

After seconds of hesitation, she did so. As she was entering, Lamborelle hit her so hard on the head with the gun that she collapsed unconscious onto the back seat.

He got in himself within seconds, started the engine and sped off.

James saw this and ran back to his car as fast as he could. Since he had already attached a tracking device to the Jaguar days ago, he simply followed the signal and caught up with the car within a few minutes.

Just after 1.30 p.m., Matthew rang Lis' doorbell several times, but she didn't answer. He immediately called Alfonse and told him.

"I'm coming over with Thomas, wait there. We're on the highway right now."

Ten minutes later they arrived. They hurriedly got out of the car.

"That's not her way, Alfonse. She knows I'm supposed to pick her up. No cell phone, no sign, I'm worried. Come on, let's break down the door," Matthew said to Alfonse.

"I can unlock it, don't worry," he said.

Five minutes later, Alfonse had opened the front door and upstairs they immediately saw that the front door was only ajar.

"Maybe she's in the shower and has already opened the door for you to be on the safe side?" asked Thomas.

"No, she would hardly do that!"

Lis' handbag was in the hallway, and even her knife, which she usually had strapped around her ankle, was lying next to it. Matthew looked in her bag, the gun was there. He didn't want to say anything about it at the moment.

"Here, her knife, she never leaves the house without a knife. Alfonse, something has happened here. Do something. This is not normal. Someone has kidnapped her. We have to call the police."

Just then, Matthew received a text message.

*Elisabeth Bouvier is with me. If you don't want someone to die, don't call the police. Further instructions will follow. PL.*

Thomas, Alfonse and Matthew stared at the message.

"Damn! What now, ex-inspector?" asked Matthew. "I hope you have a Plan B!"

"Where could he have taken her?"

"To the clinic!" Matthew shouted. "He can hardly go home and he probably can't go to the orphanage either."

Alfonse had the presence of mind to call Alan and David, who were in the clinic's cafeteria and briefly explained what had happened.

"Fantastic that you're already here. And thanks for the information in advance!" He couldn't help making this sarcastic remark.

"Don't do anything for now, keep an eye on everything; one of you stand guard at reception, the other can watch the entrance to the clinic from the underground parking lot. You both know his face as well as Lis'. So, keep an eye out, I'm sure he'll take her there."

"Okay!" was all Alan said. "What does the vehicle look like?"

"No idea! Something expensive, I should think," Alfonse shouted into the phone.

"Alfonse, this really sucks!" Thomas was standing next to him.

"I know, man! We have to go to the clinic to see your brother Jeff and your father," Alfonse looked at Matthew seriously.

"Okay, and Alfonse, leave the police out of it. Four people's lives are already in danger!" Matthew said.

"Oh boy," said Thomas, "that's not going to work."

"We have no choice if we don't want corpses," said Alfonse sharply.

"Come on guys, off to the clinic."

"Matthew, give us a description of the clinic, what's where?" asked Alfonse as they sped to the clinic.

"Downstairs in B1 and B2 are the surgical facilities, but there are also some intensive care rooms there where special diseases are monitored. There are so many rooms there, I can't list them all.

"B3 houses the morgue, an autopsy room and some other surgical facilities.

"The parking lots in these basement levels each have direct access to the clinic with a special code. Visitors must go through reception."

"Okay, better than nothing."

Alfonse pulled out his cell phone and called his former colleague Bob Wagner, giving him all the details.

"Yes, go to the clinic as soon as possible and stay outside until further notice, he said. "Bring your colleague with you. Tell him it's all top secret. I'll be in touch if it becomes necessary."

"Will do Mr. Weis, we're already on our way. And if Inspector Kraus asks me, I'll tell him that we have an urgent matter to attend to."

"Tell him what you want, just not the truth. Otherwise, we'll have him outside the clinic with a special unit with a hundred men and then there'll be a panic, I guarantee it! He could evacuate the entire clinic and we don't want that—not yet. Thank you very much!"

"Do you think your father is involved?" Alfonse asked Matthew, looking at him in the rear-view mirror.

"No, I don't think so, his clinic is sacred to him, but after everything we've seen so far, I wouldn't bet on it either."

Alfonse drove at full speed and in less than twenty minutes Alfonse, Thomas and Matthew had reached the clinic.

"We'll go after my brother now and then we'll get my father John involved too. If Lis dies, I'll kill Jeff and Lamborelle myself!" roared Matthew.

David was at the reception desk and Alan was monitoring the entrance to the parking lot.

Peter Lamborelle pulled into the driveway of the B parking lot, leaving James outside, unable to enter the private carpark.

Spontaneously, he parked on the side of the road, half on the sidewalk, got out and walked to the main entrance of the clinic. Arriving at the reception, he looked for the elevator and caught it down to the B parking lot. A map of the basement in the elevator provided an overview of the clinic. He noted that the parking lot provided access to the operating theatres, but only with the access code.

Lis slowly regained consciousness. She found herself lying on the floor of a brightly lit room and her head hurt like hell. Her hands and legs were bound, she realised. Next to her head, she saw the feet of someone standing less than a meter away from her.

"Get up, Elisabeth Bouvier! We don't have much time."

She rubbed her eyes as much as she could with the handcuffs on.

Then she stood up slowly, her head aching badly. She looked around. There were cupboards, materials, machines, and a large ceiling light, like the ones used in surgery.

"Sit on that chair there. Here, drink some water!"

Peter Lamborelle handed her a glass. "Careful, and don't make a wrong move! Then it will continue to be painless for you."

Lis sat down on the chair and drank some water.

"It's just a laceration on your head, I've looked at it. Don't worry."

The grey-blond man looked at her with his small eyes. *Just like Eric's eyes*, Lis thought, *Eric looks like him.*

"What did you do with Eric?" she demanded.

"With Eric and Caro, feel free to ask!"

"What? You have Caro too?"

"That actually went quite smoothly. Your son practically ran into my hands when he was looking for Caro, who unfortunately didn't come out to meet him after the 2 p.m. shift. If he hadn't picked her up, or let's say wanted to pick her up, he wouldn't be involved right now."

"Where is he, where are you holding them?"

"Do you seriously think I'm that stupid?"

Her heart was pounding in her throat but she had to get through this situation now.

"One question has been bothering me for a long time, you shabby scumbag." Lis looked him straight in the face. "You knew who I was from the start, didn't you?"

"Well, since we were on the flight to Santo Domingo together and I looked you in the eye, yes! And I think you knew it at the same moment!"

Lis forced herself to calm down. She breathed in and out deeply. Now, of all times, she didn't have her knife with her, and she had to rely only on her own wits. Lamborelle looked at her with amusement.

"That surprises you now, right? Of course I knew that. I also knew who you were and are traveling with. The microchip in Matthew's foot was helpful. It's just a shame he removed it later."

"How can a person become like you? What are you missing?"

"What was I missing, you ask?" he repeated in a gruff tone. "Nothing really, except that my father wasn't home for ten years and I was allowed to visit him in prison once a week. Is that what you call a bad childhood that leaves its mark? And how it leaves its mark even though I was already a young adult by then! But you know the whole story well enough. We don't need to brush up on it now."

"Do you really think you'll get away with it?" Lis raised her voice.

"You won't believe it, but yes, I think so. If you're referring to the people who are probably looking for you now, we'll take care of that, don't worry.

"If you're hanging around with my wife's lover and making appointments as Mrs. Kaufmann, I can't imagine you are wanting to come to me for adoption papers."

He continued to stare at her.

"Caro and Eric are somewhere they can't be seen or heard until we've sorted everything out. Then we'll see."

"What have you done with Mrs. Van Helden? She's no longer in Room 1112, is she?" Lis looked at him with a look that was more than contemptuous.

"Oh, do you know where she was lying? It seems as if Caro has been snooping everywhere. I should have been more careful, but I didn't know she was involved with your son until recently."

"You're such a bastard! Why couldn't you leave the whole Van Helden family alone after your father got out of prison? Everything was fine, I had come to terms with my situation, why do you want to destroy the whole Van Helden family now? Can't you even make peace with yourself? How could you?"

"If Diane had kept her hands out of my business, things might have gone a little smoother. She maneuvered her way into the situation, and I was done with Caro and her parents, too. But now you turn up and turn everything upside down."

"You snatched Caro from her biological parents just like that! Can you imagine how much her parents must have suffered for over twenty years?" said Lis.

"Sure I do! Are you getting sentimental now? I suffered too, but nobody cared at the time! Besides, Caro found good adoptive parents, she didn't mind. And it wasn't about punishing Caro, I was just aiming at her biological mother, Laetitia Van Helden, one of Gerard Van Helden's daughters."

He stared at Lis, his eyes filled with hatred and revenge.

"And by taking Caro away, I punished her grandfather, Gerard Van Helden. He was the one who set things in motion. If he hadn't put my father behind bars back then, his family would have remained untouched. But I had to punish him, I thought for years about how I could hurt him the most. In the end, I had plenty of time to come up with a plan. And I could only do that by dealing with his two daughters and causing them as much pain as I could. So, Laetitia Van Helden, Caro's biological mother and daughter of Gerard Van Helden, lost her daughter and that hurt Gerard Van Helden. But I also took Gerard's wife, Emilie Fox, away from him. That was a tragic accident. Strange how things happen!" He shook his head.

Lis loathed this man. He really seemed to have developed into more of a monster over the years.

"So left was only Diane to deal with. What would you have done with her if she had stayed with you?"

"I didn't have a concrete plan yet, but I wanted to get to know her father Gerard through her. I wanted to hear from him how much he was suffering from all these tragic family dramas. It would have been nice if he had told me everything bit by bit, his future son-in-law. But unfortunately, that didn't happen. Diane started snooping around Santo Domingo too much, wanting to adopt a little girl from there, and then finally she tried to separate from me. But that wasn't part of the plan; I needed her to get to her father. I should have killed her as soon as she was admitted to hospital. Then I'd have one less problem now."

"And who would have issued you the death certificate? You're not a doctor, thank God!"

"Jeff, of course, your master magician's brother. He really had fun the day he implanted a chip in his own brother. It was so easy to bring Jeff into the game. Plus, he really got into working with the adopted kids when I brought them here from time to time.

He was happy to help. I suddenly had a free hand at the clinic, and because he was involved, there was never a problem if we had a child who suddenly got sick and didn't have a new passport yet."

"I think his father will despise him for it," said Lis.

"It's a bit late for that, isn't it? Besides, he's been fooling his father for so long. He's going to have to find out that his favourite son isn't the ideal son. Jeff was fed up with his bossy father. He was very happy that he could cheat him with this part-time job, if you can call it that. Jeff has access to everything here, which has benefited me enormously in my work. We work hand in hand, and we don't make a bad living."

"You make me want to vomit! If you hurt my son, I will kill you, I promise you that. I would have liked to do it then, but I certainly will now. You let Eric and Caro go, and you're letting them go now!"

"No, I'm not going to do that. It's not like I'm going to put the rope around my own neck. But I will have to leave you for a while, and so you will have to stay here. I'm afraid I'm going to have to tape your mouth shut. Perhaps this reminds you of an incident that happened many years ago? Yes?"

And how Lis remembered. Back then when they put her in the room, her mouth was bound with tape and her hands and feet were bound. She couldn't think back to that now.

Lamborelle took a roll of bandages and taped Lis' mouth shut. She tried to resist, but it was no use. "I'll be right back. Make yourself comfortable!"

He put on a white coat, hung a stethoscope around his neck, switched off the light and left the room, which he locked from the outside.

Lis was in a complete panic. Locked in a dark room, she crawled towards the door and started banging her feet against it. But who could hear her here?

In the meantime, Alfonse, Thomas and Matthew had also arrived at the clinic.

While Thomas stayed at the reception desk, Matthew and Alfonse took the elevator directly to the third floor, where Jeff and John McKenna had their personal offices.

Matthew knocked on the door of Jeff McKenna's office.

"Come in."

When Jeff McKenna saw the two men, he stood up immediately. He was wearing a white coat and was slightly shorter and slimmer than Matthew.

"Good afternoon. What's this about, we haven't made an appointment, as far as I remember."

"This isn't a patient of mine, Jeff," Matthew said. "We're here to talk. I'm going to ask John to join the session now."

"What's going on here? What do we have to talk about?"

"We'll get to that in a minute," said Matthew. "Please, come on, let's sit here at the table. It's very important."

Jeff sat down after Matthew had introduced Alfonse. Under the pretext of having to discuss an urgent matter in Jeff's office, he then called John McKenna, who appeared a few minutes later.

"Good afternoon," he said, looking at Alfonse. "What's going on?"

"We have a few things to clarify, Professor McKenna." Alfonse walked up to him and held out his hand. "My name is Alfonse Weis, and I'm a retired police inspector."

"I see, I'm pleased to meet you. How can I help you?"

"Please sit down, John, there appear to be serious problems at your clinic," Matthew said and then turned his gaze to Jeff, who shrugged his shoulders and looked at his father.

"Jeff, John, there are things going on in this clinic that are not right. We've been working for quite some time to finally fix it, and my guess is that you, Jeff, are part of all of this."

John looked at his son with an angry look that Matthew remembered only too well from his childhood.

"A woman, Diane Van Helden, has been held here in the clinic since July 6. This woman was hit by a car, came here to the clinic with a friend, and has been missing ever since. We were able to find out that she never left the clinic, despite what was confirmed to her friend. She has since been moved from Room 1112 to another location."

Matthew paused for a moment. Then he focused on Jeff.

"Before you try to escape, the police are outside, so you have no chance of getting away. This is just for your information, Jeff!"

"What on earth is going on here?" asked John McKenna angrily.

"Hold on, we'll get to that in a minute," said Matthew.

"There's a certain Dr. Peter Lamborelle here in the clinic who isn't a doctor at all, but goes around in a doctor's coat and organises criminal activities under that guise. I assume Jeff is working with him and doing the dirty work, because Jeff, I saw you come out of Mrs. Van Helden's room when I was here one night. All of this has yet to be proven and substantiated.

"Someone also implanted a microchip in my foot so that we could be monitored and tracked if necessary."

"Could you repeat that?" John McKenna said sharply.

"Wait, Dad, just listen. When I was in Santo Domingo with a friend, Alan Moore, we were both kidnapped and detained. During that time, we discovered that we both had microchips in our feet. We removed them as soon as we found out about it. The chips explain why we were both knocked out and kidnapped as soon as we got to the airport terminal."

"This is the first I'm hearing about this, Matthew!" John cried.

"I know, but I wasn't sure if you were in on it or not, or if you would talk to Jeff about it, so I decided not to say anything, until ..."

"For heaven's sake, Matthew! You've got to be joking." Then he looked at Jeff.

"Jeff, what do you have to say about this? Speak now, you have one minute, is it true or not? Go ahead! Say it's not true!"

Jeff looked at his father and then at Matthew.

"I won't say anything without my lawyer!" His face stiffened.

John McKenna stood up and walked towards Jeff.

Alfonse watched the scene carefully, but did not intervene.

When John McKenna stood in front of his son, he looked at him with contempt.

"Get up!"

Without saying a word, Jeff did what his father had just ordered him to do. Then his father slapped him so hard that Jeff was thrown backwards and hit the wall.

Weis intervened now. He grabbed John McKenna's arm before he could strike again.

"Come on, Dr. McKenna, that doesn't change anything now. I understand your feelings, but please sit down again. After we've discussed everything here, we'll unfortunately have to take you and your son into custody."

"Me too? I can assure you that I had no idea about any of this."

"We have to check that, do you understand?"

"Where is this Lamborelle?" asked John.

"We don't know yet, but it seems that he taken Lis Chandler, alias Elisabeth Bouvier, with him against her will."

"Who, what? What does Elisabeth have to do with this?"

"It's a very long story, Father, but we don't have time for it now. Right now, we have to find Mrs. Van Helden and Lamborelle.

Where are they, Jeff? You know exactly! You have one minute, or I'll beat the information out of you!"

Jeff looked like a dishevelled dog that had been out in the rain and storm.

"I have no idea! All I know is that Peter Lamborelle treated her after the car accident. Doctor Michel is also involved. He had the woman transferred from 1112 to B3. He didn't know what to do after they had to bring her out of her coma."

John McKenna jumped up and before Weis could hold him back, he again slapped his son Jeff, this time so hard that he tipped backwards with his chair. The professor had tears in his eyes. Then he sat down again, while Jeff wordlessly stood up and straightened the chair.

"Why Jeff, why. Look at me, damn it, why? What a disgrace! What a fucking disgrace!"

Jeff just shrugged his shoulders.

"Talk or I'll kill you!"

Jeff cleared his throat. "It was just fun at first. I met Peter Lamborelle at a conference many years ago and we got on well. He told me about his orphanage in Santo Domingo and the good that he does there. But little by little I learned that he had orphaned almost all of the children involved and then placed them with Luxembourgian couples, rich couples, for absurd sums of money. And at some point, he had a child who needed urgent medical treatment and I told him to bring her to our clinic. And that's how it all started. When he had a child that needed treatment, I would bring it here, and then he would come regularly and pretend to be a doctor."

"I don't believe it!" was all John said, "My son, a sleazy criminal. And the chip?" he then went on.

"Matthew has been having an affair with Peter's wife for years, so one day Peter asked me if I could put a chip in Matthew if the opportunity arose. At first it was just a joke, we talked about it, joked about it, but when Matthew came to the clinic with his meniscus problem, we thought it was the perfect opportunity."

"You're a scumbag," Matthew said. "Why? What more did you need for fame, eh? After all, you already had your father's full attention, wasn't that enough?"

"It was ... It was interesting, Peter paid very well for each child to be treated. And we didn't take anything away from anyone."

"Took nothing from anyone?" asked John. "This man kidnapped children and you say he didn't take anything from anyone?!"

"The parents who adopted those children were all filthy rich anyway. So I thought I'd support him and earn some extra money."

"And how did all these children get registered here? Certainly not under their real names."

"No, they all had fake IDs when they came here. Except for a few, they got their IDs later."

John McKenna opened a window. "I need some air!" He stood at the window in silence for a few minutes. "My reputation, my clinic, my own son working against me. Oh my God, that's how low you've sunk!" He shook his head. Then he turned back to Alfonse.

"Okay, Mr. Weis, take us both with you, I have nothing to hide. I'll go with you."

"I think we'll just take your son for now, Dr. McKenna," said Alfonse. "I've never gone on a manhunt so unprepared," he mumbled a little sheepishly. "I didn't even bring any handcuffs."

"But I did," Matthew said and tossed them to Weis. "Professional habit," he joked.


With his hands in the cuffs, Jeff was led out of the room by Matthew and Alfonse. They went to the basement.

In the meantime, James Hammer had searched the parking lots

on levels B1 and B2. It was the first time he had been to the clinic, and he didn't know his way around. Apart from the parking lots, there were only operating rooms in the basement and one room that looked like it was for storage.

He then went down one floor, to B3, where the morgue was located and immediately spotted Lamborelle's Jaguar near the entrance. The door was locked with a keypad. He had to go back to the front desk and then take the elevator to B3. He had his gun ready in his jacket.

When he opened the heavy metal door, there was a long corridor behind it with doors on both sides. They seemed to lead to different storage rooms that were not labelled.

"Lis, are you here?" James shouted as loud as he could. He opened every door that wasn't locked, but to no avail. No one was there.

Just as he was about to go back, he heard a muffled noise, a kind of knocking. It was coming from a room he had already opened. He went back.

"Lis?"

The knocking became stronger. Lis could hear a voice, but she couldn't make a louder sound. She was already banging her feet against the door.

Then James found the door where the noise was coming from. "Lis?"

The knocking came again. She must be in here.

"Get away from the door," James shouted. "I have to shoot the lock open! Get back!"

The shot he then fired could certainly be heard everywhere, at least for those who had experience with this kind of sound.

Alfonse and Matthew, who were in the stairwell, stopped short and looked at each other.

"That was definitely a shot," said Weis.

"Oh no! Come on, quick!" They ran down the stairs.

The shot had damaged the door lock and James was now able to open the door. With his gun drawn, he rushed in and found Lis handcuffed, her feet bound, and bandages taped around her mouth.

He quickly ran to her and knelt down next to her.

"Lis, it's okay, just relax! I'm here now!"

She was breathing fast. Full of fear, she wanted to scream.

First, he removed the tape from her mouth as carefully as possible.

"Please don't shout," he cautioned. "We don't want any visitors here!" Finally, the tape was off.

"James! I thought I was going to die …" She looked at him with tears in her eyes.

"Come on, get up," James held out his hands and helped her up. Then he took her in his arms without a word and let her cry.

He looked at her firmly. "Everything is all right. Everything is all right. Calm down, take a deep breath and exhale."

James held her again until she relaxed a little. There was little time before someone would undoubtedly show up.

"Where are we, where is my son, how did you get here? Where is Lamborelle?" Lis was trembling all over.

"I'm going to untie your hands and feet now, but you need to try to calm down first, please! Take a deep breath."

She nodded.

While James took off her ankle cuffs, he looked at her.

"I'm afraid I don't know where your son is. We're in the McKenna Clinic, in basement B3, and we really need to keep a clear head now. Now, do you trust me? Because there's no other way to unlock the handcuffs. Put your arms out and turn your face away."

Lis did so, and with a precise aim, James shot the handcuffs apart.

Weis and Matthew had also heard that second shot.

"It's coming from further down. Go to B2 or B3," Weis instructed.

At that very moment, Weis received a text message from Alan. *I'm now at reception with David and Thomas. Lamborelle just came by in his white coat to get into the elevator. We heard gunshots.*

Weis texted back. *David, come down, we're going to B2. Tell Thomas to stay and keep an eye on the reception!*

"That Dr. Michel might be there too," Matthew said. "We have to be very careful that they don't panic and make a hasty move. You never know."

B2 was a floor with another long corridor with countless doors to the right and left.

David and Alan appeared, both out of breath.

"There are a lot of operating rooms here, she must be here somewhere. If the red light above the door is on, we're not allowed in. Please note that," Matthew explained.

"Sure," David spoke up. "Let's listen at all the doors and if we hear anything, then ..."

"Why don't you raise the alarm, Matthew, and have the whole clinic evacuated? Then we'll soon have the cat out of the bag," suggested Alan.

"Are you insane?" Matthew looked at him, stunned. "Do you know what kind of panic that will cause. We can't do that. We have to find out where Diane and Lis are. I hope they're alright."

In the meantime, Weis received a text message from Bob Wagner. *We're standing in front of the back entrance to the hospital emergency room, should we position ourselves here?*

*Yes,* Weis returned the text, *and wait for my instructions.*

*Understood, Mr. Weis.*

In the meantime, on B3, James had fetched a glass of water from the sink and handed it to Lis. "Here, drink this, it'll help you."

Lis sat down and took the water.

"Better?"

She nodded and wiped her eyes shakily.

"The morgue is next door," he explained. "We're on B3."

"That monster!" She slowly explained to James what had happened and told him about her conversation with Lamborelle.

"He also has Eric and Caro ... What should we do?"

"First we have to get out of here before he comes back. Then we'll see."

"He said he would kill Eric if someone pushed him."

"We have to find Eric. I'm sure he and Caro are down here somewhere. Where else can he hide someone undisturbed?"

Lis stood up. She felt the bump on her head, which was very painful.

"Let me see." James carefully parted her hair.

"It's quite a bump, but the wound isn't bleeding!"

Lis sat down again. James had his eyes on the door, his gun ready to fire.

"Can you walk?" He spontaneously kissed her.

"Yes, I think so." Carefully, she stood up again while he held her hand.

"Okay?"

"Yes."

"Good, then let's get out of here."

"Just a moment. My friend Alfonse should be here too, they'll be looking for me."

"Is that the ex-intelligence officer?"

"Yes, and the hospital director's son Matthew McKenna, as well as the man Alan, who is looking for Diane, and his friend David."

"Well, let's get out of here before someone else surprises us."

James looked out first, very carefully, so that he had a view of the corridor.

Alan and David followed Matthew and Alfonse as they went purposefully from door to door. Thomas had remained behind in reception, awaiting further instructions.

"Alan and David, you stay here, hide behind the door, it's a storage room. If you see anything, text me. I'll try to comb through the rooms with Alfonse. We won't get any further otherwise. I have an access code to all the rooms and a universal key in case the electronics fail," explained Matthew.

"And don't put yourselves in danger, boys. Leave the arrests to me, okay?" Alfonse winked his eye.

"If only we had a gun," said Alan.

"Don't worry, I can still defend myself very well in an emergency," said David, who had served as a soldier in a special unit in combat zones in his younger years.

He and Alan stepped into the storeroom and left the door ajar, just enough to keep track of who should pass outside.

Matthew, followed by Alfonse, arrived at the first door. He gave Alfonse a hand signal to go to the other side. Then Matthew knocked on the door.

Nothing moved. Alfonse gave him another hand signal to try to push the handle and enter.

It was dark inside. Alfonse drew his gun and took the lead, while Matthew looked for the light switch.

They found themselves in an empty operating room. Nothing seemed to be happening here.

Then they left and moved on to the next room.

A text message suddenly came from Alan. *Lamborelle just ran past, alone. Towards the elevator.*

Matthew showed Alfonse and they both quickly closed the door from the inside, leaving it open a crack.

A few seconds later, Lamborelle walked past the door in a hurry. When he was further down the corridor, Matthew and Alfonse stepped out and followed at a distance.

Lamborelle turned the corner right next to the elevator.

By the time Matthew and Alfonse reached the end of the corridor, he had already disappeared. He could only be in one of the rooms.

Alfonse gave Matthew another hand signal and pointed to the door on the left.

Matthew nodded.

Alfonse positioned himself in front of the door with his gun drawn while Matthew knocked.

"Mmmmmh?" a woman's voice called. He looked questioningly at Alfonse Weis. He gestured with his hand to open the door without saying anything.

But when Matthew tried to open the door, it was locked. He quickly dialled the code and, with a green light, the door opened for him.

Matthew opened the door carefully; it was dark in the room.

"Hello?" said Matthew. "Who's here?"

Alfonse was hot on his heels.

As he entered the room, Alfonse switched on the light.

In one corner, a blonde woman was tied to a stretcher, her mouth taped shut.

Both men rushed to her.

Matthew removed the tape from her mouth. She looked at them both with wide, fear-filled eyes. Alfonse kept an eye on the door anyway.

"Diane?" Matthew asked sadly.

The woman was visibly scared and trembling.

"Don't worry, we're here to get you out of here. I'm a doctor and this man here is a police inspector."

"Yes, I'm Diane Van Helden ... How do you know my name? Watch out when Lamborelle comes back, he's got a gun," she whispered.

"Me too," Alfonse said. "Me too!"

He quickly sent a text message to his former colleague Bob Wagner: *Keep an eye on the parking lot exit, guys. If Lamborelle escapes, chase him and keep your distance.*

Then he texted Alan too, and a few minutes later, both he and David arrived in the room.

Alan immediately ran over to Diane.

"Diane, what a relief!" He knelt down next to her and stroked a strand of hair out of her face. "I thought I'd never see you again!"

She sat up and they hugged each other long and hard.

"I'm so glad to see you, Alan. I thought he'd killed you!"

"They were close to being successful, I have to say."

Then Alfonse also approached.

"You two, Alan and David, stay here with Diane for now. Keep the door closed and don't let anyone in, okay? We have to find Lis."

Alfonse and Matthew left quickly and went into the room next door.

"An operating theatre too?" asked Alfonse.

Matthew nodded in agreement. "Yes, there are a lot of them here."

With an energetic movement, Weis opened the door and hurried inside.

The room was also pitch black. Matthew switched on the light. As they looked around, another text message from Bob arrived.

*So far, no one has left the underground parking garage.*

One by one, they checked all the operating and storage rooms, but there was no trace of Lis.

"Where the hell could he have taken her!" Matthew was worried. Alfonse leaned back against the wall and looked down the long corridor.

"Doc, if you wanted to hide someone here on the spur of the moment, where would you take them?" asked Alfonse. "Think about it, we may not have much time!"

Matthew looked at Alfonse with a serious expression.

"To the morgue," Matthew replied glibly.

Alfonse looked at him resolutely. "That's right! Come on, let's go to B3."

"But you can't leave anyone alive there for long, can you?" asked Alfonse as they hurried to the elevator.

"Yes, you could, in one of the adjoining rooms, and also in the room where the autopsies are done, but not forever either ... Oh, I'm going to be sick!" Matthew imagined Lis lying there.


"Don't pass out now, Doc. Bad timing." Alfonse patted him on the shoulder. "Come on, every second is precious now!"

He took Matthew by the arm and they both descended the stairs.

Alfonse and Matthew walked silently and carefully towards the morgue. Since Matthew had a special access code, it was no problem to get in.

Then Matthew thought of the room behind the morgue. "Come on, I think I know where they might be."

Through the hallway and then further back there was a smaller room that is quite well hidden.

They stood in front of the door, which was locked.

"Hey, someone's in there," Matthew knocked on the door, then Alfonse too.

"Help, we're locked in here," came voices from inside.

Matthew couldn't open it with his code. "Damn, Lamborelle must have changed the code."

"Okay, then we'll take this one." Alfonse drew his gun.

"Get away from the door! I have to shoot it open," he shouted. "Are you all right in there?"

"We're okay, go on," the voice called out.

One shot and the door opened.

Caro and Eric were sitting there on the floor, both with their hands and feet bound.

While Alfonse and Matthew were cutting the shackles from Caro and Eric, James and Lis suddenly appeared in the doorway. James stood there, pointing his gun at Alfonse.

"It's all right, James, this is Alfonse Weis and Matthew, the doctor."

James looked around cautiously and then put his gun away.

Lis bent down to Eric while Matthew was still cutting Caro's restraints.

"Eric! I was so worried!" Lis cried and hugged him tightly. James stopped just outside the door.

"And who are you?" asked Alfonse, looking at James.

"I'm James, a friend of Lis'. It's a long story," he said, looking at both of them.

Matthew turned his attention to Caro. "Are you all right?"

"Glad to see you guys. I thought we were going to die here."

They all looked at each other with great relief.

"Mum, I'm so happy to see you!" Eric had tears in his eyes.


Suddenly Lamborelle stood in the doorway.

"Hands up, everyone. NOW! I'm not repeating myself!"

Lamborelle grabbed Eric and held him in front of him with the gun in his back.

"Now everyone stay calm and gentle. Otherwise, unpleasant things will happen here."

"Oh, Eric! No! Let my son go!" Lis screamed in panic. "Please!"

James stood motionless and watched. Any wrong decision could be fatal for someone.

"Put the gun down, Weis, on the ground with it, NOW!" shouted Lamborelle. Alfonse did so.

Caro sat in the corner, startled. "Eric!" She began to cry.

Matthew was sitting right next to her. He was silent for a few seconds.

"Lis, I'm going to walk out of here with your son, and if anyone follows me, he's dead! I mean it!"

It was as quiet as a mouse, then Lis' voice could be heard. "Eric is your son too!"

This sentence hit hard. For a few moments, Lamborelle was completely paralysed. Eric stared at his mother.

"A bad joke!" shouted Lamborelle. "Come up with something better."

Then he tried to push Eric out of the room: "Come on, let's both get out of here now. And be quiet!"

"This is not a joke! It's the truth, do the math yourself!"

Then Lis mentioned Eric's birthday and waited.

"Get out of here," Lamborelle was now visibly confused, but he still held his gun on Eric's back. He was already halfway out the door.

Within a nanosecond, James drew his gun and shot Lamborelle in the thigh. As he slumped to the ground, Lamborelle turned and shot James, who immediately collapsed. Wriggling free, Eric jumped up and ran towards Caro.

At the same moment, Alfonse and Matthew leaped on Lamborelle together who was still holding his gun. In the confusion he fired again. The bullet hit Alfonse, who also collapsed onto the ground.

Then another shot. James had aimed at Lamborelle again and shot him in the stomach. He was now checkmated.

Matthew jumped to Alfonse's side.

"Hey, Alfonse, are you okay?" Matthew ripped open his shirt. "I think so, but it hurts like hell," Alfonse whispered.

Matthew took a quick look. "Stray shot, you're bloody lucky." He hurriedly called the emergency room.

Lis knelt next to James.

"I think it's just a shoulder injury," James whispered, though he was bleeding profusely.

"The paramedics are on their way," Matthew said. "Come on, let me see!"

Alfonse's phone rang. Matthew picked up the receiver and checked.

Bob Wagner had sent a text message: *A red Jaguar just sped out of the parking lot like a madman. It's my turn!*

Matthew pressed redial and called Bob. "Hi, this is Matthew, I'm with Weis. He's been shot. It's Dr. Michel, fleeing in the red Jaguar. Go after him!"

Bob had the presence of mind to set off in pursuit with his blue lights flashing.

In the meantime, John McKenna had also arrived at B3. He quickly took stock of the situation.

"Dad, Diane Van Helden is in Room 202 with two of our men. She needs urgent help."

"Okay, I'm on my way. I'll call the police!"

On the way out, he stopped in front of Matthew.

"Matthew! I'm so glad you're alive. I'm so proud of you!"

John McKenna hugged his son tightly. Matthew was overwhelmed. He had tears in his eyes.

James, Lamborelle and Alfonse were rushed to the emergency operating room. Two nurses and Matthew accompanied them.

"Matthew, get some rest, we'll manage," said the doctor in charge.

"No, I'm staying. I'll take care of Alfonse; I'll stay with him!"

Eric and Caro seemed to be in shock as they remained sitting motionless in the corner.

"Come up here, you two," Lis said and walked towards them.

They stood up slowly. Caro's whole body was trembling.

Another paramedic entered and approached her.

"Come with us now, we'll take care of you."

Lis stood in the doorway. When Eric was near her, he looked at her in confusion.

"What did you say earlier? Were you trying to confuse me? You certainly succeeded. A great reaction, Mum!"

Lis looked at him and tears rolled down her cheeks.

"What's wrong, Lis?" asked Eric.

"I'm so sorry, Eric, that you had to find out under these circumstances. It wasn't just a distraction ... It's the truth."

Without saying a single word, Eric walked out with Caro and the paramedic. There was no mistaking that he was also in shock.

Lis knew that she had to give him plenty of time now. He would understand, hopefully.

Shortly afterwards, Inspector Kraus appeared with two of his assistants and they had a long chat with Lis, Alan, David and Thomas while Dr. John McKenna, Matthew, and some other doctors attended to the treatment and surgeries of James Hammer, Alfonse Weis and Peter Lamborelle. One of the policemen positioned himself in front of the operating theatre where Lamborelle was being treated.


Inspector Kraus had numerous questions and asked for an explanation of what had preceded this incident. Of course, Kraus was not completely unfamiliar with the name James Hammer, but he did not know the man personally.

Lis spent several hours in the cafeteria and in the waiting

room outside the operating theatres, where James, Alfonse and Lamborelle were being treated and operated on at the same time. She wished she could crawl away somewhere and hide from the world. The last few hours had been almost unbearable.

Fortunately, Alfonse had only been grazed by the bullet. He was treated and bandaged and came out of the operating theatre less than an hour later.

"Alfonse, I'm glad to see you," Lis said and hugged him.

"I don't think anyone expected us to start a real firefight."

"You can say that out loud! And it should all be discreet, you said."

"Well," said Alfonse mischievously, "sometimes things just don't go according to plan."

"I'm going home tonight. I'll talk to you later." He patted her on the shoulder and then spontaneously planted a kiss on her cheek.

After more than two hours, the door opened and James was wheeled out by a nurse, followed by Matthew.

"He'll have to stay here for a few days," Matthew explained. It's a shoulder wound, but he'll be fine."

"Thanks, Matt!"

James was then wheeled into a room.

"As for Lamborelle, he's been shot twice. If James hadn't fired, Lamborelle would have taken Eric hostage, and I don't want to know how it would have turned out."

"Is Lamborelle seriously injured?"

"A shot in the thigh and a shot in the stomach. The operation is almost over. He'll survive. It would be too easy if he didn't!" added Matthew.

"I'm going to James's now. I'll see you later," Lis said, giving Matthew a kiss on the cheek and hurrying into his room.

Matthew noticed that something between them had changed and he guessed why.

Lis entered quietly, sat down on the chair a little way from the bed and looked at James for a long time. He looked peaceful.

Sometime later, he slowly woke up.

First, he looked around and gradually realised where he was.

"Finally!" said Lis and went straight to his bed.

He looked up.

"Hello!" he whispered.

"Hi. Welcome back." She smiled and put her hand on his, which he took and held tightly.

"Shoulder wound," she said, "but you'll be fine!"

"And you?"

"Apart from the shock, I have no injuries, thanks to you! You've saved my life twice in a short space of time!"

"I just happened to be in the right place ..." he smiled.

"And you saved my son's life too," she added, with tears in her eyes.

Their eyes met and his hand still held hers. James realised that he loved Lis Chandler. Even though, after his wife had taken her own life, he had vowed to stay alone.

He pulled Lis close and kissed her. "Lis, I love you!"

"I love you, James! I was so worried. I thought he'd shot you." She laid her head against him for a few moments.

"Well. Lamborelle has serious injuries. Shot in the leg and stomach, but he'll survive."

"And Eric. That was a huge shock for him!" said James.

"Oh yes. We haven't spoken a word to each other since then."

"I'm sure he'll be fine ..." James held her hand tightly.

"I hope so." It was the only chance to shake Lamborelle up a bit."

"But you have certainly succeeded."

"Yes."

She stayed at his bedside for some time. She held his hand tighter than ever.

"By the way, Matthew McKenna broke into Lamborelle's office here at the clinic a few days ago and found a whole file of adoption records for numerous children. I thought you might want to take a look at it before he hands it all over to the police, because it's quite possible that your daughter's file is in there too!"

"Sarah ..." he whispered. Tears welled up in his eyes. "Yes, I'd like to have a look at that. Do you have a chance to look at this file and then maybe 'borrow' Sarah's file for a while? Then we can see what's been going on? In the obituary, my little girl was called Line, and her adoptive parents were called Weyland-Lehman, from Moutfort."

"I can try that. I'll let you know, and we'll take care of it when you get out of here. Where do you live?" asked Lis.

"In Boudler, a very small village near Grevenmacher, in a renovated farmhouse. I had to get away from everything. I couldn't stand it around me anymore. The people, the police, everything."

"I understand," Lis said. "I have to go now. I'll tell you everything else when you're fully awake again, okay?"

"You'll have to!" he smiled, deliberately not letting go of her hand immediately.

"Lis, if you find something, can I ask you not to talk about it with anyone, not even Alfonse? Is that all right?"

"Yes, but then we have to do something, don't we?"

"Absolutely, but only after we have decided what we are going to do and how we are going to proceed."

They looked at each other for a long time, then she leaned over him and kissed him again.

"See you soon!" she whispered.

"We'll discuss that in detail when I get out of here."

Then he let go of her hand.

"I'll let you know tonight," he added, "when I can think clearly again!"

As Lis was leaving, John McKenna entered.

"You'll have to stay here for a few days," Dr. McKenna said.

"I thought so. I guess we'll all have to testify as witnesses about Lamborelle and your son?"

"I think that will be inevitable."

Lis already had the door handle in her hand when she impulsively turned around and walked back to his bed.

"Have you forgotten something?" he asked, his blue eyes saying more than a thousand words.

"Yes," she said softly. Then she leaned forward and kissed him again.

"It promotes healing," she said and smiled.

"Yes, I can already feel it," he whispered in return, his eyes closing.

Then she went out.


In the meantime, Diane Van Helden had also been treated by medical personnel. She was still very weak after being in a coma for so long. She would need to stay a few days longer in the hospital.

"She'll be fine, don't worry," John McKenna explained to Alan, David and Thomas, who had all been waiting in the hallway until the examination was over.

"At least today, she must have absolute peace and quiet and must not be interrogated."

Alan stayed with her in the hospital until late in the evening.

David and Thomas decided to round off the day with a good bottle of red wine.

When Lis arrived at reception, Matthew was standing there

with Brigitte, who had just arrived and was crying profusely in Matthew's arms.

"Come on, I'll take you to him, he's still undergoing intensive treatment, but you'll be able to see him for a few minutes."

Lis stood still. "I'm going to go home now and get some sleep," she said.

"I'll be in touch, okay?" Matthew said and hugged Brigitte to him. What else could he have done at that moment?

"Sure, fine."

Brigitte continued to weep bitterly. The shock was huge for her, not only was her husband fighting for his life after being shot, he was also a child smuggler and criminal, and would probably spend the rest of his life in prison.

When Lis finally arrived home, she flopped down on the sofa and closed her eyes.

The events of the day continued to play in her mind. Eric had sent a short text message to say that he wouldn't be home today. *See you soon*, he had written, but that gave Lis little hope that he would be in touch in the next few days.

Then her thoughts turned to Matthew. It was clear that he would now be more absorbed by Brigitte than ever before. But why he felt so committed to Brigitte was completely incomprehensible to her.

James Hammer had just closed his eyes and was about to go to sleep when there was a knock on the door of his room.

It was Alfonse. He stuck his head in first: "May I come in for a moment?" he asked.

When James saw who it was, he said, "Please sit down, Mr. Weis."

"Thanks, let's stick with Alfonse. I think we can call each other by our first names after last night," said Alfonse.

"I agree, Alfonse! I'm James, ex-secret service."

"It's kind of funny."

"Well," said James, "that depends how you look at it."

"By the way, thank you! You saved my ass, James! Otherwise, I wouldn't have gotten off so easily."

"I don't know. I did what I could do at the time."

"I'm guessing you didn't kill Lamborelle on purpose?" asked Alfonse. "Because you don't miss. And neither do I!"

James smiled. "Right."

"Why not?"

"Three reasons. Reason number one: I need to talk to him. Number two: He's the father of Lis' son and I don't want to be the one to kill Eric's father. Number three: Shooting him would have been far too easy for that bastard!"

"I completely understand that." Alfonse admitted. "I think Lis is struggling with the fact that Eric's father is a criminal."

"I can imagine that. I would have the same problems if I were her."

Alfonse stayed with James for a while. After a good hour, he finally said goodbye.

"I'm off then. I can go home now, I've been discharged."

"See you soon, Alfonse. Take care of Lis until I'm allowed out of here again."

"I will. Good night."


A few hours later, Alfonse contacted Lis.

"Hey Lis, I'm finally home."

"How glad I am that you survived, Alfonse. It could have ended badly for you and for all of us."

"You can say that again! Inspector Kraus visited me earlier, I gave him everything on the record. He was also briefly with Lamborelle, but he's not yet responsive. Then Kraus insisted on talking to his wife.

"I also had a conversation with James Hammer before I left. That he was also involved in such a child kidnapping. Boy, oh boy. What a story. I can't believe that the press isn't already sniffing around. Hammer says there won't be a line about it, certainly not about Lamborelle being exposed."

Lis assumed that James hadn't told him about their recent encounter in Clervaux.

Alfonse abruptly snapped her out of her thoughts.

"Hey Lis, but that's not why I'm calling. Listen, I've just finished my research. There's no longer any doubt. Caro is the biological daughter of Laetitia Van Helden and Klaus Schmitt. My researcher has the exact data, and everything matches. A DNA test will prove everything, but I wouldn't say it if we weren't already 99.9% sure."

"And now?"

"Now we have to get to Laetitia Van Helden and Klaus Schmitt as quickly as possible. I want to bring the news to them personally. They'll be shocked too, that's for sure."

"And only then will we talk to the Klein family."

"Yes, it won't be nice for them because they adopted in good faith and are sure that their child no longer has living parents. It will be brutal news for them."

"When should we go to Maastricht, Alfonse?"

"I'll call first thing in the morning and ask if we can meet them. I'll give the reason that Diane, her sister, is in hospital. Once we're there, the conversation will turn. I don't want them to get suspicious before we get there in person."

"Good idea, Alfonse."


Lis had just settled back on the couch when the phone rang again.

"Hey, it's me, James. I hope I didn't wake you up."

Lis sat up. "No, not at all. I had Alfonse on the phone. He's just come home and is already back at work."

Lis reported what Alfonse had told her.

"I'll probably be able to go home this weekend, at least I hope so. I'm not made for long rest periods. How is Dr. McKenna? I mean, the one who helped us?"

"Oh, Matthew. I haven't spoken to him yet tonight. There's going to be a lot of tension in the McKenna house. The situation is very tense as far as Jeff McKenna and his father are concerned. He has to come to terms with the fact that his son is going to end up in prison and that's going to have negative press on the clinic. Although it's only indirectly related."

"It won't be easy for Dr. McKenna to talk his way out of this or explain that he had no idea about anything."

"No, it won't. It will certainly leave a bitter aftertaste for his clinic."

"Alfonse Weis came to see me before he was allowed to leave the clinic," James said. "I told him about my Sarah, but nothing more."

"Alfonse told me that you had a conversation before he left the clinic."

"How are you?" James asked, "have you recovered from the shock?"

"I think so, but I'm really worried about Eric. And I blame myself for not telling him the truth sooner. That was the worst possible way for him to find out who his father is, and in front of everyone. But I had no other choice."

"No, you didn't, you did the right thing considering the situation."

Lis was silent.

"He'll be fine," James said. "He's a grown man and he'll come to terms with it, trust him!"

"I'm going to try and get some sleep. Take care of yourself, James, and good night! I miss you!" said Lis.

"I miss you a lot too. If everyone involved can rest for a few days now, everything will sort itself out. Also as far as the police investigation is concerned." Then James said goodbye.

Lis then spent a restless night and slept until late in the morning.


# WEDNESDAY, AUGUST 14

Alfonse called Lis just after 10 a.m. the following morning.

"You still sound pretty sleepy."

"I'm still in bed. Good morning, Alfonse," said Lis.

"We're going to Maastricht tomorrow, Lis. Are you ready?"

Lis sat up immediately. "Of course I'm ready. After all, we have to sort everything out. How did Laetitia Van Helden react?"

"I just told her that her sister Diane was in hospital, that it was nothing serious, but that we would like to come and see her to let her know. She then wanted to come to Luxembourg, but I didn't think that was such a good idea because we don't want to involve Caro right away. And if they are so close, then I see that as a possibility. So I told her that we would come to them."

"That's perfect. One more thing, Alfonse, you have the file that Matthew stole from Lamborelle's office, don't you?"

"Yes, I do."

"Can I look at it? I'd like to see if I know any names."

"I'll bring it tomorrow, but you're not doing anything weird on your own, are you?"

"Of course not, Alfonse."

With these words, they said goodbye.

# ERIC

## *THURSDAY, AUGUST 15*

Matthew arrived at the clinic just after 7 a.m. on Thursday morning. He had insisted on an open conversation with his father to clarify any unanswered questions.

John was already there, waiting for him.

When Matthew entered John's office, he was surprised by the hurt he saw in his father's face. His favourite son Jeff had been arrested and it was likely he was going to jail for being an accessory to the attempted murder of Diane Van Helden, for the unauthorised and illegal implantation of microchips, not to mention his link to an illegal child smuggling ring.

"Hello John," Matthew greeted his father, and they both sat down.

"Matthew. I'm glad you're here. There's a lot to talk about."

"I bet that's true!" said Matthew resolutely. "There's a lot to say, and that's why I'm starting now. And it's not primarily about what's happened in the last few days. It goes back many years." He didn't wait for his father's reaction, but just kept talking. He had had many days to think about his mother's revelations and to prepare himself for this situation.

"I went to see Ingrid, Mum's best friend, and she told me that you're not my biological father. That settles my first question."

John McKenna was visibly shocked. "I didn't know she knew ..."

"Yes, she knew everything, and Mum wanted to tell me before she died. Unfortunately, she couldn't talk to me that night because I was too late. But she had already agreed with Ingrid days before that she had to take on this mission and tell me. And so she did!"

"And now you want to send me to hell?"

"No, I don't really want that. But now it at least makes sense that you never loved me the way you loved your biological son, Jeff. And then when I chose medicine as my second interest instead of my first, your fatherly love was completely gone. Not that you ever showered me with love, but until then there was a tiny bit of it."

John McKenna was visibly at a loss for words; he had expected anything but not this statement from Matthew.

"At the time, it was a lot harder for me to deal with than I initially thought, and besides, I would have loved to have you at the clinic," John said. "You were always more enthusiastic about medicine than Jeff, but I really wanted a successor for the McKenna Clinic, I wanted the clinic to stay in our family. Maybe you understand my concern about that?"

"You could have asked anything of me, except exclusively on your terms," Matthew replied. "I offered you half the time to be present in the clinic and to help out, and the other half of the time to look after my magical world, but that wasn't enough for you."

"I know I've made mistakes, Matthew, and I'm very sorry! I mean it, my son. These words are coming rather late from me, I realise that, and I'm not asking you to forgive me or understand me at this stage."

"Better late than never," said Matthew, looking at his father. "Now I understand why I was always so happy with Franz when he took me fishing with him in his boat. He loved me so much and I loved being with him. That must have really disgusted you, didn't it?"

"I sensed that there was a connection between you two that I could never have with you. You were his flesh and blood, and unfortunately not mine." Now John looked very sad.

"I think Franz would have been so happy if I could have called him father. He must have suffered a lot from the whole situation, but he never said a wrong word, never made a remark about it, even when I was an adult. Even then, we met regularly for a beer, for dinner. I should have known.

"It will take me a long time to come to terms with these thoughts. Maybe he was just waiting for me to realise that there was a strong bond between us, much more than just a friendship. Mum was happy when I was out with him. It was all so harmonious when he visited us and you were at the clinic. I wish I could spend just one last hour with him. I have so much to tell him." Matthew had tears in his eyes.

"Do you think, Matthew, you and I could work on getting along a little better in the future? I mean, could we at least try?"

He stared at John. Matthew knew for a fact that his mother Claire would not have wanted him to keep fighting with John. *Claire's probably with her Franz now,* Matthew thought, smiling at the idea despite the tears in his eyes.

"I think, John, we're both trying to make the best of this situation, and if you want me to move into Jeff's office and move my practice here, I will. On one condition."

John picked up his sentence and continued: " …that you can be half magician and half deputy director of our clinic!"

"Deputy Director?"

"Yes, that would be a good start, wouldn't it?"

"Accepted," Matthew said and stood up. The two men embraced warmly, probably the first time they had ever been really close.

"I'm sorry it went the way it did with Jeff. That must be particularly disappointing for you." Matthew asked.

"Even more than that!" John admitted. "Jeff had everything, why did he have to get involved in criminal matters? I don't understand it, and I won't for a long time."

"I don't understand that either. How can you kidnap children, babies, declare them orphans and know that they have biological parents who are alive? How can you work with someone, getting deeper and deeper into this muck and slime? By the way, have you heard by now what our Dr. Michel has to do with this?" asked Matthew.

"Well, he also worked hand in hand with Lamborelle. I still can't believe it." John was visibly shaken by the events of the past few days. "Especially that it happened in my, pardon me, in our clinic, and that Jeff went along with it all, for money, for recognition, for ... I don't know, Matt. I don't think we'll ever know," he said. "I have no idea what I'm going to tell Jeff when I visit him in jail."

"I'll have to wait a while before I go to him, I'd rip his head off if I saw him now. I need time before I can face him," Matthew said.

"I completely understand, but as his father, I still need to see him soon."

After his conversation with his father, Matthew left the clinic feeling relieved. It was as if a huge stone had fallen from his heart. He felt free and he was sure that he could run the clinic side by side with John.


Lis and Alfonse had now arrived in Maastricht.

"We have to proceed very carefully. These people have been through a lot and now we are going to open up a big wound. This family are going to find their child after many years, and knowing that she has been alive all this time will be very painful.

The other parents will be very afraid that they will lose their child now, which will most likely not be the case. We won't say where Caro lives yet, I want to discuss it with the Klein family first but there will be tears on both sides."

"Yes, it will be very moving," agreed Lis. "But there also will be tears of joy. If they respond well now, I'll speak to Caro tonight."

"Go for it, Lis, in this case it's better to talk woman to woman."

They rang the doorbell and the door was opened. A smartly dressed, blonde lady stood in front of them and let them in with a friendly smile.

"Good afternoon, Mrs. Chandler, Mr. Weis, please come in."

They were shown into the salon, where Klaus Schmitt also greeted them warmly. He was a slightly shorter man, slim, with short dark hair, a full beard and a friendly look.

As they sat down, a housekeeper brought coffee.

"So you have my sister in a clinic in Luxembourg and she's been in a coma since an accident?" Laetitia asked with great concern.

"Yes, that's right. She had a concussion but her condition has improved. There was no information anywhere about any close relatives, so it's taken a while to track you down."

"Why didn't the police find us straight away? Surely that shouldn't be a problem these days?" asked Klaus.

"You're right, the situation is a trickier than it looks and we didn't want to go into it on the phone," said Alfonse.

Lis began. "We came to see you today, not just about Diane but also about something else."

"What else is there?" Klaus sounded a little uneasy. Laetitia looked at him in confusion, then at Lis and Alfonse.

"What we are about to tell you, Mrs. and Mr. Schmitt, will touch you emotionally. We have been working on a special case for many weeks, investigating and seeking clarification. A case, or a criminal case, that goes back many years. This particular case, it has also affected me personally, as we have also made other discoveries in this context."

Klaus and Laetitia looked at Alfonse and Lis with increasing astonishment.

"Are you accusing us of something now? Something criminal?" asked Laetitia.

"Oh no, not at all, absolutely not," Alfonse reassured her.

Lis took a deep breath. "About twenty years ago, you were on vacation in the south of France, and your daughter disappeared there."

"Yes, that's right," whispered Laetitia. "Our Caroline was kidnapped."

Klaus reached for Laetitia's hand.

"We have been working on a criminal case involving the entire Van Helden family. We firmly believe that your daughter Caroline is alive but she does not yet know that her biological parents are still alive. She was treated as an orphan and was adopted by loving parents."

Klaus and Laetitia were on the verge of a breakdown. Laetitia Van Helden began to tremble, then to cry.

"However, to be absolutely sure, we would have to do a DNA analysis and would need hair from you both."

"What makes you think this is true? It would be a really bad joke to come here and tell us a story like that, or to give us hope again after such a long time!"

"That is correct! But we can only confirm this once the analysis has been conducted."

The emotions that the two parents then experienced were indescribable. They cried tears of joy, laughed and hugged each other, and when Lis took out a photo and showed it to them, all three of them cried, except Alfonse.

"Oh my God!!! Our daughter! I still can't believe it!" said Klaus in tears.

Afterwards, many questions were answered and many things were explained and clarified.

Both Laetitia and Klaus were very understanding. As soon as the DNA was confirmed, Caroline would be informed and then a meeting would be arranged.

However, they would first have to speak to her adoptive parents, as they did not yet know that Caro's biological parents were still alive.

Klaus and Laetitia insisted on having lunch together, where they learned the whole true story of Lis and her life, as well as what happened to Diane and Alan Moore.

Alfonse took hair samples from Laetitia and Klaus before they left the house.

In the late afternoon, Lis and Alfonse drove back to Luxembourg, where they arrived shortly after 8 p.m..

Alfonse dropped Lis off at home and then drove straight home.

## FRIDAY, AUGUST 16

On Friday morning, Lis looked at the file that Alfonse had brought her the day previously.

She went through all the contracts, finding one folder in the name of Mr. and Mrs. Weyland-Lehman. She took this contract out of the file without telling Alfonse when he picked it up again around noon. He was required to hand it over to the police.

Alfonse told Lis that the police would take care of everything else. He had already spent two hours at the station that morning and Alfonse had then gone to the clinic with a colleague to see Diane Van Helden. She was in a good condition and would be able to go home in a day or two.

Lis had given a statement about everything that had happened, including information about family connections, but nothing had been said about Caro. Everyone agreed that a gentle conversation was needed first with Caro and then with her adoptive parents, the Klein family.

Since Alan had found Diane in hospital, he had almost never left her side. He didn't want to take any more risks and wanted to take her home with him as soon as possible. It seemed to have been the same for both of them: they were meant for each other.

Lis had just had her sushi lunch delivered and was in the kitchen when she heard the door close. Seconds later, Eric was standing in front of her.

She stood up immediately.

"Hello, Eric. I'm so glad you're here!"

Eric stood in the doorway, looking lost.

"How are you?" Lis was on the verge of tears. "I am so sorry that you had to learn the story this way. You have to believe me, Eric, that before I took off from Santo Domingo, I couldn't even imagine in my wildest dreams that I would ever see this man again. Until then I didn't even know who he was."

Eric sat down. "May I?" He took a rice roll.

"Lis, I know you did your best for me, or at least you tried. I'm just in a situation now where I really don't know what to do. When you said I was his son, something happened to me, I still don't know how to describe that feeling. There's a man in the same room who wants to take me hostage, and suddenly I discover that this man is my biological father.

"A criminal, a child kidnapper, a rapist, a successful, good-looking businessman, someone who pretends to be a doctor and isn't, a guy who wants revenge on the whole world for what happened to him, namely that his father was in prison. I'm exhausted and there are moments when I want to see him, talk to him, there are moments when I want to beat him up until he can't stand and talk anymore."

"So now you know how I feel, Mum. I can't be angry with you, of course not, how could I? What else could you have told me?"

Eric was on the verge of tears. "I've got his eyes, haven't I?"

"Yes, you do. I've noticed it too."

He got up from the table, walked towards Lis and hugged her tightly.

"Sometimes life sucks, and for me, those sometimes are right now!" Then he started to cry. Lis held him for a long time. They talked and talked for hours. They would both remember this day for a long time to come. Eric had many questions, after all. The conversation brought them even closer than they already were.

In the early evening, Eric went back to Caro. She was also exhausted from all the events, and she still didn't know anything yet about her real family situation.

After Eric had left Lis, Matthew was the next to arrive, just after 10 p.m.

"Hey, good to see you!" He hugged her and held her for a long time.

"How are you?"

Then he sat down. He looked tired.

"My father doesn't want to see or speak to Jeff. Brigitte is close to a nervous breakdown, she's afraid she'll be asked to testify even though she knows nothing and ..."

"And ...?" asked Lis.

He looked at Lis for a long time. "I don't want to leave her alone, at least not now. Do you understand?"

Lis looked at him for a long time. She nodded. "Yes, I do ... You know Matt, we had our time together, back when we were teenagers but I don't think you can move on after so many years based only on those feelings. I don't think it's possible."

"I don't know, Lis. I'd love to, but at the moment I can't break away from Biggy. And I can't just erase the last four years with her."

"That's more than we ever had together," Lis added.

"We will remain friends, very good friends, I promise." He was on the verge of tears and when he said goodbye, they both cried.

"By the way, my father wants me to be the clinic's deputy and accept a part-time position. What do you say?"

"I think it's fabulous. He must have had to work a lot on that."

"Yes, and me too. But we have a real chance of still having a kind of father-son relationship."

"We'll keep in touch," she whispered, "after all, you're my family doctor."

"I certainly hope so."

Then Matthew left.

## SATURDAY, AUGUST 17

James called Lis shortly after midday. She had just come back from the shops.

"Hey, Lis, I'm back home. I think we should talk, but preferably not on the phone."

"I could come to you this afternoon if you want to talk? You probably shouldn't be driving around. Has anything happened in the meantime?"

"Nothing dramatic, but I'll tell you later!"

Shortly after 4 p.m., Lis reached the small village of Boudler and looked for James's house. In this village with only a few streets, there weren't any street names, just house numbers.

He had already opened the door as she pulled up.

"Well, I've certainly never been here before," she said and stepped inside. He was carrying his arm in a sling.

"Come in, it's good to see you." He closed the door, and they stood opposite each other a little hesitantly.

"Hey, I'm glad you're home," Lis said.

"May I have your cell phone, please? I'll give it back to you when you leave." James held out his open hand to her.

Lis looked at him, confused.

"It's nothing to do with me not trusting you, but I don't want us to be bugged."

He put both cell phones in a metal box.

"I prefer to play it safe."

Then she hugged him for a very long time. "It's nice to feel you again," James said and kissed her passionately.

"Being able to hold you with just one arm is not ideal," he whispered.

"That doesn't matter at all. The main thing is that I can see and touch you!"

They sat down.

"Lis, there are many things I want to tell you. But there is one important condition. You must not, and I mean this very seriously, you must not talk about it with anyone. Neither with your friends, nor with Alfonse Weis, nor with anyone else. If you don't follow this rule, you'll put us all in great danger, and I mean mortal danger. Okay?"

Lis looked at James, a little confused. "What's happened?"

"Nothing so far! But it will."

Opening her handbag, Lis showed James the Line Weyland-Lehman's adoption contract. Everything was laid out in detail in the contract, and there was also a photo of a little girl.

James had tears in his eyes.

"Yes, that's her! My little Sarah, my girl." He couldn't take his eyes off the photo. Lis could only imagine how painful this was for him.

"The medical report is also in there. Sarah had been in an accident; she was hit by a car and died a week later from her injuries."

"Thank you so much for that. I needed to know what had happened to her." He took Lis' hand and squeezed it tightly. "At least now I know exactly what she died of."

Then he turned the page and looked at the adoption contract.

"This contract can only have been signed by Dr. Peter Lamborelle, because he has the power of attorney for the orphanage in Clervaux," said James.

"You found that out too," she said.

"Yes, but I've since found out more. A very good friend of mine, who is still with the secret service, told me the day before yesterday that he had found a connection between the orphanage and some members of our local government. I worked as a bodyguard for some of our ministers for over twenty years of my life and travelled with them everywhere."

"What?"

"Yes, and that's why I told you Lis, that everything we discuss now must stay between the two of us, at least until further notice. Because if any of it leaks anywhere, we're all dead! And I mean it! Okay?"

Lis looked at James; she was startled, but she nodded in agreement.

"We're dealing with a very sensitive matter here, involving someone from the State Department and someone from the government's Department for Family Affairs, and these people are working hand in hand with Lamborelle. By now they certainly know that he has been arrested and they will be wondering whether he will testify or not. I'm assuming he won't testify because if he does, he'll die. If he doesn't testify, he'll be in prison for life but still alive."

"But isn't he guarded there around the clock? There's a policeman outside his room in the clinic."

"Yes, but that's no obstacle for them, believe me."

"Aha?"

"If we are a danger to these people, it would be very easy for us to have a 'car accident' or something similar. We have to be very careful about what we do and what we say on the phone. I don't want to drag you any deeper into this."

"I'm already there anyway, and I'm on your side! But what government members are they? I still don't understand."

James continued.

"It's not that easy. There are corrupt people everywhere in the world. And if one of them is part of a government, it's easy to get access and permissions to do the things they then do sometimes. It happens everywhere in the world, not just here, everywhere. I travelled with these people, I protected them, their lives, and they kidnapped my daughter and sold her to rich people here in this country. Do you understand what that means?"

"And you didn't know who was involved beforehand?"

"No. It was only when I read the obituary of our daughter that I really started to think about it. When she disappeared in the Dominican Republic, I would never have made a connection with Luxembourg. But then I found out that the orphanage there also has a branch here in this country.

"We were still living in Germany at the time of her kidnapping, which means we were still registered there. They didn't know we were planning to move to Luxembourg. I hardly think they would kidnap a girl and later arrange an adoption in the same country where she lived before. That's far too risky.

"So, my secret friend helped me and found out that a couple had adopted my girl a year after her disappearance. He then also gave me the information that the adoption had been arranged through this orphanage in Clervaux, at least officially.

"As I had often observed the orphanage in Clervaux and had seen this man Lamborelle come and go, it was quite easy to identify him. I then followed him to the Dominican Republic. That was the flight you were on.

"I had seen you with Matthew while you were waiting for your luggage. And I followed Lamborelle at a distance. He left the airport building and went back in through a back door. I stayed outside and waited.

"Then, after about half an hour, I saw a black SUV with him as a passenger drive out of the same part of the building he had gone into. I'm now assuming that Matthew was in there when he was kidnapped.

"However, as I had to take a cab, I couldn't follow the car. I then drove to my hotel, very close to the orphanage, and tried to make further inquiries there."

James paused for a while.

"I couldn't get to Lamborelle at this time because I wanted to get to the masterminds in the government. It was already clear to me that even Peter Lamborelle couldn't operate without the help and cooperation of the government in order to carry out such missions. He couldn't possibly smuggle children into the country without official backing. That is out of the question. And he himself also works in the Ministry of Family Affairs."

"I understand," Lis said, "So there's more to this. We thought his revenge was only against the Van Helden family."

"That may have been the starting point when he was young, the start of this dirty work, but he had the plan well thought out and then there were others who became part of it. I have to think about what we can do, but it's not going to be easy."

"What about Matthew McKenna? He's clean, isn't he?" asked Lis.

"That's right. He knew nothing about any of this. There's only one connection, he's been Lamborelle's wife's lover for years. That's why he was chipped, and that's why Lamborelle knew for a fact that he was on his way to the Dominican Republic."

"Do you think Lamborelle was following him before?" asked Lis.

"Not necessarily. He seemed harmless to him, probably. And I'm guessing it didn't bother him that his wife was stepping out on him. It probably suited him fine so that he could work on building his connection to Diane," James said.

"He seems to be a very violent man, judging by what his wife said. And from what I experienced ..."

"Don't think about it," James said, looking at Lis urgently.

"I don't want to put Eric in danger."

"It would be good if he stayed away from his so-called father, at least for now."

"I wish I hadn't told him that Eric was his son!"

"It was a situation of total surprise. And in the moment you can't always control the direction of events and, above all, people's reactions. You certainly checkmated Lamborelle, at least for a good few seconds. You had to make that declaration to prevent the worst from happening. I think that was the right thing to do.

"If you still have something to talk to him about, Lis, I'd go and see him in the clinic as soon as possible if I were you, because to be honest, I don't think they're going to let him live much longer. He knows too much, and no one wants to take the risk of him talking. Besides, aren't you surprised that nothing about the shooting at the clinic was in the press or on the news?" asked James.

"Now that you mention it, yes. You're right. I hadn't even thought about that."

"Have you seen Eric yet?"

"Yes, we've talked. But it will take time, he has a lot on his plate at the moment. He still wants to talk to Peter Lamborelle at some point, too. Alan will fly to Santo Domingo with Diane as soon as possible to pick up the little girl Kim, who she liked so much from the start."

"That's great. But they should first find out whether the child really is an orphan."

"Yes, that will be arranged."

Their eyes met as they stood up almost simultaneously.

"Be very careful, Lis, please. I mean it seriously. These people are unpredictable and much more dangerous than you realise."

He played with a strand of her hair.

"When I saw you on the plane, I wondered what that man must have done to you to frighten such a beautiful woman. Now I can understand your reaction all too well."

James kissed her again and held her close to him for a long time.

"Do you think we'll get through all this?" she asked, a little worried.

"I hope so. Even if it's very quiet at the moment, we shouldn't underestimate these people and be vigilant. They never give up and will fight to the end. Even if the police get involved. It sounds unreal, I know, but it's true."

"Seriously?"

James nodded in agreement.

"You mean it's all infiltrated by corrupt people?"

"More than you can imagine, but please, I'll say it again: keep everything you learn from me to yourself; it could cost you your life and the lives of others very quickly, okay?"

"Yeah, sure. That sounds worrying, James!"

"Wait and see! We'll soon find out how things develop and who will make which move first."

"Do you know by now who is working with Lamborelle, I mean, from the government?"

"If I tell you now, yes, I figured that out, I don't want you asking me for names, okay?"

"Okay! And how did you find that out, if you don't mind me asking?"

He smiled and squeezed her hand tightly. "You would have made a good investigator. The less you know, the better it is for you."

Then he took her in his arms again. "Trust me, Elisabeth Bouvier! Will you ever go back to your real name?"

"I don't know yet. That depends a lot on Eric. If he wants to work with his grandfather in his bank, Bouvier is probably the right name for him as my father's successor."

James kissed Lis again. "You're a remarkably brave woman!"

"I guess I never had a choice if I wanted to survive."

James then took out Lis' cell phone, handed it back to her and accompanied her outside.

"I'll keep in touch. Have a safe journey home," he whispered and kissed her again as they pressed tightly against each other.

"If there's anything, send me an e-mail and I'll send you an encrypted address. And don't forget: I love you." He kissed her again.

"Okay, take care of yourself! I love you too, James. And I want to see you on safe ground soon."

While Lis was on her way home, Eric was on his way to the clinic. He tried to call his mother several times, but he couldn't reach her, there was no reception.

Eric drove to Parking Lot B and called Caro.

"Caro, listen, I need your help, and I need it now. Please call the clinic and ask where Dr. Lamborelle is. Do it under any pretence, I don't know, you need to check his meds, or whatever ... I need to talk to him and I need to talk to him now."

"I don't think that's a good idea, Eric," said Caro.

"It is what it is, I have to do this now. Please tell me how to get in there!"

"Okay, give me a few minutes. I can log into the system and check. Can you remember the storage room we were both in? You'll find doctor's paraphernalia and other things there. Take anything that makes you look like a doctor. Eric, I still wouldn't do this, do you hear me? Okay, it's Room 4222! But let's talk about it in peace, I ..." Eric had already hung up.

It was 7 p.m. and the clinic was due to close in an hour to visitors. Eric took the stairs to the storeroom and grabbed a stethoscope and a white coat. When he reached the fourth floor, he saw from a distance that a police officer was guarding a door further down the corridor.

*"Damn!"* he thought. *Of course, Lamborelle's being guarded.*

Eric cleared his throat. He had to look genuine if he wanted to be credible in his disguise as a junior doctor. He wore a stethoscope around his neck and placed one hand in the pocket of his white coat. He walked purposefully down the corridor in the direction of the police officer.

"Good evening," he greeted her in a firm voice. "Time to go home soon?"

The policeman was reading something, he looked up briefly. "Yes, it's about time, I'm really tired."

"I can imagine," said Eric. "I'll be quick, just a routine check. I'm still on my internship."

"I understand, doctor. Take your time. I'll stretch my legs for five minutes and go to the vending machine to get a coffee."

"Go ahead, take ten minutes, if you need," Eric replied confidently.

He stepped inside the room. Eric could feel his pulse in his head and throat.

Peter Lamborelle was lying in a bed in the middle of the room, connected to numerous monitoring devices. When he heard the door open, he turned his head and saw the white coat, but immediately recognised Eric.

He approached his bed. Lamborelle looked at him wordlessly. Yes, there was no doubt about it, Eric's eyes were a perfect copy of his own.

Eric was completely overwhelmed by his feelings at that moment. He was standing in front of his biological father—a criminal—for the very first time in twenty-five years. Eric searched desperately for the right words to say to him.

Lamborelle held out his open hand and asked in a weakened voice: "It was a bit of a shock for both of us, wasn't it?"

Eric nodded in agreement.

"I've spent 25 years thinking about what it would be like to stand in front of my biological father one day, and now I don't know what to say. Whether I should hate you for everything, or whether I should try to understand you, or whether I should ... I don't know. I had no idea until the shooting yesterday."

"Well, me neither!"

"You're quite a scumbag, aren't you?" asked Eric.

"You can rarely undo what you've done, so you have to live with it. You should try to do the same."

"Don't you have anything to say about the fact that you ... have a son?"

"I don't know, I don't think you're proud to have a father like me. Really, you shouldn't have come here."

"Well, I'm here now, damn it!" Suddenly Eric spoke up. "And now I expect you to say something to me, to your son, who is not at all proud of you. On the contrary, who is ashamed of what you have done to others and who perhaps just wants to understand a little why."

"Don't bother, it's much more complicated than you know."

"Why have you taken so many children away from their parents, caused them so much suffering, and so much pain?"

"They found new parents, the other parents were able to have new children, and we all made good money out of it. It's that simple, son, but I guess you won't understand. And now it's better that you leave. Get lost! I don't want to get to know you."

Eric was speechless by Lamborelle's words; he was both sad and angry with his father.

"Why did you do this to my mother?"

"Sometimes things happen, you can't control your emotions, and she was so beautiful! But she was only there for one purpose, for our money. Actually, I had nothing against her personally, but I needed to get to her father and that was the only weak spot I could find."

Eric was visibly shocked. "It might be easier for me to understand if you explain it to me, eventually. You'll end up in prison either way, the only question is how long, and then I'll come and nag you until you explain everything to me, so I understand."

"Your mother won't like that!"

"I don't care, I'm an adult and can decide for myself."

"Listen Eric, put your cell phone on record first, because you can use what I say now later if necessary."

Eric looked at him in amazement and surprise.

"Go ahead, you don't have much time before someone comes."

Eric put the cell phone on the tray next to the bed and sat down on the chair.

*"Saturday, August 17. I, Peter Lamborelle, in full possession of my mental faculties, state the following for the record. I assume that I will not get out of this hospital alive. I know too much, and the people involved know full well that if I am taken into custody, they will make me name names if they don't kill me first. And please tell your mother that I'm sorry. I realise the damage done is irreparable, but I at least want it said."*

Then he stopped the sound recording.

"You can't be serious. They want to kill you?" Eric said, stunned. "Surely that can be prevented, and there's a police officer outside for your safety."

"That doesn't mean anything, Eric. You still seem to see the world through the eyes of a child, you have no idea what reality looks like. But never mind, the main thing is that you record this conversation so you can use it if necessary."

"Who are they? Tell me, I'll take care of them."

Peter Lamborelle laughed. "Boy, they're a few sizes too big for you, believe me. Now get out of here before I get sentimental and think we could really do something together."

"We could at least try, although my mother will hate me for it."

"Out, I say. That's enough!"

Lamborelle looked at Eric one last time before turning and walking to the door.

There he turned around once more. "Take care of yourself, boy, do better than me." Lamborelle had tears in his eyes, which Eric fortunately couldn't see.

"Are you all right, Doctor?" the police officer asked immediately after Eric had closed the door from the outside.

He cleared his throat and turned to the police officer.

"Yes, everything's fine. I'll be on my way then."

"I'm being replaced now too. See you tomorrow then!"

"I'll see you tomorrow. Good night."

Eric went to the elevator. The conversation had upset him but he could never talk to Lis about it.

His biological father was a criminal, a bastard, and a brutal husband, but still he was his father. Eric's head was spinning.

Once he got to this car, he drove around for hours, letting his thoughts run free. He cried.

It was late at night before he came home. Lis was already in bed. He decided to wait to see her in the morning at the earliest, definitely not now. He sent Caro a text message to say he was fine.

## SUNDAY, AUGUST 18

The day passed rather quietly. Lis noticed that Eric was lost in thought, and he realised that his mother also had a lot on her mind. Neither of them wanted to broach the subject.

In the evening, Eric drove to Caro's and spent the night there.

At the McKenna Clinic, Matthew had taken over Jeff's practice. He had been busy all day getting the paperwork in order. It was already 9.30 p.m. and before he went home, he spontaneously decided to pay Peter Lamborelle a visit.

He was still being guarded by a police officer who was sitting on the chair in front of the door and looking at his cell phone.

"Good evening," said the friendly man, barely paying attention to Matthew.

He entered and went to his bed. Lamborelle was still awake and looked at Matthew.

"Oh, Dr. McKenna himself," he said as Matthew stood at his

bedside and briefly checked all the data on the monitors he was connected to.

"Good evening, Mr. Lamborelle. How are you?" he said very distantly.

"Don't get smart with me, Matthew, I know you're not in the mood for nice words, so ..." said Peter sharply. "You'd rather see me dead, that would have been good for you and Biggy, wouldn't it? Or did you get involved with the Bouvier daughter too? It's been a bit of an emotional rollercoaster over the last few weeks."

"I'm fine, to answer your question," he continued. "Except I almost got killed by a sniper. Who was that? No one's told me yet."

"It's not my job to explain that to you. I'm just here to provide you with medical care." There was no way Matthew wanted a face-to-face conversation with this man.

"Then get the fuck out of here. I don't need anything." Lamborelle demonstratively closed his eyes.

When Matthew had checked everything, he went out again. "Good night!"

The policeman was still sitting in his chair.

"Good night, doctor," he said.

"Are you on the night shift?" asked Matthew.

"No, my replacement arrives around 10 p.m."

"Have a good evening," Matthew said as he left.

He was still thinking about Lamborelle's words. What a strange fellow. Matthew took the elevator to the parking lot and went straight home. He was done for the day.

The policeman standing outside Lamborelle's room heard footsteps and, as he looked down the corridor, he saw his replacement approaching. A tall man was walking briskly towards him.

"Hello," he stood up. "A bit early."

"Good evening. Yes, I was in the pizzeria nearby and it's too far to drive home again," the officer explained.

"I can understand that. Well then, good night, I'm off then."

"Good night. See you next time," said the tall man. "Everything quiet and normal?"

"That's right. Dr. McKenna just visited him personally and checked everything out."

"Wonderful, then it will be a quiet night. I've brought a new book," he said with a smile.

Then the policeman left and the replacement sat down.

By now it was midnight. It had become very quiet in the clinic. This area was somewhat secluded, as the intensive care unit only had a few single rooms that were separated from the others. The patients were only separated by glass walls.

The replacement policeman stood up, entered Peter Lamborelle's room and locked the door from the inside.

It was dark in the room, with only a small emergency lamp on the floor providing sparse light.

He approached the patient's bed and pulled out the cable of the emergency call button. He took a seat next to the bed, removing his police cap and putting it in his pocket.

Lamborelle heard soft noises and opened his eyes. He saw the man in uniform sitting there.

"Shouldn't you be outside ..." he started to say before he recognised the face of the man sitting before him. It was the man with the full beard who had shot him.

"Oh," said Lamborelle when he realised who was sitting next to him. "What gives me the honour? Mrs. Bouvier's new boyfriend?"

"I'm the father of Sarah Hammer, alias Line Weyland-Lehman, if that name means anything to you. There were so many children that you can't remember every single name, can you? Sarah was my three-year-old daughter when she was kidnapped. And she died as Line Weyland a year and a half ago."

Peter Lamborelle looked at James Hammer. What should he say now? Until now, he thought it was just Lis' new friend. But that explained his presence.

"Oh!" Peter just said, "I'm glad you're visiting me now, I won't be here much longer."

"Oh, no?" asked James. "Are there any changes of plan from the elite?"

"The who?"

"Please. Let's drop the game. I know it. Who else is playing with you? You're not going to live much longer anyway. You know that and I know that. I used to be in the secret service and the special forces."

"What if I charge you tomorrow for being here and all that?"

"Nobody will believe you, you bastard. And the police detachment will be outside later and deny everything, so ...! And now to the two of us," said James.

"Do you know what you have done to all these children, the parents and everyone involved? Sure, you know that. But once you're part of it, there's no going back, and you often realise that too late."

"If you already know everything, why are you still coming here?"

"Because I want to look you in the eye when you tell me who is responsible for my daughter's death. I know I don't need to kill you because the other side will, and I strongly suspect you won't get out of here alive. I have said for the last three years that if I find the person responsible, I will kill him myself and with my own hands. But I know I don't have to do that because the elite is involved, because they will never let you testify.

"It was just bad luck that the coincidences turned against you, and that was all set in motion by the disappearance of Diane Van Helden. Who would have thought that she would have met the love of her life that night on the bus? A man for whom I have the greatest respect. His courage and determination led to this rotten game being exposed. He and his friends will never know how deep the swamp really is. And that's a good thing, otherwise they would be in danger too."

Then James stood up. "That's what I wanted to tell you. And remember the karma thing. If that's true, then you don't have a good time ahead of you."

He plugged the emergency power cable back in and said to Lamborelle: "Sarah would have been six years old this month." He gave him one last disdainful look, went to the door, and quietly walked out.

Peter Lamborelle was silent. He had tears in his eyes.

The real replacement was already outside. Everything had happened in silence.

James handed him back his badge. "Thanks Mike, I owe you one," he whispered as he gave the policeman a friendly pat on the shoulder and walked to the elevator. There he wiped away his tears.

On the way home, James listened to one of his favourite Boyz to Men songs at full volume: One sweet day.

*I could never have imagined living without your smile, feeling and knowing that you hear me, that keeps me alive ...*


# *MONDAY, AUGUST 19*


Lis was just about to leave the house when James called her cell phone.

"Hey Lis, do you have a moment?"

"When?"

"Now? I'm in the neighbourhood. May I come in, I won't be long?"

"Absolutely!"

Five minutes later, the doorbell rang, and he was there.

He was wearing a black leather jacket, a black T-shirt and jeans, and when Lis closed the door, he hugged her without words and held her tighter than ever.

As usual, he took Lis' cell phone with him and put it in a special case.

"I'll leave you this case here, and if you talk to anyone here about sensitive matters, from now on you put your cell phones in here, all of them. Don't forget!"

"What's happened?" Lis asked anxiously.

James looked at her seriously and put his hand on her cheek.

"Don't worry, nothing has happened yet." Then he looked deep into her eyes.

"Lis, I've fallen in love with you! But I hadn't planned to fall in love with someone, not so quickly and certainly not in the middle of my investigation."

"It wasn't my plan either," she whispered, "but when I saw Mr. Winther enter the orphanage, I knew we had something in common."

"Yes, I had that feeling at that moment too. But ..."

"But what?"

"I have a job to finish, and to do that I'm going to go into hiding for a few days or maybe weeks, which means no phone, no texting, no contact at all. I want to tell you this in person, because if you were looking for me, that wouldn't be good. I'll get back to you when I can and if I can."

"What are you doing?"

"Just let me keep quiet, without asking questions and, above all, without looking for me. This is very important, if not vital. And I want you to trust me!"

"You have some time now, don't you?"

"Sure!"

They sat down in the living room.

"You're not putting yourself in danger unnecessarily, are you?"

"No! Everything is fine. And if anyone asks you where I am, you won't know!"

"Okay, no problem. But is it really inevitable that you'll take matters into your own hands? Now that Lamborelle's been caught, he'll have to testify, and then everyone connected to him will be arrested too, don't you think?"

"Unfortunately, no, I don't think so, beautiful lady. I'm afraid I don't believe it. I have been through three painful years searching for my daughter, followed by my wife's suicide. It's one thing to lose a child through death. But it's a completely different situation when your child simply disappears, when she is kidnapped. I know you understand, and I certainly don't want to trivialise what you have been through. But a ransom was demanded from your father, which at least gives hope and reassurance that the child is still alive and that you will probably see them again.

"But when a child is kidnapped and there is no money involved, no ransom, then thoughts of the worst kind that parents can imagine arise. You go through hell every day, every night, every minute. Is my child being abused or tortured? Is she locked up, is she still alive, and so on."

"What are you going to do?"

James took her in his arms and kissed her without answering her question.

"Do you want to talk to Lamborelle again?" asked James.

"No, we had our talk at the clinic when he left me tied up after all. I never want to see that man again, and I hope so much that Eric doesn't try to contact him."

"And if he does?"

"I don't know, but it won't do him any good." Lis was convinced about that.

"No, I don't think so either. I had a visit from Inspector Kraus and I put everything on record about what had happened, why I was involved and that no one was interested in my story three years ago. He took it all in, but he also seemed very relaxed. But I'm not surprised."

"You don't think he's somehow complicit, do you? He would have to use his common sense to realise that more than just one or two people could be behind the kidnapping of children in this way."

"Lis, think about it: a large part of our society lacks common sense, that's just a fact. In a case like this, special care needs to be taken about how to proceed, how much you can investigate and still stay alive. Having said that, I would like to end our discussion, please."

It was quite clear that James didn't want to talk about this subject any further.

"Will you contact Sarah's adoptive parents?"

"No. I considered it, but at the time they were so dismissive and the DNA test that was done was negative. That says enough, because if I hadn't been one hundred percent sure, I would have said so from the start. So they presented a fake DNA test too. Besides, I don't want to have any contact with them. I couldn't bear it if they showed me pictures of their time together with my daughter.

"They knew that they had agreed to an illegal adoption, or at least that there was something fishy about the whole thing. But that didn't bother them, the main thing was that they could have a white, pretty girl. I don't want them to know that I'm still alive. I'll have to come to terms with that.

"When are you going to talk to Caro and then bring her two families together?" James asked.

"Alfonse and I will discuss it with Caro tomorrow. We'll make sure that Eric will be with her because it's bound to be very emotional. One family will lose their adopted daughter, so to speak, and the Schmitt-Van Heldens will regain their daughter again after more than twenty years."

"Is your son definitely going to stay here in the country now?" asked James.

"Yes, he had already planned that before all this came up. And Bernard will welcome him with open arms. Maybe that will bring us a little closer together, me and my father, and we can finally break down the wall that has stood between us for so long."

"What about Matthew?"

"He has spoken to his father, and they are making a fresh start in their relationship, with him as deputy director of the clinic and Brigitte very likely at his side. She will certainly separate from Peter and divorce him.

"Thomas, Alfonse, Alan and David never dreamed what would be set in motion when Alan met the woman of his life on the bus that night. Actually, the Van Heldens owe him and you a lot for uncovering all this. And I do too, because without the trip there I would probably never have met Peter Lamborelle."

Lis snuggled up to James. "You know what, I'm glad this is all over. The trial of Jeff McKenna is going ahead, and I can well imagine him going to prison for many years."

"I hope so too, although he only knew part of the whole story. He is so naive and believed everything Peter Lamborelle told him. I don't think this will lessen his sentence though. He took his Hippocratic oath when he became a doctor and nothing will excuse his actions."

"It will take John McKenna a long time to come to terms with all this. Jeff, who he thought was so loyal, correct and committed. Matthew, on the other hand, will get another chance to build a better relationship with his adoptive father. It's never too late for that.

"You and Matthew, were you..?" James looked at Lis. Maybe it wasn't appropriate to ask this question, but he felt like it.

"For a while, we thought we could start again where we had lost ourselves many years ago. But it's not that easy. He has this relationship with Brigitte, and since I met a man who somehow magically attracted me from the very first moment, the decision wasn't difficult."

"Oh yeah? That's interesting! I think you need to tell me all about it in detail. I need to know!"

Then James took her in his arms and kissed her passionately. He spent the night with Lis and late at night they both fell asleep, snuggled up close together.


# TUESDAY, AUGUST 20


Lis was already out of bed when James woke up. She was in the kitchen making coffee. James got up too, walked over to her, put his arms around her and leaned his chin on her shoulder.

"Hey!" he whispered. "Are you okay?"

She turned around and kissed him. "Oh yes, very good! I just have to tell you this now, I'm sure you've heard this before, but you have eyes that mesmerise me. I could look at them for hours."

He smiled. "You're welcome to do that. My father had the same eyes, I guess I inherited them from him."

He hugged her tightly. "Lis, you make me feel good." Then he kissed her again. "I'd like to spend more time with you when this is all behind us."

"I'd like that too. I would love that." They stood facing each other, embracing tightly.

They had breakfast together and then James said goodbye.

"See you soon," was all he said. "Just a little patience, okay? I can't give you a schedule, I really can't."

They looked at each other for a long time and Lis nodded in confirmation.

"Take care of yourself!" she whispered.

"Trust me! I'm serious, trust me no matter what!"

Then he went out.


Lis had invited Caro and Eric to lunch, and when they arrived home, Alfonse also dropped by.

As they sat together over a cup of coffee, they were already wondering what new information Alfonse would bring back this time.

"Caro," Lis began after a while, "we've made some very moving discoveries with evidence, and what we're telling you today has all been verified."

Eric and Caro looked at each other and then both looked rather confused at Lis and Alfonse.

"You're making it exciting," said Eric, surprised that she hadn't informed him yet.

"Okay," Caro said simply and waited to hear more.

"Caro, you yourself once told me that you came from an orphanage in Clervaux and that the Klein family are your adoptive parents, as your biological parents were fatally injured in a car accident."

"That's true, but it's not so bad because I didn't even know my birth parents, I was so young and can't remember them."

"Well, there's more to this adoption than you've been told," said Alfonse, clearing his throat. "More than anyone knew at the time."

Alfonse waited a moment to see Caro's reaction. She appeared relaxed and curious at the same time.

"What does that mean?" she asked.

"Well … It will be an unsettling discovery if I explain it to you now, but hopefully it will also be a positive thing for you."

"Okay, I'm listening." She looked at Eric.

"Your biological parents didn't die in a car accident; you were kidnapped by an organisation."

There was silence for a few moments. Eric and Caro looked at each other questioningly and rather shocked.

"I … was … kidnapped? As a baby? By whom and for what purpose? Who would say that?" Eric sympathetically took Caro's hand and squeezed it tightly.

Then Alfonse explained very slowly and clearly the connection to Diane Van Helden and also the organisation of Peter Lamborelle and the connection to Gerard Van Helden, Caro's grandfather.

As Caro gradually realised that she would soon see her birth parents, but also that her adoptive parents would sadly learn the truth, she burst into tears. It took quite a while for them all to get through those hours after the declaration.

Alfonse told her to decide for herself when she was ready to see her real parents, and that he would also inform the Klein family, which was inevitable.

Lis had arranged to meet Thomas for lunch that Wednesday. Since the incident at the clinic, they had only been in contact by phone. She wanted to talk to him about what had happened in peace.

Just as Lis was saying goodbye to Thomas, she received a text message from Matthew: *"Peter Lamborelle dead, cardiac arrest."*

She immediately called Matthew. "What's happened? I thought he was fine and would survive?"

"That's what we thought too. I have no idea. He was found dead in bed this morning. We had only moved him from the intensive care unit to a normal room yesterday, and there was a police officer at the door day and night. An autopsy has already been ordered."

A conversation with Alfonse in the afternoon did not bring any new insights either.

"I thought he would be released from hospital within the week and then remanded in custody," Lis said.

"That's what I thought too," Alfonse agreed. "I can't wait to see what the autopsy reveals."

Lis would have liked to speak to James, but she had no way of reaching him.

Eric came home later that afternoon. He hadn't been home since Sunday evening.

"Hello Mum, good to see you." He kissed his mother Lis.

"Hello." Eric made himself a coffee and sat down opposite Lis.

"Eric, I've just received a message that ... well ..."

"What's happened?" He could tell by the look on Lis' face that something was wrong.

"Peter Lamborelle died in hospital this morning, from cardiac arrest."

"Say that again!"

"Yes, unfortunately it is ..."

"He was killed, Lis. They fucking killed him." Eric put his head on the table and began to cry. He banged his fist on the table.

"I didn't even have the chance to get to know my biological father under normal circumstances. That's not fair. It's so damn unfair."

Lis went over to him and put her hand on his head. She didn't know what to say.

"Everything is unfair," he cried out in tears, "what happened to you, what happened to all the children. Why am I involved in all this crap? I don't want this! All I ever wanted was to lead a normal life. And now that I've seen my real father, who's a criminal, was or whatever, now he's died without me being able to sort it out with him."

Then he looked up and wiped his tears away. He stared at Lis.

"I went to the clinic and visited him on Sunday night! He already knew he was going to be killed."

"You ... wanted to see him?" Lis was shocked.

Eric took his cell phone and put it on the table.

"Sit down, Lis, and listen to this."

Then he played the recording from Lamborelle.

That same evening, Alfonse Weis came by and Eric gave him the recording, which he then took to Inspector Kraus in person.

# THURSDAY, AUGUST 22

Biarritz, South of France. The former Luxembourg Minister for Family Affairs, Alexander Merten, had taken part in a golf tournament and was returning home late at night.

Merten's vacation home was located outside Biarritz on a large plot of land. When he was still a few hundred meters away from his home, he had to brake quite abruptly because a car was parked across the country road, blocking his progress.

It was dark and there were no street lights. Merten switched off the engine. Someone must have fallen ill here, or a drunk driver was still at the wheel, he concluded as he opened the car door.

Then everything happened very quickly. Within a few seconds, someone was holding a gun to his head.

"Get out, close the door, put your cell phone on the floor and your hands behind your head, without trying anything, you know, because otherwise you'll be dead. And all without making any noise," demanded a man wearing a black hood.

The minister had no other choice. He put his cell phone on the floor, the man took it and put it in a case.

"Who are you ... Your voice sounds familiar!" said Minister Merten.

"I bet it does! Come on, let's go into the forest for a bit, to the left please and after you!"

After the two men had walked a few hundred meters further into the forest, the man with the rifle said: "Sit here on this tree trunk, then we can talk."

Alexander Merten did this without protest. Drops of sweat dripped down his forehead. He knew that he couldn't call for help here, nor could anyone locate him.

"If it's about money, I'm sure we can find a solution."

"It's not about money!" said the man. "Now you listen to me carefully and without interruption. Then there will be the usual round of questions and then we analyse the answers."

The minister nodded in agreement and didn't say a word.

He tried to remember who this man was, because he was sure that the voice was familiar.

The man was standing about three meters away from Minister Merten and had his gun with silencer pointed at him.

"It's about human lives, it's about human trafficking. My name is James Hammer, I was in the secret service and special forces for a long time. My three-year-old daughter was kidnapped three years ago, when my wife and I were on vacation in the Dominican Republic. We turned the whole world upside down to find her and yet not a single trace was discovered.

"The police in Luxembourg and abroad used all their capacities and connections to find our little Sarah, but to no avail. When I did my own research into the official police systems, I was suspended from my job. And then, a year and a half after her kidnapping, an obituary with Sarah's photo appeared in the Luxembourg daily newspaper. She had died in a car accident. The only strange thing was that her name in the ad was Line Weyland-Lehman."

The minister was drenched in sweat and staring at James Hammer. By now he had a very good idea of what was going to happen and knew that he would not leave this forest alive. Why else would this James Hammer show his face and reveal his name? No, he realised, unless they came to an agreement. Maybe there was a way. Minister Merten was afraid.

James continued. "My wife commited suicide because she couldn't bear the thought that our daughter had ended up with another family in Luxembourg, that she had been adopted, and that she had been so close to her all this time. That was probably an error of judgement on the part of your organisation, because children are never given up for adoption in the country where they were born. That would be too risky.

"However, as we were still living in Germany at the time of the kidnapping, this was not known. I then contacted the adoptive family, who were not very happy about my appearance, whereupon, at my request, a DNA analysis was carried out via a lawyer, and I was told that the test was negative. From that day on, a court order forbade me to have any contact with this family. Please don't tell me now that it wasn't my daughter in the newspaper, because I'm telling you, it was our Sarah. But I'll come back to that in a moment.

"Do you have anything to say so far, Minister Merten?"

"What does all this have to do with me? I couldn't have helped you either, but I would have done my best if I had been contacted or informed."

"It's a shame that you haven't yet understood the seriousness of your situation and that you're even lying. But that doesn't matter. I'll refresh your memory. It may be that you don't know the individual names of the children, that's possible."

James looked the minister straight in the eye and pointed the gun right between his eyes.

"I did some research on my own, which wasn't easy. It was a bit unfortunate that the adoptive parents, unaware of the consequences, noted in the obituary that their special thanks went to the McKenna Clinic for the care they provided in the last days of her life. It was only through this connection that I came to the orphanage in Clervaux through a very good friend and through him to the orphanage in the Dominican Republic.

"My friend, or rather his wife, had contacted the adoptive parents under false pretences and asked them in the course of the conversation where their adopted daughter came from. Although all of these parents had signed a contract agreeing to absolute confidentiality, these parents were in so much pain and grief that they forgot about this confidentiality agreement and told him. And then the rest was pretty easy, I'll cut the story short here.

"I just didn't know yet what scum of humanity in the

government our Peter Lamborelle was working with, or rather who was covering his ass. Because getting kids across borders and giving out fake DNA tests is not that easy to do. You need connections in higher circles.

"And you, Minister Merten, are one of them. Of course, only rich and upper-class citizens are eligible for such adoptions, that goes without saying! Besides, all these parents know exactly that something is wrong, but that doesn't seem to bother them. The main thing is that they can adopt a child with white skin colour. Or am I wrong?"

James paused for a moment. The minister was now completely white in the face, sweating and trembling slightly.

"Do you have something to say, Minister Merten?"

Merten looked at James Hammer and thought about it. "You're assuming that I had something to do with this because I was responsible for this department? That doesn't give you the right to even assume that I was involved!"

"I knew you'd tell me an outright lie to my face. It's just that I have all the proof I need. Whether I let you live or not doesn't change anything. I just want to know who else is involved. And I don't think you're going to tell me. But I will find out. Because if you're found shot dead tomorrow, and no one will know by whom, then one or other of your associates—if I may call them that—will get cold feet.

"Whoever injected Lamborelle with lethal insulin—and I'm assuming a well-paid policeman here—he did his job well and there's no proof. But they are just little puppets who are proud to serve the elite. What they don't know is that when they're no longer useful, they'll suddenly die in an accident or commit suicide, right?

"One day, I hope you will have to take responsibility for the immeasurable suffering you have caused so many parents. You have destroyed their lives and that is irreparable, you have taken children from their biological parents, and the adoptive parents have been part of this mess.

"I'm going to stop now because I have to leave you. Is there anything else on your mind?"

"Mr. Hammer, please, let's talk, I … We … there's a solution for everything. Please, give me a chance to help you!"

"No. I'm sorry for your wife, for your children, because they hardly know anything about your dirty work, but others have suffered too. Maybe your family will find out the truth, I haven't decided yet."

James stepped towards the man. The shot that hit Alexander Merten between the eyes was completely silent. The minister was killed instantly and fell backwards.

James Hammer then continued to wander through the forest, creating a confused trail that would be impossible for forensics to trace. After all, he had enough professional experience to know how to avoid such things.


# *FRIDAY, AUGUST 23*


Alfonse Weis sat at the breakfast table and listened to the news.

Yesterday evening, the body of the former Minister for Family Affairs Alexander Merten was found in a forest near his summer residence, not far from Biarritz. He had been killed at close range by a well-aimed shot to the head. An investigation has been opened. Further details are not yet known.

Alfonse quickly picked up the phone and called Lis.

"Yes, I just heard it too. Tell me, what was going on? First Lamborelle dies in hospital, now Merten gets shot."

"It's all very strange. I think there's more to it than we suspect."

"I think so too," said Alfonse, "but I don't think we should talk about it on the phone."

Later that evening, another surprising announcement was made on the local news: Foreign Minister Jean-Joseph Lavoine had announced his resignation from his post with immediate effect for personal reasons.

This time Lis called Alfonse. "What's going on here, Alfonse? What are they doing there? It can't be a coincidence, one after the other."

"I don't think so either. We'd better stay in the background for a while and discuss the state of things when we see each other. Not on the phone."

"You're right. Thank you very much. See you then."

Then Lis hung up. She was now very worried, especially because she hadn't had a chance to speak to James.

## SUNDAY, AUGUST 25

That Sunday morning, Lis was visited by Matthew. Days ago, she had asked him for Line Weyland-Lehmann's medical records, which he wanted to hand over to her discreetly, without his father's knowledge.

He had brought her a bouquet of flowers. Beautiful white roses, which he held in his hand when she opened the door.

"Thank you, Matt." They hugged warmly. "For the beautiful roses and for the report from James's daughter, I think he has a right to know what his Sarah died of."

"That's for sure. What a story," Matthew commented. "They're copies, he's welcome to keep them." Matthew had also been deeply affected by the events of the last few days.

"And in our clinic of all places. I am ashamed to call Jeff Mc-Kenna my half-brother. It is simply incomprehensible how a wealthy young man could consent to such acts. He didn't need any more money. He has more than enough. Then what was it, I wonder?"

"Well, he was always under pressure from his father, he had to be the best and be everything his father wanted him to be. You managed to say no instead."

"I guess that's true, Lis. Why didn't he ever talk to me about it? I would have supported him."

"How long will he have to spend in prison, what do his lawyers think?"

"Ten years at least, they estimate. But maybe they can reduce the sentence, we'll have to wait and see how the whole thing develops."

Lis looked at Matthew. "How are you and Brigitte?"

"That's okay. She has to learn to stand on her own two feet again and she's aware of that. We'll never move in together, that's my condition."

"Oh, that surprises me now."

"I don't want to give up my freedom for anyone. You know that better than anyone."

He looked at her lovingly. "And you and James?"

"He's a somewhat extraordinary person who I fell in love with the first time I met him. I couldn't do anything about it."

"I know. I'm happy for you!"

Matthew then said goodbye with a warm hug and kissed Lis.

"See you around!" he said.

"I promise!"

Lis closed the door. Could there have been a future with Matt? It was hard to say.

She went back inside and looked at the file on Line, alias Sarah.

The girl had suffered severe bleeding on the brain after being hit by a car and taken to hospital. She was still alive two days after the accident, but had not regained consciousness.

Lis put the file aside and lay down on the couch. Her thoughts revolved around James. When would she see him again? Would she see him again? Trust me, was all he had said. That was a very vague statement. But she had no alternative. She loved this man, and she was ready to share a life with him. Was he ready for that? She didn't know at this stage.

## SATURDAY, SEPTEMBER 7

On Saturday evening, everyone involved in the events of the last few weeks was invited to Thomas' house. Thomas, Alfonse, David, Alan, Diana Van Helden, Eric, Caro, Matthew and Brigitte, John McKenna, Bernard Bouvier and Lis were there.

Once these turbulent weeks and events were over and everything had calmed down, they all wanted to spend a nice evening together. After all, it was thanks to Thomas and Alfonse's initiative in looking for Alan that this whole chain of events had been triggered and the culprits could be arrested.

The fact that Peter Lamborelle did not survive was due to an overdose of insulin that someone had given him. An investigation was launched, but would there ever be a concrete lead? Alfonse doubted it.

Lis was rather quiet and reserved throughout the evening. She was worried about James. He hadn't given her any sign of life for almost two weeks, and if she had wanted to look for him, she wouldn't have had the slightest idea where he was. And she wasn't allowed to, as he had instructed.

It was a great evening and they chatted until 3 a.m. There were so many things to say, so much to decide.

## SUNDAY, SEPTEMBER 8

In one week, Lis was due to start her job as a Spanish teacher at the local university. Life would somehow take its everyday course.

Caro and Eric were in the process of looking for their own apartment, and Eric had told his grandfather that he would take the job at the bank on a trial basis for a year. Eric didn't want to go by the name Bouvier for the time being, but he was open to changing it later if he followed in his grandfather's footsteps and took over the bank. But he didn't know that yet.

Caro now had two sets of parents and it would take a long time for everyone to get used to the new situation. On the other hand, she was so happy to meet all her blood relatives and to have a real aunt in Diane Van Helden. It was all new and so unimaginable. Her grandfather Gerard Van Helden had even considered meeting Bernard Bouvier to talk about old times. The name Auguste Lamborelle would also play a role.

## MONDAY, SEPTEMBER 9

Monday morning began with a headline on the local radio: *Thirty-nine-year-old doctor Jean-Donnat Michel, who had been arrested for some incidents that were not reported to us, was found dead in his cell last night.*

Alfonse was having breakfast when he heard this. He wondered who still wanted to get rid of all the people involved in all these adoption scandals. And of course, none of this scandal had been reported in the press. That was probably to the McKenna Clinic's advantage, but still. Usually, the press reports before something happens and here ... Already very disturbing.

John McKenna was immediately informed of the unexpected death of Dr. Michel and asked his attorney to immediately request increased police surveillance and protection for his son Jeff to prevent a possible next murder or 'sudden death', as it was officially called.

"What do you think?" Lis asked Alfonse later over lunch.

"I'm not sure, but it's easy to see that all the people who are or were somehow involved in the child smuggling scandal, which still seems to being kept out of the press, are dying or resigning."

"Don't you think they'll start investigating now and close the two orphanages?" Lis asked in astonishment.

"No, I don't think so. Who else is going to testify? Peter Lamborelle is dead, Dr. Michel is dead, ex-minister Merten is dead."

Lis was silent for a few moments and thought about Alfonse's words.

"Jeff McKenna?" she then said.

"I'm sure he's afraid for his life and that of his family. But I assume he only knows the tip of the iceberg."

"I see ... Yes ... But someone is active behind the scenes, or am I wrong? Who do you think is cleaning up here?" asked Lis.

"One possibility is that the upper echelons are getting rid of those who could be dangerous or that someone else is sorting things out. Or it's a mixture of both. But we're unlikely to find out, because everything is being done carefully and professionally. No leads, no clues, no suspicions, all clean, right?"

"Hm ...." Lis propped her arms on the table and rested her head in her hands. "You're right!"

"Is there a dessert?" asked Alfonse.

"Gladly, with coffee," said Lis.

The waiter served a delicious portion of ice cream.

"Have you heard from James lately?" Alfonse asked after a while.

"He's busy, he told me."

Alfonse looked at Lis with loaded eyes.

"Lots to do! I see." Alfonse repeated.

"What, you mean?" Lis said with a raised index finger.

"I don't mean anything. I just know that I like this man. By the way, my ice cream is delicious. How is yours, Lis?"

That was Alfonse's way of not wanting to go any further into the subject.

"It's delicious, thank you!"

"You know," Alfonse began, "when I first met you, and I mean when you were just fifteen, I had the impression that you had remarkable stamina. And after the way everything has turned out, I also felt that you would later emerge from all this with a very strong personality.

"I think that almost any girl your age would have accepted your father's suggestion to terminate the pregnancy and to lead a simple life with enough money for everything. But you defied all of that and have chosen to go your own way. I can hardly imagine how difficult this path must have been at the beginning, but I hope you know you did the right thing. I am very proud of you and I am very proud to know you. I sincerely hope that your father will be able to tell you that one day too."

Alfonse raised his glass.

Lis had tears in her eyes. "Thank you, Alfonse!"

"And I've been thinking about something else, too. In my opinion—and this is just my opinion, please don't get me wrong—it's good that Peter Lamborelle died, for your peace of mind, for Eric, for all of you."

"I thought that too, Alfonse. I couldn't express it to Eric like that. But you're so right. It would have been torture for Eric because he would have always been torn between the father figure and the criminal. It would have torn him apart in the long run, and it would have torn me apart too."

"I see we understand each other."

Lis and Alfonse had become very close during this conversation, and they were both aware of it.

In the days that followed, Lis prepared for her new position at the university. She was glad for the distraction that kept her busy and occupied her thoughts. Not a single day went by when she didn't think about James Hammer. She hadn't heard from him since that last morning—no phone call, no e-mail, nothing. But she was confident that he would get back to her when he decided it was the right time.

# FRIDAY, SEPTEMBER 13

It was raining cats and dogs on Friday morning. Eric had gone away with Caro the day before for a long weekend. They both needed some distance from everything and a lot of time to talk.

Lis woke up when someone rang the doorbell. Surprised, she jumped out of bed, it was only 9 a.m. Who wanted to see her so early?

She put on her bathrobe and went to the intercom.

"Yes?"

"Do you have time?" Lis couldn't believe it. It was James's voice that she heard on the intercom.

"What do you mean?" She opened the door and within a few minutes he was standing in front of the apartment door.

In one hand he held a huge bouquet of red roses and with the other hand he made a sign, put his finger over his mouth and then held his open hand in front of Lis. She understood immediately.

She took the flowers and immediately handed him her cell phone. He put his and hers back in the special case. He closed it and put it in the hallway.

"I've missed you so much," she said as he hugged and kissed her tenderly.

"I love you, Lis," he whispered to her and slowly undid the belt of her bathrobe. He could finally feel her bare skin.

Without asking, he took her hand and led her into the bedroom.

"James, over the last few days I've been wondering if I'll ever see you again. I've been so worried, especially after all the recent news."

"I believe you. But hopefully that time will soon be over."

After Lis had opened his shirt, he stripped off the rest of his clothes and they ended up lying close together.

"Is your shoulder still very sore?" asked Lis when she saw the bandage.

"That's no obstacle!" he said with a smile.

The rain lashed against the window panes as they were finally able to act out their feelings and desires for each other.

After hours of intensity, they lay close together.

"So, do we dare to start together?" Lis said and stroked his hairy chest.

"It seems so!" He sealed this statement with an intense kiss. "It wasn't easy for me to come to terms with everything that has driven me in the past year and at the same time moved me forward. I thought long and hard about whether I was ready for a new life."

"I can understand that," Lis said sympathetically. "I had a long talk with Alfonse about Peter Lamborelle and the fact that he's dead. We agreed that it was the best thing for Eric and for me, and he's right. It sounds harsh, but it is."

"I think so too, but it's not for me to judge. There were so many things I wanted to ask that man, but unfortunately, I didn't get around to doing it. Maybe it was for the best, I don't know. Life goes on and there's nothing we can do about the past."

"Who do you think killed him in the hospital?"

"It's hard to say, but this organisation has people infiltrated at all levels. It's just a routine job for them."

"Really?"

"Really!"

"And the murder of the former family minister Merten is also very strange. So that's part of it too?"

James was silent for a while and looked at Lis with his striking eyes. "I think so!"

"And shortly afterwards the resignation of Foreign Minister Lavoine. I assume that was also connected then?"

James nodded in agreement. "But let's not dwell on it. Let's hope the orphanage has at least been closed or is being used for something useful to help children."

"Are you hungry?"

"Oh yes, I could do with something."

They both stood up and he spontaneously took Lis in his arms and carried her into the kitchen.

"We'll have plenty of time," he said, hugging her as if he still had a lot to say to her.

"That sounds wonderful," Lis said, enjoying every second. "I have so much time, my whole weekend is free."

"That's a good start." He kissed her passionately.


Later that afternoon, James set off to meet Alfonse Weis.

The two men met near the Kopstal, parked their cars at the

edge of the forest and then walked deep into the woods. Their cell phones were switched off and securely wrapped so that it was impossible to locate them.

"James, I can't help but ask you a few questions. We haven't seen each other since all this happened, and since we both have the same job, you know …"

"Alfonse, what can I do for you. I'm glad you're well."

"And your shoulder?"

"Soon as good as new," joked James.

"We have lost four people in the last few days. Peter Lamborelle, Dr. Michel, the former family affairs minister Alexander Merten, and the former foreign minister Lavoine is resigning. Well, we didn't lose him in that sense, but still. And none of this was a coincidence, that's for sure."

"I agree," said James. "I suppose they had to remove Lamborelle because he could have testified and the elite can't afford that. Not even if the risk is small. The same thing will have happened to Dr. Michel. Whether he did it himself or was helped is irrelevant. He has disappeared from the stage, that alone is important. And Lavoine's resignation is just to pull the wool over the eyes of the few people who suspect something, so that they think everything has been cleared up. As always."

"But that's not all, is it?" said Alfonse.

"No, that's not it. It will never be like that. You know that, I know that. And that's where it has to end."


"And Merten? Shot in the head at close range?" Alfonse looked at James questioningly. "That was a professional shot."

"Yes. Any more questions?" said James. Alfonse had a good sense of when it was appropriate not to ask any more.

"Shall we have another beer together?"

"I would like that, Alfonse. I think we really deserve it."

"And do you know what I think?" said Alfonse.

"Shoot!"

"This could be the start of a wonderful friendship!" said Alfonse.

"That's it!!!" James put his arm around Alfonse for a minute.

The two men then walked back through the woods to their cars and met up shortly afterwards in a nearby pub, where they spent the rest of the evening.

Around 10 p.m., James called Lis' house. "Can I stay with you one more night?"

A few minutes later, she opened the door for him and fell into his arms.

"Not just one night, I can last a lifetime with you if you can take the risk," she whispered.

He kissed her tenderly. "Mmm ... I would say that you're taking the big risk!"

"When I look into your eyes, I can forget the whole world. And I want to have that feeling every day," she said.

James hugged her tightly. "I love you, Lis Chandler, Elisabeth Bouvier, Martina Kaufmann. From the moment I took a photo on the plane, I've thought of your face so often; it's been with me every day. And I just knew that one day we would meet."

## SUNDAY, SEPTEMBER 15

Sunday evening was a special kind of evening. Lis and James wanted to spend it with Caro and Eric and to talk in private. So much had happened in such a short space of time, and no one had

had time to talk about what they had experienced. From Monday, life would resume its usual course.

"I'm looking forward to seeing how I'm received at Bouvier Bank on Monday," said Eric, who had signed an employment contract there. "One year on probation as Eric Chandler. If it goes well between grandfather and grandson, I will change my name to Bouvier after a year and then Bernard will officially declare that I will become his close assistant and later his deputy director and thus his successor."

But until then, he wanted to take his time and carefully consider whether this would be his future or not.

"There will be adjustments for all of us," James said. "I'm going back to work for the Secret Service and I've finished my unpaid leave. I've missed the job, if I'm completely honest, but I couldn't concentrate on other cases until I'd solved my own private case. And now I'm at peace with that."

"Do you still want to talk to your daughter's adoptive parents one day?" asked Caro.

"No, I don't want that. I don't want to open a wound any further. It won't bring Sarah back to me, and it would only make the pain worse to hear about their life with her. No one can undo what happened, but the fact that these adoptive parents knew full well that something was wrong with this adoption, that they had to sign a confidentiality agreement, not just them, but all the adoptive parents involved with Lamborelle and his company, that's bad enough. And we'll never find out the whole story, because they're all protected by higher authorities."

"It's incomprehensible," Eric agreed. "I've experienced more in the last few weeks since I've been back from London than in my entire life so far. But amongst it all, I've found the love of my life," he said, looking at Caro.

"It has been a very intense time for all of us," said Lis, "which will leave a bitter aftertaste for a long time. But we have all become stronger as a result."

James put his arm lovingly around Lis and kissed her.

"If I hadn't gone after Lamborelle, we would never have met," he added.

"Do you think that he also had something good or human in him?" Eric asked with a sad undertone, looking at James and Lis at the same time.

"I think everyone has something good deep down inside," said James. "But Lamborelle chose the wrong side at some point and eventually had to face the consequences of his decisions. You can't heal pain by inflicting more pain on others. It doesn't work that way."

"I also have some very surprising news," Caro said. "My aunt Diane and Alan wrote from Santo Domingo this afternoon to say that little Kim has finally been found and that Diane has been able to submit a legal adoption application, with the help of the local police. Her parents really had died and so nothing is standing in the way of the adoption.

"On the other hand, I still need a lot of time to get used to my birth parents. I don't know if I'll ever succeed, but at least the two sets of parents have become friends, which makes everything a lot easier. The Kleins had no idea why they had to sign the confidentiality agreement, they thought it was normal. As they weren't part of the rich elite, they came to this connection by chance and actually had to take out a large loan to finance my adoption."

It was a very personal evening during which they all became much closer to each other. They came to the conclusion that their lives had changed for the better after everything they had been through.